TRUSTING
MOLLY

Rescuing Harley
Marrying Emily
Rescuing Kassie
Rescuing Bryn
Rescuing Casey
Rescuing Sadie (novella)
Rescuing Wendy
Rescuing Mary
Rescuing Macie
Rescuing Annie (February 2022)

Delta Team Two Series

Shielding Gillian
Shielding Kinley
Shielding Aspen
Shielding Jayme (novella)
Shielding Riley
Shielding Devyn
Shielding Ember (September 2021)
Shielding Sierra (January 2022)

Badge of Honor: Texas Heroes Series

Justice for Mackenzie
Justice for Mickie
Justice for Corrie
Justice for Laine (novella)
Shelter for Elizabeth
Justice for Boone
Shelter for Adeline

Shelter for Sophie
Justice for Erin
Justice for Milena
Shelter for Blythe
Justice for Hope
Shelter for Quinn
Shelter for Koren
Shelter for Penelope

SEAL of Protection Series

Protecting Caroline
Protecting Alabama
Protecting Alabama's Kids (novella)
Protecting Fiona
Marrying Caroline (novella)
Protecting Summer
Protecting Cheyenne
Protecting Jessyka
Protecting Julie (novella)
Protecting Melody
Protecting the Future
Protecting Kiera (novella)
Protecting Dakota

SEAL of Protection: Legacy Series

Securing Caite
Securing Sidney
Securing Piper
Securing Zoey
Securing Avery

Securing Kalee

Securing Jane (novella)

SEAL Team Hawaii Series

Finding Elodie

Finding Lexie (August 2021)

Finding Kenna (October 2021)

Finding Monica (May 2022)

Finding Carly (TBA)

Finding Ashlyn (TBA)

Finding Jodelle (TBA)

Beyond Reality Series

Outback Hearts

Flaming Hearts

Frozen Hearts

Stand-Alone Novels

The Guardian Mist

A Princess for Cale

A Moment in Time (a short-story collection)

Another Moment in Time (a short-story collection)

Lambert's Lady

Writing as Annie George

Stepbrother Virgin (erotic novella)

TRUSTING MOLLY

Silverstone, Book 3

Susan Stoker

 Montlake

Published by Montlake, Seattle

www.apub.com

Amazon, the Amazon logo, and Montlake are trademarks of Amazon.com, Inc., or its affiliates.

ISBN-13: 9781542021449
ISBN-10: 1542021448

Cover design by Eileen Carey

Printed in the United States of America

TRUSTING
MOLLY

Chapter One

Mark "Smoke" Chamberlin was tired of the jungle. He and his fellow Silverstone teammates had been in Nigeria for weeks, attempting to find the Boko Haram terrorist group. Months ago, they'd kidnapped seventy-two girls and young women from a local school. They'd also taken an environmental engineer who'd been at the school that day. Molly Smith.

Molly was thirty-five, but at first glance, Smoke supposed she could've been mistaken for a teenager by the terrorists. She was petite, almost a foot shorter than his own six-foot-one frame. In the pictures he'd seen of her, she'd had long black hair and eyes that seemed to harbor too much anguish for someone so young.

There had been reports of a few of the kidnapped schoolgirls reappearing in various places, but most were still unaccounted for. Silverstone had arrived in Nigeria a month ago and, using the information they'd gathered from the FBI and local authorities, had been searching the jungle for any signs of either the terrorist group or the remaining girls.

And they'd finally found them.

Smoke, Bull, Eagle, and Gramps lay in the thick foliage, observing the crude camp. It was no wonder helicopters hadn't been able to spot the group. The tents were camouflaged, and the area of the jungle where the terrorists had brought the girls was dense with trees and almost inaccessible. There were no roads in or out; the thought of the girls being forced to walk the twenty miles or so into the area was abhorrent.

It had been hard going for Smoke and his teammates, and they were in their prime. It couldn't have been easy for a group of terrified schoolgirls.

There was a trio of large tents set up in the middle of the camp, one side of each open to the hot, humid air of the jungle, and Smoke could see girls inside all three. Smaller tents surrounded the larger ones. Smoke assumed they were for the men, a way to safeguard the camp and to prevent the girls from running. Although escaping the out-of-the-way camp would be almost impossible. He had a feeling, once in the jungle, the girls would have no idea which way to go to find safety.

Looking through his binoculars, Smoke observed most of the girls lying in the tents listlessly, as if they had no energy to do much of anything. Three fires were lit off to one side, and fifteen girls were gathered around them, obviously cooking and preparing food.

As for the kidnappers . . . there were more of them than Smoke had thought there'd be. He counted at least two dozen. All armed to the teeth. They had machetes strapped to their chests and rifles slung across their backs. They were quick to yell at their captives if the girls stepped out of line, and Smoke watched as one girl, who couldn't have been more than eleven or twelve, got smacked so hard she fell to her back.

Witnessing the abuse was bad enough. But also, no matter how carefully he looked, Smoke saw no evidence of Molly Smith.

There was no telling what may have happened to her during the last three months. His stomach rolled as he thought about what the kidnappers could've done with her, but he forced himself to put it out of his mind.

"Any sign of Abubakar Shekau?" Gramps asked Eagle.

"I'm guessing that's his tent over there," Eagle responded softly, indicating a fourth large tent that sat a few dozen yards from the others.

It seemed to be of better quality—and there were two men standing guard outside.

As they continued to observe, two of the kidnappers dragged a young woman—Smoke guessed she was probably around fourteen years old—toward the tent. She was crying and pleading with the men to let her go. They ignored her, holding her biceps so tightly they were practically carrying her.

They stopped outside the tent, then one of the men leaned down and said something to the girl. She shook her head, and the man smacked her. The crack of skin hitting skin was loud in the dense jungle.

Smoke's teeth clenched. He wanted to leap out of the trees and snatch the girl away, save her from what he knew was going to happen inside that tent. But he couldn't. His hands were tied.

The two men laughed at the girl and, after the guards opened the flap of the tent, shoved her inside. Smoke saw her fall to her knees just inside the tent. A man loomed over her, pointing toward a spot in the dirt. The girl quickly crawled to where he was pointing, staying on her knees.

The man reached for the drawstring of his pants as the guards closed the tent flap.

"It was him," Eagle said in a tight, tense growl. "Shekau."

Smoke knew if Eagle said the man was Shekau, then he was Shekau. Eagle had the unique ability to remember every person he'd ever met or seen a picture of. Even though the interior of the tent had been dim, Eagle had still been able to identify the man.

They all knew how lucky it was that Shekau was there. He could've easily made the members of his terrorist organization do his dirty work while he stayed hidden elsewhere. Having him at the camp was a huge stroke of luck.

Silverstone had come to Nigeria specifically to kill the man.

Smoke wanted to move right then. Slip into the back of the tent and kill the bastard. It was apparent the girls had been abused in every way one human could abuse another during the months since they'd been taken. But he was forced to wait. Now that they had confirmation both the girls and Shekau were there, they had to report back to the Nigerian officials.

As much as Silverstone wanted to kill Shekau and slip away, they couldn't leave the girls at the mercy of the remaining Boko Haram members. No, this had to be a rescue mission as well as a mission to kill the terrorist leader.

All they could do for the moment was watch and wait for their backup to arrive. Silverstone would kill Shekau, and any of his followers who dared to resist, and the Nigerian forces would back them up and gather the girls and return them to their families, who were frantic to find them.

Two days. That was how long it would take for the Nigerian forces to get into place for the raid.

Smoke wasn't sure he could stomach sitting back and doing nothing while children were being abused. But he didn't have a choice. None of them did.

Bull slipped off to notify their Nigerian contacts that they had visual confirmation Shekau was at the camp and to give them coordinates. Smoke knew he'd make sure everyone understood time was of the essence.

"This is going to sound harsh, but . . . I've never really thought too much about the people we rescue on missions like this," Eagle said in a low tone. They were far enough away from the camp that they wouldn't be overheard, but they didn't want to push their luck.

Smoke looked over at his friend. Eagle was frowning and looked extremely stressed out. All four of them were more than ready for this mission to be over. The jungle was hot, they were exhausted, and he knew his friend was missing his wife. Eagle was clearly worried about how Taylor's pregnancy was progressing. When they'd left, she'd been about fourteen weeks; it had to be hard missing the milestones of their first pregnancy.

"I mean, I feel bad for the victims," Eagle clarified, "but I never think much about them afterward. Remember when we went to Peru and took out del Rio?"

Smoke nodded, and next to him, Gramps did as well.

"I was disgusted by what he'd done, how many lives he'd ruined, but after we left, I didn't think about his victims again. Lately, though, I can't help but wonder how they're doing. If they found their families. If they were able to reacclimate to their former lives, or if they're too traumatized by what happened to have any kind of normal life again.

"Now that I'm married, and have a child on the way, I can't stop thinking . . . what if that had been Taylor? What if that serial killer who'd targeted her had managed to get away with her? I look at the girls in this camp and wonder what their lives are going to be like after going through this. It . . . haunts me."

Smoke wasn't sure what to say. He wanted to empathize, but since he wasn't married, hadn't been in a serious relationship in years, wasn't expecting a child . . . he really couldn't. Of course he felt bad for the girls who were being abused by Boko Haram, but once his team killed Shekau, their part was done. They'd all go back to Indianapolis and their towing company and continue with their own lives.

Eagle turned to Gramps and Smoke. "I look at these girls, and now I see my own child. I hear stories about women being raped and held against their will, and imagine Taylor being in their place. I don't know if that makes me better at what I do or worse."

"Better," Gramps said without hesitation. "My grandparents came to America from Mexico to escape a drug cartel. They were forcing everyone in their small town to work for them, and anyone who balked was simply shot. Children, grandparents . . . no one was safe. So my grandparents packed what they could carry and walked across the Sonoran Desert to get into America. It wasn't easy, but they knew whatever that future held was better than working for the cartels. They wanted the children they hadn't had yet—and grandchildren, and great-grandchildren—not to have to live in fear. Wanting what's best for the ones you love is *never* a bad thing."

Eagle nodded.

Gramps didn't talk about his background much. They'd all known his grandparents had lived in Mexico, but hadn't known the details about how they'd gotten to the United States.

"It took a long time, and a lot of hard work, but they got their citizenship," Gramps went on. "They just wanted to pay their taxes and live freely in this country, and now they do. I think if we lose empathy for others, then we might as well hang up our hats. Yes, we kill people. We happen to be damn good at it. But we don't kill simply for the sake of it. We do it to make the world a tiny bit better. I hate that you see Taylor in the faces of those we're freeing from tyranny, but in my mind, that makes what we do more personal."

Eagle took a deep breath. "Thanks. I needed to hear that."

"Smoke and I are happy to deal with the civilians if that makes things easier for you," Gramps said.

"I'm good," Eagle told him. "I just miss Taylor. I haven't talked to her in a month, and it feels as if a part of me is missing. I'll get through this, because I know my wife misses me just as much. Having a connection like that with someone else is something I really hope you guys find. It's different from the bond we have, and even more satisfying."

Smoke hated the pang of jealousy that hit him. He was happy that Bull and Eagle had found women who could stand by them and be proud of what they did. But Skylar and Taylor were unique, and he wasn't sure he'd ever get lucky enough to find someone like them.

"I love that you have that," Smoke said honestly. They were all quiet for a moment, then he asked, "Anyone seen the American?"

Gramps put the binoculars back up to his eyes and shook his head even as he rescanned the area. "No."

"They might've killed her already," Eagle said quietly.

Smoke sighed. He'd had the same thought. He didn't like to think about the woman being dead, but at this point, there wasn't evidence to suggest otherwise. She'd simply disappeared into thin air. No rumors that she'd been sold into the sex trade, no sightings of her in any nearby villages. It was likely Molly Smith had been killed when Boko Haram had discovered her among the schoolgirls, then left to rot in the jungle.

She didn't have anyone advocating for her search. Her grandparents had been found dead in their burned-out house back in a suburb of Chicago, and the company she worked for, Apex, had packed up all their employees working in Nigeria and sent them home.

No one was looking for Molly Smith.

A shout sounded from the camp, and Smoke turned his attention back to the situation at hand. He had to focus on what he'd come to do: kill Shekau and free the dozens of girls who'd simply been in the wrong place at the wrong time.

～

Molly Smith licked her lips, but it didn't help moisten them. The water in her hole had dried up overnight, and no matter how deep she dug to find more, she hadn't had any luck. Her time was coming to an end, and she knew it. She couldn't last long without water. And the assholes who'd captured her hadn't bothered to bring her any in a very long time.

She tried to calculate how long she'd been in the jungle, but couldn't do that either. She'd kept track at first, but after she'd tried to escape the first time—and been beaten unconscious for her effort—she'd lost count of the days. After her second escape attempt, she'd been thrown into this hole, and she hadn't thought about anything other than surviving since.

Maybe she'd been stupid to try to run the second time, but she refused to sit and wait for someone to hurt her, or force her to be someone's "wife." At least down here, she was isolated from the kidnappers, and no one had tried to touch her inappropriately.

She was used to being alone—liked it, in fact—but after not talking to anyone for so long, she thought she was literally going crazy. Once or twice, she'd tried talking to the men who appeared above her prison every so often to throw down some stale bread, but they'd simply laughed at her. Asked her why she wasn't dead yet, then left.

The hole she was in wasn't that deep. Probably only around seven feet or so. But it might as well have been a mile. She'd tried climbing the walls, but it was impossible to get any traction. And when she jumped, she couldn't get a good grip on the edge of the hole. It was maddening to be so close to freedom, but not be able to get there.

She'd been let out of the hole only a few times since being forced to climb down a crude, rickety ladder that had been fashioned out of sticks from the forest and fraying rope. Once, she'd been paraded in front of the girls, probably to show them what would happen if they defied their captors.

The last time, she'd been forced to witness the "marriage" of a ten-year-old girl to a middle-aged man. It was sickening . . . and there was literally nothing Molly could do to stop it.

Feeling helpless and hopeless, she rested her head on her updrawn knees. She was going to die here. In the middle of nowhere. All her kidnappers would have to do was throw dirt over the hole—she was already in her grave.

The thought was morbid and depressing, but without being able to get out of the hole, she was as good as dead.

Later that evening, when she was at her lowest point yet, Molly heard something. A sound she hadn't heard in a week.

Rain.

In the jungle, the sound of water falling on leaves was surprisingly loud. Standing up in anticipation, Molly tilted her head back, opened her mouth, and waited.

She was rewarded with light droplets at first. Then, without warning, the gentle rainfall changed into a torrent.

Laughing with joy, Molly swallowed as much of the rain as she could. It tasted delicious. Pure and clean. Kneeling, she dug at the hole at the bottom of her prison and watched as it slowly filled with water. It was muddy, but at this point in her captivity, Molly didn't care. Water was water. She'd drink from the contaminated rivers if only to keep herself alive a little longer.

Next, she stripped off her shirt and cleaned herself as best she could. It had been forever since she'd been *truly* clean, and the rainstorms that moved through the area were her only chances of removing some of the dirt that had accumulated on her body.

A vision of Andy in the movie *Shawshank Redemption* came to mind. It was after he'd crawled through the pipe filled with sewage. He'd ripped off his shirt and thrown his head back, letting the rain cleanse him of both the stench from the shit he'd crawled through, and the stink of the prison he'd been unfairly kept in for so long.

That was how Molly felt. Of course, she was in Nigeria in a hole in the ground, and had only been held prisoner for months and not years—and she wasn't free—but the rain falling over her body somehow felt like a sign from a higher power.

Though . . . that was doubtful. Rarely in her life had she ever thought someone was looking out for her from above. In fact, more often than not—and her grandparents aside—she felt as if she was on her own. Especially when her frequent tough luck again reared its ugly head.

Her grandmother always said that if she didn't have bad luck, she wouldn't have any luck at all. She'd even been nicknamed Folly

Molly by classmates because of the bad luck that seemed to follow her everywhere.

Even in the middle of a jungle on another continent.

Her grandparents had never used the nickname themselves . . . but they'd also never actually said they didn't believe it was fitting. They loved her, as she did them, but they all knew she had the worst luck.

However, she'd been at the end of her rope, needing water to stay alive, and now it was raining. Pouring.

Maybe, just maybe, things were looking up, and she could shake the bad luck that had plagued her throughout her entire life.

After struggling to put her shirt back on, Molly sat in the mud at the bottom of the hole. She leaned against the side and tilted her head up. With her mouth still open to catch as much clean water as she could, she closed her eyes.

She wasn't going to give up. Not yet. The rain had given her flagging psyche a boost. The next time her captors came to get her out of the hole, she would make another attempt to run for it. She wouldn't stop until she was sure no one was following her. She didn't care how far she had to walk, she was going to get out of the jungle and back to her grandparents in the suburbs of Chicago. She longed to see Nana and Papa again. They loved and supported her without reservation. Without the hope of seeing them again, without that goal, she might have given up already.

Molly was going to live through this, no matter what. Her death would destroy her grandparents, and she didn't want that for them. She'd never been the most positive person in the world, but she was beginning to understand that out here, positive thinking was the only thing keeping her going.

Molly fantasized about her reunion with Nana and Papa. She'd barely reach the end of the drive before they'd come rushing outside, eyes watering with joy. They'd hug and cry and then lead her inside. After eating a huge homemade meal, Molly would snuggle into her grandmother's side, and they'd watch game shows on TV, just as they'd done regularly since Molly's recent move back into their home. Papa would kiss her on the temple, and Nana would tuck her into bed like she'd done when Molly was younger.

Her grandparents had always been her safe place, and Molly fell asleep thinking about how happy they'd be to see her home at last.

Chapter Two

This was it.

Smoke was crouched in the thick foliage on the edge of the Boko Haram camp, ready to spring into action. He and his Silverstone teammates had been tasked with taking out Shekau. The rest of the Nigerian security forces would be responsible for making sure the kidnapped girls weren't targeted by the terrorists, and taking out any of Shekau's supporters if they tried to fight back.

Looking over at Gramps, Smoke waited for the signal. The plan was to enter the tent Shekau was holed up in from the back. They'd quickly slice through the canvas and take the leader out by any means necessary. Ideally, they'd be able to do so without the use of a gun, because the shot would alert his followers that they were under attack, but all four of them were ready for almost anything.

Smoke had gotten his nickname because he was so good at getting in and out of tricky situations without anyone being the wiser. It had been said he could disappear like smoke. And Silverstone considered stealth their greatest asset, but with the two dozen Nigerian security forces in place—who were jittery and on edge—they all knew this job would be anything but stealthy.

As if to prove that point—before any of them could make a move, before Smoke could make good on his nickname—shots rang out from the other side of the compound.

Their Nigerian comrades had obviously been spotted, and their plan to be stealthy was all shot to hell.

"Fuck," Gramps swore as the four of them left their positions, hurrying toward Shekau's tent.

But just seconds after that first shot, the shit had already hit the fan. Bullets were flying from both the Nigerian police and the terrorists. Children were screaming and crying; a few of the girls fled into the jungle when the guards assigned to their tents abandoned their posts to focus on fighting the Nigerian security forces. The situation was complete chaos.

It was nothing like what Silverstone was used to. They liked control in all things, and currently they had literally *nothing* under control.

Smoke was doing his best to take out any threats as he moved as stealthily and quickly as he could, even while keeping an eye out for Shekau. Luckily for the team, the camp was in such a densely forested part of the jungle, they could remain mostly hidden until the last minute . . . but it also made it easier for the members of Boko Haram to hide and dodge bullets.

Several yards out from Shekau's tent, Smoke saw the guards panic and flee their posts, running into the jungle. Then Shekau himself exited his tent, his expression one of rage as he shot off a few rounds with a pistol before running for the cover of the jungle.

"I'm going right," Gramps said via radio. "Smoke, go left. Eagle and Bull, stay on course. We need to make sure he doesn't veer in either direction and catch him before he disappears."

Smoke didn't bother to respond; he didn't need to. All four of them knew that if Shekau escaped, he'd just find another group of schoolgirls to kidnap in the future. This time bringing more guards to ensure any rescue attempt would fail.

Peeling off to the left, Smoke weaved his way through the trees and saw the larger tents up ahead, still filled with girls who were too scared to run. He would approach from behind, then veer around—and hopefully Shekau would decide to turn toward the camp, running into Smoke in the process.

Concentrating on scanning the area ahead of him, trying to make sure the coast was clear, Smoke wasn't watching where he was putting his feet.

One second he was moving as quietly as he could—and the next he was falling.

His head smacked against the edge of a huge hole he'd stepped into as his body fell. Smoke didn't have time to swear or do anything to slow his fall before the wind was knocked out of him as he landed hard.

His mouth opened, and a grunt escaped—but it was the frightened feminine squeak that had him scrambling to get to his feet, off the person he'd landed on top of.

Smoke turned and looked down, shocked to the very marrow of his bones. He might not have had the ability to remember every single person he saw, like Eagle did, but he knew without a doubt who he was looking at right that second.

Molly Smith.

She looked the worse for wear, but she was alive. Her hair was matted, and she appeared even more petite than in the photos he'd seen. The T-shirt she was wearing was filthy and filled with holes. The cargo pants on her legs were ripped, and she was barefoot. She was currently sitting motionless in the mud at the bottom of the hole he'd fallen into, looking up at him in clear confusion.

"Molly?" Smoke asked, the disbelief easy to hear in his tone.

At his question, the woman seemed to shake off her shock that he'd literally fallen on top of her, and she jumped to her feet.

Jumped might've been an exaggeration. She put her hand on the wall of the hole and weaved on her feet when she stood. One hand went to her waistband, probably to keep the baggy pants from falling around her ankles. "Yes! I'm Molly Smith! You know who I am?"

"Yes," Smoke told her. "We weren't sure you were still with your kidnappers."

"I am. I'm here!" she cried, then winced. "But you can see that."

"Why are you—"

Smoke's question was interrupted by Bull's voice through his earpiece. "Smoke? Where the fuck are you?"

"Shit," Smoke muttered, then he looked up at the edge of the hole. It was only a few inches above his head, and he should be able to climb out without too much difficulty. He looked back down at Molly. "I need to get back out there."

Her eyes widened. "Okay. Help me out, and I'll come too."

Smoke reluctantly shook his head. "You're safer in here, believe me."

"No! Please! I need to get out of here."

Smoke knew he didn't have time for this, but he couldn't leave without assuring the woman. "My team needs me. We have to find Shekau, the guy who organized the kidnapping of all those kids. Once we deal with him, I'll come back and get you."

Molly stared up at him, and he could tell she wanted to protest. Wanted to insist he take her with him right now. But instead, she took a deep breath and asked, "Promise?"

In response, Smoke activated his radio and, without breaking eye contact with Molly, said, "I found Molly Smith. She's alive but is being held hostage in a fucking hole in the ground about twenty-five feet behind one of the large tents. I'm coming to help now, but if something happens to me, make sure to get her the fuck out of here."

"Ten-four," his three teammates said at the same time.

Smoke placed a gentle hand on Molly's shoulder. "We won't leave without you. But I really *do* need to get back out there and help my team."

He saw her swallow hard, then nod. "Okay. What can I do to help? You're pretty tall, so you might not need help getting out of here, but I can get on my hands and knees, and you can step on my back to give you a boost."

Smoke stared at her, shocked, for a moment. He *really* needed to get the fuck out of there, but he was awed by her response. She looked as if she weighed no more than the pack on his back—and she was offering to let him use her as a fucking step stool? No way in hell was that going to happen.

"I appreciate the offer, but I can make it," he told her. Making a split-second decision, Smoke shrugged off his pack and dropped it to the ground next to him. "Inside, there are gel packs for instant energy. I've got some water in my canteen, and there are a few MREs . . . meals ready to eat. I've got some rope in one of the pockets you can use for a belt, and if you want to change your shirt, I've got an extra in there as well. It's not clean, but it doesn't have holes in it."

Molly's eyes were huge as she whispered, "You're leaving your stuff?"

"Yes. I'm going to be back," he told her before glancing up at the edge of the hole again.

"Okay," she said bravely, but Smoke still heard her voice quiver.

He reached out and cupped her cheek. He was taking a risk touching her like that. She could've been raped and abused by her captors, but he couldn't have stopped himself if he tried. He *needed* to touch her. Needed to show her even a brief moment of kindness.

"Thanks for cushioning my fall," he said quietly with a smile. "I'll be back, Molly. Believe me, you're safer here than anywhere up there right now."

He waited for some sort of reaction to his words, and got it when her head tilted slightly, giving him a bit of her weight. It wasn't much, but even that small amount of trust almost did him in.

"Watch out. I'm going to jump," he said as he dropped his hand.

"Be careful," Molly replied.

Smoke didn't answer. He put his back against the wall of the hole, then pushed off with his foot and leaped for the top. He easily got his hands over the edge, but the dirt was slippery, and he immediately felt himself sliding backward.

But then Molly wrapped her arms around one of his legs and pushed upward with all her might.

She gave him just enough leverage that Smoke was able to swing his other knee up and over the edge of the hole. Once he was out, he glanced down. Molly had her head tilted back, and she was looking up at him. From this angle, she looked even younger than in her pictures. And desperate.

With a quick nod, Smoke rolled away from the hole and got to his feet. He still had his rifle across his back, and he pulled it into position. The knives in his holsters were in place, and he had two extra handguns on his person as well. Leaving his pack wouldn't make him more vulnerable in the least. If anything, it would make him stealthier.

"I'm on my way," Smoke said tonelessly into the radio, letting his team know he was back in action.

But a part of him was still in that hole with Molly. He wanted to know how long she'd been there. What her captors had done to her. When the last time she'd had anything to eat was. How she'd slept, because she sure as hell couldn't lie flat in that hole. He had a hundred questions, but no time to ask them.

He'd hated seeing the defeat in her eyes when he'd said he had to leave her. Notifying the team that she was there and letting her have his pack were the only ways he could think of to prove he was serious about coming back. Someone would be rescuing her, and Smoke hoped like hell it would be him.

A terrorist surprised Smoke by almost running straight into him as he dodged around a tree. The man started to raise his gun, but Smoke reacted faster, pulling the trigger on his rifle. The man fell like a sack of potatoes.

Listening to his team strategize as they closed in on the spot where Shekau had ducked out of sight, Smoke quickly jogged to catch up with them. He'd wanted to take out the leader of Boko Haram for a long time, but now all he wanted was for this to be over so he could get back to Molly. Reassure her that she wasn't alone anymore, and prove he hadn't forgotten her.

～

Molly stared at the large backpack sitting at her feet. She'd heard the gunshots earlier and had been sitting in a ball, her back against the wall of the hole, her heart hammering in her chest, when a man had literally fallen from the sky. Dirt and debris had rained down at the same time he'd landed on top of her, taking the wind from her chest. All she'd been able to do was squeak out a protest.

For a moment, she'd been afraid it was one of her captors. Never in her wildest imagination would she have thought an American soldier would fall into her hole. She had no idea what his name was, where he came from, or who he was working with, but honestly, she didn't give a shit.

He'd known her name, which had to mean he was one of the good guys . . . didn't it?

And he'd recognized her. Even without a mirror, Molly knew she looked awful. Her hair was a mess, she was filthy, and she'd lost a lot of weight. So much that her pants wouldn't stay up. She had to clutch them every time she stood. But he'd still recognized her.

And when he'd looked at her, it hadn't been with pity or disgust.

She would've sworn she'd seen admiration . . . but that couldn't have been right.

She was probably delirious from lack of food and water.

Speaking of which, Molly looked down at the man's pack. He'd promised to come back for her, but if he didn't, if her captors killed him and whoever he'd talked to over his radio, they'd take the backpack away from her.

She was torn between eating everything she could get her hands on and trying to make it last. Looking around, she wondered if she could bury some of the things she found in his bag so her kidnappers wouldn't find them.

Taking a deep breath, she shook her head. "No, he's coming back," Molly said. "He promised."

It was rather childish—saying the words wouldn't make them true—but it still made her feel better.

Feeling as if she was snooping, Molly forced herself to get on her knees and slowly unzip the pack. Reaching in, she pulled out a small dry bag. Curious as to what it contained but more interested in finding food, Molly put it back inside and rummaged around some more.

A minute or so later, she'd found the promised canteen, an MRE, the energy gel packs, and a T-shirt. He might've thought the garment was dirty, but to her, it was almost too good to be true. Not even thinking twice, she struggled out of the damp shirt she was wearing and threw it to the ground. She supposed she should salvage it just in case, but honestly, if she never saw it again, she'd be happy.

Molly pulled the man's plain black T-shirt over her head and inhaled deeply. It smelled like sweat. But it didn't repulse her. Under the sweat, she could faintly smell the scent of detergent.

Tears sprang to her eyes. She was being so stupid. But the scent of something so normal, so everyday, made her vow to never take being clean for granted again.

The shirt was ridiculously large on her. Her emaciated frame swam in it. Molly quickly gathered the extra fabric at her hip and tied it into a knot. She couldn't stop herself from also smelling the sleeve once more as she rolled it up.

It was official; she'd lost it.

Forcing herself to stop smelling the poor man's shirt, Molly struggled to open one of the gel packs. She'd never had one before, but she'd take any calories she could get right about now. She imagined her cells soaking in the nutrients like the ground sucked in the rain after a drought.

Not wanting to litter—even if that made her feel ridiculous, under the circumstances—she tucked the top of the plastic back into the man's pack and brought the gel to her lips. Squirting a bit into her mouth, she paused to assess. Her taste buds exploded from the sweetness, and she involuntarily puckered.

Molly could still hear gunshots above her, but she was too engrossed in what she was doing to give them more than a cursory thought. Food and water took precedence over everything else.

She swallowed the gel and decided that it was actually pretty good. She forced herself to consume the rest of the packet slowly, even though she wanted to gulp it down. She tried to unscrew the cap of the canteen next, but couldn't get it open.

She hated that she was so weak she couldn't even open the container to get to the contents. Frustrated, she wanted to cry, her mouth salivating at the thought of the clean water that was probably inside, but she reluctantly put the canteen aside and reached for the MRE. She ripped open the top and inspected the contents. She had no idea how the spaghetti was warmed up; right now, it felt like maybe it was freeze dried inside one of the packets—but when she saw the small bite of chocolate that was included in the meal, she forgot all about the pasta.

"Chocolate," she breathed.

The candy felt like mush inside the small wrapper, but that didn't deter her. She slowly peeled it open and brought it to her nose. The familiar smell of the chocolate made her want to cry yet again. Nana had always kept a bowl of chocolates in her dining room. She'd let Molly pick one out whenever she'd gone to visit with her parents . . . before they had died.

Molly licked every bit of chocolate off the wrapper, feeling sad when she'd finished. But then the crackers in the pack caught her attention. Knowing it might be a mistake to eat those without something to

drink, she decided to go for it anyway. There was also a piece of banana bread, but the crackers seemed easier to eat at the moment.

She ate one, then another, before her stomach began to rebel. It had been a very long time since she'd eaten as much as she just had, so Molly carefully put what she couldn't eat back into the MRE bag and tucked it inside the man's backpack. As she did, she saw the rope he had mentioned and pulled it out.

Standing slowly, Molly fed the rope through her belt loops and tied it tight, leaving the rest to dangle. She wasn't sure when she'd realized how much weight she'd lost. But one day she'd stood up, and her pants had literally fallen to her ankles. Her hip bones were sticking out, and knowing she'd lost so much weight was disheartening.

It was crazy how having something as simple as a belt somehow made things look brighter.

Putting another gel pack into her pocket, Molly placed everything else back into the pack and zipped it closed. She had no idea how much time had passed, but surely he'd be back soon.

She no longer heard gunshots above her, but that didn't make her feel any better. Had the kidnappers overpowered the man and his team? Were the schoolgirls all right? Had everyone fled the jungle and left her there alone?

Folly Molly . . .

The hurtful nickname came back to her in a rush. Maybe the man who'd dropped from the sky had been killed. It seemed as if everyone she came into contact with somehow ended up hurt. Look what had happened to the schoolgirls. And her parents.

Then there was Preston. Her bad luck had definitely been in charge when she'd met *him*.

Maybe her bad luck had rubbed off on the man who'd fallen in her hole, simply because he'd touched her.

Shaking her head, Molly tried to dispel the thought. She remembered how gentle his touch had been against her cheek. It had been

long since someone had touched her without the intent to hurt her. The hugs from Nana and Papa had been the last gentle human contact she'd known. Until the man had put his hand on her cheek.

Looking up, as if that would somehow conjure the man from thin air, Molly did her best to stay calm. "He said he'd be back, so he'll be back," she whispered. She just had to be patient. He'd come back for her. He'd promised.

Chapter Three

Smoke glanced at the carnage around him and sighed. So far, nothing on this mission had gone as Silverstone had hoped. Their usual MO was to sneak in, kill their target, and get out. But with the schoolgirls to protect and two dozen members of Boko Haram willing to do whatever it took to make sure their captives didn't escape, things had gotten crazy fast.

The only thing that had gone according to plan was eliminating Shekau. The team wasn't going to let him get away or allow the Nigerian forces to arrest him. He had enough supporters that even if he went to jail, there was a good chance he'd be able to get out to terrorize innocent girls once again. They hadn't given him a chance to beg for his life or use any of the girls as shields. After receiving confirmation from Eagle that the man they'd captured was actually Shekau, the head of Boko Haram, and not a decoy, Bull had put two bullets into his heart—and another in his head for good measure.

But that hadn't been the end of the job—not in the least.

When the dust finally settled, there were dead men lying all around the jungle hideaway. A few from the Nigerian security forces had been killed along with the terrorists. The girls were hysterical, crying and huddled together in the larger tents.

But throughout the bedlam and all the bullets flying, Smoke hadn't stopped thinking about Molly. He'd honestly not expected to find her.

It made no sense for Boko Haram to keep an American woman. He had no idea if they'd planned on ransoming her or what else they may have wanted to do.

"You said you found Molly?" Gramps asked.

"Yeah. I need to go back to her," Smoke said. He turned and headed behind one of the large tents, straight toward the hole where she was being held. His teammates followed close behind. Smoke knew he should be paying attention to the jungle around him, as it was more than likely some of the terrorists had fled into the dense foliage, but his eyes were glued to the ground.

The hole wasn't exactly hidden. Her captors hadn't tried to camouflage it.

"Holy shit, are you fucking kidding me?" Bull asked as they neared Molly's prison.

"Please tell me she's not in there," Eagle added.

"Assholes," Gramps threw in for good measure.

Smoke didn't blame his friends for their reactions. They'd seen many of the horrible things one human could do to another during their stint in the Army and as Silverstone. They definitely hated to see anyone, especially a woman, put into a hole and left to rot.

Lifting the strap of his rifle over his head and shoulders, Smoke got down on his hands and knees and crawled the remaining few feet to the hole. He didn't want to risk any debris falling in on Molly.

He peered over the edge—and blinked in surprise. Molly had obviously been through his pack, as she was now wearing one of his extra T-shirts. She'd tied it in a knot at her waist, and he could also see the ends of the rope he'd told her to use as a belt dangling down her legs. She was sitting on his pack, and her head was resting on the dirt wall behind her. Her eyes were closed . . . and she looked as if she was sound asleep.

"Molly?" Smoke called out.

She jerked as if he'd bellowed her name right into her ear, losing her balance and falling off his pack and into the mud at the bottom of the hole.

"I'm here!" she called, then looked up. "Are you all right?"

Smoke frowned. She was asking *him* if he was okay? Admiration bloomed in his chest. "I'm good. You want to get out of there?"

"Yes!" she practically shouted as she stood up. "There should be a makeshift ladder somewhere in camp. That's how I got in here, and how the assholes who kidnapped me got me out whenever they wanted to make a point."

Smoke didn't like the sound of that, but he let it go for now. "No need for a ladder," he told her. "Can you scoot over until your back is against the wall?"

She looked confused but immediately did as he asked. Smoke turned to look at his teammates. "I'm going down. I'll give her a boost up, then I'll need a hand."

"Of course," Gramps said, shrugging off his own pack and getting ready to assist.

"I'm coming down," Smoke warned Molly.

"What? No, wait—"

But Smoke was already moving. He sat on the edge of the hole, then hopped back down into the pit.

"I don't know whether to be impressed or pissed that you make that look so easy," Molly complained.

Smoke grinned, then ran his gaze over her, assessing. She looked rough. There was no denying that. But then again, so did he. He hadn't shaved in a month, and other than using a washcloth to clean himself, he hadn't had a real bath in that same amount of time. He and his team had been scouring the jungle for any signs of Boko Haram and the kidnapped girls. While they'd had the option to stay in a few small villages, they'd decided to rough it instead, just in case they came across any Boko Haram sympathizers.

But he hadn't been starved. Hadn't literally slept in the dirt. He'd washed his clothes in a couple of the small streams they'd come across, and he'd had plenty of water, thanks to the filters and purification tablets he and the others carried.

Molly hadn't had any of that. He had no idea how long she'd been kept in this hole, though it was obvious it had been more than a day or two. But amazingly, she stood in front of him right now, upright and unwavering.

If Smoke was being honest with himself, he was a little bit intimidated by her strength.

"You ready to get out of here?"

"Yes."

Her answer was short, but the emotion behind that one word was clear.

"Right. My friends will help you at the top, all you have to do is put your foot in my hands, and I'll lift you. Easy peasy. You ready?"

Molly looked up and saw Bull, Eagle, and Gramps standing at the top, waiting to help her. Then she looked back at him. "Am I allowed to ask what your name is?" she asked quietly.

"Shit. I haven't even introduced myself to you. Wow, is *that* rude. I'm Mark Chamberlin. But everyone calls me Smoke." He held out his hand.

"I'm Molly," she said politely as she shook his hand. "It's *very* nice to meet you."

Smoke held on to her hand for a beat, then squeezed it gently before letting go. He interlaced his fingers together and leaned over. "Put your foot here," he told her, gesturing to his hands with his head.

She put her hand on his shoulder to steady herself, then placed her tiny bare foot into his hands trustingly. Moving slowly so as to not startle her, Smoke stood as Molly walked her hands up the side of the hole, and the second she was within reach, his teammates took hold of her arms and pulled her up and out of her prison without fanfare.

Once she was out, Smoke picked up his pack and shrugged it on. Then he held up a hand, and Gramps grabbed hold. Within seconds, he, too, was standing beside the hole.

"Well, that was almost a little anticlimactic," Molly said, running a hand uneasily over her hair.

"Trust us, anticlimactic is good," Gramps said. "We prefer things to be unexciting, if possible. I'm Gramps."

Molly looked up at him. "I think you're taller than that hole I was in," she noted as she shook his hand.

He smiled back at her but didn't comment.

"I'm Eagle," Eagle said, as he extended his hand.

Bull then introduced himself, and Molly smiled at them all. "And I'm Molly, but I'm guessing you all knew that."

Everyone nodded. "We're very glad to see you alive and well," Eagle told her.

"Well . . . alive. I'm not sure about well," Molly quipped.

"You're sick?" Smoke asked, concern lacing his voice.

She shrugged. "I just meant that I'm a little worse for wear."

Smoke knew he should've relaxed at her explanation, but he couldn't seem to. Why he felt so bothered by her discomfort about the way she looked, he had no idea.

"What size shoe do you wear?" Bull asked.

Molly furrowed her brow. "Six. Why?"

"I'll be back," Bull said, then turned and headed for the mess on the other side of the tent.

Smoke knew he was going to search the dead men to see if he could find a pair of shoes that would work for Molly. He had no idea if she'd balk at wearing a dead man's shoes, but he didn't think so. Thus far, she'd been extremely levelheaded for someone who'd been through such an ordeal.

"Are they all dead?" she asked, her gaze flicking to the large tent nearby.

"The terrorists? Yes," Gramps told her bluntly. "You're safe. The Nigerian authorities will transport the girls who are still here back to the town of Askira to be reunited with their families. They'll also question everyone to see if they can get a lead on where the remaining missing girls might be."

"They married them off," Molly told them. "Before I pissed them off enough to put me in that hole, they made us all watch the ceremonies."

Smoke's blood boiled. Everything about stealing underage girls and then selling them off to the highest bidder was wrong. And to make the others watch, knowing that was likely going to be their fates as well, made it all worse.

"Come on, let's get you back with the others," Smoke said gently, gesturing for Molly to walk ahead of him.

She didn't look excited about the prospect of being reunited with the other girls, but she nodded and started walking gingerly toward the noise coming from the other side of the tent.

Smoke and Gramps shared a concerned look, following behind her.

"Did you get enough water?" Smoke asked as they walked.

"I couldn't get it open," Molly admitted.

"Fuck," Smoke swore under his breath. "Eagle, hang on a sec," he told his friend.

Everyone stopped walking as Smoke put his pack on the ground and rummaged through it. He pulled out his canteen and easily unscrewed the lid before handing it to Molly. "Sorry, I always crank the top extra tight. There's nothing worse than a leaky canteen."

Her hands shook as she reached for the water, and Smoke got pissed all over again. They all watched as her eyes closed when she took a sip of water. It was lukewarm and probably tasted funny because of the purification tablet, but Molly gave no indication that she was disgusted. She didn't guzzle the water, which was good, because it probably would've come back up. Instead, she took small sips, her enjoyment easy to see.

When she opened her eyes and saw that she was the center of attention, she smiled a little self-consciously. She capped the canteen and tried to hand it back, but Smoke waved her off. "Keep it."

"But I can't. It's yours."

Smoke shrugged his pack back onto his shoulders and shook his head. "And I'm giving it to you."

"Oh, well . . . thank you."

He liked that she didn't continue to try to refuse. She simply ducked her head and put the strap over her head and one arm so it was slung around her body.

"You look like a warrior," he commented.

Molly wrinkled her nose and gave a little self-deprecating laugh. "Oh yeah, a warrior wearing clothes that are falling off her body and who hasn't seen a bottle of shampoo in months."

"I'll take a warrior over a princess any day," Smoke said, not knowing where that had come from, and suddenly feeling embarrassed that he'd actually said it out loud. "Come on," he said quickly, trying to cover any awkwardness. "I'm sure the others will be thrilled to see you."

He heard Molly mumble something under her breath, but she'd already turned and started walking, so he missed what she said.

The second they stepped around the large tent, the noise hit him once more. The Nigerian forces were trying to organize the girls and get them ready for the walk to where the trucks had been left. Unfortunately, Boko Haram had set up camp where no trucks could go. They'd all have a long walk through the dense forest to get to their transportation.

Smoke and his teammates had planned on going in the opposite direction, back to where they'd left their own truck, but now suddenly that didn't seem like the best idea. Leaving Molly wasn't something he felt comfortable doing.

He opened his mouth to ask Gramps if he could talk to him privately to discuss a change in plans when one of the older girls began screeching. She pointed at Molly and ran toward her, yelling in Hausa and gesturing wildly.

Smoke had no idea what was going on, and he looked at a group of Nigerian officers standing nearby. They were staring at the girl in mild bewilderment but didn't seem overly concerned.

By the time Smoke looked back at Molly, the girl had reached her. She was standing right in front of her, still speaking rapidly and pointing at Molly's chest.

Molly's lips were pressed together, and her fists were clenched at her sides, but she didn't say anything in the face of the girl's obvious displeasure.

Then the girl's hand whipped up, and she slapped Molly across the face.

Before Smoke or anyone else could react, she did it again.

Her hand was raised to smack her a third time, but Gramps swiftly reached out and grabbed hold of the teenager's wrist, preventing her from making contact. The girl struggled against Gramps's hold as Smoke moved to Molly, putting his arm around her chest and pulling her away from the irate girl.

"What the fuck?" Eagle asked.

One of the Nigerian officers came over and grabbed the girl, who was clearly still spewing angry words at Molly, and dragged her back to the group. Now that Smoke took the time to study them carefully, he saw that none of the schoolgirls looked happy to see Molly. Most turned their backs to her; it was obvious she wasn't going to be welcomed with open arms.

"Are you okay?" Smoke asked, turning Molly so she was facing him.

She wouldn't meet his gaze. "I'm good." She brought a hand up to her face and rubbed her now-red cheek.

"Talk to me," Smoke ordered. "What was that about?"

He didn't think she was going to answer, but eventually she sighed. She still wasn't meeting his eyes, staring at his chest instead, but she explained, "They blame me for being kidnapped."

"That makes no sense," Bull said as he approached. He was holding a pair of battered sneakers and a pair of socks. "Why?"

"I'm bad luck," Molly said.

Smoke waited for her to say more, but when she didn't, he put his fingers under her chin and lifted her head until she had no choice but to look at him. "Explain."

"Folly Molly. That's what I'm called. I've *always* had bad luck. Apparently that didn't change even when I traveled halfway around the world. I was at the school to talk to the girls about what I do, about being an environmental engineer. I hadn't had a chance to speak before the school was overrun with kidnappers. Since I was the only thing different about that day . . . they blamed me."

"You know that's ridiculous, right?" Smoke asked.

She shook her head. "You don't understand," Molly whispered.

"What I understand is that Boko Haram had planned on kidnapping these girls long before they'd hit the school in Askira. There was chatter on the Homeland Security channels that proved it. You were in the wrong place at the wrong time, and you were in no way responsible for these assholes."

Folly Molly. The nickname was ridiculous. There was no such thing as someone being bad luck. Bad things happened to everyone.

"But they think I am," Molly said quietly. "They hate me. When I tried to get some of them to escape with me, they were too scared. They said I would bring the wrath of the kidnappers down on all of them if I tried anything. But I couldn't just sit in the tent all day and night, wondering what horrors our captors would do to us next. After I tried to escape the first time, they all turned on me. Refused to share any food with me. Didn't want to sleep near me. Then, after my second escape attempt, the kidnappers put me in that hole. The girls were probably relieved."

Smoke couldn't believe what he was hearing. "They turned *against* you?"

Molly shrugged. "I'm not like them. I'm white . . . an American. I'm an outsider. And I don't blame them for not wanting to do anything that would have made them a target to our captors."

"Fucking hell," Gramps muttered.

"Guess our plans have changed," Eagle said.

"Good thing I found these shoes," Bull added.

Smoke mentally sighed in relief. He wouldn't need to try to talk the team into letting Molly go with them, after all. But before he could reassure her that they would get her home safely, and that she wouldn't have to worry about the other girls, she took a step back from him.

"I appreciate you coming to help us all," she said a little stiffly. "I don't know what would've happened to us if you hadn't." She looked at each one of them. "Eagle, Bull, Gramps . . . Smoke. Thank you. I'll never forget you." Then she started walking toward the very group of girls who'd turned their backs on her.

Smoke moved quickly, grabbing hold of her upper arm and turning her around.

Molly looked at his hand, a question in her gaze.

"You aren't going with them," he told her.

"I'm not?" she asked. "Oh, right, because I'm not Nigerian. I get it. I'm guessing someone from my company will be meeting me and helping me get back to the States?"

Smoke shook his head slowly. "They evacuated the country after you were taken," he told her gently.

"They *left* me?" Molly asked in a small voice.

Smoke heard Gramps swearing behind him, but he didn't take his eyes from Molly's. He hated that she thought she'd been left behind—but that was exactly what they'd done. "They didn't abandon you," he hedged.

She stared at him, and Smoke had a feeling she could see right through his empty words. "Who hired you to come find me, then?"

Smoke pushed on, even though he was uncomfortable as fuck with this conversation. "We were tracking Abubakar Shekau. The leader of Boko Haram," he told her honestly.

He saw the moment his words registered. "You didn't come for me," she whispered.

"We didn't," Smoke agreed. "But that doesn't mean you weren't on our minds. We knew you'd been taken along with the schoolgirls, and we prayed that you'd be found with them."

Her eyes dropped. "Right. So what now? How am I supposed to get out of Nigeria? I don't have any money. Don't have my passport. I've literally only got the clothes on my back, and my company has deserted me. I suppose I could call my grandparents. They'd help me."

Smoke's heart nearly shattered at those words. It hadn't occurred to him before now that, of course, she had no idea her grandparents were dead. He did the mental math and realized that they'd been killed after she'd been taken hostage. She wouldn't have had any way of knowing what had happened.

He surreptitiously held up a hand to his teammates to keep them from saying anything.

The last thing this woman needed right this minute was to learn that her grandparents had been murdered.

"You're coming with *us*," Smoke informed her.

Molly looked at him for a beat, then at his teammates. "I am?"

"Yes."

Smoke had no idea what was going through her mind, but she shocked the shit out of him when she said, "Are we going to have to walk all the way back to Askira? I mean, I suppose after spending the last who knows how long in a hole, I can do that, but I was hoping for some sort of limo service or something."

Bull and Eagle burst out laughing, and even Gramps smiled at her.

The admiration Smoke had felt earlier bloomed in his chest once more. "No limo, but you won't have to walk all the way back. It's over a hundred miles, anyway."

Her eyes widened. "It is?"

"Yeah. But we stashed a truck about twenty miles from here. We're going to go to Maiduguri and catch a plane to the Murtala Muhammed International Airport in Ikeja. Then we'll head back to the States. We *will* need to walk a bit, but not a hundred miles." He wished she didn't have to walk even twenty. It almost felt like too much to ask of her after everything else she'd been through.

"I found you some shoes," Bull said, approaching them and holding out the sneakers. "They aren't Louboutins, but they should do."

Smoke saw tears form in Molly's eyes for the first time. "First a canteen and now shoes. You guys sure know how to treat a girl."

Deciding not to mention the tears, Smoke watched as she sat on the ground right then and there and pulled on the socks—which had holes in the toes—and the shoes. The shoes weren't in great shape, but they were better than her walking through the jungle with bare feet.

Smoke reached a hand down, and she grabbed hold and let him help her stand.

"How do they feel?" Bull asked. "I can go find others if those don't fit."

"They're good," Molly told him. "Thank you."

"Excuse me."

The words startled Smoke, and he realized that his sole focus had been on Molly, which hadn't happened to him before. He'd never gotten so distracted by someone they'd rescued that he'd forgotten anyone else was around.

Turning, Smoke saw one of the Nigerian officers standing nearby. "The American needs to come now. We're leaving."

Looking over, Smoke saw a line of girls walking out of the camp. Bodies still littered the jungle floor, but no one seemed the least bit interested in giving the terrorists any kind of burial. The few Nigerian officers who had been killed were being carried away by their comrades.

"She's coming with us," Gramps informed the man before Smoke could.

The man frowned. "That wasn't the plan. She needs to come with *us* now."

"Well, the plan's changed, and we're taking care of her from here on out," Eagle said, stepping in front of Molly.

Smoke put a hand on her hip and pulled her back toward him. "I don't think—"

"The girls are traumatized. You saw how they reacted to her. Do you really want to have to deal with trying to keep them apart while you travel back to Askira? It's better for everyone if they're separated."

"But she needs to be interrogated," the officer insisted.

"Interrogated?" Bull growled. "You're forgetting she's a victim in all of this too."

"I only meant that she might have information we need to find the missing girls."

"If she does, we'll pass it along," Eagle said. "We want them found as badly as you do. But you have to admit that things will be easier if we take her with us. It's obvious you can't house her in the same place as the other girls, not with the animosity between them. And what are you going to do with her once you get to Askira? Where is she going to stay? Who's going to take care of getting her home to the United States? It's going to cost money. We're volunteering to take responsibility for her. She's not your priority; only those girls are."

The man considered Eagle's words. "I don't like this," he said after a moment.

"You don't have to like it," Gramps said. "She's coming with us, and that's that."

Smoke stood close to Molly, ready to fight anyone who dared try to force her to go with them, but after a few very tense seconds, the man finally nodded. He spun around without another word and headed back to the others.

"Holy crap," Molly said. "That was intense. But you guys aren't responsible for me. I mean, I'm sure I can figure out how to get home."

"But now you don't have to," Gramps said, turning his back on the camp.

"I . . . thank you," Molly said.

Smoke was once more reminded of how grateful he was to have Silverstone. They had each other's backs, no questions asked, and seeing how the others had stood up for Molly made him proud to call them his friends.

"How about we get the hell out of this jungle?" Gramps suggested.

Eagle pulled out a GPS and took point. Bull followed, then Molly and Smoke, and Gramps was last.

As they walked away from the camp, Smoke glanced back. There were lots of things to look at. The tents, the dead bodies, and the tail end of the line of girls heading into the trees—but the only thing Smoke could concentrate on was the hole he'd fallen into, where he'd found Molly.

He didn't know what was in store for *her* future, but he had a feeling that his own had just irrevocably changed.

Chapter Four

Molly couldn't stop thinking about how the men she'd just met had stood up for her. Bull, Eagle, and Gramps had actually put themselves between her and the Nigerian officer, as if they'd fight before allowing him to take her. And the feel of Smoke's—no, *Mark's*—hand on her hip, pulling her slightly behind him as he'd also remained between her and what he'd obviously perceived to be a threat, had been a balm for her battered soul.

She'd thought she was going to die in that hole. Alone and forgotten. And now, here she was, with four champions.

Molly wanted to glance back at Mark as they walked, but she was too embarrassed to be caught staring. Besides, if she turned, he'd want to know what was wrong, and he'd probably make them all stop so she could rest, or eat and drink. He'd already proven to be keenly aware of her moods.

It was weird to have someone's undivided attention. She wasn't the kind of woman who'd ever made a man do a double take. She blended into the background, which was fine with her. Usually the only time someone noticed her was to make a comment on her size.

She'd always been slight, and she wasn't sure why it seemed to be such a big deal. Her mom had only been five feet tall, and her dad hadn't been all that tall himself, so it wasn't a surprise that she'd stopped growing at five-three.

"How're you holding up?" Mark asked from behind her.

Molly didn't turn her head, not wanting to trip over her feet or run into anything. "I'm good," she told him. She wasn't. Not really. After being held captive in that hole for so long, she wasn't used to walking so much. But she wasn't going to complain. She was alive, and not still *in* said hole, so she was good. Peachy. Perfect.

But something in her tone must've alerted Mark to the fact that she was being less than truthful. He whistled, and the others stopped. Everyone turned to stare at her.

Feeling uncomfortable with the attention, Molly fidgeted. "What?" she asked.

"We'll stop here for the night," Gramps said.

"No, I—"

But Molly's words went unheard as Gramps, Eagle, and Bull fanned out and disappeared into the foliage around them.

She looked at Mark. "I can keep going."

"I know," Mark said, which made her feel a little better. "But there's no need. We aren't on a timetable here. There's no reason to exhaust ourselves trying to get back to the truck. We've made good time today, actually better than I guessed we would. No one's after us, we don't have to hide or evade anyone as we head to our truck and Maiduguri. You aren't used to this, and we need to be careful with your health."

Molly swallowed and looked away, trying to keep her composure. Her thoughts inevitably turned to Preston. When they'd first started dating, he'd seemed equally attentive.

But it wasn't long before he began snapping at her, frequently calling her *stupid* and other names. And while at first he seemed so sweet and funny, he quickly became a jealous, possessive jerk who would just as soon scowl at her as smile.

She wasn't even sure she'd wanted to go out with him in the first place. But Preston was persistent. Feeling lonely—and as if her time to find someone to spend her life with was growing shorter and shorter—Molly eventually gave in.

Just a month later, while out at dinner, she told him she wanted to be just friends, and Preston refused. He hurt her. Holding her arms too tightly as he hurried her out of the restaurant, then slamming her against his car.

From that night on, he'd started stalking her in earnest.

Now, she couldn't help but wonder about Mark. What he was like in his normal life. He seemed protective now, but would that protectiveness morph into something different later, like it had with Preston? Until he wanted to know where she was every second of the day, calling her relentlessly until she picked up?

Did he hide things about himself as well?

"What are you thinking about so hard?"

Molly jerked at the question. Shit, she'd been so lost in her head, she'd forgotten where she was for a second. She did that all the time . . . and, of course, Preston had hated it.

"I'm sorry," she apologized.

"You don't have anything to be sorry about," Mark said with a small smile. "If you want to stand there all night and think, you go right ahead."

Well. That was certainly a different reaction than she was used to. "I just . . . I *am* tired, and if it's really okay, I wouldn't mind stopping."

"It's really okay," he reassured her. "You've done an amazing job today."

Molly wrinkled her nose. "I've had to stop every ten minutes for a break, and I'm sure if I wasn't here, you could've already been at your truck."

"If you weren't here, then we'd still be trying to find you," Mark said without hesitation. "Come on, let's find you a place to rest while we get things ready for tonight."

She let him lead her through the trees in the direction his friends had gone. Amazingly, they had found a small clearing, had already started gathering wood for a fire, and had also made room for a place to sleep.

"This is actually kind of fun," Eagle said with a smile as he dropped an armful of wood. "I mean, so far we've had to be stealthy. I like that we can simply camp and not have to worry about being quiet or seen."

"Are you sure we're safe?" Molly asked. "We aren't that far from the camp."

"We're safe," Mark answered for his friend. "There were a few men who escaped into the woods, but if they decide to give us shit, they aren't going to last long. They have to know their best bet is to get as far from the camp as possible."

"And while we're not trying to keep quiet, we're also not disregarding our safety altogether. We'll take turns staying up and standing guard. You're safe, Molly," Gramps said, the sincerity easy to hear in his tone.

"Thanks," she said softly. Then she watched as the four men worked in tandem; it was obvious they'd done this many times before. Not long afterward, there were four lean-tos set up, a fire was ready to be lit, and she was sitting on a crinkly blanket-type thing someone had pulled out of their pack.

Now she studied the sleeping arrangements with a wary eye.

"We only need four, since one of us will stay awake at all times," Mark said, obviously seeing her discomfort.

"Oh. I didn't mean to be rude," she told them.

All four men snorted.

"You aren't being rude," Eagle said. "We should've explained earlier to put you at ease."

"I didn't even ask . . . are you hurt? Did those assholes . . . violate you?" Mark asked gently.

His blunt question didn't offend her. While it was embarrassing to talk about, she preferred to have everything out in the open. "No. I don't think they had any idea what to do with me. They couldn't marry me off to one of their supporters, I was a grown woman, and I also stick out like a sore thumb. Being the only white woman, and an American at that, seemed to make them wary. I think they were happy to put me in that hole. Out of sight, out of mind, you know?"

"At the risk of sounding flippant, honestly, you were better off hidden away. The last thing you wanted was to bring attention to yourself. Being on Shekau's radar would not have been a good thing," Bull told her.

Molly nodded. "I know." And she did. Before she'd been put in the hole, she'd seen the Boko Haram leader in action. He'd walked around with a group of men trailing behind him, catering to his every whim. "One night, he came into the tent I was in," she told her rescuers, "and pointed out about five girls. The next day, they were gone." She shivered. "I'm sure he knew I was there—I definitely stuck out among the other girls—but he never laid a hand on me, and I guessed he was holding on to me for *some* reason. Maybe to ransom me? Or sell me? I think he had me put in that hole to make sure I didn't try to escape while he . . . did what he did with the other girls."

The looks on the men's faces told her that they probably agreed with her. She'd had a close call, and they all knew it.

"So . . . you've got a choice to make," Mark said with a small smile.

Molly was relieved he was changing the subject. "About what?"

"Dinner. We've got spaghetti, chicken with egg noodles and vegetables, beef taco, or meatballs in marinara sauce."

Molly's mouth watered at the thought of *any* of those options. "Anything is fine," she said. "I'm not sure how much I'll be able to eat. I pilfered a few crackers from your pack and thought they wouldn't even make a dent in my hunger, but after only a couple, I was stuffed."

Eagle nodded. "It'll take a while for your stomach to stretch back out. The key is to eat small meals several times a day."

"The beef taco tastes like shit," Bull added with a smile. "I suggest the spaghetti or the meatballs."

"Meatballs," Molly said. "I could probably use the protein. But don't count on me eating more than one. I don't want to waste any food."

"No worries. We've been rationing because we weren't sure how long we'd be gone. We have plenty to last us until we get back to civilization," Mark reassured her.

She watched as he pulled out a flexible card-looking thing—which he said was a heater—and added a bit of water to it. Then he put the heater and the meatball pouch back into the box the pouch had come from, and held it closed.

"That's kinda cool," Molly said, her eyes fixed on the pouch.

She heard laughter and looked up to find four pairs of eyes fixed on her. Knowing she was probably blushing, she asked, "What? It *is*."

"It's fun to see the reaction of someone who's never eaten an MRE before," Bull said.

"I bet Skylar would get a kick out of it too. She would probably arrange an entire lesson around it," Eagle said.

"Very true," Bull agreed.

Mark leaned over and said, "Skylar is Bull's girlfriend. She's a kindergarten teacher."

Molly had never thought she'd go from being trapped in a hole in the ground to sitting around the jungle with four men she probably would've found scary as hell if she'd met them anywhere else talking about MREs and their girlfriends.

"I'm thinking we need to challenge Archer to make something edible out of these things," Smoke said with a smirk.

"Are you *insane*?" Gramps asked. "No fucking way."

"And Shawn Archer is one of our employees back in Indianapolis. He was hired to clean, do the landscaping, and cook, but pretty much just cooks now. He's amazing, and I hope to God we never lose him," Mark explained.

Molly glanced at him. "One of your employees?"

"Yep, you're looking at the owners of one of the most successful towing companies in Indianapolis," Eagle said with a smile.

Brows drawn down in confusion, Molly asked, "If you own a towing company, what in the world are you doing in a jungle in Nigeria?"

Bull, Eagle, and Gramps all looked over at Mark, making it clear he was to answer that question.

"This is kind of our . . . second job," Mark offered.

"What? Rescuing damsels in distress?" Molly asked.

"That's sometimes a side effect of our missions. We used to be in the Army. Special Forces. We do the same thing now that we did when we were active duty. We track down and eliminate the dregs of society. The FBI and Homeland Security assist us with logistics."

Molly nodded. "So you weren't lying when you said I wasn't your mission. You were here to kill Shekau."

"Yes."

"That makes sense. I'm just glad you fell into my hole in the process," she said wryly.

"No comments about what we do?" Gramps asked.

Molly shrugged. "Not really. I have more questions about your towing company, actually. How many employees do you have? Why did you decide to start it? Does being out here affect it? And you have a *cook*? That must mean you're pretty successful. Why did you choose Indianapolis?"

For a second, no one said anything—then all four men laughed.

"What?" she asked yet again. She was asking that question a lot.

"I'll never understand women," Gramps said with a small shake of his head.

"Why?" Molly asked, totally lost now.

"When Bull told Skylar what he did, she couldn't handle it, and he almost lost her. When Eagle told his girlfriend about Silverstone—that's what we call ourselves—she pretty much didn't blink. And now you, after finding out that we're basically assassins, just want to know about our towing company."

Molly wrinkled her nose. "Sorry, should I not have asked about your business?"

"No! I just find it fascinating. We agreed never to tell anyone about these missions in order to protect ourselves and our families. It just seems that people care less than we thought," Gramps said, trying to explain.

"I'm impressed. And in awe of you. I mean, I'm sitting here trying not to attack Mark and steal those meatballs—which smell delicious—out of his hands, but even *that's* because of what you do. I'd still be in that hole right now, wondering if they'd remember to feed me today.

"And I saw firsthand how horrible men like Shekau can be. How they have no compassion toward their fellow human beings. Anyone who would sell women like slaves deserves to die. What you do is important. I'm just a science nerd myself. I want to go back to my boring life in Oak Park, outside of Chicago. Back to my grandparents. They've got to be worried sick about me, and I want to reassure them that I'm okay. I find it a little surprising that you four do what you do, but I'm not going to judge you for killing the man who was responsible for me almost dying in a hole."

The men were throwing glances at each other left and right, and Molly couldn't figure out what she'd said that had them looking so uncomfortable. "I'm sorry if I said anything offensive."

Mark cleared his throat. "No, it was perfect. I think dinner is ready."

Surprised at the change of subject, Molly let it go after smelling the meatballs once again. Mark pulled the pouch of food out of the minioven he'd made with the materials of the MRE packaging and handed it to her, along with a spoon.

Steam rose from the pouch, and Molly inhaled deeply. Her stomach growled, and she couldn't help but grin. To go from believing she was going to die to sitting here with hot food in her hands less than eight hours later was a hard adjustment.

"Careful, it's hot," Mark cautioned unnecessarily.

Nodding, Molly kept her attention on the food. She spooned up a piece of meatball and blew on it impatiently. She noted that the others were also eating meals they'd prepared. She was glad they weren't staring at her as she ate.

They dined in silence, and even though Molly could only eat one meatball, as predicted, she did her best to nibble on some of the other items in the MRE. Mark finished off the remaining meatballs and packaged up the rest of the food for her to eat later.

The jungle got dark quickly; it was something that had surprised her when she'd first gotten to Nigeria. One second it was dusk, the next it was pitch dark. The men got the fire going, and if she closed her eyes, she could almost pretend she was sitting in her grandparents' backyard, making s'mores around their firepit.

"I need to tell you something," Mark said gently.

Molly turned to look at him. She was sitting on the blanket thing, her arms around her knees, enjoying the feeling of a full belly. But that belly suddenly rolled when she saw his expression—it was obvious whatever he wanted to tell her wasn't anything good. "What?" she asked.

"It's about your grandparents."

Everything within Molly froze. Except for her breathing. That sped up, and she wanted to put her hands over her ears like she was three years old again.

"I'm really sorry, Molly, but . . . they passed away while you were in captivity."

45

Molly instantly flashed back to when she'd been in junior high, and a police officer had said almost the exact same words about her parents.

Her body began to shake, and she couldn't do anything but stare at Mark and pray he was mistaken.

"There was a fire at their house. Their bodies were found in the rubble. The police . . . they believe they were deceased before the house was set on fire."

Molly wasn't even aware he'd moved until Mark put his arms around her. She turned her face away and squeezed her eyes shut, resting her forehead on his arm and shaking her head.

"I'm *so* sorry," Mark murmured.

She couldn't believe it. Not Nana and Papa. They were the last people she had in the world. Without them, she had no one.

"Breathe, Mol," Mark ordered.

She hadn't realized she wasn't, and she gasped in a large breath. But that just made the pain more acute. Sobs wracked her body then, but no tears fell. She wasn't hydrated enough, even with Mark and his friends pushing water and those gel packets on her all day as they'd walked.

Molly had no idea how long she sat in Mark's arms, but when her mind cleared, she realized that the other three men had moved closer. Bull's hand was resting on one of her knees, and Eagle's was on the other. Gramps was sitting on her other side, his arm around her lower back.

She might have normally been uncomfortable surrounded by four large scruffy men, but she was just . . . numb. She appreciated their support, and was surprised by it; she was a stranger, after all. But she couldn't really concentrate on anything other than the fact that her beloved Nana and Papa were gone.

"What happened?" she whispered finally, not moving her head from Mark's arm.

"All we know is what the report said," Bull answered. "That fire personnel were called to a house with flames coming out of the roof.

The house was fully involved, and it took several hours to completely douse the flames. When the fire inspectors went inside, they found your grandparents in an upstairs bedroom. It wasn't until the autopsies, when no smoke was found in their lungs, that they realized they'd been murdered before the fire was set."

Molly's throat closed, and she was afraid the food she'd eaten earlier was going to come up.

Murdered. Nana and Papa had been *murdered*. It was bad enough thinking they'd perished in a fire, but to know someone had killed them was far worse.

"The house was a complete loss," Eagle said.

Something else occurred to Molly. She had nothing. Literally *nothing*. She'd moved in with her grandparents after Preston had started harassing her. All of her belongings had been in her grandparents' house. Not only had she lost the only two people in the world who gave a shit about her, but she now had just the clothes on her back, literally . . . and the shirt didn't even belong to her.

"Do you have somewhere to go when you get home?" Gramps asked. "Someone you can stay with?"

"I'll figure it out," Molly whispered. "All my things were in the house. I can go to Goodwill to get clothes to tide me over. I'll have to avoid Preston—"

"Preston?" Mark interrupted, his tone . . . deeper? "Who's Preston, and why do you need to avoid him?"

"My ex," Molly admitted. "He wasn't happy I broke up with him, and he was actually the reason I took the job overseas."

"Not happy *how*?" Gramps asked.

"He followed me everywhere. Literally *everywhere*. Including the one time I tried to go on a date with someone else. Preston interrupted our dinner and accused me of cheating on him. I think he was drunk, which isn't a surprise; he drank pretty heavily while we dated—something I had no idea about beforehand—and it just got worse after we broke up. I tried to convince my date that we weren't together, hadn't been for a long while, but he said I wasn't worth the hassle and left me at the restaurant."

"He left you there? With your ex?" Mark snapped.

For some reason, Molly wasn't scared of this man. His ire wasn't directed at her. She knew the difference. "Yeah."

"Focus, Smoke," Bull said. Then asked, "You scared of this Preston guy?"

Molly nodded.

"Could he have been so mad he couldn't find you that he'd hurt your grandparents?" Eagle asked.

Molly hated to even think about that . . . but she nodded again.

"Fuck," Gramps swore.

Mark's arms tightened as he said, "You can stay with me in Indianapolis when we get back to the States."

Even though Molly felt as though she was swimming through molasses, she raised her head in surprise. "What?"

"You can stay with me," he repeated. "I've got a house on several acres, and it's just me. I know it's not home, but you won't have to worry about this Preston asshole finding you, and it'll give you time to figure out what your next steps are. I'm sure there will be stuff you've got to figure out with insurance and your grandparents' estate. You can do that from Indianapolis as easily as you can from Chicago."

Molly was flabbergasted. She couldn't believe this man, whom she'd just met, would offer something so generous. She just stared at him, speechless.

"He's got plenty of room," Bull assured her when she didn't answer. "He can more than afford to have you there. And I'm sure Skylar would love to meet you."

"Taylor too. And if your ex somehow finds out where you are, Smoke won't let him get near you," Eagle added.

"You can come hang out at Silverstone Towing during the day, if you aren't comfortable being at his place by yourself," Gramps said.

"Thank you, but . . . I *can't*," Molly said, her head spinning.

"Why not?" Mark pressed.

She didn't really want to get into this, but figured she should be honest. The last thing she wanted was for something to happen to Mark's house—or Mark himself—because of her. "I'm bad luck," she said simply.

The four men, who hadn't moved away from her, glanced at each other in obvious confusion.

"Seriously, why not?" Mark asked.

"I *am* being serious. Everyone I've had any lasting contact with has suffered because of me."

"You honestly believe that?" Mark asked.

Molly nodded.

"I'll take my chances," he said, as if it was already decided.

"You don't understand. My parents died because of me. My grand-parents died because I made a shitty choice in a man. Those girls were kidnapped because of me. I'm like a good-luck charm in reverse!"

"Bullshit," Mark growled.

Molly was so surprised at his gruff response to her lifelong shame, she could only stare at him.

"I read your file. Your parents died in a freak train accident. It had nothing to do with you."

She was briefly surprised there was a "file" on her somewhere, but she had to make Mark understand why being anywhere near her wasn't a good idea. "They were coming home after working late, on a train they didn't usually take, because I'd badgered them to take me to a show the next day," Molly protested.

"You weren't responsible for that train derailing," Eagle told her.

Molly shook her head. "I'm ninety-nine percent sure my ex killed Nana and Papa. There's no one else who would hate them enough to murder them. He was probably trying to get them to tell him where I was, and they refused. So *they* died because of me too."

"That's on Preston, not you," Mark insisted.

"But—" Molly started, but she was interrupted by Mark again.

"No *buts*. Your ex being a douche is on *him*, not you. Those girls being kidnapped had nothing to do with you—it had to do with Shekau being a grade A asshole who got off on enslaving others and profiting from their pain."

"Folly Molly," Molly whispered. "It's what I've been called my entire life. Even my parents joked about it."

Mark took her face in his palms. "Cruel childhood names don't mean shit to me. I'm not scared of you, Molly. If anything, you should be worried about *me*."

As Molly looked into the heated brown gaze of the man holding her, she wondered for the first time if she'd gotten out of the frying pan only to land in the fire.

"I see you're finally getting it. You don't know anything about me. I could be as much of an asshole as Preston."

Molly swallowed. Well . . . Mark had certainly gotten her to think about something other than her precious grandparents' deaths. She knew she'd obsess over what happened to them later, but for now, her focus was on the man holding her.

"You aren't," she said softly, despite having wondered the same thing herself.

"You're right, I'm not. Your instincts are good, Mol. You've had some shit happen to you, but—and I'm not trying to be harsh here— shit happens to everyone. Bull's mom left when he was a baby, and his dad died when he was seventeen. Skylar was taken captive by a pedophile and almost killed. Taylor has a condition where she can't recognize anyone's faces, including her own, and her mom couldn't deal, so she just gave her up. She grew up in foster homes, never connecting with anyone. Gramps's family came over from Mexico illegally and definitely didn't have an easy time of it. And my parents were *also* killed, and I was raised by my uncle. I'm very sorry about everything that's happened to you, but you aren't the first woman to be stalked by an ex, and you aren't the only person who's suffered a loss."

Molly stared at him. His words *were* pretty harsh, but he didn't give her a chance to comment, just kept talking.

"But dwelling on the bad stuff that happens to you means you miss out on seeing the good things. Yeah, you were in the wrong place at the wrong time and got kidnapped by Boko Haram, but you're alive right now. You weren't violated, and you're going home. Your parents were killed, but that gave you a chance to know your grandparents in a deeper way. I'm guessing you wouldn't have been nearly as close to them if they hadn't taken you in. There are two sides to every coin, Molly, and I know it's hard, but you have to look on the positive side. Otherwise, you'll drown in your own negative thoughts."

Molly swallowed hard, and Mark let go of her face. She dropped her forehead to his shoulder and inhaled deeply. He smelled like sweat, but it wasn't repulsive. She knew she probably smelled much worse than he did.

He was right. She was alive. It hurt more than she'd ever thought possible to think about Nana and Papa, but they'd been the best grandparents she could've asked for. They'd taken her in without a second thought. If Preston had tried forcing them to divulge where she was, she knew with every fiber of her being they wouldn't have said a word. They wouldn't take any chances that Preston would track her down, even on the other side of the world.

They loved her. Completely and without reservation. She knew if they were here right this second, they'd tell her to accept Mark's incredibly generous offer.

"Preston's probably going to find me," she warned.

"I hope he does," Gramps growled.

Molly glanced at the other man. "He's dangerous," she said.

Gramps stared at her for a beat, then grinned. "Honey, look around you. We aren't exactly slouches ourselves."

Molly realized he was right. These men had been in the jungle for a month looking for Abubakar Shekau. A man no one had seemed to be able to locate. They'd not only found him, but had killed him—and had helped rescue most of the kidnapped girls. Even *she* knew how low the odds of them accomplishing this mission had been. "You have a point," she said.

Mark's body shook against hers. She looked up at him. He was chuckling. "My house is big and on quite a few acres, but the security is top notch. I've got cameras everywhere. They're a pain in the ass, but a squirrel can't fart on my property without me being notified. And you'll see that Silverstone Towing is just as secure. You'll be safe with me, Molly. I swear it."

"If you get sick of me, or want me gone, all you have to do is say the word, and I'm out of there."

"I won't, but okay," Mark said.

"I'll talk to Skylar about getting her some clothes to tide her over," Bull said.

"And I'm sure Taylor won't mind taking her shopping when we're home," Eagle added.

"Archer will be thrilled to have the chance to fatten her up," Gramps threw in.

Molly had no idea what was happening. Why these people, who she didn't even know, were being so generous.

"You'll get used to us," Mark told her. "You tired?"

Amazingly, she was. She'd thought there would be no way she could sleep after everything that had happened, especially after hearing about her nana and papa, but at the moment, her eyes felt so heavy she thought she could sleep sitting up. "I haven't slept lying flat in I don't know how long," she muttered.

Before she could move, Mark had stood, with her in his arms. Molly quickly clutched at him.

"Easy. I'm not going to drop you."

She did her best to relax, but couldn't stop the words from leaving her lips. "One night when he was hammered drunk, Preston picked me up once, then *purposely* dropped me, laughing at the way my ass bounced off the floor."

"Fucker," Mark growled, his arms tightening. "You're safe with me."

Those four words seeped into her psyche. She *was* safe with Mark. How she knew that for certain, she had no idea, but she had no doubt he'd do whatever was necessary to protect her.

And that sort of scared her. She didn't want him getting hurt because of her. Too many people in her past already had.

She had to make certain he wasn't caught up in her drama. She owed him that much and more.

He carried her over to the lean-to closest to the fire. Going down on one knee, he gently lowered her to the ground. What she could only call a *sleeping bag liner* had already been spread out.

"Your castle, milady," he joked.

Molly put her arms over her head and arched her back, stretching muscles that were tight and achy after everything her body had been through the last couple of months. "Thank you," she said softly.

"I really am sorry about your grandparents," Mark said. "Maybe tomorrow while we're walking, you can tell us about them."

Molly had no idea if he was serious or not, but she respected him all the more for offering. "Thanks again."

"And you have nothing to fear from me or the others," Mark told her. "I swear you're safe with us, Molly."

"I know." And she did. Not once had she worried about being attacked or taken advantage of. Bull, Eagle, Gramps, and Mark had been nothing but gentlemen. They might've looked a little scary with their bushy facial hair and dirty black clothing, but they'd acted more decently than any of her captors had.

Mark studied her for a long moment before he nodded and stood. He walked back to the fire and sat. Gramps was no longer anywhere to be seen, so Molly assumed he was already patrolling, making sure they were safe to let down their guards.

She knew she *shouldn't* have felt safe. Not after discovering Preston had killed her grandparents, and knowing some of her captors were most likely still lurking around the forest. But somehow, even in the middle of the dark jungle, she'd never felt safer.

～

"She took that well. Almost too well," Eagle observed when Smoke sat back down at the fire.

"I think she's in shock after everything that's happened," Smoke said, resisting the urge to turn around and check on Molly. He'd literally just left her, she was fine. "I told her if she wanted, we'd love to hear about her grandparents tomorrow."

"Good thinking," Bull said.

"You think the ex did it?" Eagle asked.

Smoke shrugged. "No idea. But her fear of him is certainly real."

"I fucking hate bullies," Bull said with a scowl. "If you need any help with anything, let us know. We may not have a fancy house, but Skylar and I are more than happy to stand guard if necessary."

"I know, and I appreciate it," Smoke told his friend.

Conversation waned, and he thought about everything that had happened earlier that day. He hadn't thought they'd find Molly Smith, but they had. And she'd turned out to be so much more than he'd expected. Yes, he'd read her file, and he'd also seen her picture . . . which didn't do her justice. But even down in that hole, he'd been impressed with her. Especially the way she'd put her fear aside when necessary, and her obvious concern for everyone but herself.

She was also . . . real. Very down to earth. He appreciated that more than he could say.

He'd never had a problem catching a woman's eye. He'd gotten the best of his parents in the looks department, and women had often told him that he was handsome. But after they'd gotten to know him—specifically, once they'd learned about his substantial inheritance from his uncle—their interests had always changed, sometimes in less than subtle ways. They suddenly began to prefer more expensive restaurants. Oohed and aahed over pricey clothes and jewelry. One had even flat out asked him, "You can afford it, what's the big deal?"

They'd stopped being interested in *him*, instead falling in love with his money.

He couldn't know for sure . . . but he suspected Molly might be different. She didn't know about his inheritance, although Bull had implied he had plenty of money. And she would've been happy to meet *anyone* who could get her out of that hole, but he hadn't imagined the shy glances she'd been giving him throughout the day. Or the way she'd clung to him after hearing the awful news about her grandparents, and not Gramps or the others.

They'd already connected, starting the moment he'd fallen into that hole. In a way that was different, deeper, than if they'd met in a bar or club. In a way that had nothing to do with what he could buy for her.

He vaguely wondered if this was what Bull and Eagle had felt upon meeting Skylar and Taylor. This instant need to know them better. Oh, Smoke wasn't ready to get down on one knee and propose—not by a long shot; he hardly knew the woman.

But for the first time in ages, he was excited to *get* to know a woman.

Losing his internal battle not to look behind him, Smoke turned. Molly was still lying on her back, her legs spread just slightly, and her arms stretched out to her sides. She was taking up as much space as possible on the poncho liner they'd spread out. He smiled. It had to feel good to be able to sleep like that after being cooped up in a small hole for so long.

He was suddenly glad he'd decided to put a king-size bed in one of his guest rooms. She'd have as much space as she wanted.

His offer to let her stay with him was definitely out of character. He didn't go around offering a room in his house to everyone he rescued. Yes, he felt bad about the situation with her grandparents, and he was worried about that ex of hers, but plenty of other people he'd helped out in the past had issues as well.

No. His offer wasn't just a kind act from one stranger to another. There was something special about this woman, and he had a feeling if he let her go *without* attempting to offer help, he'd regret it the rest of his life.

And thinking about Molly living in his house didn't freak him out in the slightest. The big ole house had gotten lonely over the years. He'd loved the space at first, had grand plans for filling it, but as the years had gone by, it had started to seem more and more like a waste, and he'd considered selling everything, lock, stock, and barrel. He'd thought he'd be married with children by now, but that hadn't happened.

After thinking long and hard about moving into a smaller place, he'd realized he couldn't. It was the house he'd grown up in, and it held memories of his uncle everywhere he looked. It might've been a pain in the ass to clean and to manage the grounds, but it wasn't as if he didn't have the money for upkeep.

He had no idea if Molly could cook . . . if she was clean or messy . . . what she liked to do in her free time. All he knew was that she was an environmental engineer who needed someone to offer a helping hand. He could do that and more.

He'd also find out about this Preston asshole—and if he truly was a danger to Molly, Smoke and his friends would mitigate that danger.

Smoke's turn at patrol was after Gramps's, so he nodded at Eagle and Bull and headed for the lean-to next to Molly's. Lying down, positioning himself so he could see her, he closed his eyes. It would be a long trip back to Indianapolis, but he was anxious to get her back to the States and on his home turf. He had a feeling Molly could change his life . . . if she was brave enough to try.

Chapter Five

It took another few days to get to where Mark and his friends had stashed their truck. Molly hated that she'd slowed them down so much. She'd heard Bull talking about Skylar, and knew Eagle was worried about his pregnant wife, but no matter how hard she'd tried to push, her body—so deprived of nutrients and exercise—just wouldn't let her go more than four or five miles before it began to shut down.

It was hard work walking through the jungle. There were no paths, and it wasn't like walking down the street. The hot weather and humidity sapped her strength even further, and she'd had a hard time eating as much as she needed to replenish her energy.

The men had reassured her over and over that it was fine, that they were in no hurry. But that made Molly feel even more guilty. Because *she* was in a hurry. She wanted to go home. Even if she didn't *have* a home anymore, she was ready to put Nigeria in her rearview mirror.

Most of the people she'd met before her kidnapping had been amazing. Kind and friendly. They'd been enthusiastic about her job, and about water purification, and she'd been welcomed with bright smiles and open arms just about everywhere she'd gone.

Then everything had gone to shit, and even her fellow captives had hated her.

Regrettably, she'd forever associate Nigeria with her terrifying kidnapping—and worse, with learning about her grandparents' deaths. That was a blow she knew would never heal.

But Mark and his friends had helped more than she could say. He'd asked about Nana and Papa and let her talk about them nonstop the day after they'd given her the news. She'd told them about what a wonderful cook her nana had been, especially how amazing her pound cake was. Molly told them all about how her papa had loved Christmas and started decorating at the beginning of November. He would've kept their tree up all year if Nana would've let him.

The more she talked, the less it hurt. Well . . . the pain of never seeing them again was still unbearable. But somehow, just hearing Mark and the others laugh at some of the things her grandparents had said and done made Molly feel a tiny bit better.

The plan was to spend the night at the Dujima International Hotel, then catch a plane to Murtala Muhammed International in Ikeja. Gramps had said they'd probably have to spend a night there as well while they waited on a replacement passport for her. Molly had no idea how they were going to pull that off so quickly, but she didn't ask. Since none of the men seemed concerned about getting her out of the country, she tried not to be either.

She'd spent a *lot* of time thinking about what Mark had said, about being positive, and Molly realized that all her life, she'd been *that* person. The one who saw the negative in everything. She reluctantly had to admit her parents had done the same thing, and her grandparents frequently had as well. Negativity was learned, and while she hated always seeing the bad around her instead of the good, it was a very hard habit to break.

During that long hike, Molly decided she was going to try to turn her thinking around, but she knew it wouldn't be easy. She was thirty-five and had lived her entire life being Folly Molly.

When she'd told Mark she wanted to be more positive, he'd smiled and told her that he'd do what he could to help.

Which blew her away even more than the offer of a place to stay.

Mark was the type of man who could have any woman he wanted. She was sure of it. Why he was bothering with *her* was a mystery. She figured he felt responsible for her for some reason, or maybe considered her a project. After they'd been back in the States for a while, he'd come to his senses and wonder why he'd taken her in as if she were some lost little girl.

Then again, wasn't that what she was? She might be educated, and definitely old enough to make decisions on her own, but the idea of trying to figure out what to do next—when she basically had zero possessions to her name—was almost paralyzing.

Regarding a job, she supposed she still had a position at Apex, but after everything that had happened, she wasn't sure she wanted to go back.

If not, she really *was* going to have to start her life over in every way.

When they finally reached the truck, Molly had never seen a better sight. The vehicle itself was a piece of crap, and she wondered if it would even start.

"Don't worry, it'll get us to Maiduguri."

Molly frowned, realizing she'd done what she'd always done—automatically thought about what could go wrong rather than being thankful for what she had. She nodded. "That's good, because I'm not sure I could walk for much longer."

Mark smiled at her—and Molly's breath froze. His smile completely changed how he looked. More approachable. More open. And she hadn't fully registered exactly how good looking he was until right that second. Now she couldn't help but wonder what he looked like without the bushy beard. Some men simply looked better with facial hair, but she had a feeling a naked-faced Mark would blow her away.

Gramps got behind the wheel, and they all climbed in with him. Molly was sandwiched between Mark and Eagle in the back seat, and Bull took the passenger seat. When they were all settled, Gramps turned around and asked, "So, who has the keys?"

Oh God, what if no one had them? What if they couldn't start the truck?

But then Gramps smiled at her and winked. "Gotcha," he said, holding up a single key.

It took Molly a second to realize he was teasing her. "Not nice," she said, attempting to scowl at him . . . but she couldn't hold the mean face and instead burst out laughing.

When she pulled herself together, she realized she was the center of attention—again. All four men were staring at her.

"What?" she asked.

"Nothing," Bull said with a grin, turning around to face the front.

Gramps did the same, putting the key in the ignition and starting the truck.

Molly looked at Eagle, who just winked at her, then she turned to Mark and raised an eyebrow.

"It's just good to see you laugh, Mol," he told her softly.

Molly bit her bottom lip. She couldn't remember when she'd last laughed. Not a full-body laugh. Or when someone had last teased her as Gramps had. Not while she'd been a captive, and certainly not in the last couple of days while her thoughts had been full of Nana and Papa.

The truck lurched as Gramps put it into gear and slowly pulled out of the heavy overgrowth and onto the road. *Road* was probably an overstatement. What they were driving on was more like a rut in the forest, but Molly was too glad to not be walking to care about being jostled.

Closing her eyes, she stretched her legs; sitting felt so good right now.

She heard Eagle snort next to her, and she opened one eye before turning her head to look at him.

"Being short has some advantages," he said, nodding to her stretched-out legs.

Molly glanced down and saw that both Eagle's and Mark's knees were touching the seats in front of them. She couldn't help but grin. Seeing the positive side of things really *did* feel good. She could've been concentrating on how much her legs hurt from walking. How dirty she was. How desperately she missed her grandparents . . . but instead, in that moment, she was just grateful she could stretch her legs out and not be cramped.

"You know what else is good about being short?" she asked.

"Nope, what?" Eagle asked.

"I don't have to worry about how big bathtubs are; I always fit. Same for showerheads . . . they're never too short for me. The water always runs over my head instead of hitting me in the chest."

"Both good things," Gramps said from the front. "I can't tell you how many deep knee bends I've had to do in showers simply to get my head under the spray."

That comment sparked a long and boisterous conversation about showers, and the various places where the men around her had taken them during missions.

Molly didn't participate, simply sat back and listened. She knew she had a goofy smile on her face, but she couldn't help it. The conversation was so . . . normal. Which in itself was weird, considering the men around her were anything *but* normal.

As the conversation waned, the rocking of the truck and the late-day heat began to put Molly to sleep.

Right before she went under, she felt Mark pick up her hand.

She opened her eyes to see her fingers interlaced with his. She couldn't remember the last time she'd held hands with anyone, let alone a man.

Feeling safer than she had in a very long time, tucked between Eagle and Mark, with her hand held firmly by the latter, Molly let herself relax and fall asleep.

She jerked awake when Gramps turned off the engine outside what looked like a motel. The stucco walls were cream colored, and everything about it looked fresh and clean. "We're here," he announced.

"Where's here?" Molly asked, trying to get her brain to function. She felt spaced out after her nap.

"Dujima International Hotel in Maiduguri," Gramps told her. "Home sweet home, at least for the night."

"I'll go in and grab some rooms," Eagle said, hopping out of the back seat.

"Once we get you settled, I'll head out and see what I can find for you clotheswise," Bull said, turning around to speak to her.

"Oh, I don't need much," Molly protested.

The men completely ignored her.

"Don't forget shampoo. And conditioner if you can find it," Mark told Bull.

"I'm not going to forget shampoo," Bull said with a raised brow. "I'm the one who lives with a woman, I think I know what she needs."

"Shoes too," Gramps threw in.

"Size six," Mark reminded him.

"Six. Got it. I'll figure out what size that is over here," Bull answered with a nod.

"Seriously, I don't need much." Molly tried to interject. But once again they talked over her.

"She's probably going to be cold on the plane. Since she's been in the jungle for so long, her body's gonna have a hard time reacclimating to air-conditioning. So grab a sweatshirt or sweater too," Gramps suggested.

"Right, since she's lost weight, she'll feel even colder," Bull agreed.

"And food. We're running low on supplies. She'll need to keep eating every couple of hours," Mark reminded his teammate.

"Guys!" Molly said as forcefully as she dared.

All three stopped talking to stare at her.

She sighed. "I appreciate your help more than I can say. I can't exactly go out and buy anything right now, as I don't have any money. But I really *don't* need much. I don't want to put anyone out. A pair of pants, a shirt, maybe some underwear, and a pair of flip-flops. That should tide me over. I can use the motel's toiletries."

"Not happening, sweetheart," Bull said with a shake of his head. "I'm not sure what the selection will be here, but I've been with Skylar long enough to know that she feels better about herself when she's feeling pretty. Now, as far as we're concerned, you're already fucking beautiful—we value strength over everything else. And someone who's survived what you have is fucking Superwoman. It's not a hardship to find you some clothes that will fit better than Smoke's T-shirt. You've got a hard road ahead of you, and making sure you feel comfortable will go a long way toward making that road easier."

Molly's eyes filled with tears for the first time since her rescue. The water Mark had been pressing on her had obviously done a good job rehydrating her tear ducts.

"I'm not sure whether we can salvage your hair or not, but I'll help," Mark said softly, fingering a strand of her absolutely filthy locks.

"And while I'm sure we can scrounge up an extra toothbrush between the four of us, you're out of luck with moisturizer and all the other smelly shit women seem to like," Gramps told her.

Molly was at a loss for words. It had been a very long time since anyone had been so generous. These men might've been violent and deadly to those who killed and kidnapped others, but they were actually big teddy bears.

"Thank you," she choked out softly.

Mark squeezed her hand, and Gramps and Bull simply nodded.

Then the three men started talking about all the things Bull should get for her once more. Molly's tears dried up—and she couldn't help but blush—when Mark told Bull to get *good* underwear, not the cheap shit.

"What do *you* know about women's underwear?" Bull griped. "You haven't seen any on a real live woman in years. Looking at magazines isn't the same thing."

"Fuck off," Mark growled. "All I'm saying is, don't grab a three-pack and call it done. Molly deserves better."

"Of course she does," Bull agreed. "I'm not an idiot. And I'll have you know, Skylar has no complaints about the lingerie I buy her."

Molly brought a hand to her mouth and did her best to hide her amusement. They sounded more like ten-year-old brothers than grown men. She caught Gramps's eye in the rearview mirror, and she couldn't hold back her laughter when he rolled his eyes.

"Sorry," she managed to say when both Bull and Mark glanced at her in confusion. "I'm sure whatever Bull finds will be fine. I'm really not that picky." She wasn't going to explain how having *anything* clean against her body would be heaven after wearing the same clothes for so long.

Luckily, Eagle returned then, interrupting the argument and Molly's equal parts of embarrassment and amusement over everyone talking about her underwear. He had three keys. He gave one to Gramps and another to Mark. "No connecting rooms, but we're all next to each other."

Molly had no idea what the plan was for rooms, but she figured the men would each share a room, giving her the third one.

Eagle pointed out where their rooms were located, and Gramps steered the truck in that direction. He parked, and they all got out, the guys grabbing their packs from the bed of the pickup. The rooms were on the first floor, and Mark gestured for Molly to go to the one in the middle of the others. She did, and he unlocked the door for her.

Stepping inside the room, she briefly panicked at the thought of being alone, especially at night—but Mark surprised her by entering and shutting the door behind him. He put his hands on her shoulders and moved her to the side, then walked through the room, looking under the beds and in the bathroom.

"All clear," he told her.

Molly stared at him as he put his pack on the floor next to the bathroom and began to dig through it. He started pulling everything out, placing items on the floor. Clothes, dry bags, an MRE, a pistol, ammunition, three knives . . . it was as if the bag was magical and bottomless. She had no idea how he'd managed to stuff so much in the thing, but by the time the pack was empty, he was surrounded by gear.

He rummaged through his stuff, then stood. He held out a few items. "A clean toothbrush, toothpaste, and some liquid soap. It's nothing fancy, but I wasn't sure if you wanted to wait for Bull to get back to shower. I mean, you can certainly take two showers, one now and one when he returns."

Molly studied him . . . and realized Mark seemed nervous.

She looked around the room. There were two double beds in the somewhat dingy space, but the sheets looked clean. As did the carpet. The more she thought about it, Molly realized that this was probably the cleanest cheap motel she'd ever stayed in.

"Are you staying here with me?" she blurted.

Mark stepped inside the bathroom and put the toiletries on the counter, then walked toward her.

Molly held her ground, tilting her head back as he got closer and closer. He stopped about two feet away. Not so close as to make her uncomfortable, but close enough that he definitely had her complete attention.

"Yes. Though, I can go stay with Gramps if you—"

"No!" Molly interrupted. "I mean . . . if it's okay?"

Mark slowly lifted a hand, and Molly didn't flinch as he brushed her hair over her shoulder. "When I was in the Army, before I was a Delta, my platoon and I were captured by the Taliban. They beat the hell out of us, then dragged us into the mountains. They separated all of us, and it took a week before we were found. When we got back to base, the Army thought they were doing us a favor by giving us our own rooms in the barracks. But I'd just spent the last week alone with my thoughts, and the last thing I wanted was to be by myself.

"I quickly figured out that most of my platoon felt the same way. We couldn't all fit in one room, because they were pretty damn small, but we managed to get seven of us wedged into my room anyway. Someone's feet were in my face, and one of the guys snored like a fucking chain saw . . . but I slept better that night than I had in ages. If you want to be alone, I'll head out. But I thought that maybe you might like some company."

Molly hated thinking of Mark being held captive, and her heart melted at his understanding. "I was trying to come up with a way to ask one of you to stay with me," Molly admitted. "I was going to resort to freaking out over a fake spider if I had to."

He smiled at her. "Somehow, after what you just went through, I don't think a spider would freak you out."

She shook her head. "No, but staying by myself in this room might."

"Then it's a good thing you don't have to," Mark said. "Now, do you want to jump into the shower or wait until Bull gets back?"

It wasn't a hard decision. "Wait. I don't have anything clean to put on afterward."

"No problem," Mark said, turning to head back to his pack. "How about a snack, then?"

Molly smiled. "Are you going to make it your next mission to feed me?"

"I just might," Mark said, and she heard nothing in his tone to indicate he was joking.

He stared at her for a long moment, and Molly could feel her heart beating double time. She felt oddly connected to Mark, but she had no idea if it was simply because he'd rescued her, or if it was more.

"You can at least brush your teeth," Mark said, breaking the spell between them. "It was one of the best feelings when I finally got to scrub the fuzz off my teeth after being freed."

Nodding, Molly headed for the bathroom. She closed the door behind her and picked up the toothbrush. She stared at it for the longest time, tears forming in her eyes once more. It was stupid. It was just a toothbrush. But for a woman who had literally nothing, it was so much more.

Taking a deep breath, getting her emotions under control, she picked up the tube of toothpaste.

~

Smoke knew his teammates would be doing what needed to be done to get them out of Nigeria and back home to Indianapolis. They'd report back to Willis about the success of their mission, and he'd pull strings to get a replacement passport for Molly.

His only concern right now was for the woman herself. He was very glad she'd been all right with him staying in the room. Even though no one thought Boko Haram, or what was left of it, would be after her for any reason, Smoke didn't want to take that chance.

She was still a woman alone in a foreign country, and until they were back on American soil, he wouldn't let down his guard. Hell, even *then* he'd be on alert. America had its share of violence . . . and he definitely didn't like the sound of her ex. If what Molly had said was true—and Smoke suspected she hadn't even told him the worst of it—the man seemed like a douchebag of the highest order.

And if he had killed her grandparents? He was crazy as well as obsessed.

Molly would have a lot of things to take care of when she got back to the States. She needed to talk to the Oak Park Police Department. They were likely the ones doing the investigation into her grandparents' deaths, since that was the suburb where they'd lived. Then, if she hadn't already, she needed to file a restraining order against her ex. It wouldn't keep him from fucking with her, but it would be a tool in the case against him if he ever crossed the line.

And again, if he had killed her grandparents, Smoke had no doubt he *would* cross that line. Obsessed men didn't care about restraining orders, and he might even see it as a challenge.

His mind spun with everything Molly needed to do, and how he could help her.

Why he *wanted* to so badly, Mark couldn't explain. But from the second he'd laid eyes on her in that hole, something had clicked for him.

He already knew he respected her. She'd been through hell yet was making a concerted effort to focus on the positive.

The door to the bathroom opened behind him, and he turned.

Molly had obviously done her best to wash her face and hands. They actually looked a shade lighter than the rest of her skin. "Feel better?" he asked.

"I will never take toilet paper for granted again," she said with a wry grin.

Smoke chuckled and held out his hand before he thought about what he was doing.

She immediately came toward him and put her hand in his. It seemed so natural, which should've surprised him, but instead, he felt a measure of calm he hadn't experienced in a long time. He walked her over to the small picnic he'd set up on the floor next to the window. The curtain was drawn, as he didn't want random people walking by to be able to look inside, but the sunshine still shone through the edges of the curtain.

"A picnic?" she asked.

"I didn't think you'd want to sit on the bed and get the covers dirty."

"You're right. This looks perfect," Molly told him.

Smoke helped her sit and then got down on his knees next to her. He reached for his canteen, opened it, and handed it to her. The water in the hotel should be fine to drink, but he'd learned over the years to be safe rather than sorry. He'd keep purifying it until they were back home. While he heated up his last MRE, she nibbled on some crackers. "Bull will bring back something to eat when he comes with the clothes for you," Smoke told her.

"Honestly, this is fine," Molly said.

That was another thing he'd noticed; she hadn't complained once— not that she was tired. Not that her legs hurt. Not that the MREs sucked . . . because honestly, they weren't that great. But they were full of calories, which she definitely needed.

"It's not, but I appreciate you being so cool about it."

"I've thought a lot about what you said a couple days ago. It's hard for me to believe that I'm *not* bad luck. Everyone's always teased me about it, even Nana and Papa, for as long as I can remember. It's become ingrained in me. But I'm trying really hard to not always think so negatively. Instead of concentrating on how bad I smell, I'm trying to concentrate on how good this food smells. Instead of bitching about how sore I am, I'm trying to remember how much I wished I could stretch my legs when I was in that hole, and now I can. If I have to cut off all my hair because I can't get a brush through it, it'll just give me a chance to try out a new, fun, short haircut when I get home. And . . . maybe Preston won't recognize me, and he'll leave me alone. He always said he wanted my hair to be longer, so cutting it off will irritate him, which is a good thing in my eyes."

"I've found over the years, and especially in Delta training, that being positive is always better than being negative. It just makes things easier," Smoke said. He didn't want to think about her ex at the moment. The more he learned about him, the more he hated the other man. He couldn't wait to get back to Silverstone Towing and their secure computers to be able to do an in-depth search on the guy—and find out all his vulnerabilities. If the jerk thought he could continue to harass Molly, he'd find that she wasn't such an easy target . . . not with Silverstone at her back. "And I'll think you're pretty whether you have long or short hair."

Molly rolled her eyes.

Smoke couldn't help but chuckle. "What? You don't believe me?"

"Mark, I haven't showered in months. There's probably a family of rats living in my hair, and there's so much dirt under my nails, I may never get it out. I'm a mess. Besides, I've *never* been pretty, even when I wasn't being held hostage in a tropical jungle."

Smoke shifted so he was even closer to Molly. "Listen to me. Are you listening?"

She nodded slightly.

"There's pretty, then there's *pretty*. I couldn't care less about someone's outward appearance. I've known classically beautiful women who were so ugly inside, they made me feel slimy simply standing next to them. I've also known women who have been disfigured by fire, or by a car accident, or by a bombing, or at the hands of someone who was supposed to love them . . . and because of who they are inside, they're some of the most gorgeous women I've ever seen. It's not what's on the outside that matters, but the kind of person someone is deep down. And you, Molly Smith, are one of the most amazing people I've ever met . . . and I've met a *lot* of people. But believe me, you're damn easy on the eyes as well."

She stared back at him, the desire to believe him easy to read in her face.

"Are you sure you aren't married? Or dating anyone?"

Smoke frowned in confusion. "I'm sure. Why?"

"Because I don't understand why someone hasn't snatched you up. You're nice, perceptive, generous, polite . . . and you make me feel safe even when you aren't doing anything."

He shrugged. "I haven't found anyone who makes me feel like she truly wants *me*. Ever since I inherited my uncle's estate, it seems as if that's all women see. I could be a fucking troll, and they'd put up with me just to get their hands on my money."

"You're rich?" Molly asked. "I mean, you mentioned during our hike that you inherited the house you live in, and that you helped start Silverstone Towing, but I didn't assume anything."

"A hundred million dollars," Smoke said matter-of-factly, praying he wasn't ruining a good thing by telling her.

Molly's eyes almost bugged out of her face. "Seriously?"

"Yeah."

"Well . . . yeah, I can see how that might make women act completely stupid around you. Men too, I bet."

Smoke chuckled, but there was no humor in the sound. "Yeah, I used to think I needed more friends, but after inheriting all that money, I realized that most people only want to hang out with me because they think I'll pay for everything."

"When I get access to my accounts, I can pay for the hotel room," Molly replied softly.

Smoke shook his head. "I didn't say that to make you feel guilty about anything," he told her.

"I know, but still . . . I'm not broke. I can buy my own clothes, and food, and even afford to stay in one of those long-term-residency hotel things when I get back to the States."

"No," Smoke said, not caring how stubborn he sounded. "If your ex killed your grandparents, you could be in danger. I've got more security than you could even imagine. You'll be safer staying with me."

Molly stared at him for so long, Smoke got nervous. For the *second* time in the last hour.

But then she blew his mind with her next words.

"It's their loss," she said quietly. "Those women who only wanted to be with you because of the money. Money can't hug you. It can't tuck you in at night and hold you tight when you're hurting. It can't make you chicken noodle soup when you're sick, and it can't make you laugh until your sides hurt. Would my life have been easier after my parents died if I'd had money? Maybe materially. But having Nana and Papa there, hugging me when I had a bad day and taking a gazillion pictures when I went to my senior prom, was worth more than all the money in the world."

Her eyes teared up, and she looked down, clearly trying to compose herself.

Smoke hated when she cried. Even though she hadn't shed a single tear out in the jungle after she'd learned of her grandparents' fate, she'd still sobbed harder than anyone he'd ever seen.

Moving slowly, so as to not alarm her, he sat on his ass and reached for her. He pulled her into his side and did his best to ease her pain.

Molly's arms went around him, and she put her head on his chest and cried.

She was right, of course. About all the things that were more important than money. Which was why he hadn't bothered to try to get into a serious relationship in the last five years. He wanted to be more than a bankroll for a woman. He wanted to be her best friend, just as she'd be for him. He wanted to go camping with nothing more than a tent and a sleeping bag and eat s'mores and watch the stars while they lay on a scarred picnic table. He wanted a big family, kids he and his wife could spoil—not spend a fortune on *others* to keep them occupied and out of their hair. He couldn't see any of the women he'd met in recent years being willing to do any of that . . .

Except maybe Molly.

The knock on the door was so unexpected, it made them both jump.

Chuckling, as it was rare that Smoke was surprised, he looked down at Molly. "You okay?"

"Yeah."

The knock sounded again, but Smoke didn't move.

"Shouldn't you get that?"

"It's Bull," Smoke told her. "He can wait. I want to make sure you really are okay, and you aren't just saying that because you're uncomfortable."

"I am. It just hits me at weird times that Nana and Papa are gone. I hate that I didn't get to tell them how much they meant to me. How much I loved them."

"They knew," Smoke said with conviction.

"Thank you."

"You're welcome."

"And seriously, I can pay my way," she said.

Smoke rolled his eyes. "You're one of those women who make it really hard to buy presents and to do nice things for, aren't you?"

"I just don't want you to think I like you because of your money. I mean, I didn't even know you *had* that kind of dough until just now, and I liked you anyway."

"I know. That's why I told you. Believe me, giving details about my inheritance isn't the kind of small talk I usually engage in."

"Come on, Smoke, open the door!" Bull called from the other side. "These bags are heavy!"

"We should let him in. I mean, you do need to approve the underwear he bought, right?" she teased.

"Damn straight," Smoke said, quickly standing. He held out a hand and helped Molly to her feet. "Humor me, and please go wait in the bathroom."

"What? Why?"

"Precaution. I recognize Bull's voice, but I don't know who else might be hanging around out there. And the last thing I want is someone walking by to see you, then think you might be vulnerable and they can take advantage."

"But you're staying here with me. Why would someone come after me?"

"Because they're stupid. Because they think Americans are dumb and an easy mark? I don't know. But please? Just go in there long enough for me to let Bull in," Smoke pleaded.

For a second, he didn't think Molly was going to do as he'd asked, but then she turned without another word and walked across the room. He waited until the bathroom door had shut behind her before he opened the other door.

Bull was standing there, his hands full of packages.

Smoke grabbed a paper bag that was about to fall sideways out of Bull's grip, and closed and locked the door behind his friend.

"You can come out now!" he yelled, and seconds later, Molly peered out of the bathroom.

"The coast is clear?" she asked.

"Yup."

"Are you suuuure?"

"Yes, smart-ass," Smoke said with a smile.

She came out of the bathroom and stopped short when she saw all the things Bull had purchased. "Holy crap, Bull . . . what did you buy?"

"A little of this, and a little of that," he said with a smile. "And I've got a duffel bag out in the truck so you can carry all this. I'll bring it by later."

"You find anything edible?"

"Smells like you already ate," Bull said.

"MREs don't count as eating, and you know it," Smoke complained.

"Just fuckin' with you. Of course I did. Decided to go safe and got some traditional Nigerian fare . . . akara, moin moin, and puff-puffs for dessert."

Smoke turned to translate for Molly, but she was grinning and reaching for the bag Bull was holding out. "Oh my God, I love moin moin! I didn't think I would when I was first introduced to it. I mean, cooked bean pudding doesn't sound appetizing at all, but there's something about the spices they add to it, and it's like crack. Gimme!"

Both Smoke and Bull smirked as she grabbed the bag as if she couldn't wait a second longer to taste the delicacies inside.

"And you like the akara, the bean cake?" Bull asked.

Molly shrugged. "It's fried, what's not to like?" she asked as she pulled out one of the moin moins. It was wrapped in a large leaf, and she not so delicately pulled it back and took a big bite of the traditional Nigerian street food. "Oh my God . . . so good," she moaned.

Bull nudged Smoke. "Looks like all you have to do to keep her happy is feed her," he joked.

Smoke reached for the bag, picking it up from between Molly's feet, where she'd put it after getting her hands on the moin moin. He plucked out one of the fried sugary doughballs—otherwise known as a puff-puff—and shoved the whole thing into his mouth. As he chewed, he smiled over at Molly, whose cheeks were similarly stuffed. She smiled back.

"I got you three shirts—two short and one long sleeve. I decided against going with a regular pair of pants, because I didn't want to guess at your size. So I settled for a pair of leggings and a loose, flowy pair of cotton pants with an elastic waist. The shoes were harder, but I found some flip-flops and a pair of Nike knockoffs. They'll probably fall apart the first time you wear them, but they should get you home at least.

"There's a sweatshirt in there, too, and, as per the request, some silky-soft underwear. The woman who was helping me probably thought I was a pervert since I insisted on feeling the material before I bought them. There are two sports bras as well—again, I figured that was a better bet than me guessing on your size and failing. Then I got some deodorant, lotion, shampoo, and something the lady promised was just like conditioner, although I have no idea if she really understood what I wanted. I got you a comb and a brush, fingernail clippers, a nail file, ChapStick, socks in case your feet get cold, two razors, and a necklace . . . because the brown stone reminded me of your eyes. It's probably fake as shit, but I didn't care."

Molly stood stock still now, the moin moin forgotten in her hands, threatening to drip all over the floor. She stared at Bull, her eyes wide from obvious shock.

"Having a girlfriend has taught me a lot about what women think is necessary when it comes to toiletries," Bull said.

Smoke wished he'd been the one to shop for Molly, but he had to admit that Bull had done a much better job than he probably would've. "Thank you," he told his friend.

"You're welcome. Molly?" Bull asked.

"Yeah?" she whispered.

"You're pretty amazing. I'd be honored to introduce you to Skylar when we get back to Indianapolis."

"I'd like to meet her too," Molly said.

"Great. Enjoy the food. Gramps is working on logistics. I'll call later and let you know when our plane leaves," Bull told Smoke.

"Thanks."

"If you need anything else, anything I might've forgotten, just let me know."

"Will do," Smoke said, then he turned to Molly and gestured toward the bathroom with his head once more.

"Oh jeez," she mock complained, but headed for the small room without another complaint, taking a bite of the bean pudding as she went.

"She okay?" Bull asked when she'd closed the bathroom door.

"As okay as she can be at this point, I'd say," Smoke told his friend.

"All right. Seriously, if there's anything else she needs, just yell. It's not a problem for me to head back out to see if I can find it."

"I will."

The second the door closed behind Bull, Molly popped back out of the bathroom before he could tell her it was all clear. She walked right up to Smoke and into his personal space.

Surprised, he opened his arms and wrapped them around her when she hugged him with one arm. The other hand was still holding her food.

"Thank you," she muttered into his chest.

Her head only came up to the top of his pecs, and she felt delicate and frail against him. But he knew she was anything but. "You're welcome."

Then she backed up, and he had to suppress any sign of disappointment over how short the hug had been.

She thrust the rest of the moin moin at him. "I want to eat the whole thing, but I'll puke if I do. Besides, I want to eat some akara later. And some puff-puffs."

Smoke accepted the food and took a big bite. "It's good," he agreed when he could speak again, but Molly wasn't paying any attention. She'd knelt on the ground and was looking through the things Bull had purchased for her.

Smoke wasn't sure about the quality of the clothes, but it was obvious Molly didn't care. The smile on her face told him she was more than pleased with what she'd received.

It took three trips to get all the toiletries into the bathroom as well as the clothes she wanted to put on after her shower. She paused at the door, looking at him a bit sheepishly. "I'm sorry, do you want to go first?"

Smoke laughed. "No way am I getting between you and that shower, Mol. Go ahead. Do your thing. I can wait."

"It might take me a while," she said as she bit her lip.

"Take as long as you want. We don't have anywhere to be until tomorrow at the earliest."

"You might regret telling me that," she said softly. "But thank you. Again." Then she shut the door.

Smoke heard the water from the shower turn on, but noticed she hadn't locked the flimsy door. Not that the lock would keep him out if he really wanted to get inside. But that simple show of trust in him shook Smoke to his core. Whatever this thing was between them, he hoped her trust was a sign it wasn't one sided.

It both excited him and scared the shit out of him all at once.

"One step at a time," Smoke told himself as he eased himself back down to the floor to await his turn in the shower. He wasn't as dirty as Molly, but he was still pretty ripe.

He stared at the bathroom door as he finished off the moin moin. It was almost scary how protective he felt toward Molly already. This had to be how Bull and Eagle had felt after meeting their women. As if they'd do anything to keep them safe, happy, and healthy.

The thought should've set off some alarms . . . *something* . . . but instead, Smoke felt contentment steal over him.

This was *right*. He'd bet all the money in his account on it. He'd invited Molly to stay with him impulsively, out of compassion, but if things worked out the way he had a feeling they might . . . hopefully she'd never want to leave.

The best things in life never came easy. That had been his uncle's motto, and Smoke had never believed in it as much as he did right this moment. Convincing Molly to stick around, to let him help her with the asshole ex, and to deal with the death of her grandparents and everything that came along with that wouldn't be easy. But in the end, Smoke suspected more and more that she'd be worth it. He just had to hope she thought the same of him.

Chapter Six

The trip back to Indianapolis was long and tiring. Molly had forgotten how exhausting traveling could be. It didn't help that every other second, Mark or one of his friends was hovering over her, asking if she was all right and if she needed anything. She appreciated their concern, but her nerves were officially shot. She was stressed about being back in the States.

She was happy to be back, but because she had no home and no belongings, and she had to face the reality of her grandparents' deaths, she felt overwhelmed.

They'd had to take an extra day in Ikeja as they'd waited for her passport. Molly had wanted to know how in the world they'd gotten a brand-new passport for her on such short notice, especially since it had seemed to take forever when she'd renewed it before she'd left for Nigeria, but since it was getting her out of the country, she didn't dare ask too many questions.

It was dark when they landed in Indiana, and Molly felt as if she was going to keel over with exhaustion.

"Come on, Mol, you're dead on your feet," Mark said, taking hold of her elbow.

"Are you sure you're okay with me staying with you?" she asked for about the hundredth time.

"I'm sure," Mark answered patiently. "I wouldn't have offered if I wasn't."

"It was great meeting you, Molly," Bull said.

"We're glad you're all right," Eagle added.

"And thanks for breaking Smoke's fall into that hole," Gramps joked.

The men had given Smoke no end of shit after they'd heard he'd literally fallen on top of her. Apparently, the idea of the man who could be so sure footed and sneaky falling into a hole was hilarious to them.

"See you guys tomorrow afternoon," Bull said, then hurried off in the other direction.

Mark had already told her that after they got home from a mission, they always met the next day, after getting some rest, to discuss what had gone right and what they could do better next time. She was impressed with their professionalism and dedication to bettering themselves.

"I'll bring Taylor to Silverstone Towing tomorrow," Eagle told her. Then, with a smirk, added, "If she can walk."

Gramps and Smoke chuckled, but Molly simply rolled her eyes. She'd heard all about Skylar and Taylor over the last day and a half they'd been traveling. Bull and Eagle were head over heels in love with their women, and hearing how much they'd missed them sort of made her heart hurt.

"We'll talk tomorrow about what to do about your asshole ex," Gramps said.

She'd also told the men more about her situation with Preston. None of the men were happy with her ex, and they were all prepared to make sure he knew she was now off limits.

There were a lot of things that Molly had to do now that she was back in the United States. She needed to talk to the police and see what was going on in the investigation of Nana's and Papa's deaths. She had to call their lawyer to see if she needed to do anything to settle their estate.

The insurance company would have to be contacted about the house as well as an accountant to deal with her inheritance. Her grandparents hadn't had a lot of money, especially compared to Mark, but Molly assumed there would be taxes to deal with.

And she needed to go shopping. Flip-flops and cheap sneakers wouldn't last her long, not in Indiana. But thinking about everything she needed to do was too overwhelming, and all Molly wanted was to lie down and sleep for a month.

"I know I've said Preston may have killed my grandparents, but maybe I wasn't thinking straight. It's just so hard to imagine *anyone* wanting to kill them," Molly told Gramps.

"We'll find out what the cops know and go from there," he said. "If your ex had anything to do with it, we'll make sure he's put behind bars, where he belongs."

Molly studied the tall man. She couldn't really get a read on him. One second he was frowning and looking pissed off at the world, and the next he was teasing her like a big brother might. Either way, she couldn't help but like him. She liked all Mark's friends.

"If Bull and Eagle are going to be late tomorrow, let me know," Mark told Gramps.

"Will do. If you need anything, just yell," Gramps said.

"Thanks."

"Molly?"

"Yeah?" she asked, turning to face Gramps.

"I'm really glad you're all right. You're one tough cookie," the older man said.

"Thanks. You're not so bad yourself."

"You remind me of another woman I knew once. She was pretty strong too." They smiled at each other for a second, then Gramps nodded at her and turned to walk away.

"He sounded sad," Molly mused after he was out of earshot.

"Thinking about the one who got away is never a good feeling," Mark told her.

She wanted to know more, but pushed down her curiosity. "I like your friends," Molly told him.

"I'm glad. They like you too," he said. "Now, come on. I'm exhausted, so I know you have to be as well."

They walked out of the small regional airport and headed for the parking lot. Mark knelt by the back corner of what looked like a brand-new Ford Explorer, then stood with a small box in his hand.

"Seriously? A hide-a-key?" Molly asked with a smile.

He returned her smile and shrugged. "This parking lot is monitored, and Silverstone pays a pretty penny to make sure nothing happens to our cars. And I don't want to take a chance that I'll lose my pack and the key while I'm on a mission."

It made sense, but it still seemed hilarious to Molly. She started giggling . . . and couldn't stop. She knew having the key in a magnetic box stuck to the underside of his car wasn't *that* funny, but Molly was beyond tired at the moment.

Mark didn't comment further, but the grin on his face said he wasn't upset with her laughing at him. He walked her around to the passenger side of his car and helped her in. She was still giggling when he climbed into the driver's seat.

He started the engine, then turned to face her. His grin widened. "What?" she asked.

"Nothing," he said with a shrug. "I just like hearing you laugh."

That sobered Molly up. She couldn't believe she was laughing and having a good time when her life was in such turmoil.

"Fuck, I should've kept my mouth shut," Mark muttered as he put the car in gear.

Molly reached out and put her hand on his arm. He stilled and turned his gaze to her once again.

Even though they'd been alone together before, this time it seemed more intimate for some reason. Maybe it was because it was dark outside. Maybe it was because they were back in familiar territory in the United States, or because she knew they were in his personal vehicle. Whatever the reason, Molly felt goose bumps rise on her arms. "Nana and Papa would've liked you," she said quietly.

Mark's shoulders relaxed. He reached out a hand and smoothed her hair back. "I know I would've liked them right back."

Then, without another word, he pulled out of the parking space and headed toward the nearby road.

Molly put her head back on the seat and closed her eyes. She was tired, but she couldn't seem to stop thinking about everything that had happened in the last several days since meeting Mark.

She wasn't entirely clueless. She could tell he had a soft spot for her . . . but she wondered if that was solely because of the situation. Because he'd rescued her.

When she'd come out of the bathroom after her first shower back in Maiduguri, he'd still been sitting on the floor. He stood and walked over to her, his eyes glued to the straight black hair brushing her shoulders. She'd changed into one of the T-shirts Bull had bought for her, and the leggings. They were both a bit big, but having clean clothes felt incredible. She'd washed Mark's T-shirt as best she could, not wanting to throw it in the trash as she had her filthy pants and underwear.

"It looks good," he said, referring to her hair.

"I'm lucky it's thin," she replied. "I shampooed it three times."

"May I?"

Molly nodded.

His hand was gentle when he ran it over her head. "It's soft. Beautiful."

How long they'd stood there staring at each other, Molly had no idea. But eventually he'd shaken his head, as if to clear it, and declared that his stench was going to scare away the bugs. "Stay inside, don't answer the door. I'll be out soon." And with that, he'd disappeared into the bathroom himself.

Ever since then, she'd found his gaze on her hair more than once. He'd even touched it, as he had a minute ago, a few more times. Molly had no idea why he was so fascinated by her hair, but she had to admit she loved his touch. Every time he stroked her, she wanted to lean against his hand and purr.

Despite knowing she probably should have been paying attention to where they were going, Molly couldn't force her eyes open. She floated in a half-asleep state, thinking of Mark, until the car stopped.

"We're here, Mol," he said.

Taking a deep breath, she sat up and pried her eyelids open. They were stopped outside a gate, and a bright light was shining down on the car from above.

"I wanted you to see my security firsthand so you'd feel safer," Mark said.

Doing her best to shake the fogginess from her brain, Molly nodded.

"This road is the only one that leads into the property. The fence goes all the way around. The light is motion triggered, and there's a camera that will take a picture of the license plate of any car entering." He leaned over and hit a long sequence of numbers on the keypad, and the gate opened.

After he drove through, Molly looked back and saw the gate begin to close the second the back bumper cleared it.

"It's designed to detect when the vehicle has gone by and close right afterward. I didn't want two cars to be able to get in at a time. The gate at Silverstone Towing is set up the same way."

Molly nodded, impressed.

As she was by the property itself. There were large trees everywhere, but they seemed fairly evenly spaced out, as if their placement had been carefully planned. As they headed toward the house, her eyes widened.

It was beautiful.

The two-story house looked welcoming but not pretentious, despite its size. The covered porch on the front caught her attention right away, as did the white shutters and large windows. There were some bushes around the perimeter of the house, but not close enough—or big enough—for someone to hide in, which didn't surprise Molly, not after seeing the gate at the end of the driveway.

As they drove down the gravel drive, Mark continued to talk about the security measures on the property. "Most of what's here, my uncle put in. I simply enhanced everything when I inherited the place. He was paranoid, but then again, he'd been the victim of a home invasion three times before he got tired of being a target. There are cameras placed strategically all around the house. Notifications are sent to me via an app on my phone. I can view the video right then to see if it's just an animal or someone up to no good. Everything is controlled by a box inside the house. With one touch of a button, everything can be turned on or off. The system can't be turned off by cutting any wires outside, and even if there's a power outage, it'll stay armed for up to eight hours."

"Wow," Molly said. "I think I'm intimidated," she told him honestly. "With both your house, and the security you've set up."

"That wasn't my intention," Mark said. "I made my house as comfortable as I could, and of course I wanted the outside to be pleasing to the eye as well. And as far as the security, I just wanted you to know that you're safe here. I'll teach you the system tomorrow, when you aren't half-asleep. Tomorrow morning, I'll also take you out and get you a phone. We can grab anything else you need immediately, but I'm sure Skylar and Taylor will take you shopping to get more clothes."

"I don't need a phone right away," Molly insisted.

"Yes, you do. You need an immediate way to get in touch with me, or any of the other guys."

"I'll pay you back," Molly said.

"No need. Did you *not* hear how much money I have?" Mark asked.

That irritated Molly just a bit. "I don't want your money," she told him. "I'm not like those women you date who are only interested in the size of your bank account. I've got my own money, Mark. I'm not helpless. And if you think I am, you can just turn around and take me to a hotel."

He was polite enough to not point out she had no money to rent a room.

Instead, he pulled into a four-car garage and turned toward her as the door was shutting behind them. To her surprise, he was smiling.

"What?" she asked a little belligerently.

"Nothing. I just never thought you'd be so . . . prickly."

"Well, if you'd stop being an ass, I wouldn't be," she retorted. Then immediately thought maybe she should've kept her mouth shut. Nana had always hated how she spoke without thinking . . . but when Mark chuckled, she relaxed a bit. "I'm sorry. I'm exhausted, and that was uncalled for, especially when you're helping me. I know you don't have to."

"It's okay. It's been a long time since anyone has turned down my offer of assistance. Most people just go with it when I offer to pay for anything."

"Well . . . I appreciate it, I do. But I really *don't* want your money. And I feel horrible at the moment that I need as much assistance as I do."

"I just want to help you, Mol," Mark told her.

"Thank you. I appreciate it. I've got a cellular account already, I just need a replacement phone. You don't have to add me to your friends-and-family plan or anything crazy."

"Deal. Now . . . wanna see the house?"

"A siren isn't going to start going off if we step inside, is it?" Molly asked, glad they seemed back on neutral ground.

"Only if I don't input the password into the system within thirty seconds."

"Thirty seconds? That's it?"

"That's actually a really long time. You'll see."

"I'm totally gonna set that thing off, and you're going to get sick of having to tell your alarm company that it's just your clueless guest who can't seem to get the hang of inputting the correct code."

Mark burst out laughing as he got out of the car.

Molly hopped out on her side and walked around to Mark, smiling the entire way.

"My alarm company is me," he told her when she reached his side.

"What do you mean?"

"Just that. I'm not hooked into a corporation or anything. I get the notifications on my phone. And if I don't happen to have my phone on me, my watch alerts me as well."

"I wondered why it looked like you were wearing a desktop computer on your wrist."

"Funny girl," Mark said, bumping his hip lightly against her.

Molly pretended that his nudge was more powerful than it was and fake stumbled to the side. She loved seeing the smile on his face. She imagined that without his bushy beard, it would be even more electric.

"I can notify the cops with the touch of a button if, after I check out the cameras, it looks like I have an intruder. I do have to admit, though, no one's lived here other than me since I set it all up. We'll have to figure out some sort of system. I don't want to irritate the police and have them showing up if there's an accidental trigger of the alarm, but I also want to make sure you're protected at all times."

"Why?" Molly blurted, then blushed at her rudeness. "I mean, I appreciate it more than I can say, but . . ." She sighed. "I guess I'm still confused about why I'm even here."

"You're here because you've gotten the short end of the stick lately. And no, that doesn't mean I think you're Folly Molly, so don't even suggest that. I just mean with your grandparents being gone, your abusive ex, and being held captive in a foreign country . . . you need a break. And I can offer it."

"You said no one else has been in the house since you set up the security stuff? I don't know how long that's been, but since you and your friends started Silverstone Towing five years ago, I'm assuming it wasn't yesterday. I'm sure you've helped other victims of . . . bad stuff since then?"

"We have, but no, I don't invite random victims to stay with me."

"Then why?" she pressed.

"You have to ask?" he asked quietly, reaching for her hand and pulling her close when his fingers tightened around hers.

Molly swallowed hard. She was scared to say the wrong thing.

"I'm not offering a diamond ring. Or even my letterman jacket . . . not that I have one. You impress me, Molly. You're strong and smart. You aren't prone to hysterics, and you've dealt with everything amazingly well. You aren't afraid of me or my friends, or what we do. You might think you always look on the negative side of life, but believe me, you really don't. You've held up much better than nine out of ten people would've. All of that is attractive as hell . . . and I'd like to see where things might go between us. I know that's presumptuous of me, as you might not want anything to do with me romantically, but even if that's the case, I still want to see you safe.

"And we can't forget . . . someone killed your grandparents. Maybe it was a random burglary that got out of hand, or maybe it was your ex, like you suggested. Either way, you'll be safe here, from anyone who might want to hurt you, for as long as you want."

Tears formed in her eyes, and Molly closed them, trying to beat the tears back. She wasn't a crier and hated to be weak in front of Mark.

"Don't," he said softly. "If you want to cry, cry. I'm not going to freak out over a few tears."

"I hate crying," she said with a sniff.

"I'm actually relieved to see your eyes watering. You kinda scared me in the jungle when you cried without shedding one tear."

Molly smiled slightly and looked up at him. He was a bit blurry because of the water swimming in her eyes, but she held his gaze. "Have I thanked you yet?"

"Yes."

"Then, thank you again."

"You're welcome. Now, come on, let me show you the house so you can lie down."

Molly was well aware Mark hadn't let go of her hand, but she didn't tug it out of his grip.

She also hadn't missed the huge garage with the motorcycle in the corner and a sleek red convertible Alfa Romeo. There was also a gym setup in the garage. Mark had a treadmill, a stationary bike, and lots of free weights.

His wealth intimidated her a bit, but he was so down to earth, she often forgot about it.

She let him escort her inside, then watched as he put a code into the alarm box on the wall. It didn't look all that complicated, but she was also tired, so she might not've been paying enough attention. He then rearmed the security system.

They walked down a short hall, and she caught a glimpse of a washer and dryer in one room off the hall and a half bath. The hallway opened into a dining room with a huge table, big enough to seat at least twelve people. The wooden table looked old and had large, chunky legs, and the top was worn, as if it had seen thousands of meals.

"Most of the stuff in the house was my uncle's. He wasn't much for the modern look," Mark said with a grin.

He kept walking, and they entered a large family room. The space looked much more comfortable and laid back than the stuffy dining room. There was a huge brown leather sectional, a couple of recliners, a glass coffee table, and a massive television on the wall.

"How many times have you hit your shins on that coffee table?" Molly asked.

"More times than I can count. I have no idea why I haven't chucked it by now," Mark said.

"Because it was your uncle's?" Molly guessed.

"Yeah. He loved that thing. He even made me use a coaster when I was growing up. He polished the thing every Sunday."

"You miss him," she said softly.

"I do. He could be an ass. We lost touch after I graduated from high school and joined the Army, which I regret. But he took me in when my parents died. He could've refused; he was older, and I know he didn't want to raise a smart-mouthed teenager. But he stepped up, and I loved him for it."

"That's how I felt about my grandparents. I mean, I was already close to them, so there really wasn't a question of whether they would take me in or not. But it's hard to find yourself in the role of a parent when you thought all that was behind you."

Mark squeezed her hand gently. It was almost weird how much they had in common. They'd both lost their parents and had been raised by a family member. It was the sort of thing that created an instant bond.

He walked her to the edge of the kitchen—and Molly could only stare in surprise. "Wow, it's like a different house altogether," she said after a moment.

"Yeah, I had some parts of the house updated. I couldn't bear to touch the dining room—it totally reminds me of my uncle when I look at it. But I wanted a modern kitchen, not the disaster that it was before."

"What else did you update?" she asked.

"A bunch of stuff over the years. The master suite. A lot of the electrical, and of course all the security. The house is big—five bedrooms and six and a half bathrooms. It's way too large for just me, and I considered selling it, but in the end decided not to. I think my uncle wanted to have a large family once upon a time, but it wasn't to be. He and I kinda rattled around in the house, but I've learned that I like my space. Back to the updating . . . it took a while, as I did a lot of it myself, but I think you'll like the bathrooms."

Her eyes lit up. "Ooooh, sounds intriguing." Molly couldn't wrap her mind around five bedrooms and so many bathrooms. Her grandparents' house had been small and older. It'd been cozy, and she'd loved it. But something told her after being stuck in a hole for weeks, having so much space wouldn't be hard to get used to.

Mark smiled and led her up the stairs. At the top, there was a small landing.

"I've got a home office, and there's a big media room in the basement. Up here are mostly all bedrooms. The guest rooms are that way," Mark said, pointing to the right. "I'll show those to you in a second, and you can pick which one you want. Although, may I suggest the one with the king-size bed? I've seen how much of a bed hog you are."

"Hey!" Molly mock complained, secretly enjoying how it made her feel to be teased by him.

"I'm serious. I've never seen someone as small as you take up so much space. It's as if you can't get comfortable unless you're touching every edge of the mattress."

"Whatever," Molly said, but she knew he was right. She'd always been kind of a crazy sleeper. The covers were usually askew when she woke up, and she never woke in the same place in the bed or the same position as when she'd gone to sleep. "One of the good things about being short is that no bed is ever too small for me," she said.

"Um . . . I think for any other five-foot-three person, that would be true. But not you."

"Shut up," Molly protested, but she smiled when she said it.

Mark grinned and preceded her down the hall toward the master bedroom. He pushed open a door . . . and Molly could only stare.

He didn't turn on the overhead light, but she could see everything by the light coming in from the bathroom. Not only was the room huge, but it looked comfortable and cozy while at the same time not being overly masculine.

But it was the floor-to-ceiling windows that drew her in. Mark dropped her hand, and Molly walked toward the glass as if mesmerized.

"This was one of the rooms I remodeled," Mark said quietly. "I felt cooped up in here before. There was only a small window. And after living through the things I did in the Army, and with the missions we've been on since then, I realized I needed more openness."

"Aren't you afraid people will see you from out there?" she asked, not taking her eyes from the millions of stars shining brightly overhead.

"No. They're one-way windows. We can see out, but no one can see in." Mark walked over to a pad on the wall and pushed a button. Immediately, the glass in front of her turned gray. "They've also got internal shades, as you can see. That lets me sleep during the day if I need to." He pushed the button again, and the stars were once again visible. Then he went into the bathroom and shut off that light, too, plunging the room into darkness.

Molly put a hand on the glass and leaned close. She stared at the stars for a long moment. Without looking away, she said, "When I was in that hole, I'd stare up at the sky and take comfort in the fact that Nana and Papa could be looking at those same stars. Oh, I knew our time zones were completely different, but that didn't matter. The stars gave me hope. Night after night, they'd sparkle and shine above my head without fail."

She felt Mark come up behind her, then his hands rested gently on her shoulders. The heat from his body made her want to lean back against him and soak it up, but she steeled her spine and stayed upright.

"That's how I feel when I look at them too," he said quietly. "No matter what goes on down here on earth, they return, night after night. It sounds stupid, but it gives me hope for the future."

"It's not stupid," Molly said quietly.

They stood there looking at the stars for a long time. Neither speaking, just soaking in each other's presence and taking comfort from the night sky.

It wasn't until Molly jerked and realized she'd fallen asleep standing up that Mark moved. "Time for bed," he said.

Molly didn't even protest when he leaned down and picked her up. One arm went behind her knees and the other under her back. She buried her nose against his chest and closed her eyes as he walked.

He stopped and asked, "You need to use the bathroom? Brush your teeth?"

Molly didn't have the energy for either. "No." She'd gone months without cleaning her teeth—one more night wouldn't make a difference at this point.

She felt herself being lowered onto a mattress and immediately stretched out. She flung her arms above her head and spread her legs slightly.

Mark chuckled, but she didn't open her eyes. She felt him taking off her sneakers and socks, then bringing the covers up and over her. "Sleep well," he whispered.

Molly felt pressure on her forehead and realized that he'd kissed her.

Smiling, she sighed. Then knew no more as she fell into a deep sleep.

∼

Smoke paused at the doorway of the guest room and watched Molly sleep. She'd taken over as much of the bed as she could . . . and he couldn't help but wonder what she'd do if he crawled under the covers with her. Would she cuddle up next to him or push him away so she could have her space?

He'd wanted to tuck her into *his* bed so she could wake with the view of his property. But he didn't think she'd be happy if he gave up his room.

He was heartened to know she loved the stars as much as he did. It was just one more thing that made him suspect they might be great together. Neither were ready for a full-fledged relationship, but he hoped over time, their connection would morph into more.

Forcing himself to turn away from her room, he went down the stairs to the garage. He disarmed the alarm, headed out to grab their bags, then went back inside. He turned on the alarm once again, checked the cameras on his app to make sure everything was working properly, then went back upstairs.

He put Molly's bag just inside her room, where she'd see it when she got up, then closed her bedroom door. It took him longer than he would've thought to fall asleep. It felt amazing to be back in his own bed. Usually after being gone for over a month on a mission, he would've crashed the second he lay down. But tonight, he stared out at the stars for what seemed like forever.

He couldn't stop thinking about the woman down the hall. She had almost nothing, and he had more money than he'd ever be able to spend in a lifetime. But despite that, they just clicked.

He hadn't fully understood Bull's and Eagle's connections to their women. He *liked* women, and wasn't averse to a relationship. But the things he felt for Molly after such a short time seemed so much bigger than he could've imagined possible. He wanted to do everything for her. But in reality, all he could do was hope to stand by her side as she navigated her new life.

Vowing to do just that, and to make her life as easy as possible in the process, Smoke finally closed his eyes. He had no idea how long he'd slept before he began dreaming.

Molly was wearing a white dress, walking toward him in the great room at Silverstone Towing. They were surrounded by his teammates and their Silverstone Towing family. Eagle was holding a baby, and Bull was standing next to Skylar, grinning like a fool. Gramps was holding hands with a Hispanic woman, someone Smoke didn't recognize, looking more relaxed and happy than he'd ever seen his friend before.

Just as Molly was about to reach him, a man wearing a mask burst into the room and pulled out a gun.

He heard Molly gasp "Preston!" before she was shot in the heart, the red blood quickly spreading, covering her beautiful white gown—

Smoke jerked awake, his skin dewy with sweat. He immediately threw back the sheet and checked in on Molly. She was sleeping soundly, her arms and legs stretched out toward the four corners of the bed. Smoke went back to his room and took a long hot shower before going downstairs and grabbing his laptop. He settled on the couch in the living room and opened his computer.

He needed to find out everything he could about this Preston asshole. He was going to do whatever was necessary, pull as many strings as needed, so Molly would be safe to reclaim her life.

Chapter Seven

Molly rolled over and groaned. It felt as if she'd been asleep for days. When she looked around, she didn't recognize the room she was in, but after inhaling deeply, she immediately remembered she was in Mark's house. The sheets smelled like the shirt he'd given her to wear. She recognized the detergent.

She was lying on a king-size bed, and like usual, the covers were in complete disarray. Realizing she was still wearing the clothes she'd been traveling in, Molly wrinkled her nose. Seeing her bag by the door, she padded over to it and hauled it over to the bed. After straightening the sheets and blanket, she rummaged through her bag, pulling out a change of clothes and the toiletries Bull had bought for her.

She stopped in her tracks and stared with her mouth agape when she opened the bathroom door.

It was absolutely amazing.

Granite countertops, two sinks, a walk-in closet through an open door on one side, a little room with a toilet, an oversize shower with a Jacuzzi tub nearby. The room looked like it had come straight out of a multimillion-dollar home.

"Holy crap," she mumbled, making her way inside and putting her things down on the expansive counter. "I could live in here."

After brushing her teeth twice, and vowing never to take a simple thing like a toothbrush for granted ever again, she turned on the water in the shower and smiled in contentment when it warmed almost immediately.

She stood in the hot spray for several minutes, enjoying the simple pleasure of hot water raining down on her. Eventually, she sighed and got to work getting clean.

Ten minutes later, she stepped out of the shower feeling like a completely different person. It was amazing what hot water and a long night's sleep could do.

But then she made the mistake of looking in the mirror.

The woman staring back at her was a stranger.

Molly had known she'd lost weight during her captivity, but seeing herself naked was something of a shock. Her hip bones stood out significantly, as did her ribs. Her boobs were even smaller than they'd been before, which was somewhat sad considering she'd already been only an A cup. She had absolutely no muscle contour on her arms . . .

The gaunt woman looking back at her was almost frightening.

Turning her back on her reflection, Molly quickly pulled on her clothes. She'd always been slight, but seeing how much weight she'd lost was still distressing.

She headed out of her room, immediately confused by the silence in the house. She went down the stairs and didn't see or hear Mark anywhere. She was starting to feel a little freaked out until she saw the note on the kitchen counter. It was propped up against a coffee machine.

She unfolded the note and saw that her suspicion she was alone in the house was spot on.

> Molly,
> I'm sorry that you had to wake up alone, but I woke up early and decided to head in to Silverstone Towing and check on things. We've been gone a long time, and while I trust our employees implicitly, I still want to make sure nothing's gone wrong.

I apologize if I overstepped, but I checked on you this morning and you were completely out of it . . . taking up as much of the mattress as humanly possible too. ;)

The coffee is ready to go, just hit the start button. There's sugar and sweetener on the counter. I don't have any cream or milk, but can pick those up later.

Make yourself at home. Snoop in my drawers, judge my DVD collection, and if you want to use my computer, feel free. The password is H4sdqkq830BnM@7

May I suggest, however, that you not do any extensive searches on yourself or Preston? As of right now, no one knows you're back in the States. I have no idea if your ex is computer savvy or not, but maybe it's better not to chance it just yet.

You're safe, Mol. I wouldn't have left you alone in my house if I didn't think so. The alarm is on, though, so if you need or want to go outside, call me on the landline (there's a receiver in the kitchen behind you, near the sink), and I'll walk you through how to turn the alarm off.

I'll go to the grocery store and pick up some basics on my way home. I know there's not much to choose from at the moment.

Take a deep breath and relax, Molly. Enjoy your first day back. There will be time to figure out everything in the coming days and weeks. You don't have to do everything in one day. And I'll help you in any way I can. So for now, just revel in the fact that you're alive and well and safe.

—Smoke

Molly read the note three times before she folded it back up and held it to her chest. She closed her eyes and tried to remember a time when she'd felt like she did right then . . . and couldn't. Her parents had loved her, but she'd still been a kid when they'd died. Nana and Papa had taken her in and helped make the pain of losing her parents not quite as sharp. She'd dated over the years, but no one and nothing had ever made her feel like Mark just had with that simple note.

Safe.

Content.

Cared for.

As if she were the most important thing in the world at that moment.

He'd checked in on her and, after seeing she was still sleeping, hadn't woken her. He'd made her coffee. He'd given her the password to his computer. She couldn't help but smile thinking about the latter. It was completely random . . . and everything she expected from the security-conscious Mark.

After everything that had happened to her recently, Molly wasn't as uncomfortable being alone in Mark's huge house as she'd thought she'd be. Especially when she remembered how much security he had. She was in a strange house, in a strange town, in a state she hadn't lived in before . . . but remarkably, she felt at ease.

She liked Mark and his friends. Had seen firsthand how much they cared about each other, and how much Bull and Eagle loved and worried about their women. All that, along with the sweet note Mark had left for her, made Molly not nearly as anxious as she might've been otherwise.

She obviously hadn't met the right kind of men previously, because not a single one had made her feel as taken care of as Mark had with just a note. And she knew he wasn't acting out of character. That note was exactly who he was.

Molly pushed the button on the coffee maker to start the brew, then headed back up the stairs. She had no idea what was in store for her future. She had no home. No belongings. And she wasn't ready to think about her job yet. But for the moment, she didn't have to think about anything at all, because Mark had given her a safe place to hole up until she was ready.

Molly opened her bag and put the note at the bottom, hoping it wouldn't get too wrinkled. She covered it up with her clothes, then headed back downstairs. It was already past noon; she'd slept for almost twelve hours. She couldn't remember when she'd last slept that long. But it was obvious her subconscious knew she was safe and she could let down her guard to get the rest she'd so badly needed.

Her belly growling, Molly headed into the pantry to see what she could scrounge up for lunch. Recalling the state of her body, she knew she needed to put more of an effort into building her weight back up. She grabbed a jar of peanut butter and a few cans of tuna. It wasn't the most nutritious of meals, but it would have to do for now.

Mark had obviously cleaned out his fridge before he'd left for his mission, and there wasn't much in there to help make the tuna more appetizing, but Molly forced herself to eat it anyway. Then she took a mug of coffee and the jar of peanut butter and a spoon into the living room. It took a while for her to figure out the remotes and how to get the TV to work, but once she did, she sat back to enjoy a mindless rerun of *The Big Bang Theory*. She was going to do just as Mark had suggested—try to relax and forget about everything she needed to accomplish. At least for a little while.

~

"Good to see you back, man," Archer said when Smoke came upstairs around two in the afternoon. The employees were used to them going to "conferences" and other work-related travel for extended periods.

And if they had a suspicion there was more to the owners of Silverstone Towing than met the eye, they didn't bring it up.

Smoke had spent the morning going over the jobs his employees had been on while he and his team had been away. There hadn't been any issues or problems, and it looked like everything had run smoothly.

Hiring Shawn Archer had been one of the best decisions they'd ever made. The man was the father of one of Skylar's students, and he fit in with everyone as if he'd always been there. He'd been hired to cook, clean, and do the landscaping, but it'd quickly become obvious his greatest talent was in the kitchen.

"Thanks," Smoke said. "It smells good in here."

"I made Thai chicken lettuce wraps for lunch," Archer said. "They're easy to eat on the go for anyone who doesn't have time to stop and eat, and they're healthy too."

Smoke felt guilty about not bringing Molly to the garage. He knew there wasn't much to eat in his house, and after everything she'd been through, she was probably starving for some good homemade food.

But after peeking in on her that morning and seeing how relaxed she'd looked, he simply hadn't had the heart to wake her up. *He*'d slept like shit. He couldn't get the dream he'd had out of his head. He hadn't known Molly all that long, but seeing her bleeding out, even if it was only in a dream—a nightmare—had left him rattled.

Smoke knew it was weird that he was becoming so attached to the woman already, but knowing his buddies had become obsessed with their women just as fast, he felt a little better about it. He just needed to not freak Molly out. Give her time to get to know him and feel safe with him. After her abusive ex, he figured it would take a while for her to trust him fully.

That was another reason he'd left her at his house this morning. He didn't want to pressure her into anything, and he wanted to make it clear that he had nothing to hide. He hoped she'd snoop into his stuff. There wasn't anything he was ashamed of in his house.

Okay, he had some *Penthouse* magazines stashed in a drawer next to his bed, and he had plenty of lube as well, but he was in his late thirties. And he wasn't a monk.

He wondered what she was doing right that second. If she was relaxing or stressing about replacing her things. Maybe she was thinking about her grandparents and crying. Or maybe she was worrying about her job.

And just like that, Mark wished he could go home and be there for her. He considered ditching the after-action review, but just then the door opened, and his friends walked in.

"I'll put together a tray for you guys," Archer said, turning toward the refrigerator.

Even though he hadn't been there long, the man knew how much the owners of Silverstone Towing liked to eat—which was a lot. They also worked out hard. Archer did an amazing job of making fancy-looking food that actually tasted good, and was also good for their bodies. He was a godsend, and everyone knew it.

"Hey," Smoke said, turning to his friends.

"Hey," Bull, Eagle, and Gramps said in unison.

"How's Molly?" Gramps asked.

"She's good. I came in a few hours ago—couldn't sleep—and instead of waking her up to bring her with me, I left her sleeping," Smoke said.

"She settle in all right?" Bull asked.

"How could she not?" Eagle answered before Smoke could. "You've seen Smoke's house."

Everyone chuckled.

"For someone so small, she sure can fill up a bed," Smoke said with a smile.

Three pairs of eyebrows lifted at his words, and Smoke quickly explained. "I mean because she spreads herself out from corner to corner."

When his friends simply continued to smirk at him, he rolled his eyes. "I looked in on her this morning," he clarified. "She was in a guest room, and I stayed in the master. Jeez, I just met her, and I'm giving her a place to stay while she figures out her life."

"Un-huh," Bull said. "That's how it starts."

"Then she gets under your skin, and you don't want her to leave," Eagle added.

"That's how it was with my Sasha," Archer added as he prepared a huge tray with lettuce wraps, pastries of some kind, and three large bowls of mixed fruit.

Smoke wanted to explain that it wasn't quite like that with Molly. But deep inside, he wanted it to be *just* like that, so he ignored his friends and gave his attention to Archer instead.

"The first time I met her, I knew I wanted to make her mine," their cook went on. "It didn't matter to me that she was Black and I was white. It didn't matter that I grew up on the wrong side of the tracks and her parents had money. It didn't matter that *both* our parents were against our relationship from the start. We clicked in a way that I'd never clicked with a woman before. We got married within a month and a half of meeting, and every day I had with her was a blessing. It wasn't ever easy, and I experienced firsthand how bad discrimination still is in this country. But together, we could face anything. Then we had Sandra . . . and life was perfect."

"How did Sasha die?" Eagle asked.

Smoke was definitely interested in hearing Archer's response. They hadn't asked about his personal life before, not wanting to pry. Their newest employee was still so young—his thirtieth birthday was just around the corner—so they were curious about his wife's passing.

"We put Sandra to bed one night, then watched some TV. We made beautiful love before going to sleep. When I woke up in the morning, she was just . . . gone. The second I touched her, I knew. The coroner said she'd had a massive heart attack in the middle of the night.

Said she didn't suffer, which I'm thankful for. I miss her every day, but Sandra helps keep me going. She looks so much like her mom. I want to raise her to be a strong woman, proud of her heritage, like Sasha was."

"I have no doubt she will be," Bull said.

"I'm sorry for your loss," Smoke said, feeling the words weren't adequate.

"Thanks. I didn't mean to bring the mood down. All I'm sayin' is that sometimes you just know. My advice is to just go with it, and don't fight it."

Smoke's lips quirked. "Noted."

"Good. Now, go on. The faster you get your work done, the faster you can get home to your women. Except you, Gramps. I'm making your favorite for dinner. Enchiladas."

"Yum," Gramps said with a grin.

The four men headed down the stairs, into the safe room they'd built in the basement. It was a place where they could talk about Silverstone business without fear of being overheard.

"How's Taylor?" Smoke asked Eagle when they'd all gotten seated and were attacking the lunch Archer had made.

"She's good. I'm stunned by how much her body's changed in just the month we were gone. Pregnancy is fucking mysterious and amazing and miraculous . . . and I'm glad it's women who give birth, and not men."

They all laughed.

"Her cravings are both hilarious and disgusting at the same time. But I still find them fucking adorable. Last night, I walked in on her eating yogurt with Cheetos mixed in."

"*Ewww,*" Gramps said, his nose wrinkling in distaste.

"Yeah. It gave me pause for a second, but when she burst out crying at seeing my reaction, I realized that I don't give a shit *what* she eats as long as she's happy. I'd do anything, literally *anything*, for her," Eagle said.

"I know the feeling," Bull said. "Last night, when Skylar and I were lying in bed together after . . . well, you know, she randomly said that she wished their school district had the budget to get more digital tablets. They're given to the older kids, but not the kindergartners. I swear to God, I got up naked as the day I was born to get my laptop. I ordered three right then and there because I couldn't stand to see her sad."

"If she needs more, let me know," Smoke said. "I'm happy to donate them."

"Thanks. I think she wants to start off with just a few to see how things go," Bull said.

"I guess Taylor and Skylar hung out quite a bit when we were gone," Eagle said. "And when I told Taylor about Molly, about her grandparents being killed and all her things being lost in the fire, she was ready to go straight out last night to shop for her."

"Skylar was the same way," Bull added. "I'm sure they'd be happy to pick some things out to tide her over."

"I think she'd prefer to pick out her own clothes. I mean, she's more than grateful for what you got her in Nigeria, but I have a feeling she's pretty independent. She's also a little prickly about other people spending money on her."

The guys stared at him for a moment—then burst out laughing.

"What?" Smoke asked, irritated.

"That's gonna suck for you," Gramps said, still laughing. "You're the king of buying shit for people."

"I am not!" Smoke protested.

"Um, not two seconds ago you offered to buy Skylar's entire class tablets," Bull noted.

"That's different—"

"And before we headed to Nigeria, you decided we needed another pinball machine so Taylor and Eagle could both play at the same time," Gramps added.

"And don't think we missed the new car seats you donated to the police department when their supply got low," Eagle threw in.

"*Fine.* But I've got the money, and I don't need ninety-nine percent of it. Why not use it to help others?" Smoke defended.

"I'm not saying it's a bad thing, but you just need to make sure Molly doesn't feel like a charity case," Bull said.

"She's not," Smoke said firmly.

"*We* know that, but if you're constantly throwing money at her or buying her things, she's gonna feel obligated . . . which I'm guessing isn't what you *want* her to feel when she thinks about you," Eagle said with way too much insight.

"I don't," Smoke said quietly. It was the first time he'd even hinted to his friends what he was feeling toward the woman they'd rescued, but none of them gave him any shit about it.

"Maybe this weekend she could go to the mall with Taylor and Skylar," Bull suggested.

"I'll talk to her. There's a lot of shit she needs to do in regard to her grandparents' deaths."

"Right. You'll remind her about Taylor's pregnancy?" Eagle asked.

"Of course. I'm sure she won't let her overdo it," Smoke told his friend.

"I didn't say she would, but I wouldn't mind an extra pair of eyes on Taylor just in case."

"Is she having any morning sickness?" Gramps asked.

"Thankfully, no," Eagle said, sighing in relief.

"Good."

"Right. So, let's get on with the AAR so I can be home when Skylar gets there after work," Bull suggested.

As the talk around the table turned to Nigeria and their search and discovery of Shekau, Smoke couldn't keep his mind from returning to Molly. Wondering what she was doing right that moment. He was itching to be done with work so he could get to the store and find some things he hoped she'd like to eat. Later, they could go together, and she could choose her own food, but for now, he wanted to make it clear that she didn't have to go anywhere, or do anything, until she was ready. It would take time for her to deal with the death of her grandparents, the ordeal she'd gone through in Nigeria . . . and he was determined to help with that process.

Chapter Eight

Smoke couldn't believe how much he was looking forward to getting home. He couldn't recall feeling like this—this anticipation—even after a tough mission. Of course, it was all because Molly was at his house. He'd made a couple of stops after leaving Silverstone Towing and was later than he'd wanted to be by the time he finally pulled into his garage.

He climbed out of his Explorer and grabbed a few of the bags. He went inside the house, turned off the alarm, and headed to the kitchen.

Putting the bags down on the counter, he went on the hunt for Molly. It took him a minute or two, but he finally found her in his bedroom. She'd moved the recliner from the corner to the middle of the floor so it was facing the large windows. She looked tiny in the oversize chair, and he couldn't help but love the fact that she enjoyed the view from his room so much that it was where she'd chosen to spend her time.

"Hey," he said.

She jerked in surprise—and the second her gaze met his, she screamed and leaped out of the chair.

"It's me!" Smoke said, holding up his hands and taking a step backward.

"Holy shit . . . *Mark*?" she asked.

"Yeah. Who else would it be?" he asked in confusion.

"Good God, you look *nothing* like you did the last time I saw you!"

Smoke finally clued in to why she was so scared. That morning, before he'd left the house, he'd hacked off a month's worth of facial hair. He ran a hand over his clean-shaven chin. "Sorry, I should've realized how different I look without the beard, and how it might scare you."

"I didn't hear you come in," Molly said, a hand on her chest as if to slow her heart rate.

He felt horrible about scaring her so badly. "I'm really sorry."

"No, it's okay," she said with a shake of her head. "You really *do* look different. For a second, I thought you were an intruder. I wasn't paying attention, was just enjoying your view."

Turning, Smoke looked out his window. He understood. Every time he saw his view, it calmed him. His property backed up to a nature reserve, and all he could see at the moment was trees and the occasional bird flying overhead. It always relaxed him when nothing else could. He hoped the land did that for Molly too.

"Want to help me unload the car?" he asked with a smile.

She stared at him a moment before shaking her head. "Of *course* he has a dimple," she murmured under her breath.

That made Smoke's smile widen. "If it makes you feel better, it was the bane of my existence when I was little. All my parents' friends thought it was 'so cute' and couldn't stop commenting on it. I don't think I smiled at all for two years."

"But you got over that?" Molly asked.

Smoke nodded. "Yeah. Once I figured out that chicks dug it, I perfected smiling just wide enough to bring it out and make the girls swoon and trip over themselves trying to impress me."

Molly chuckled, as he'd intended. "Not vain at all, I see."

He laughed. "Hey, I was fifteen," Smoke defended himself. "Eventually I realized that the girls who wanted to be with me because of the way I looked weren't the ones I was attracted to, so I stopped using my dimple to entice them."

"And who were the girls you were attracted to?" Molly asked.

"The quiet ones. The smart ones. The girls who stood back and watched everything going on around them. I wanted someone who liked me for me, not because of a damn dimple in my cheek."

They stared at each other for a long moment before Molly said quietly, "I think you know I liked you before I saw your dimple."

Smoke wanted to jump up and down and pump his fist in the air a few times like he was fifteen again, but he restrained himself and said, "And I like you too. Come on, I've got frozen food in the car. The ice cream's gonna melt all over the place if we don't rescue it."

"Ice cream?" Molly asked. "Why didn't you say so in the first place? Come on!" She ran by him and snagged his hand on the way, pulling him out of the room and down the hall.

Smoke could only grin at the small but mighty woman. He made a mental note to always have ice cream on hand in the future.

They gathered the rest of the bags from his car in the garage, and she helped him put everything away. It was clear from the way she didn't hesitate to put items away in their proper spots that she'd examined his kitchen.

"I wasn't sure what you liked to eat, so I got a bit of everything," Smoke said a little sheepishly after seeing how packed his fridge and freezer were by the time all the groceries had been put away.

"Honestly, I'm not that picky. Never have been," Molly said with a shrug. "I do have a bit of a sweet tooth, and with the amount of weight I need to put back on, that's probably a good thing."

Smoke hated hearing the self-deprecating tone in her voice. He put his hands on her shoulders, turning her so she was facing him. "Don't be so hard on yourself," he ordered. "You haven't even been out of the jungle a week."

"I know, I just . . ." She sighed. "I accidentally looked in the mirror after I got out of the shower this morning. Oh, and you were right—your bathrooms are amazing."

He raised an eyebrow, not letting her change the subject.

"Right. Anyway, I realized just how much weight I'd lost. I've never been a big person, but seeing what those assholes did to me really hit home."

"You'll gain it back," Smoke told her.

"I know. But I've always been made fun of because of my size. It's not just overweight people who get comments about their bodies when they're out in public. You wouldn't believe how many people have told me I need to eat more. I've even had people tell me flat out that I'd be more attractive if I wasn't so skinny. It's not that I haven't tried to eat to gain curves either. I just have a high metabolism, I think. And I don't really get all that hungry. I forget to eat when I'm working, and a lot of times when I get home from work, I'm too tired to do more than grab a sandwich or something. Preston also said—shit . . . never mind."

"No. What did that asshole say? Get it all out," Smoke urged. He knew overweight people frequently got comments about their weight and were put through hell, but he hadn't thought about the other side of the coin. About how slender people could be treated to the same kind of harsh words.

"He told me once that if I didn't look like a prepubescent teenager, I'd be a lot more attractive."

"That's such bullshit," Smoke growled. "You're perfect the way you are. Any issues your ex had are *his* issues, not yours. The way you look didn't make him be a jerk. Didn't make him say mean things. He sounds like he's a controlling asshole, and *that's* what made him treat you unkindly. You might be slight, but believe me when I say it's *not* a turnoff." He wanted to say more, but it was too soon. He didn't want to do or say anything that would make her feel uncomfortable around him, or in his home.

"As far as you gaining weight, I can help with that. I've learned a lot about nutrition over the years . . . what kind of fuel is best for sustaining muscle strength and what's good to eat when I've needed to gain weight myself. I've spent my fair share of time in out-of-the-way places tracking bad guys, and it's not unusual for me to lose twenty pounds or more in a short period of time as a result. I can help you remember to eat . . . and think about how fun it will be to eat all the ice cream you can stomach."

She swallowed hard before saying, "Thank you."

"No need to thank me. You've been through something not many people have experienced. It'll take some time to reacclimate to your normal life and to feel like yourself again. Cut yourself some slack. Okay?"

"I'll try," she said.

"Good. Now, why don't you open that last bag over there while I make us something to eat?"

"What's in it?" she asked.

"Go and see," Smoke said with a small smile.

Molly frowned at him, but he could see the sparkle in her eyes. She was excited about receiving a present, even if she tried to hide it.

He leaned against the counter as he watched her open the bag.

"A phone!" she exclaimed, turning to face him with the box in her hand.

"Yeah. It's not activated yet, so you'll need to go online to your provider and get it set up, but I didn't want to let another day go by without you having a way to get in touch with people. Email is all well and good, but sometimes it's necessary to talk to others."

"You didn't have to get the latest-and-greatest one," she scolded gently.

Smoke shrugged. "I wasn't going to get a used one," he retorted.

"But it would've been just as useful," Molly insisted.

Knowing he needed to get this out of the way, Smoke said, "I've got money, Mol. Lots of it. You already know this. Spending an extra four hundred bucks to get the latest model of phone isn't a hardship, especially if it lasts longer. And even if I didn't have millions of dollars in the bank, I still would've gotten you the same phone. I don't like being used for my money, but I *do* like giving things to people who deserve it. I give to charities. I spoil my friends. Just ask Bull, Eagle, or

Gramps. They've learned not to talk about anything they want around me because they know it'll end up in their bag, or mailed to their house, or stashed in their car. You're going to have to put up with me giving you things, and buying the foods you like, and cooking for you, because that's who I am."

"I seriously don't know how you're single."

Her response was surprising, but Smoke wasn't going to stop being honest now. "Because I tend to be very black and white. I'm not the most forgiving person either. I'm intense and overly protective. I have a bit of a temper, and I sometimes act before I really think about what I'm doing. I work too much, and I put my relationship with my friends before almost anything else. If Bull, Eagle, or Gramps call for my help, I'll drop everything for them.

"I also like my alone time. And there are times when I want to sit by myself in my room and stare at my view and just think rather than talk or entertain other people. I don't care for eating out—because I have no idea who's made my food or if they've washed their hands before doing so—and I rarely have the attention span to watch movies. Because of those things, and a lot more, I'm a horrible date. In addition to all that, when I'm sick, I'm the biggest baby around."

When he was done listing all his faults—both the ones he could think of off the top of his head, and those that other women had thrown at him when they'd broken up with him—Smoke wasn't sure what Molly would say. He didn't like painting himself in a bad light, but he wasn't a saint, nor did he want her to think he was.

Molly set the brand-new phone on the counter and walked around the kitchen island.

Surprising the hell out of him, she walked right into him, putting her arms around him and hugging him. Hard.

She rested her cheek on his chest and said, "I'm an introvert. I don't trust that easily. I got my master's degree because I had no idea what I wanted to do with my life after graduating from Northwestern. It was just easier to stay in school than to find a real job. And I prolonged that for as long as I could. It took me four years to get a degree most people get in two. I definitely hate confrontation, which is why I took the job in Nigeria. It was better than dealing with Preston and being scared all the time. I eat too much junk food, which I already told you, and I've never had a long-term relationship with anyone. I'm bad luck—which you know, but refuse to accept—and I have a really hard time seeing the positive in situations."

Smoke smiled and held her tighter against him.

"But I've never cheated on anyone, and I've never shoplifted anything. I'm a rule follower, and if you're my friend, I'd do anything for you. I'm trying to be more positive, but I'm not sure it's working. I miss my grandparents, and I hate that I didn't get to say goodbye to them. I can't help but wonder what they went through and what they were thinking . . . if they blamed me."

"They didn't," Smoke said immediately.

"You don't know that," Molly protested.

"I do. From everything you've told me about them, they loved you. So much. They would've done whatever was necessary to protect you. And if your ex killed them, I can guarantee the only thing they were thinking was how glad they were that you weren't in the States."

Molly nodded and sniffed, but she didn't move out of his arms.

A minute or two went by, and Smoke was more than fine with that. He *never* wanted to move. He wanted to stand there in the middle of his kitchen and hold her forever.

"I thought of something else good about being short," she said quietly.

"What's that?" Smoke asked.

"I can hear your heartbeat when I hug you," she said.

Smoke chuckled. "Very true."

Molly lifted her head and looked up at him. "I'm not good at accepting gifts, but if you don't go overboard, I'll try to get better at it."

"Deal," Smoke said. "And I'll text when I'm on my way home so I don't scare you again."

"I'd appreciate that."

"And I'll make sure you have Bull's, Eagle's, and Gramps's phone numbers too."

"Will Skylar and Taylor mind?"

Smoke wrinkled his brow in confusion. "Why would they?"

"Because another woman is calling or texting their men?"

"Ah, no. Bull and Smoke are head over heels in love with their women. We all know they have eyes for no one but them. Besides, Taylor and Skylar have *my* number. Does that bother you?"

Molly shook her head.

"Right. Because now that they're with my friends, I'm just as devoted to them as I am my teammates. If something ever happened to them, I'm not sure Bull and Eagle would be able to handle it. Eagle still hasn't forgiven himself for being knocked out a few months ago when Taylor's stalker crashed into his car and tried to kidnap her."

Molly's eyes widened. *"What?"*

"Long story. And I know both women are hoping to meet you sooner rather than later, anyway, so they'll fill you in. They want to take you shopping so you can start to replace your things. I told them not to go overboard, but you need to be prepared for them to be a little overenthusiastic."

"I'm not sure how long I'm going to be here," Molly replied a little hesitantly.

"There's no need to rush to get back up to Chicago, is there?" Smoke asked, a little anxious about the answer.

"Not really."

"Have you been in contact with your boss?"

"No."

He wanted to ask why, but decided that was a conversation for another time. "We still don't know what the deal is with your ex, so it's probably better for you to stay away for the moment."

Molly sighed. "I don't want to be a mooch."

"You aren't a mooch. You did hear me earlier when I said I liked to help my friends, right?"

"But we just met, Mark."

"We did," Smoke agreed. "But . . . you can't tell me you don't feel this bond we seem to have."

For a second, he thought she was going to deny it, but eventually she shook her head.

"Right. So why not stay for a while? There are no strings to you staying here," Smoke reassured her. "Promise."

"If you get tired of me being in your space, you have to also promise to tell me," Molly said.

"I don't see that happening, but yes, I'll say something if it does," Smoke replied.

"Okay. I'll stay. I like your house, Mark."

"Thanks. Did you snoop?" He smiled when he asked so she wouldn't think he was upset with her.

"Yup," she said without hesitation.

"And?"

"Well, I haven't found all your hiding spots yet, or the secret rooms, but from what I can see so far, you don't have any bodies hiding in your closets."

"I save those for the barn outside," he deadpanned.

When Molly threw her head back and laughed without any self-consciousness, Smoke grinned.

"Seriously, this house is awesome. The media room downstairs intimidated me, but I was glad to see you have a junk room like most normal people."

"Junk room?"

"Yeah, that storage room in the basement. The one with all the boxes and stuff. With how neat the house was, I was beginning to think you were a freak or something."

Smoke smiled. "Hey, I need some place to put all the holiday decorations."

"You decorate for the holidays?" she asked.

"Of course. My uncle had this huge-ass Christmas tree he made me haul upstairs the day after Thanksgiving every single year. Then he forced me to decorate it with him. It was a pain in my ass."

"And you loved it."

Smoke nodded. "Yeah. I did. And putting it up now reminds me of him and the good times."

"I like that for you. And . . . anyway, yes, I snooped. And I love your house. It's amazing. And big. Kids could play hide-and-seek in here and never be found."

"I've thought about that too," Smoke said honestly. And he had. Frequently. He still wanted children. Lots of them. But he'd started to think the opportunity had passed him by. "How about some dinner?" he asked, changing the subject.

"Okay. I can help."

"I got this. You can test out the ice cream I bought, though," Smoke told her, reluctantly dropping his arms and stepping away.

"Ice cream before dinner? Aren't you afraid it'll ruin my appetite?"

"Nope. Because I'm going to make the best baked chicken you've ever tasted."

"Baked chicken is boring," Molly teased.

"Not the way I do it. It's all in the spices that you cook the breasts in. And it'll take at least an hour for it to be ready. You can snack on the ice cream. I figure you'll be full in fifteen minutes. Then your stomach will have time to settle, and you'll be ready to eat again by the time the chicken is finished cooking."

Molly nodded. "Yeah, you're probably right. What kind did you get?"

"Chocolate chip cookie dough, mint chocolate chip, and rocky road."

"Cookie dough is my favorite," she told him.

"Why am I not surprised?" Smoke said as he turned to grab the pint out of the freezer. He handed it to her with a spoon. "Have at it."

"Mark?" she asked, pausing on her way out of the kitchen.

"Yeah?"

"News flash . . . that dimple of yours is still cute."

He saw the smirk on her face as she turned and headed for the couch.

Smoke loved that she felt comfortable teasing him. He knew he was smiling like a fool as he turned to grab the chicken breasts from the fridge, but he didn't care. Having Molly in his house was fun.

He just hoped he didn't get so used to it that it would break him when she left to get back to her life.

~

Molly's heart was beating double time as she sat on the couch to eat her ice cream. She'd never felt this . . . *giddiness* . . . around a man before. Especially not right after meeting him. She was always cautious and hyperaware of everything she said and did, especially after Preston.

It had been her experience that men didn't like to be teased. They certainly didn't want her to know any of their faults, so they pretended to be perfect. Then the veneer eventually wore off—sometimes sooner rather than later—and the real person behind it was revealed.

But Mark had laid out his faults without hesitation. She had already experienced the overprotective side of him. But for someone who'd lived through a kidnapping and an abusive ex who couldn't seem to get over the fact that she'd broken up with him, overprotectiveness wasn't exactly a turnoff.

Like Mark, she also wasn't very forgiving. Once upon a time, she'd bent over backward forgiving friends in school for being mean and giving boyfriends the benefit of the doubt, but she was done with that. So she couldn't hold that against Mark. And she was glad that he put his friends first. She didn't need to be the center of anyone's life. His solid relationships with Bull, Eagle, and Gramps just reinforced that he was the kind of man who was worth getting to know, that he could stick by someone no matter what life threw at them.

As the blend of chocolate, vanilla, and cookie dough exploded in her mouth, Molly practiced her positive thinking. She'd spent a lot of the day crying over her grandparents—including in Mark's room, shortly before he'd returned—which wasn't going to bring them back. She was exhausted as a result.

I was kidnapped, but I didn't die. I was rescued by one of the most generous men I've ever met. He's got a core group of friends, which means he's loyal. I've got a safe place to live. No one knows where I am right now. I have a phone, so I can call Nana and Papa's lawyer and start figuring all that out. I can get in touch with the cops to find out more information about both Preston and what happened at the house in Oak Park. And . . . chocolate chip cookie dough.

She took a bite of the ice cream and smiled. A week ago, she never would've guessed this was where she'd be. Sitting in a huge house with an insane amount of security, eating ice-cold perfection from a spoon.

Then she remembered something else Mark had said.

You might be slight, but believe me when I say it's not a turnoff.

Her smile grew. When she'd left for Nigeria, she'd decided she was better off being single, and that she wasn't going to date anyone for a very long time. But since meeting Mark Chamberlin, she was already changing her mind. If there was ever anyone she'd consider breaking her no-dating vow for, it'd be him.

But she wasn't going to rush things. One day at a time. She had a lot on her plate right now, and she had to figure her life out before she could jump into any kind of relationship with anyone. She was grateful Mark was letting her crash in his house, and she didn't want to take advantage of his generosity . . . or be a convenient lay for him.

Though somehow she knew he wouldn't do that to her.

Taking a deep breath, Molly realized she was full already. Mark had been right, she hadn't eaten nearly as much of the ice cream as she'd thought she might. Putting the container on the coffee table in front of her, using a coaster so she wouldn't leave a mark on the shiny glass, she sat back and closed her eyes. She could hear Mark puttering around in the kitchen, and it reminded her once again that she was safe.

She awoke with a jerk. She was lying down on the couch, with Mark kneeling in front of her.

"Dinner's ready," he said softly.

"Oh, how long was I asleep?"

"About an hour. I came over to check your progress on that ice cream, and you were out. I put the pint away for later and left you to sleep."

"Thanks. I didn't mean to fall asleep."

"I know. It'll take a while for you to work through the jet lag and for your body to recover from the stress of the last few months."

Molly abruptly sat up—and closed her eyes as the room spun for a second.

"Hang on, I've got you," Mark said.

Molly felt herself being picked up, and she wrapped her arms around Mark's neck. "Another perk to being small . . . I can be carried everywhere," she teased. She supposed she should've been annoyed that he felt the need to cart her around, but that would've been hypocritical, since she totally didn't mind when he held her.

She admired his dimple when he smiled. It was almost hard to believe he was the same man she'd met in the jungle. She didn't prefer one look over the other, though. He was good looking with a beard and without.

"Hey, did the other guys shave too?" she asked.

Mark chuckled. "Yup."

"Crap. Now I'm going to have to figure out who's who," she joked.

"Gramps is the tall one," Mark said. "Bull's hair is black. But you won't have to figure out anything when you see them at the garage, because they'll be wearing name tags."

"Really?"

"Yup. Skylar thought it would be easier on Taylor if everyone wore one so she wouldn't constantly have to wonder who everyone is."

Mark had told her about Taylor's condition. How she didn't have the ability to recognize faces . . . even those of people she knew and loved. "Oh, I hadn't thought about that. It *would* be hard, huh?"

Mark leaned over and placed her on a chair at the small table that sat right off the kitchen. He'd already plated their dinners, and Molly inhaled deeply, loving how good everything smelled.

"Yup. But now she can relax at the garage, which was the intent."

Molly nodded, her attention already on the food. The chicken looked delicious. It had some sort of sauce over it, and the green beans and fresh rolls looked just as good. "Wow," she said. "This looks amazing."

"The beans are from a can, and the rolls are from a tube," Mark said with a shrug. "I just don't want you thinking I'm a chef from one of those baking shows. Now, if this was a meal Archer made, everything would be from scratch."

Molly picked up a fork and took a bite of the beans. The buttery garlic flavor made her moan in appreciation. "He's the cook at Silverstone, right?" she asked once she'd swallowed.

"Right."

The next thirty minutes went by in a flash as they ate and talked about the employees of Silverstone Towing. By the time she'd finished eating—and had amazingly cleaned her plate—she knew about everyone who worked for Mark.

She helped carry their dishes to the kitchen sink. "You really like them, don't you?"

"Our employees? Yes. They work hard and are loyal to Silverstone Towing. We started the company kind of on a wing and a prayer, and without them, we'd still be four guys running in circles trying to catch our tails, like we were at the beginning. Leave the dishes, I'll do them later."

Molly froze midreach for the sponge in the sink. She looked at Mark. "Um . . . they'll be gross if we leave them. We might as well put them in the dishwasher now."

"You're one of those, aren't you?"

"One of what?" Molly asked.

"Someone who has to rearrange the dishwasher after her man stacks it because he didn't 'do it right.'"

Molly smiled. "I've never been accused of that, but it's probably because I've never lived with a man, and if I had dinner with someone, I was always the one taking care of the dishes."

"I'm not that guy," Mark said. "I admit that there are times when I adhere to the traditional male and female roles, but I'm perfectly able to clean a dish, sweep a floor, and I've been doing my own laundry for years."

"Good to know," Molly told him. "But I'm going to feel weird knowing the dishes are sitting in the sink with the food hardening on them."

Mark chuckled. "By all means, then, let's get them in the dishwasher so we can go veg on the couch."

They worked in tandem, and within a minute and a half, the dishes were neatly arranged and ready to be washed when the dishwasher was full.

"I'm looking forward to meeting them. Your employees," she told Mark, referring to their previous conversation.

"Good. Because I thought you could go with me to the garage tomorrow," Mark said. "Taylor and Skylar want to meet you, and I figured that would be the easiest place. Then, if you feel comfortable, you can go with them to get some clothes and stuff. They'll bring you back to Silverstone, and then we can go home."

Molly was nervous about meeting the other women, but would rather get it over with than put it off. If they clicked, great, but if not, at least she'd know sooner rather than later.

They sat on the couch. Molly took one corner, and Mark sat at the other side. "I need to call my grandparents' attorney."

Mark nodded. "I know. We can do that tomorrow afternoon."

"I just can't believe they're gone," Molly said softly, wondering if she was talking too much about her nana and papa.

"I wish I could've met them," Mark said. "From everything you've said so far, they sound like they were wonderful."

"They were." And just like that, Molly felt tears well up once more. "Shit, I'm sorry," she said, turning her head away.

"About what? About loving them? About being sad they're gone? You have *nothing* to be sorry about," Mark said. "My God, it's only been a few days since you learned about their deaths. Give yourself a break, Molly. Tell me more about them."

"Are you sure?" she asked.

"Yes. Your loved ones shouldn't be pushed into the background. They were loved and loving, they deserve to be remembered."

"Will you tell me about your parents and uncle?"

"Yes."

For the next few hours, they talked about the people they'd loved and lost. And surprisingly, Molly felt much better afterward. It felt good to tell Mark about the times her grandparents had made her laugh, and even when they'd made her mad. She loved hearing about Mark as a kid and the trouble he'd gotten into. By the time she was so tired she couldn't keep her eyes open anymore, the extreme pain of losing Nana and Papa had faded a bit. For now. Though anger still filled her. Anger that someone had not only killed them, but burned down their house, destroying any physical mementos she might've had of them.

"It's going to be all right," Mark said softly.

Molly realized she'd said that last part out loud. "I hope so."

"I know so. You aren't alone, Molly Smith. You've got me and Silverstone at your back. If it turns out that your ex *did* have something to do with this, we'll find out. And if he thinks he can continue to stalk you, he's going to be very surprised at the reinforcements you've gotten since the last time he saw you."

"You don't know how he is," Molly protested.

"I actually do. You forget that my team and I deal with the worst of humanity. We have to delve into the messed-up psyches of terrorists and murderers all the time."

"He's upset that I broke up with him," Molly said. "I think it was a blow to his ego more than anything else. He didn't love me, and I certainly didn't love him."

"Some men are like that. They treat people as objects and throw a fit if someone takes their toy away before they're ready. I'm going to make sure he knows you're off limits and needs to move on."

"Are you going to kill him?" Molly asked baldly.

Mark didn't look upset at her question. "Not if he takes the hint and stops harassing you."

"And if he doesn't?" she pressed.

"I'm going to do whatever's necessary to make sure he doesn't hurt you again."

Molly knew she should've been appalled that Mark had basically just hinted he *would* kill Preston if he hurt her . . . but deep down, she'd known he'd say that.

She wasn't an idiot; she was well aware of what Mark and his friends did, having witnessed it firsthand. She may have balked before, but after living through being a captive of a crazy bastard like Shekau, and just knowing her grandparents may have been killed for no reason other than that she'd broken up with someone . . . she was *glad* there were people out there like Silverstone. Forget the superheroes in the movies;

she was sitting next to a real-life superhero right this second, as far as Molly was concerned.

That didn't mean she wasn't scared for him. Mark could still be killed, and she knew, deep down, Preston wasn't going to like the fact that anyone had taken her side. He'd be even more determined to get to her once he learned where she was, no matter *who* was protecting her. But she had to trust that Mark knew what he was doing. That she really was safe. The alternative, constantly being worried about Preston, was terrifying. "Thanks," she said softly.

"You're welcome. I think it's time for you to head up to bed."

"What time are we going to Silverstone tomorrow?"

"It's Saturday, so Skylar doesn't have to work. And there's no need to get there at the crack of dawn. You can sleep in. If you're not up by nine, I'll wake you, though, if that's okay."

"It's hard to believe before I left for Nigeria I was a morning person," Molly said with a rueful grin. "Now, it's a struggle to drag myself out of bed at all."

"As I said, it'll take time. But for now, there's no reason for you to get up with the sun."

"You're a morning person, aren't you?" Molly asked as she pushed herself to her feet.

Mark got up as well and nodded. "Guilty. Comes with being in the Army. I still work out most mornings. Sometimes I run, other times I just do weights in the garage."

Molly's eyes ran over his body, appreciating how in shape he was.

"Stop ogling me, woman," Mark mock complained.

Molly chuckled. "Hey, can't blame a girl for looking. Besides, you all but invited my stares. Talking about doing weights and working out and stuff."

Mark merely shook his head. "You need anything before you head up?"

"No, I'm good. Thank you for all you've done for me, Mark."

"You're welcome."

"Seriously. I needed tonight's talk."

Mark reached out and surprised Molly by pulling her into his arms. She held on tightly, loving how she seemed to fit against him perfectly.

She felt his lips on the top of her head, then he stepped back. "I'll see you in the morning, then."

Molly nodded and headed for the stairs. She looked back once, when she was halfway up, and saw that Mark was still watching her. She gave him an awkward wave and saw his lips twitch. He gave her a chin lift and turned to sit on the couch. He reached for the remote as Molly continued up the stairs.

When she was once again sprawled in the king-size bed, Molly closed her eyes and smiled. It was safe to say that she liked Mark Chamberlin. Probably more than she should, considering her circumstances. But she couldn't bring herself to care about that. With a full belly, a comfortable place to sleep, and the knowledge that she was safe behind the walls of Mark's home, she was more content than she could remember being in a very long time.

Chapter Nine

Molly was having second and third thoughts about going to Silverstone Towing that morning. She'd gotten very used to being by herself over the last few months, and being around other people had always been exhausting and awkward for her. Why she'd thought it would be a good idea to meet Taylor and Skylar was beyond her. She could've just bought clothes online and had them delivered. Shopping had never been one of her favorite things, and now she'd committed herself to shopping with other people. Strangers at that.

"It's going to be fine," Mark told her, looking over at her from the driver's seat of his car.

How he always seemed to know what she was thinking, Molly had no idea. "I know," she lied.

"They're really nice," he added.

Molly was embarrassed that he felt the need to prep her for the upcoming meeting. "I'm sure they are. Look, just because they're with your friends doesn't mean we're going to get along. I mean, women are weird. Sometimes we just don't click with other people. I'm not going to be rude or anything, but if we don't end up BFFs, I don't want you to think it has anything to do with you or your friends."

"BFFs?" he asked.

"Best friends forever," Molly said. "You've never heard that?"

"I'm thirty-eight. Haven't dated in forever. And don't forget I was in the Army, and now I only hang out with the Silverstone guys. So no, I haven't heard that term."

Molly chuckled. "Right. Anyway, I'm just saying that if we don't hit it off, don't take it personally."

"You're going to be fine," Mark repeated, his tone full of confidence.

Molly didn't want to contradict him again. She'd warned him, and that was all she could do. All her life, she'd had a hard time making friends. She wasn't sure why. Most of the time, she'd only *thought* she was tight with someone, then when something bad had happened, she'd discovered most of the connection had been on her side. It was one reason she was so leery of what she felt for Mark. She'd lost enough people in her life that she'd thought would stand by her when the shit hit the fan. She'd learned to be cautious.

"You are," Mark insisted. "I told you about Skylar's experience with being kidnapped by a child predator, but I don't think I told you about Taylor."

"You said something about Eagle being upset when she was taken right under his nose after a car accident," Molly said.

"Yeah, well, she had a stalker. He'd become interested in her when he found out she had prosopagnosia."

"Pro-so-what?" Molly interrupted.

"Prosopagnosia. Facial-recognition blindness. That condition I told you about? That's what it's called. So this guy found out about it, and he thought she'd be fun to fuck with. He finagled meetings with her to see if she recognized him, and when she didn't, he actually managed to get into her apartment by pretending to be a maintenance man. He even delivered a pizza to Eagle's place when she was staying there. Turns out he was a serial killer. He'd kidnapped and tortured eleven other women before her, and when she and Eagle were on their way to Bloomington for an awards dinner for one of her clients, the guy wrecked their car and tried to take Taylor."

"Holy shit, what happened?" Molly asked. "Was she hurt? How'd she get away from him? Why does Eagle blame himself? That's crazy!"

Mark was smiling.

"What? This isn't funny!" Molly scolded.

"It's not, but *you* are. If you give me half a second, I'll finish the story."

"You're taking too long," she complained. "Hurry up!"

"Sorry. So, while Taylor didn't recognize the man from all the times she'd met him before, she *did* recognize his smell. And his car. So she ran into the trees alongside the road and hid until Eagle regained consciousness and came after them."

Molly bit her lip. "What happened to the guy?"

"Eagle killed him."

"Did he get in trouble?"

"Mol, the man was a serial killer. No, he didn't get in trouble."

"And Taylor's okay?"

"Yeah. My point in telling you this is just that Taylor and Skylar aren't like a lot of women. They're compassionate, and even a little introverted themselves. They've been through hell, just like you have. I'm not saying you need to be best friends with them, but I think if you give them a chance, you might just be surprised at how much you have in common."

Molly thought about that for a moment and realized Mark was probably right. She was doing surprisingly well mentally after being freed, but that didn't mean she wouldn't have a flashback or wouldn't want to talk to someone about what had happened to her. And while Taylor and Skylar hadn't been kidnapped and thrown into a hole while in a foreign country, they'd still experienced situations just as horrible as hers.

"Has there ever been any . . . weirdness . . . between you guys because of women?"

Mark glanced at her, then turned his attention back to the road. "I'm not sure what you're asking, but I'll tell you this: at no time have Gramps or I been upset because Eagle or Bull were dating. And at no time have any of us secretly harbored any feelings for someone else's woman. Apparently when a Silverstone man falls, he falls hard."

She hadn't missed the wry tone of Mark's voice . . . or the look he'd thrown her way.

Go slow, she admonished herself. *Remember all those other friends who you thought were lifelong buddies, and how quickly they turned their backs on you when you needed them most.*

But hadn't Mark already proven that he wasn't like that? It would've been a lot easier to let her go with the other girls after they'd all been rescued. She wasn't his problem, yet he and his friends had taken it upon themselves to arrange her passport and get her back to the States. And Mark had given her a place to stay, had fed her, had gotten her a phone, and was introducing her to the most important people in his life . . . namely, his Silverstone Towing employees, and Taylor and Skylar.

It certainly felt as if she could count on him, but only time would tell.

"We're here," Mark announced.

Molly looked surprised. "*This* is Silverstone Towing?" She couldn't avoid the note of disbelief in her own voice.

But Mark didn't take offense. He merely chuckled. "I know it looks bad, but looks can be deceiving." He leaned out his window and punched in a very long security code before the gate in front of them began to open.

"Let me guess, you helped with the security for this place," Molly said dryly.

"Yup."

Yeah, she'd known that. He'd told her that he'd been heavily involved in setting everything up at the garage. But even if he hadn't, with how secure he'd made his own property, it wasn't hard to guess that he'd made his business safe as well. He'd flat out told her he was protective, and she was beginning to understand just how far that protectiveness extended. Not only to himself, but to those he held near and dear.

He drove around the back of a decrepit-looking building and parked his Explorer at the end of a row of vehicles. The butterflies were back in her belly, but Mark didn't hesitate. He cut off the engine and opened his door. Taking a deep breath, Molly followed his lead. She hopped out of the car and walked around to meet him on the other side.

Mark took hold of her hand and squeezed. Then he led the way to the door at the back of the building. He punched in another long security code, and she heard the lock click as it disengaged. Then she was inside—and immediately the smell of something delicious wafted their way.

"Oh wow, that smells like fresh bread," she said.

"It probably is. Archer bought a bread maker, and he's been going a little crazy trying it out. He's made just about every type of bread you can think of, including a loaf of gluten-free stuff, which was just as good as the regular." Mark dropped her hand and reached for a name tag on a metal board just inside the door. He attached one onto his chest that had the word SMOKE in large easy-to-read letters . . . then he smiled as he reached for another and held it up.

Molly was surprised to see her name on the tag.

"May I?" Mark asked as he gestured to her chest.

Molly nodded, wondering how and why there was a name tag with her name on it.

"Skylar made it for you. She didn't want you to feel left out by being the only one not wearing one. And, of course, it helps Taylor."

Ah, that made sense . . . and suddenly it didn't matter, because Molly couldn't think about anything other than how close Mark was. Even though he towered over her, she didn't feel hemmed in at all. One of his hands reached just inside the neckline of the T-shirt she was wearing, and she could feel the backs of his fingers brush against the naked skin of her upper chest. He wasn't copping a feel—he was just attaching the name tag to her shirt—but it still felt extremely intimate.

She shivered as he pulled his hand away.

Then she blushed, confused beyond belief. She shouldn't have been so turned on by such a simple touch. She wasn't sure what it was about this man that was so different from anyone else. Why she'd felt like she might go up in flames when he'd touched her so innocently.

Mark brushed a lock of hair behind her ear but didn't say anything. Then he put his hand on the small of her back and gently propelled her down the hall.

Molly could hear people talking, and it took her a second to get her bearings once again. It was almost scary how much she liked Mark touching her. She'd gone thirty-five years or so without *needing* a man's touch, but now she seemed to come alive when his skin came into contact with her own.

"Smoke!" someone called out as they entered a huge room. A kitchen was on one side, and everything about the space seemed cozy despite its size. The room wasn't shabby in the least, as the outside of the building might have suggested. But it also wasn't over-the-top fancy. The couches and chairs looked comfortable and inviting, and the scent of bread didn't hurt the welcoming atmosphere either.

Mark walked them over to where a group of people was standing near a granite bar separating the kitchen from the rest of the room. It was obvious the kitchen was the domain of the man standing on the other side of the bar. Molly assumed this was the famous Archer she'd heard so much about. He had black hair that was a touch too long, and he was very skinny, especially for a cook. It was surprising how young he looked. She'd had a picture in her head of an older man, maybe in his fifties, but Archer looked younger than *she* was, maybe even in his late twenties. An apron covered with flour was wrapped around his chest and waist, and he smiled when he saw them, nodding in greeting to Mark.

Everyone was indeed wearing a name tag, and somehow that made Molly relax a fraction. She wouldn't have to try to memorize everyone's names right off the bat.

Mark made introductions. "Molly, this is Leigh, Jose, and Bart. They're on shift at the moment, and probably stocking up on some fresh bread before they head out on their first calls of the day, am I right?"

Leigh laughed. "If you think I'm leaving without some of Shawn's delicious bread in my belly, you're insane. It's nice to meet you, Molly. I'm sorry about what happened to you, but you couldn't have hooked up with a greater group of people to help you get back on your feet."

She looked up at Mark in surprise.

"They know about your grandparents and the house burning down," Mark said gently.

Molly nodded. She'd thought for a second that Leigh had been talking about her being kidnapped in Nigeria. She and Mark had talked a little bit about how his employees weren't aware of what he and his friends did, the fact they traveled overseas eliminating bad guys. He'd had to explain so she wouldn't inadvertently let something slip that would spill the beans.

"Thanks," she told the other woman.

"Welcome to Silverstone Towing," Jose said. "It's an amazing place to work, and it has even more amazing people working here."

"Watch it, Shawn's food is addictive. If you aren't careful, you'll never want to go back to Chicago," Bart threw in.

Molly couldn't argue with him, but if she didn't want to go back to Chicago, it wasn't going to be because of any food. She looked over at Mark, and saw he was studying her intently. She gave him a small smile, trying to reassure him that she was fine, and he nodded back at her.

"I'm Taylor," a woman with the most gorgeous curly brown hair said as she held out her hand. "I know Smoke told you about my condition, so don't feel weird about it. And if you have questions, I'm happy to answer them. I'm a lot less self-conscious about it these days, and everyone here at Silverstone is a big reason why."

"Hi," Molly replied, thinking the other woman was very brave to be as open as she was about her prosopagnosia.

"And I'm Skylar," added a woman who wasn't much taller than Molly. She had beautiful auburn hair and green eyes that seemed to sparkle. "I'm the kindergarten teacher. I know that makes me a glutton for punishment, but I love spending time with my kids. They're inquisitive and energetic, which is great . . . though I can't deny I'm happy to send them home at the end of the day!"

Molly couldn't help but smile at that. "I'm Molly," she said a little awkwardly.

"It's good to see you again, Molly. You settling into Smoke's giant house all right?" Bull asked as he stepped forward and gave her a short hug.

"Oh yeah, it's a real hardship," Molly quipped.

Everyone chuckled, and Eagle leaned down and gave her a kiss on the cheek. "Welcome to Silverstone Towing," he said.

"I think you should come stay with *me*," Gramps said, wrapping Molly in an embrace once Eagle had stepped back.

"Enough," Mark told his friends, rolling his eyes and tugging on Molly's hand, pulling her against his side.

Everyone around them laughed, and Molly was relieved to see how at ease everyone was with each other.

After a bit more small talk, Jose, Bart, and Leigh all said their good-byes and headed for the door, obviously going to work.

"We'll head downstairs," Bull said. "Smoke, come down when you're ready." He then kissed Skylar. Eagle did the same to Taylor, then followed his friend toward a hallway off to the side of the room.

Gramps was still smiling, but he nodded his head at Smoke and Molly and followed his friends.

"Give us a second?" Mark asked the other women. They agreed and headed over to one of the couches behind them.

"Try to relax with Taylor and Skylar today. They'll take good care of you, and I think you'll have fun. You have your phone?"

Molly nodded.

"Good. It should be working fine after you activated it this morning, but if you have any issues, tell Skylar to stop by the store so you can talk to someone in person about it. That's always easier than dealing with someone over the phone. And if you get too tired, don't be afraid to say something. Both women know the truth about what happened to you. Get Archer to pack you a snack for later if you want. You need to keep your caloric intake up. And lastly, don't skimp when you shop today. You'll eventually get a check from the insurance company to cover what you lost in the fire, and if you need money to tide you over until they pay up, I've got you covered."

Molly just stared at Mark. She wasn't sure what to say. It felt good to have someone so concerned about her, but it was also a little weird. She wasn't a kid, and she kinda felt like Mark was treating her like one. But before she could tell him that she wasn't helpless, that she could take care of herself, he spoke again . . . as if he'd read her mind.

"I know you're a grown woman and have been taking care of yourself for a long time, but I can't help it, Molly. I told you that one of my faults is that I'm too protective—this is a part of that. Have fun, but take care of yourself, too, okay? And don't try to be too responsible when it comes to budget. You need clothes, shoes, and lots of other stuff."

He *had* told her he was protective. And after a moment's hesitation, Molly decided she could live with this brand of protectiveness. It wasn't anything like Preston's obsessiveness. "Okay," she answered somewhat lamely.

"And again, if you get too overwhelmed, just say so. Taylor and Skylar will understand."

"I will."

Mark stared at her for a long moment. Then he leaned forward and kissed her on the forehead.

His lips felt warm against her skin, and Molly didn't want him to move away.

He smiled and said, "Another good thing about you being pocket-size . . . you're the perfect height for forehead kisses." Then he took her hand in his once more and brought her over to where the other two women were doing their best to pretend they hadn't been staring at them.

"Here she is, ladies," Mark said. "Try to take it easy on her today. It's been a long time since she's had a marathon shopping trip. And don't forget to take a break for lunch. And Mol has a sweet tooth, so make sure she eats something healthy before she has dessert."

Both women were smiling and nodding.

"And . . . have fun," he said. Then he squeezed Molly's hand and turned to head down the same hallway where his friends had disappeared earlier.

Molly sank down into a chair next to the couch.

"Holy wow," Skylar said, fanning her face with her hand.

"I mean, I've always thought Smoke was intense, but that was . . . whew!" Taylor added with a smile.

"I've only known him for a week," Molly said, not sure what she was protesting.

"Sometimes that's all it takes," Skylar retorted with a smile. "Bull was the same way."

"Eagle too," Taylor chimed in.

"But anyway . . . we've got some shopping to do," Skylar said, rubbing her palms together. "Where do you usually shop? What kind of things do you like to wear? Jeans? Leggings? Skirts? And what else do you need? Shoes, of course. At the moment, you don't need kitchen stuff or sheets and towels, but I'm sure you could use a suitcase, and purses, and—"

"I don't want to go crazy," Molly said quietly, interrupting the other woman.

Skylar blushed, and Molly felt bad for saying anything. She'd been so excited, and now she looked embarrassed. "But I'm so grateful that you guys are going with me. I mean, if it was up to me, I'd just go to Target and call it done."

"I love Target," Taylor said.

"Me too. Although I always spend way too much when I go in there. I don't know if they pump some sort of buy-me juice through the air filters or what," Skylar said.

"Buy-me juice?" Taylor asked, then burst out laughing.

Molly joined in. Maybe this shopping trip wouldn't be so bad after all.

～

Five hours later, Skylar pulled back into the parking lot of Silverstone Towing, and Molly couldn't remember when she'd had a better time. Her new friends had convinced her to buy way more than she'd ever need. They'd walked the mall as if they were a trio of high schoolers with their parents' credit card. Molly had bought shirts, pants, shoes, jeans, pajamas, underwear, socks, purses, bags . . . even a winter coat that she wouldn't need for at least another few months.

They'd gone into a home store, and Molly had bought a Keurig with Skylar's urging. She could now have a cup of froufrou coffee while Mark had his manly black stuff.

It had been Taylor who'd insisted that she needed the picture of the turtle swimming off the waters of Hawaii. Molly hoped she could hang it in the guest room at Mark's house until she found a place of her own.

They'd stopped by Target after they'd left the mall, and Molly had found herself buying wrapping paper, a cute little donkey planter, envelopes, pens, a couple of pairs of earrings—and a stuffed animal, of all things. It was nothing she needed, but all of it made her smile, so that made it worth it.

After leaving Target, Skylar had convinced them to stop at a thrift shop, and Molly had filled a shopping cart with even more stuff there. She'd bought a dozen books for a buck, found even more clothes, and even picked up a present for Mark. She had no idea if he'd like it or not, but Molly had seen it and thought it would be perfect as a thank-you gift.

They'd stopped to eat lunch, and Skylar and Taylor had refused to let her eat her peanut butter chocolate cake before she'd finished her fettucine Alfredo. She was still so full, she felt as if she was going to burst, but she couldn't remember being happier.

They'd then gone to the grocery store, and Taylor had told her the story of how she'd met Eagle at that very same one—the same store where the serial killer who'd become obsessed with her had first seen her. She admitted that she still didn't really like shopping there, but since she had both Skylar and Molly with her, it was a lot easier.

Molly had also bought way too much crap at the grocery, but to be fair, she'd been encouraged by both Skylar and Taylor. When Molly had mentioned that she needed to gain back the weight she'd lost, they'd gone a little crazy throwing all sorts of sugary foods into her cart.

Mark had checked in quite a few times during the day, and each time her new friends had given her "I told you so" looks. When she'd tried to insist that Mark was just concerned for her safety, they'd merely laughed and said, "If you say so."

"I have no idea how we got everything in here," Molly said, turning around and looking in the back of the Jeep Wrangler Taylor had borrowed from Eagle.

"I'm just glad Smoke has an Explorer," Skylar said from the front passenger seat.

As they pulled around the back of the garage, the door opened, and Bull, Eagle, Mark, and Gramps appeared.

They were all grinning at how full the Wrangler was.

Mark was standing by Molly's door by the time Skylar parked. He opened the door and held out his hand. Molly took it, and he helped her out. "Have fun?" he asked.

Molly smiled and nodded.

"They all look like they survived," Gramps teased.

"We did!" Skylar said happily.

"Did you leave any doughnuts in the store for anyone else?" Eagle asked as he peered into the grocery bags in the back of the Wrangler.

"Nope," Taylor replied with a huge smile. "Although, I was nice and let Molly have the last bag of the spice-cake Krispy Kremes."

"You look happy," Mark said quietly, for Molly's ears only.

"I had fun," she told him.

"Good." It looked like he wanted to say more, but after a moment, he turned and began to help his friends sort through the packages and move everything Molly had bought to his Explorer.

"I had such a great time!" Skylar said as she approached Molly.

"Me too," she told her.

"We need to do this again," Taylor added. "Well, maybe not go on such an extreme shopping spree, but definitely hang out."

"Yes!" Skylar said enthusiastically. Then she frowned. "But, of course, I work during the week."

"We can do dinner or something," Taylor said. "I mean, Smoke's got that big ole house. We could meet up there."

"That would work," Skylar enthused, nodding. "He's got that huge, amazing kitchen, and definitely enough chairs for us all."

"Um . . . I'm not sure how long I'm going to be here in Indianapolis," Molly said almost apologetically.

Both Taylor and Skylar turned to look at her.

"You're not? I thought you were staying here," Taylor said.

"I mean, my life is in Oak Park," Molly said without any real confidence.

"It was," Skylar agreed. "I'm sure your friends and stuff are all there, huh? And your job."

"Well, I didn't really have any close friends. Just my nana and papa. And they're gone now. And I'm not sure what to do about my job . . ."

Molly couldn't believe she'd just admitted that. She hadn't had a lot of time to think about her job, but after hearing that the company had pulled out all their employees from Nigeria and essentially left her to her own devices . . . she was still hurt. She'd been thinking about doing something different even before she'd gone overseas. She'd been an environmental engineer her whole career, but she'd started to realize months ago that she didn't really *like* it.

"Then you can stay here in Indianapolis until you figure out what you want to do," Skylar said. "Smoke's not going to kick you out, and you can hang with us while you're here. And if you want, you can come visit my classroom, see if teaching is something you might like. You've got your master's degree, so you'd probably just need to take a few classes, and I'm sure you'd be snatched right up. The teaching profession needs as many awesome teachers as it can get."

"I'm not sure I'm cut out to be a teacher, but I'd like to see your classroom," Molly said honestly.

"I love working from home," Taylor said. "I like being by myself . . . it's just more comfortable for me. But since meeting Skylar and marrying Eagle, I enjoy getting out more, as long as I have someone with me. Though it's still uncomfortable to come face to face with someone I'm supposed to know but don't recognize."

"I'd love to work from home, but I have no idea what I'd do," Molly admitted. In the back of her mind, she did know what she *wanted* to do.

But this wasn't the time or place to get into it . . . and it wasn't exactly something she could just decide to do on her own . . . maybe.

"You've got time to figure it out," Skylar said.

Molly knew she didn't really. She wasn't rolling in money and couldn't afford to pay rent unless she figured her life out pretty quickly.

"And I'm thinking it's probably best you didn't go back to Oak Park right now anyway," Taylor said. "I mean, I've had a stalker, and it's scary as hell. If this Preston guy is really as bad as you've told us he is, it's probably better that you keep lots of miles between you."

Molly couldn't disagree with that. "True."

"Great, so it's settled. Dinners at Smoke's place, and we'll see when we can hang out on the weekends too," Skylar said.

"What's at my place?" Mark asked, coming up behind them.

Molly turned and tried to think of a way to tell him that his house had been volunteered for get-togethers.

"Dinners. We want to hang out with Molly, and since you have the biggest place, we decided it was perfect," Skylar said.

"Sounds good to me," Mark replied, not fazed in the slightest.

"Not all the time, just now and then," Molly clarified.

Mark looked down at her, then at the other women. "You are all welcome to my house any time you want to come. You'll just need to let me or Molly know ahead of time so we can turn off the security system."

"That's right, nothing gets in without Smoke's say-so," Skylar said with a chuckle.

"Damn straight," Mark muttered.

"You done inviting yourself over to other people's houses?" Bull asked Skylar as he put an arm around her shoulders.

"For now," she answered breezily.

"Thanks for keeping my girls entertained today," Eagle said, pulling Taylor into his side.

"Your girls? Something you aren't telling us?" Gramps asked with a raised eyebrow.

Taylor rolled her eyes. "He's convinced this baby is a girl. I keep telling him there's no way he can know that, but he insists." She put a hand on her still-flat stomach, and Molly loved how Eagle immediately covered it with his own as well.

"You gonna be upset if it's a boy?" Bull asked.

"Fuck no," Eagle said immediately. "I don't care if it's a three-headed monkey. It'll be ours, that's all that matters."

"So romantic," Taylor said, rolling her eyes once again.

Everyone laughed.

"Thank you, guys, for convincing Molly to buy out the stores. Appreciate it," Mark said.

Molly turned toward him, ready to playfully smack him for being facetious, but when she looked into his face, she saw that he was completely serious.

"You say that now, but wait until all the crap I bought is strewn around your house, cluttering it up," Molly told him with a laugh.

But again, he didn't even crack a smile. Simply looked down at her and said, "It'll probably make it feel more like a home."

No one said anything for a long moment until Gramps broke the silence. "On that note, I'm out of here. Don't forget that Willis told us he's sending us something to look over soon. He's still researching whatever it is, and said he'd send it when he had more solid intel."

The men all nodded and said their goodbyes to Gramps.

Skylar came over and hugged Molly. "Thanks for coming out with us today. I had fun."

"Me too," Molly agreed.

Taylor hugged her next. "I'm home all the time, so please don't hesitate to call or text if you need anything. To talk, to whine that you don't have any more doughnuts in the house, if you get scared being alone . . . just anything. Okay?"

Molly swallowed hard. The day had been mostly lighthearted and carefree, but Skylar and Taylor had discussed what had happened to them. How scared they'd been. And Molly and Taylor had commiserated over having a stalker. Before she'd left for Nigeria, Preston had been showing up literally everywhere she'd gone, and it had terrified Molly. She felt a definite connection with Taylor and appreciated her offer to talk.

"Thanks."

Then Mark put his hand on the small of her back and guided her over to the passenger side of his Ford Explorer. He helped her in, lingering by the open door as she buckled her seat belt. "Mark? Is everything okay?"

"Yeah. I'm just relieved that today worked out."

"You didn't think it would?"

"I did, but . . . Taylor is pretty introverted. And you aren't exactly Miss Outgoing yourself. Skylar is friendly, but she tends to see the world in black and white, good and bad. I had no doubt you'd all get along, but there was the possibility that none of you would be able to open yourselves up enough to really connect."

Molly swallowed hard. Mark was very perceptive, and it was almost intimidating sometimes. "I really liked them."

"Good. You hungry? Want to stop on the way home?"

Molly groaned. "God, no. I swear all I did today was snack."

"Okay, Mol. I can't wait to see what you bought."

She wrinkled her nose. "Honestly, I'm kinda scared to look myself. After the first few stores, it's all a blur. I can probably return most of the crap I bought."

Mark shook his head. "Nope. If you bought it, there had to be a reason. Probably because it made you smile. I saw the turtle picture; it's gorgeous."

"I don't need it . . . ," Molly hedged.

"It makes you happy, so in my eyes, that means you need it," Mark told her. "Watch your feet." He shut the door and walked around to the driver's side. He got in, clicked his seat belt in place, and expertly backed up before heading toward the exit.

"I like your business," Molly said. "You and your friends have done an amazing job with it."

"Thanks."

"I envy you," Molly told him quietly. "Knowing you have the kind of friends and employees who would bend over backward to help you when you need it is rare."

"It is," Mark agreed. "I don't want to pressure you, but I overheard a bit of your conversation with Taylor and Skylar. They could be the same kind of friends for you, too, if you stayed."

Molly didn't respond, but she knew Mark didn't really expect her to. He held his hand out, and she took it in hers. They held hands the rest of the way to his house.

Molly hadn't even been in Indianapolis for three full days, and somehow she felt more at home here than she ever had in Oak Park. She also felt she was really connecting with the men and women of Silverstone.

She knew she needed to go back to Chicago at some point. But she was perfectly content to put it off for a while longer. She had a bad feeling that when she *did* go back, the contentment and safety she felt at this moment would be shattered. Not only would she have to face the fact that Nana and Papa were truly gone, but it could give Preston a chance to harass her again.

For the time being, she was going to stay with Mark and try to gain back the weight she'd lost. The longer she could live in this fantasy bubble, the better.

Chapter Ten

Something was bothering Molly, but she wouldn't talk to him about it . . . and it was making Smoke crazy. It had been a week since she'd gone to Silverstone Towing and met Taylor and Skylar. The three women texted all the time, and he was as pleased as he could be that they were getting along. They'd even already had a get-together at his house with everyone. Gramps, Bull, Eagle, Taylor, and Skylar. They'd hung out, laughed, and generally had a fantastic time.

But now something was up, and Molly wasn't being honest with him about it . . . wasn't talking to him. And while he knew he had no right to demand she tell him what was bothering her, Smoke still wanted to.

They might not have known each other very long, but their time together had been intense, and Smoke felt as if he understood Molly better than most people would. They'd both lost their parents at a young age and had been raised by a relative. They'd bonded in the jungle, and he knew without a doubt that she felt safe with him. Not to mention the nights they'd spent hanging out in his room, watching the stars and talking about nothing and everything.

So the fact he knew something was wrong, yet she wouldn't talk to him about it, really bothered him.

He'd left her at his house a couple of times while he'd gone to Silverstone to meet with his team; other days, she'd come with him.

She'd spent her time either watching TV, playing pinball, or keeping whoever was on dispatch duty company.

Molly had said she found the towing business fascinating, partly because she hadn't really thought much about it before. She'd even accompanied him on a job here and there as well.

Today, however, she'd stayed at his house, claiming that she had some stuff she needed to do.

Smoke texted to let her know he was on his way back to the house; he never wanted to scare her the way he had that first time he'd come home, when she hadn't recognized him with his clean-shaven face.

He let himself into the house, happy to see the alarm was on. She'd been intimidated by the security at first, but she'd ultimately had no problem getting used to it. It didn't smell like she'd started anything for dinner, which was fine; he'd left Silverstone earlier than usual, and he liked when they cooked together. He'd spent so much time alone in his house, it felt . . . *right* . . . to have her puttering around in the kitchen with him. Laughing when they bumped into each other, talking about how their days had gone.

When he entered the great room, Smoke spotted Molly sitting at the table off the kitchen, staring at her phone. Her hands were under her butt, and she was hunched over, glaring at the device, as if it had somehow offended her.

"Mol," he called out as he walked toward her.

Her head whipped around immediately, and she watched him as he neared.

"What's wrong?" he asked.

"Nothing," she said, a beat too fast.

Smoke crouched next to her and put one hand on her thigh and the other on the back of the chair, effectively pinning her in place. "You were glaring at your phone so hard, if it was a person, I'm sure he or she would've been crying in terror."

She didn't even crack a smile, simply turned back to look at her phone. "I've been trying all day to psych myself up to call my boss. I purposely went back to sleep after you left this morning. Then I did my laundry and organized all the crap I bought last week with Taylor and Skylar. *Then* I decided to make a cake. From scratch. Then I vacuumed. The entire house. I ran out of things to do . . . and I still can't make myself call."

"Why not?" Smoke asked quietly.

"I don't know," she said flatly.

Smoke didn't comment, simply waited her out.

Molly sighed. It was a deeply frustrated sound. "I've been putting off *everything*. You've been so patient with me, and I know I need to get back to Chicago, but . . . I've liked everything about being here so much *more* than my previous life."

Smoke moved then, standing and picking Molly up. She squeaked but didn't otherwise protest. "Grab your phone," he ordered, bending so she could reach it. After she'd picked it up, he walked over to the couch and sat, holding Molly on his lap.

She fit there perfectly.

"What's keeping you from calling your boss?" he asked. "Specifically?"

Molly was looking down at the phone in her hand and not at him as she spoke. "Nana and Papa were so proud of me when I got my master's degree. They told all their friends that their granddaughter was an environmental engineer and talked about me all the time. When I got my first job trying to improve the water quality around Chicago, they threw me a huge party. But I never really *loved* what I did. It was just a job for me. Not a passion. I only took the job in Nigeria to get away from Preston. But they couldn't stop gushing about how I was saving the world and all that." She paused.

"Go on," Smoke encouraged.

"They left me," Molly whispered. "Apex. My employer. A part of me knows why, and understands. But another part is upset. I mean, it wouldn't have been smart to keep the rest of the employees there, just in case they were targeted. But . . . it hurt to find out they'd just left me behind. That they didn't do anything to try to find me. Didn't hire anyone to go looking for me or anything. Like, maybe I wasn't that important to them or something."

"Do you want to continue working there?" Smoke asked.

Molly shrugged.

It wasn't an answer, but Smoke didn't push. "You need to at least call them and let them know you're back in the States and safe."

"I know."

Smoke looked at his watch. Three thirty. They should still be open. Molly should be able to get ahold of someone. "Would it be easier if I left you alone to make the call, or would you prefer I stay?" he asked.

"Would you think less of me if I asked you to stay?" Molly asked quietly.

"Of course not," Smoke told her.

"Will you make that homemade cheesy mac and cheese for dinner tonight?" she went on.

Smoke smiled. "Of course."

"And one of those milkshakes you made me the other night? You know, the chocolate one with the strawberries mixed in?"

"Yes." He'd made her the protein shake to help her gain weight, and had been pleased by how much she'd enjoyed it. Granted, he'd thrown in a few extra ingredients to make it sweeter, but he couldn't deny the satisfaction it gave him to feed her.

"Okay," Molly said, then inhaled deeply and unlocked her phone.

Smoke hadn't thought she would make the call right that second, but he figured it was a good idea to get it over with, especially if she'd been dreading it all day.

She dialed a number, then put the phone on speaker. It rang three times before a woman answered.

"Hello, Apex Environmental. How may I direct your call?"

"May I speak to Walter Morris, please?"

"One moment."

Smoke could feel Molly shaking, and he tightened his arms around her.

"This is Morris."

"Walter, this is Molly. Molly Smith."

There was a momentary pause before her boss spoke.

"Molly? Are you all right? Where are you?"

"I'm okay. I'm actually in Indianapolis."

"Wow! I heard that those schoolgirls had been rescued, but I had no idea if you were still with them or not."

Smoke could understand his confusion. For all he knew, Molly was still somewhere in the jungle. Silverstone previously had no idea if the Nigerian security forces had notified anyone from Apex of her rescue. Obviously, they hadn't.

"Yeah, I was. I haven't been back long, but I wanted to touch base," Molly said.

"Well, I'm very glad you're all right. When will you be coming back?"

"Um, that's what I wanted to talk to you about. I don't know if you heard, but my grandparents were killed while I was overseas."

"Oh. I'm sorry for your loss."

Smoke ground his teeth together at the man's lack of sympathy. It was obvious he was saying what he thought he should, but there was no true empathy in his voice.

"Thanks. The thing is, after everything that happened, I need to take some time off."

"We *did* need to hire someone to take your place after . . . well, you know. We weren't sure if you would be returning or not. So if and when you're ready to come back, just let me know, and I'll find a slot for you somewhere."

Molly was so tense on his lap, Smoke wanted to seriously hurt her boss. With every word out of his mouth, he was hurting Molly more.

"Right," Molly said softly.

"I'll get with human resources," Walter continued. "We didn't stop your pay while you were gone, but now that you're back, we obviously can't continue to pay your salary if you aren't working. We'll need documentation on when you arrived back in the United States so we can use that as your termination date."

"So . . . I'm fired?" Molly asked.

"No, no, of course not. Bad choice of words," Walter told her. "I just meant we need a date for legal reasons. I'm sure you understand."

They heard someone say Walter's name in the background and remind him that he had a meeting starting in five minutes.

"I need to go, I've got a meeting," Walter said, without a trace of apology in his tone. "Glad you're okay, Molly. Give me a ring if and when you're ready to come back."

"I will," Molly said hollowly.

"Bye," Walter said, then hung up.

Molly inhaled deeply, then melted against Smoke.

"What an ass," Smoke growled as he held Molly against his chest.

"I guess I knew that was how it was going to go," Molly said quietly. "And why I didn't really want to call. But you know what?"

"What?" Smoke asked, making mental plans to go up to Chicago and kick Walter Morris's ass.

"I'm relieved."

At her words, Smoke relaxed a fraction.

"I mean, Apex is a huge corporation. They couldn't hold my job forever. They had no idea how long I'd be held hostage, or if I'd ever be released. And it was pretty generous of them to keep paying me while I was missing."

Smoke closed his eyes and wanted to argue otherwise. But he knew as well as Molly did how large companies worked.

"I have no idea what I'm going to do now, but I'm kind of glad I don't have that job hanging over my head anymore," she continued. "Mark?"

"Yeah, Mol?"

"Thanks for helping me through that." She sighed. "Now I need to go up to Chicago and talk to Nana and Papa's lawyer. I also want to go by the house and see it for myself. Do you think I could borrow your car? I promise to drive safely and not wreck it."

"Look at me, Molly."

She lifted her head to look at him.

"I've been waiting for you to be ready to go to Chicago. If you think I'm going to let you go by yourself, you're seriously delusional."

"But you have work," she protested.

"Which is not more important than you," he countered.

She stared at him for a long minute, then licked her lips. Smoke forced himself to not pull her closer. He wanted nothing more than to cover her lips with his own, but he didn't want to take advantage of her vulnerable situation.

"Say the word, and we'll head up there. You'll need to talk to the police as well. Find out what they know about the fire and your grandparents' deaths. If they don't already know about him, you need to tell them your suspicions about Preston," he told her. "And we need to find out where your nana's and papa's bodies are, and make arrangements for them."

Molly nodded. "I just . . . seeing the house will make things more real," she admitted. "Right now I can pretend that they're alive and well and waiting on me to visit. I've been putting off going up there because that means they really *are* dead, and I'll never see them again."

"I know," Smoke said softly. "I'm sorry."

"And . . . even though Oak Park is a big place, I can't help but think that Preston will find out I'm in town, and he'll start up his harassment all over again. I left because he scared me. I've felt safe here knowing he has no idea where I am and can't get to me. If I go up there and he sees me, I'm afraid he'll find a way to hurt *you*, or Silverstone, or Skylar and Taylor."

"It's time to tell me everything about your ex, Mol."

She laid her head back on his chest. "I don't want to."

"I know, but you know what I do. Who I am. Do you think I'm going to let him get to you?"

"No. But you don't know him like I do. He's crazy, Mark. He'll do whatever he can to ruin Silverstone Towing."

Smoke snorted. "He won't get the chance. I promise. Now close your eyes, and tell me about him. Start with how you met him, and go from there."

"Promise you won't think less of me?" she asked.

"Never," Smoke vowed.

She didn't say a word for five full minutes, and Smoke didn't break the silence. He'd let her gather her thoughts for as long as she needed.

"His full name is Preston Weldon. I met him one day at work," Molly said, not moving from her position on his lap. "Well, not *at* work, but in the coffee shop nearby. He's a security guard and was on break from his job at the building next to mine. He was funny and charming. He was focused completely on me, which I found flattering at the time. He asked me out right then and there, but I said no.

"We kept running into each other at the coffee shop. He kept asking me out, promising to be on his best behavior. He said we could start with lunch, something light and easy. I eventually agreed, more because it was becoming awkward to keep saying no than because I really wanted to go. I figured it couldn't hurt. We went out to lunch, and he was very nice. He held my chair for me, brought me a rose, and paid without making things weird. I gave him my number, and he started calling and texting.

"We dated for a month or so. Going to dinner and lunch, and once he even took me to a show in downtown Chicago. He wanted to get a hotel and stay the night, but I wasn't ready for that. I think I knew pretty quickly that something was off about him. I'd smelled alcohol on his breath, but just once. Then Nana and Papa wanted to meet him, so I invited him over for brunch one day. After he'd left, Nana told me she didn't like him for me, but I told her not to worry, that we weren't serious.

"But apparently *he* thought we were serious. He began calling me every night. And if I didn't answer, he'd continue calling until I had to turn off my phone. He'd leave multiple messages wanting to know where I was and what was wrong. Then, I started seeing his car now and then. Outside my apartment, in the parking garage at work when I knew he wasn't working. It just got to be too much. I told him over dinner one night that I didn't think things were working out and that we were better off being friends.

"He got *really* mad and didn't say another word throughout dinner. He dragged me out of the restaurant by the arm when we were done. I told him he was hurting me, and he said, 'Well, you hurt me first.' He was holding my arm so tightly, I knew he was leaving marks. When we got to his car, he slammed me up against it and kissed me so hard his teeth cut my lip. He shoved his hand up my shirt, mumbling something like it was about time he put me in my place.

"I managed to knee him in the balls and run away. But that wasn't the end of things as I'd hoped. His stalking got far worse. I changed my phone number three times, but he always found it. He said he didn't accept my breaking up with him and we were still boyfriend and girlfriend. The day I came home from work and found him *in* my apartment, waiting for me, was the day I moved back in with my grandparents."

"Did he hurt you again?" Smoke asked through clenched teeth. He wanted to kill the motherfucker for threatening and scaring Molly.

"Yeah," Molly said softly. "He hit me, and he would've raped me, but I screamed so loud, I think he got scared someone would come looking to see what was wrong. He took off, but I knew he could get inside my apartment now. It was probably only a matter of time before he'd do it again, then overpower me and take what he wanted."

She was quaking in his lap, and he hated it. *Hated* it. "Shhhh, you're okay," Smoke said, running a hand over her hair. "You're safe."

"Anyway . . . so I moved in with Nana and Papa, and they did what they could to keep me safe. But I knew I was probably only endangering them. When the opening in Nigeria came up, I took it. I hoped that the time away would make Preston forget about me."

"You said he's a security guard?"

"Uh-huh. I think he majored in criminal justice in college. He has a two-year degree from Ivy Tech Community College in Indiana. He worked at Willis Tower, downtown, last I knew."

Smoke nodded and made a mental note. He needed to find out everything he could about this Weldon fucker. He had no idea if he was still infatuated with Molly, but if so, he needed to understand she was off limits to him, now and forever.

"I'm so sorry that happened to you. You know it's his problem, and not yours, right? That him becoming obsessed has nothing to do with you and everything to do with the asshole he is. You did *nothing* wrong."

"I shouldn't have said yes to that first date when I didn't really want it," Molly said.

"No," Smoke countered. "I mean, maybe, but him becoming a stalker isn't an appropriate response to anything you may or may not have done or said when you were with him. He should've simply moved on."

"I don't understand guys who won't take no for an answer. I mean, if I don't want to be with him, why on earth would he still want me? It makes no sense."

"I agree," Smoke said. "But it's *his* issue, not yours."

"Well, he certainly made it my issue," Molly said dryly.

"All I meant is that you didn't do anything wrong. You need to believe that."

Molly looked up at him. "The old Molly would disagree. Would nod to your face, then rehash everything over and over, wondering where she could have done things differently. But you know what? You're right. I went on some dates with him. Introduced him to my family in good faith and, instead of stringing him along when I knew I didn't want to be with him anymore, broke it off. I didn't deserve his crazy, and if he *did* hurt Nana and Papa, they didn't either."

"That a girl," Smoke praised.

"But it doesn't change the fact I'm scared to go back. To see him," Molly admitted.

"Would it make you feel better if I asked Gramps to go to Chicago with us?" Smoke asked.

"Yes," Molly said immediately.

"Consider it done. How about next week? That will give you time to call the lawyer and the coroner, and I'll see if I can use my connections to see what's going on with the investigation into the fire and your grandparents' deaths."

Molly inhaled deeply. "Okay."

"Okay," Smoke agreed. He had a million things going through his mind that he needed to do to help her, but for now, she needed his full attention. "Want to help me make the mac and cheese?" he asked.

Molly thought about it for a moment, then shook her head. "If it's okay, I think I might take a bath in that amazing tub in my room. Skylar made me buy some bubble bath the other day, and I haven't had a chance to try it out yet."

"That's more than all right," Smoke said, willing his body not to react to the thought of her naked in the tub.

"Mark?"

"Yeah, Mol?"

"Thanks again. For everything. And if we do see Preston and he focuses his crazy on you . . . I'm sorry."

"I hope he does," Smoke said firmly. "He'll find out that Silverstone doesn't put up with bullies."

For the first time since he'd come home, Molly smiled. "Yeah, you guys don't, do you?"

"Nope."

She leaned forward and brushed her lips against the very corner of his mouth. "Thank you," she said again, a little shyly. "Who knew that something as horrible as being stalked, almost raped, kidnapped by rebels, and losing my grandparents could lead me to you? And before you say anything . . . that's actually me being positive."

Then she climbed off his lap and headed up the stairs.

Smoke sat on the couch for a full minute after she'd disappeared. He'd wanted to move his head so she could kiss him on the lips, but he'd take any gesture of affection she wanted to give.

He finally heaved himself to his feet and headed into the kitchen. Molly wanted homemade mac and cheese and a shake, and that was what she was gonna get. There would be time later to talk to the others about this Preston asshole; first, he needed to feed his woman.

It didn't even feel weird thinking about Molly that way. She *was* his. He'd do whatever it took to hopefully get her to see him as more than just a safe haven. He wanted to be her everything, and he just needed to be patient.

Chapter Eleven

"How did you get the nickname Smoke?" Molly asked as they headed north to Oak Park. She'd never felt anxious about driving to the Chicago suburb before, but now that she was going to come face to face with her grandparents' burned-out house, she dreaded the trip. Her life felt as if it was out of control with everything that had happened recently, but she was doing her best to stay as positive as she could.

It had been a relief to tell Mark about Preston and what he'd done to her. She was scared of him, but Mark didn't seem to think less of her because of it. He'd told her over and over how brave he thought she'd been when they'd met, and she didn't want any of her past actions to change that opinion.

He'd asked if he could share her story with his friends, and she'd agreed, though she'd worried that Bull, Eagle, and Gramps would look at her differently afterward. But they'd been just as understanding about everything as Mark had been. They truly were good men.

Not long afterward, both Skylar and Taylor had called, pissed off on her behalf. They'd even offered to go up to Oak Park with her today, but Molly had declined. She didn't want them anywhere near Preston, and even though the chances she'd see him were low, she wasn't going to risk it.

She felt much safer with both Mark and Gramps with her, and they'd both been extremely supportive so far. She had a meeting with the detectives on her grandparents' case; an appointment with Maggie Melton, the lawyer; and a meeting with a funeral home to discuss arrangements for Nana's and Papa's burials.

Just having the two men at her side made her feel safer, and somehow made what she knew was going to be a very tough day more bearable.

"How I got my nickname isn't the most interesting story," Mark said.

"Are you stalling?" Molly teased. "Is it that bad?"

"No and no," he said. "Fine. It was in basic training. That's where most people get their nicknames, except for Gramps; we gave him his when he joined our team. Before that, people called him Giant, but that was just stupid."

"And Gramps isn't?" Gramps asked from the back seat.

Molly giggled.

"Anyway, I was in basic training, and we were on our last big thing we had to do before graduation. The three-day field training exercise. We road marched into the forest around the base and then spent a couple nights sleeping in the wilderness. One afternoon we were doing drills, basically playing war in the woods, where half of us were the 'bad guys' and the other half were the 'good guys.' I was able to double back and infiltrate the defenses of the other side without anyone seeing me. Not even the drill sergeants. I don't even know how I did it, I just did. Some of the guys accused me of cheating, but in the AAR—after-action review—one of the drill sergeants told everyone they should take a page out of my book, to be like a magician and disappear in a puff of smoke, like I had. The name stuck."

"What he's not telling you," Gramps said, leaning over the back of her seat, "is that he's able to sneak around like no one else can. He's *literally* like smoke. One second he's there, and the next, he's gone. I can't tell you how many times we've lost him on missions. We'll all be standing there talking, and the next thing we know, we look around, and he's just not there. He's sneaky as hell, and I don't know what we'd do without his unique skill."

"Except for that one time he fell into a hole in the jungle," Molly teased.

Both Mark and Gramps laughed.

"Yeah, except then," Gramps agreed.

They laughed and joked the rest of the way to Chicago, but as soon as they got on the outer loop, Molly's stomach tensed, and she felt a little sick. She suddenly wanted to tell Mark to turn around, that she wasn't ready for this.

As if he could hear her thoughts, he reached over and took her hand in his. Even that small connection made her feel better.

Their first stop was her nana and papa's house. Molly knew she needed to see it for herself. It would prepare her for the rest of her difficult appointments.

The car was quiet now except for Molly telling Mark where to turn. Before she was ready, he'd turned down the very familiar street. Everything looked exactly as it had when she'd last seen it, which somehow hurt even more.

Her eyes glued to the right side of the street, Molly saw the house for the first time—and she gasped in pain.

There was still yellow police tape around the yard. The charred, half-standing structure was obviously a complete loss.

"Oh my God," Molly whispered.

Mark stopped two houses down and parked on the side of the road.

Molly couldn't take her eyes from the house. Her chest was tight, and it was difficult to breathe. She didn't move when Mark and Gramps got out of the car. She didn't move when Mark opened her door.

"Hold on to me, Molly," he said as he took her hand in his.

She grabbed hold of him as if he were her lifeline, the only thing keeping her from exploding into a thousand heartbroken pieces. He all but pulled her out of the car, and they walked slowly up the sidewalk, Gramps at their backs.

She stopped in front of the house and stared at the destruction in front of her, feeling as gutted as the house itself. All sorts of memories were shooting through her brain.

Pictures in the yard with friends before a homecoming dance, Christmas mornings in the front room with the tree's lights burning bright, watching *Jeopardy* with Papa and laughing when neither of them could get any answers right, and Nana cooking in the kitchen.

Now there was nothing but rubble. Black, charred, melted pieces of her life. Gone.

Molly took a step forward, needing to get closer. Mark didn't hold her back; he held up the yellow police tape and stayed right by her side. When she got to the front door, she saw that it had been broken down, probably by the firemen. The crazy thing was that the welcome mat seemed almost untouched by what had happened here. The large yellow sunflower between the words WELCOME FRIENDS seemed almost obscene, shining amid the destruction.

Molly started to walk inside, but Mark grabbed hold of her arm this time. "It's not safe," he said softly.

She wanted to turn and rail at him. Tell him to let go of her, that she didn't care if it was safe or not. Her nana and papa had been inside when the fire had started, and *they* hadn't been safe either.

But deep down, she knew Mark was right. The floor in front of her had holes in it from where the inspectors' or firefighters' boots had gone through the boards. The entire second floor had collapsed onto the first.

From where she was standing, Molly could already see there was nothing worth salvaging in the home. She'd harbored a distant hope of finding a few mementos, but everything she saw was ruined from all the water used to put the fire out or burned beyond recognition.

"God, I hate seeing you cry," Mark murmured, and Molly felt his fingers on her cheek, wiping away the tears she had no idea she'd been shedding.

Turning her eyes up to him, she said, "It's gone. It's really gone." Mark didn't respond verbally, he only nodded.

How long she stood at the front door staring at the wreckage of her grandparents' home, Molly didn't know. A good long while. She was overwhelmed with memories, and the enormous loss she'd suffered was finally sinking in. She'd known this would happen, which was why she'd put off the visit. It was easier to pretend that everything was fine. That she was just visiting Mark and his friends.

But this was her new reality, a life without her grandparents, and it was so hard to come to terms with.

When she was ready, Mark and Gramps walked her around the house, and Molly was heartened to find that some of the rosebushes Nana had loved so much had somehow survived. "Papa hated those rosebushes," Molly said softly. "Said the things had it in for him. Every time he came inside from tending them, he had scratches all up and down his arms. I asked him once why he didn't have them removed, and all he said was, 'Because Pauline loves those flowers.' He would've done anything for Nana. They were completely devoted to each other. He took her to every one of her doctor's appointments, and she went out of her way to make his favorite foods. They bickered all the time, but they never fought. Not really."

"They sound like they were soul mates," Mark commented.

"They were," Molly agreed.

"You want to take some of those roses back with us?" Mark asked.

Molly stared up at him in surprise. "Really?"

"I've heard rosebushes are pretty easy to transplant. Of course, I know nothing about gardening, but we can see what we can do about digging up part of it, and we can plant it in my yard."

Molly inhaled, deeply moved by such kindness.

And it was in that moment when she realized she was head over heels in love with Mark Chamberlin.

It was crazy. Insane, really. But she recalled a conversation she'd had with her nana once. She'd been telling Molly all about how she'd met Papa, and how she'd known almost immediately that she wanted to marry him. She'd said, "When you meet the one person in this world who is meant for you, who's the other half of your soul, you'll just know."

Molly hadn't believed her grandmother then. She'd blown her off, telling herself that just because Nana had a good marriage that had lasted didn't mean that was always how love worked.

But just like that, standing in the backyard, Molly knew Nana hadn't lied.

Realizing Mark was the man for her hadn't exactly happened immediately, but it might as well have. She'd been attracted to him almost from the start, though normal people didn't fall in love in two weeks. It was ridiculous. But she *knew* what she felt for him was love. Anyone who'd offer to dig up a rosebush and plant it in his yard when he had no idea where she might be in a week was someone she wanted to keep in her life.

"Mol?" Mark asked, bringing her attention back to him. "What do you think?"

"Yes," she said softly. "I'd love to bring Nana's roses with us."

"Right. I'm sure I can borrow a shovel from a neighbor or something," Gramps said. "I'll be back."

Then Molly and Mark were alone in the backyard.

"How you holding up?" Mark asked gently, brushing the backs of his fingers down her cheek.

"Not good," she told him honestly.

"I think you're doing great," he said. "I know this isn't easy."

"It's not . . . but . . . I needed to do this first today. It's a huge shock. And even though intellectually I already knew the house was gone, seeing it firsthand is horrible. But it also makes me more determined to talk to the police. To find out what happened. And if this wasn't an accident, someone needs to pay." The more she talked, the stronger her voice got.

"I'm in awe of your strength, Molly," Mark said.

She shook her head. "I'm not strong. I'm just desperate to get answers so Nana and Papa can rest in peace."

Gramps reappeared around the side of the house holding two shovels. "Got 'em!" he said. "Spoke for just a moment with the neighbors two houses down. They said they'd love to see you if you had a moment," he told Molly.

"Oh, the Byrds?"

Gramps grinned. "No clue what their names were. Older couple, probably in their early sixties? The woman had beautiful blue dreads, and the man was Black and bald."

"That's them," Molly said with a laugh. "While you guys are doing this, I'd like to go talk to them, if you don't mind?"

Mark stared at her for a long moment, as if debating.

"I'll be careful. I won't be far, and I promise not to stay too long."

"I didn't see anyone around," Gramps told his friend.

Mark took a deep breath and finally nodded.

Molly wasn't sure why she was even asking for his permission. She was a grown woman able to make her own decisions. But she trusted him, and if he hadn't thought it was safe, she probably wouldn't have gone.

"I'll be fast," she told him. "The Byrds and my grandparents were good friends. I just want to reassure them that I'm okay."

"Be careful. Watchful. If you see anything that makes you nervous, scream your head off, and Gramps and I will come running."

"I will," Molly said.

Mark pulled her closer, leaning down and kissing her lightly on the forehead.

She leaned into him for a moment, absorbing as much strength from him as she could. She was a little nervous. Wasn't sure she had the inner fortitude to hear condolences about Nana and Papa from the Byrds. But she wasn't the only one hurting. Other people had loved her grandparents too.

She pulled back and did her best to smile up at Mark.

He could obviously tell she was forcing it, because he tucked a stray lock of hair behind her ear and said, "You've got this, Mol."

Taking a deep breath, she nodded at both men. "Thanks for getting the roses."

"No problem," Gramps said, rolling up the sleeves of his long-sleeved shirt.

Molly turned and headed across the backyard and around the house. She hadn't seen the Byrds in ages, and she'd always liked the somewhat eccentric couple. They'd lived on the street since before she'd moved in with her grandparents as a kid, and had always had the best candy at Halloween and the most lights up at Christmas.

As she came around the side of the house, she was totally unprepared when someone grabbed her by the shoulders and shoved her up against the blackened siding of her grandparents' house.

The man put his hand over her mouth and pressed down hard. She still tried to scream, as Mark had told her to, but all that came out was a muffled grunt of sorts.

Blinking, Molly looked up—right into the hazel eyes of her ex.

"Where the fuck have you been?" Preston growled. "Your fucking grandparents *died*, and you weren't here! How could you have abandoned them like that?"

Molly's heart began beating a million miles an hour, even as the rest of her froze.

This was her worst nightmare coming true. And Mark and Gramps were right around the corner, but she couldn't even scream.

Belatedly, she clawed at Preston's hand, but before she could make any noise—pound against the side of the house, *anything*—he leaned in and said, "If your fuck boy comes to your rescue, I'll kill him. I'll blow his fucking head off. His *and* his friend's. Stay very quiet, Molly, otherwise they're dead."

Molly was fairly confident Mark and Gramps could take Preston . . . but it was the small sliver of doubt that made her stay quiet. What if he surprised them? What if he got in a lucky shot?

She could smell alcohol on his breath. The occasional slurred word also told Molly that he was likely drunk, making him even more dangerous. She hadn't known he was a drinker when they'd first started dating, but it'd become clear to her fairly quickly that he had a problem.

"I've been looking for you, sweetheart," Preston hissed. "Worried sick. You left without a word. I searched everywhere for you, and no one I talked to would tell me *anything*. You can't just disappear like that on your boyfriend. I was about to file a missing person report."

Molly stared up at him in disbelief at the word *boyfriend*. Over the last couple of months, he'd morphed into this scary thing in her mind. It was almost disconcerting to find he hadn't changed at all. Clean cut as usual, his clothes immaculate. He was taller than her, but then again, most people were. He wasn't overly muscular, and Nana had said after meeting him that he had a "weak chin," whatever that meant.

His brown hair was cut short in a military style, and his cheeks and nose were flushed, probably because of the alcohol in his system. He had on his security uniform from his job, and the utility belt he wore around his waist was filled with things such as a Taser, flashlight, and handcuffs. It dug into her belly as he crowded her.

She tried to say his name, but all that came out was a muffled croak. The hand over her mouth tightened even more, preventing even one sound from escaping, her teeth pressing painfully against her lips.

"You miss me, love?" he asked, nuzzling the side of her neck.

Molly tilted away from him and tried to shake her head.

"Don't be like that," Preston admonished in a low voice that obviously wasn't carrying to the backyard, where Mark and Gramps were still busy. "I missed *you*. And it's obvious I'm gonna need to keep a better eye on you. I've been waitin' for months for you to come back to me. I even put a camera on the fence next door. You know, one of those motion-sensor cameras with an app that alerts you if it's triggered? The dumb assholes who live there never even noticed. I knew you'd come back to mourn those old shits you were so attached to. They never really loved you, you know," he purred.

Molly closed her eyes and prayed someone would see them. But there were some trees alongside the road that she had a feeling would block them from anyone driving by.

"They didn't," Preston insisted, as if he could sense her denial of his words. "I came to see them after you disappeared, and they wouldn't tell me anything. Didn't even seem concerned that you were missing. Their deaths are on *you*," he went on.

His words were shredding her, but she knew he didn't care.

"If you hadn't left, you might've been there when the space heater in their bedroom overheated. Such a tragedy. You might've smelled the smoke and been able to get them up and out of the house. But because of *your* selfishness, they were overcome by the fumes and died. Died knowing you were a selfish whore who didn't care about your own grandparents. They gave up everything to raise you, an orphaned brat, and this is how you repaid them."

He was lying. Molly knew that. The detective Mark had talked to hadn't said anything about a space heater, and she knew Papa refused to use those things. He always said they were a fire hazard, and joked that he had his wife to keep him warm.

Now Molly struggled against Preston, wanting to get his hand off her mouth. She tried to lift her leg, to knee him in the balls, but he merely laughed quietly and tightened his hold on both her arm and face. He pressed her cruelly against the charred wall and bit down on her earlobe, hard enough to make her squirm in pain.

"You're *mine*, Molly. You can't hide from me. No matter where you go, I'll find you. No one will keep you from me. I'll kill anyone who tries. Understand? I think you've gotten a firsthand lesson on that, haven't you? I've missed you so much. Now that you don't have a home, you can live with me. I'll give you everything you need and more."

Molly winced at the hatred she saw in his eyes. She didn't understand at all. If he hated her so much, why was he so intent on pursuing her? They'd only kissed once, for God's sake, and she definitely hadn't slept with him. It made no sense.

"*No one* dumps me," he said in a low, menacing tone that made the hair on the back of Molly's neck stand up. "*I* decide when a relationship ends. And we aren't done—not by a long shot. You aren't in charge in this relationship, and you have to be punished for leaving without telling me where you were going."

Before she even understood his intentions, Preston let go of her mouth and cocked an arm back.

He punched her in the face, and Molly's head whipped back, smacking against the house. The scent of burnt wood wafted around her as she made contact. She would've gone flying, but the house kept her upright.

She dazedly hoped Mark or Gramps might have heard the thump of her head against the wall.

Her legs gave out, but Preston got in a couple more punches before she crumpled to the ground.

She saw him cock his leg back, as if to kick her, so she curled into a ball as she opened her mouth and let out the loudest, most gut-wrenching scream she could manage.

"Fuck!" Preston swore. Then he leaned down and spoke fast, his words running together. "I wrote down that Indiana plate number on the Explorer. There's *nowhere* you can hide from me—remember that."

Then he turned and ran.

Molly tried to get up, to go get Mark and Gramps, but her legs wouldn't hold her. She was shaking too badly.

She'd known there was a possibility of Preston finding out she was back in Oak Park, but hadn't expected him to find her so quickly. Every one of his words had sent fear coursing through her. She wasn't safe, and neither was anyone around her. He'd all but admitted to killing Nana and Papa. He wouldn't hesitate to take out Mark or anyone else to get to her.

A shout to her left got her attention, then she heard the pounding steps of someone running toward her.

"Holy fuckin' shit! Molly! What the fuck happened?" Mark shouted.

Molly opened her eyes—well, her one eye that wasn't quickly swelling shut—and stared at him. He was kneeling on the ground, holding her shoulders gently.

"Preston," she whispered.

"Damn it!" he exclaimed.

"On it," Gramps said as he jogged toward the road to try to see where Preston had gone.

Molly jerked slightly when Mark picked her up. She snuggled into his chest and wrapped her arms around his neck, holding on for dear life. She knew she should've pushed him away for his own good, but she wasn't strong enough.

"How did he know you were here?" Mark asked as he strode away from the house toward his Explorer.

"He said he put up a camera on the neighbor's fence," Molly said quietly.

Mark stopped in his tracks, and she saw his head swiveling around as he tried to spot it.

"I'm sorry I didn't scream sooner. I tried, but he had his hand so hard over my mouth. And he said he'd kill you both if I made a sound," Molly sobbed, apologizing.

Mark pressed his lips together, then said, "It's okay, Mol."

Gramps jogged toward them as they headed for Mark's vehicle. "I don't see him."

"Shit," Mark swore. "Mol said he put up a security camera on the fence next door."

"I'll find it, you take care of her," Gramps said. "I'll get the rosebush too. Give me a few minutes, then we can go to the hospital."

Molly wanted to laugh. Tell him not to worry about the fucking roses—and that she wasn't going to the hospital—but he was gone before she could say anything. Mark walked double time toward his Explorer. To her surprise, he opened a back door and gently placed her on the seat. "Can you scoot over? Or does it hurt too much?"

"I'm okay," Molly said. She hurt, but nothing was broken as far as she could tell. Preston had been more concerned about scaring her than truly hurting her, thank God. She moved across the seat, and Mark climbed into the back with her. As soon as the door was shut, he turned to her. He gently lifted her chin with one finger and frowned as he inspected her face. "Fuck, Mol."

"I'm okay," she repeated, wanting to comfort him.

"You aren't okay," he said, shaking his head. "Your eye is swelling shut, and you've got bruises around your mouth. Tell me every single thing he did and said."

So Molly did just that, not holding back in the least. When she was done, she whispered, "He practically admitted to killing Nana and Papa to try to get information on where I was. And he was right about one thing . . . it *was* my fault. If I hadn't fled like a coward, they'd still be alive."

"No," Mark said harshly. "Do *not* do that. We've talked about this. If you hadn't gone to Nigeria, it's likely *you* would be dead. Weldon is unhinged, and he wasn't ever going to go away."

Molly swallowed hard and took a deep breath, trying to control her emotions. Then Mark gently gathered her into his arms once more . . . and she broke.

She cried for her grandparents. She cried because she was physically hurting. And she cried because she knew she'd never be able to love Mark the way she wanted. Preston would always be there between them. A threat she couldn't overlook or dismiss.

"I'm sorry I wasn't there. I shouldn't have let you go off by yourself," Mark said softly.

Molly swallowed hard and looked up at him. "What?"

"He never would've touched you if I'd have done what I promised to do—keep you safe."

"He would've gotten to me some other time."

Mark gave a small shake of his head. "Not if I'd been doing what I should've been doing."

God. She really did love this man. He was so different from anyone else she'd ever met. If someone had told her the rough-looking soldier who'd fallen on top of her when she'd been in that hole in the jungle would come to mean so much to her in such a short period of time, she would've scoffed and told them they were crazy.

But now she dreaded the day she was going to have to leave him. And that day was coming soon. Preston hadn't been able to find her when she'd been overseas, so she'd just have to go somewhere else, somewhere just as far away.

"I'm going to stop him," Mark said, as if he could read her mind. "You're going to be able to live your life without fear."

Molly didn't respond, just stared at him, trying to memorize his beautiful features. His slightly crooked nose, as if it had been broken at some point. The lines on his face from both the sun and hard living. The adorable dimple in his cheek.

The back hatch opened, scaring her so much, Molly screeched a little and ducked below the level of the back seat.

"Sorry, Molly," Gramps said as he placed a huge portion of the rosebush in the back of the car. Then he slammed the hatch and climbed into the driver's seat. Mark passed him the keys. "Find it?"

"Yeah," Gramps said, holding up a cheap security camera, then throwing it onto the seat next to him. "I'm assuming he hacked into the Wi-Fi of the residents to connect it."

"We can give it to the cops, and they can see what they can get off it," Mark said as Gramps started the engine.

"Cops?" Molly asked, sitting up straight again. Mark hadn't let go of her, and she wasn't about to suggest they move to put on their seat belts. It wasn't safe, she knew that, but she also didn't care at the moment.

"Yup. You're going to file a restraining order against this asshole," Mark said matter-of-factly.

"I'm not sure he's gonna care about a piece of paper," she said hesitantly.

"He's not," Mark agreed. "But that's not the point. We need evidence to show that he's stalking you and that he's a piece of shit. If we see him again, we'll report it. They'll have more than enough evidence to throw him in jail if he dares to fucking touch you again."

Molly realized that when Mark was upset, he swore a lot more. Even when they'd been in Africa, she hadn't heard him use as many swear words as he had in the last twenty minutes or so.

"We were going to go talk to the police anyway," he continued. "We'll do both things at once. I know we were going to spend the night here, and you have a meeting with the lawyer tomorrow, but I'm thinking it might be a better idea to get back to Indy as soon as possible."

"I can call Maggie," Molly said immediately. She didn't want to spend one more second in Oak Park or the Chicago area. Knowing Preston was aware she was here gave her the creeps. And she knew that Mark would be safer on his own turf. At least, she hoped so.

"Do I need to stop at the hospital first?" Gramps asked, looking at them through the rearview mirror.

"No," Molly said before Mark could respond. "I'm okay. Sore, and I don't deny I'm hurting, but nothing's broken."

"Stop at a pharmacy," Mark told his friend. "Get an ice pack or something, it'll help the swelling in her face."

Folly Molly.

The old nickname echoed in Molly's head, but she did her best to block it out. This *wasn't* her fault. It was Preston's.

It was much easier to hold the negative thoughts at bay when she was in Mark's arms.

The stop at the pharmacy was quick. Mark insisted she stay in the car with him while Gramps went inside. He came back with a huge bag filled with stuff. He'd bought painkillers, ice packs, ointment, and a box of Skittles. It was the candy that made her want to cry. The man knew she had a sweet tooth and was doing what he could to make her feel better.

Gramps pulled up to the door of the police station instead of parking in the lot. Mark opened his door and held out a hand to help her climb out. Moving slowly, because the adrenaline she'd felt when Preston had attacked her was gone and she was feeling sore and shaky, Molly was grateful for his assistance.

He wrapped an arm around her waist, and they walked slowly into the station.

Apparently the bruises on her face and the way she was slightly hunched over quickly got the attention of the clerk, and they were ushered behind the locked security door in seconds.

She tried to explain why they were there—to report an assault and to find the detective in charge of the investigation into her grandparents' deaths—but a female officer waved off her words.

"Come on, hon, let's get those bruises taken care of first, then we can talk about what happened." She looked up at Mark. "I've got her, sir. If you can go with my partner, we'll get to the bottom of this."

Molly was surprised at how quickly the officer was moving, but she didn't feel like arguing. She was exhausted all of a sudden and feeling every bruise. She looked at Mark, who wasn't letting go of her waist. "It's okay," she told him. "When Gramps comes in, you guys can find me."

He nodded and reluctantly dropped his arm.

The female officer guided her down a hall and into a small room. It had a desk and a chair, and it was obviously an interrogation room. Sighing, wishing there was at least a couch with comfy cushions, Molly lowered herself into a chair. Looking up, she saw a security camera with a blinking light in the corner of the ceiling. Yup, definitely an interrogation room.

The officer sat on the edge of the table next to her. "You're safe now, hon. He can't hurt you here."

Molly nodded.

"Did you have an argument?"

Molly nodded again.

"Did he just hit you in the face?"

"No. I mean, yeah, he punched me. A few times. He also held his hand over my mouth so I couldn't call out."

The officer patted her hand. "We don't look kindly on domestic abuse. He's being asked for his side of the story right now, but as he doesn't have a mark on him, and you do, he'll probably be spending a few nights in jail. You're going to file a protection order against him, right?"

"Yeah, that's why we're here."

"Good. It's not foolproof, it's just a piece of paper, but it'll work against him if he touches you again."

"Yeah, I—wait . . . how do you know Preston wasn't hurt?"

"His name is Preston?" the officer asked.

"Yes. Do you already have him in custody? How did you know he was the one who hurt me?" Molly's head was spinning.

It was the officer's turn to look confused. "Honey, I have eyes in my head. The man you were with didn't have a mark on him."

Molly's eyes widened. "Mark? He didn't hurt me. He'd *never* hurt me."

The pity in the officer's eyes was easy to see. "That's what everyone says."

And just like that, everything clicked.

Molly stood abruptly, and the chair she'd been sitting on went flying. She backed up until she hit the wall behind her. "You think *Mark* did this to me?" She shook her head, and stabs of pain shot through her skull, but she ignored them. "He didn't! He *wouldn't*! Where is he? He's not being interrogated, is he? No—just *no*! Take me to him. Right this second!"

The officer stood and held up her hands, as if she were trying to approach a wild stallion. "Easy. It's going to be all right."

"No! Not if you think Mark hurt me. It was *Preston*. Preston Weldon. *He's* the one who hurt me. He's the one who I think killed my grandparents! God, this is so messed up!" She took a few steps toward the door, wanting to get out of this room and to find Mark, but the officer took hold of her arm.

Molly screamed.

"Calm down," the officer insisted.

But Molly was done. She was scared to death. Scared Preston would find her again. Scared that Mark was going to be thrown in jail for something he didn't do. And scared this woman was going to keep him from her.

"Mark!" she yelled at the top of her lungs.

"Molly—" the officer said, but Molly ignored her.

"Mark!" she screamed.

The door opened, and another officer stuck his head into the room. "What's going on in—"

Molly didn't give him a chance to finish his sentence. She pushed past him and called Mark's name again.

She was in a hallway with nothing but doors. She had no idea where they might've taken him, but she wasn't going to let them accuse him of something he didn't do. "Mark? Where are you? Mark!"

Three doors opened in the hallway, but it was the one farthest away that caught her attention. Mark came barreling out of the door, striding toward her. There were two officers right on his heels, but he only had eyes for Molly.

She threw herself at him, and he gathered her close. They clung to each other in the middle of the hallway for a second before he took her head in his hands and asked urgently, "Are you hurt? What's wrong?"

"They . . . they think *you* did this to me. They were going to arrest you!" she told him, gripping his wrists as hard as she could.

"Yeah, I figured that out about two seconds after they got me into a room," he said dryly.

"You wouldn't hurt me. Ever," she said with complete conviction.

"Never," he vowed.

"Well, I'm thinking we were mistaken," one of the officers said.

"It happens more than you'd think," the female officer added. "Women come in with their abusers, forced to make a false statement against someone else. It's protocol to separate the parties just to make sure the female is safe."

"I'm safe with Mark," Molly said, wrapping her arms around him once more.

"There's obviously been a huge misunderstanding here," Mark said, and Molly could feel the tension in his body. "We came in to report an assault by her *ex*," he stressed. "We also believe he had a hand in killing Pauline and John Smith, her grandparents. There was a fire a month or so ago, and their bodies were found in the rubble. We want to find out more information about that as well. Discuss the investigation."

His tone was calm, but also stern and demanding, and Molly couldn't help but notice how the officers reacted to it.

"Oh, and my friend Leo Zanardi is here somewhere. Six-four, muscular, Latino, you can't miss him. He should be in on this conversation as well," Mark insisted.

"I remember that fire and the discovery of the bodies inside. Those were your grandparents?" one of the officers asked.

Molly nodded.

"I'm sorry for your loss."

She nodded again, then rested her cheek on Mark's chest. The sound of his heart beating under her ear calmed her. Grounded her.

"We'll go find your friend," someone said.

"If you'll follow us, we can figure out this mess," said a man in slacks and a white button-up shirt.

Molly hadn't seen him before now, but it was obvious he was some sort of supervisor or investigator or something. He led them into a much more comfortable room, an office of some sort.

Instead of taking one of the chairs in front of the large desk, Mark sat on the love seat under a window, pulling Molly down with him.

After a minute or so, Gramps appeared in the doorway. He was frowning. "What the hell is going on?" he growled.

"Tell you later. Is that Molly's ice pack?" Mark asked.

Gramps nodded and handed it over.

Molly jerked when Mark pressed it gently against her eye before she once more leaned against him.

The next hour went by quickly for Molly. Two other detectives had joined them, making the room quite full. She was barely listening as Mark and Gramps told the officers everything they knew. She added details here and there. Her grandparents' deaths had been determined to be a homicide, and the detectives were highly interested in what she had to say about Preston, as they didn't have many leads on who might've killed them. They took copious notes, and she could only hope they'd be able to find some sort of evidence against her ex.

They talked about what had happened earlier, and how Preston had assaulted her. Gramps handed over the camera, and the detectives promised to keep in touch with anything they found.

"We advise you to lay low," one of the men told her. "If this Preston guy is as obsessed with you as it sounds, a restraining order isn't going to do much to keep him away."

"I know," Molly said.

"She'll be with us in Indianapolis," Mark told the men. "She'll be safe there."

"Don't let down your guard," one of them warned. "Stalkers like Weldon will take advantage of the slightest slipup."

"I'm aware," Mark said in a low, harsh tone . . . one she hadn't heard since Nigeria.

Molly suddenly remembered she was sitting with Smoke, the badass former Delta soldier, the man who hunted down and killed terrorists and other bad guys.

She'd actually forgotten about that side of him. After spending so much time with him, after witnessing his kindness and patience, his loyalty to his friends and employees, she'd pushed to the back of her mind the real reason why he and his team had been in Nigeria. They hadn't been on a rescue mission. They'd gone to kill Shekau.

But she wasn't afraid. Not in the least. Smoke . . . Mark . . . would do everything in his power to keep her safe.

∼

Molly Smith wasn't going to dump *him*. No fucking way.

Preston Weldon paced back and forth in his condo. His computer screen mocked him as he speared a hand through his hair in agitation.

She'd hooked up with a fucking *mechanic*. Maybe he wasn't a mechanic exactly, but he might as well have been. The asshole owner of the truck she'd arrived in worked at a towing shop. What a fucking loser!

Preston was a respected cop. A security officer wasn't *exactly* a cop, but it was as close as he could get, thanks to the asshole psychologist who'd rejected him when he'd applied for a police officer position in Chicago. He *wasn't* unstable like the bastard had implied, not in the fucking least. He'd had no right to judge him like that. He hadn't even known him!

He was better than every single cop on the street. He wasn't afraid to use his weapon like most of them were. He'd fucking shoot a perp between the eyes without a second thought if he had the chance.

Preston snatched up the bottle of bourbon on the table as he passed and took a long swig as he continued to pace. His phone rang, and after seeing it was his boss, he threw the device on the table, not wanting to talk to the man.

He was supposed to be at work today, but when he'd gotten a notification on the security camera app and seen that Molly had *finally* shown up at her fucking grandparents' house, there was no way he could have let the opportunity to confront her, to *show* her she couldn't hide from him, slip away. He'd deal with his asshole boss later, come up with another excuse why he hadn't shown up for his shift again.

He'd been fucking busy. Spending months looking for the stupid bitch—only to learn she'd gone and shacked up with someone who wasn't fit to clean his boots!

The thought of Molly in the other man's bed made Preston see red, and he punched his living room wall, grunting at the satisfying dent in the cheap drywall. Molly was *his*. He hadn't even gotten to fuck her before she'd tried to dump him.

That wasn't how things worked. He was Preston Weldon. Women begged to go out with him. They respected his authority, and they never, *ever* tried to hide from him.

Molly was going to pay for making him look bad. He'd bragged about his girlfriend to everyone at work, and when more and more time had passed and no one had seen them together, they'd thought he was lying. The more he'd protested, the more they'd laughed at him. Molly had *humiliated* him.

He'd bring her back to Chicago kicking and screaming if it came to that. She'd do exactly what he wanted her to do . . . or she'd suffer.

Taking another deep swallow of the bourbon, Preston sat at his computer, then slammed the bottle down on the table next to the keyboard. Liquor splashed out, but he didn't even care. He was already focused on learning everything he could about Mark Chamberlin.

To discover his weaknesses and exploit them.

That was what Preston was good at.

He'd been called a nerd in high school, been made fun of, but now he was a respected security officer, practically a cop. People did what he said because of the authority he wielded.

Molly would also do as she was told—otherwise she'd have to go. Just like her disgusting old grandparents.

Chapter Twelve

After another thirty minutes of paperwork and other administrative details, they were once more in the Explorer. Smoke was pissed at himself. He'd known from what Molly had said that this Weldon guy was bad news, but he honestly hadn't expected him to be as batshit crazy as he clearly was. And his underestimating the guy had gotten Molly hurt.

Never again.

He and Molly were in the back seat once more, but this time they were both strapped in, since they were headed back to Indianapolis.

Molly was obviously tired, and Smoke could tell her head hurt by the way she winced with every bump, but she was also doing everything she could to keep herself from falling asleep. She had something on her mind, and he patiently waited for her to spit it out.

"He said he wrote down your license plate number," Molly said softly.

"Good," Smoke said. "I hope he comes to Silverstone to confront me."

"He won't," Gramps said from the front.

"I know," Smoke growled.

"Why not?" Molly asked.

Smoke squeezed her shoulder. He was sitting with his arm around her. It was a bit awkward with the seat belt, but he didn't care. He couldn't stop touching her. The sound of her terror when she'd called out his name in the police station still reverberated in his mind. She'd been completely terrified . . . for *him*.

He'd known what the two cops had thought the second they'd gotten him into the interrogation room. He hadn't been concerned, knowing the truth would come out, but when he'd heard Molly screaming his name, he'd pushed past the officers to get to her. He'd been lucky they hadn't pressed charges against him. He'd heard the one guy hit the wall hard after Smoke had slammed him out of the way.

"Because your ex is a coward," Smoke said, answering her question. "He won't confront me because he knows I can kick his ass. He had no problem harassing and most likely killing your grandparents because they weren't a threat to him. But I am."

"So he'll do what he can to harass *you*, to try to make you go crawling back to him in fear. But he's not counting on Silverstone having your back," Gramps said firmly.

The thought of Molly being at her ex's mercy made Smoke crazy. He felt like shit because she'd gotten hurt while under his watch.

"I wanted to fight him, but he was really strong," Molly said softly.

Smoke inhaled deeply, getting himself under control before he responded. "I wish I could tell you exactly what to do if anything like that ever happens again," he said after a moment. "But I can't. Every situation is different. Some women have gotten away from someone who was assaulting them by being docile and compliant. Some made their attackers see them as humans. They might mention their children, or talk about how their mother is missing them. But in other cases, a woman fighting as hard as she can is what saves her. Screaming, thrashing, and not letting the attacker relax for a second. Sometimes they give up to find someone easier to assault."

Smoke felt sick even talking about this, because inside, he was thinking of Molly being in that kind of situation. But she was obviously second-guessing what she'd done, and he hated that.

"I'm not sure I could've fought him off."

"Then being acquiescent is what you should've done," Smoke told her. "You didn't do anything to make him angrier than he already was."

"I was going to bang against the house to get your attention, but that's when he threatened you and Gramps."

Smoke tensed, then he consciously did what he could to relax. "Right, so you let him talk, and it worked in your favor. If—and that's a big fucking if," Smoke said, "anything like this happens in the future, you have to assess the situation. If you can, get away; that's always your best bet. Are there people around to hear you if you scream and fight? If so, it could be an option to go that route. But if you can't escape, and there's no one who can come to your assistance, you might need to try to be docile. Say whatever you have to in order to calm him. Lie your ass off, tell him you missed him, that you want to be his girlfriend again. Then be on the lookout for your chance to escape."

Molly looked up at him. He hated the vulnerability he saw in her gaze. "Why are some men so whacked? I mean, we didn't even get along. Why would he want me? Why wouldn't he just want to be rid of me?"

"I don't know," Smoke admitted. "It's never made sense to me either."

"My grandmother came to the States from Mexico," Gramps said. "She and my grandfather walked across the desert, swam across the Rio Grande, and literally started with nothing. They were everything to each other. Loved each other so much, I never saw one without the other. You'd think with that kind of example, their children would be the same way. But my uncle is in jail for domestic abuse. He beat his first wife and did time. Then he stalked her when he got out and did time for that too. She eventually moved away, and he got married again. And the cycle continued."

Smoke had known that Gramps didn't get along with his uncle, but he hadn't known the extent of it.

"My aunt has the worst taste in men. She picks the men who treat her like shit," Gramps went on. "She complains about it but refuses to change, to leave them. I've never understood it. My own parents have been married for a very long time, but I don't even think they like each other. They live in the same house yet don't talk much. It used to drive me crazy, but now it just makes me sad. I want what my grandparents had. I still remember going over to their house and listening to them speak Spanish to each other. They were so loving. Back then, I thought it was gross . . . but now I can look back and feel a bit of envy for what they had. Even when they had nothing, literally nothing, they had each other."

Molly leaned forward and put her hand on Gramps's shoulder. He lifted his own hand and squeezed hers. She eased back, and Smoke wrapped her in his arms once more.

"All I'm saying is that people are wired differently. Why do some kids find pleasure in torturing animals? Where does that come from? And yes, many times those are the same people who, as adults, take delight in hurting and even killing other humans. Why do some people just shrug off a breakup and others literally go stark raving mad? I don't know. All you can do is stay positive, be safe, and live your life."

"I'm trying," Molly said. "But what if others don't *want* you to live your life?"

"Then you let us help you. And let karma do her thing," Smoke said firmly.

Molly smiled then. "And you guys help karma out sometimes, don't you?"

"When needed, yes," Smoke told her. "That doesn't scare you?"

"No," Molly said firmly. "But I have to admit, Preston coming after you does."

"Did you not hear me earlier?" Smoke asked. "He's a coward and a bully. And bullies pick on those weaker than them. He's not going to hurt me."

"But what about Silverstone Towing? Or the other employees? Or Taylor and Skylar? I'd never forgive myself if something happened to any of them."

Smoke took a deep breath. She had a good point, but he had a gut feeling that her ex was going to make Molly his sole target. "Look at me," he ordered gently.

Molly turned her face up to his.

"Trust Silverstone. Trust *me*," he begged. "I'm not a man who normally believes in omens or soul mates or any of that stuff. But you *were* put in my path for a reason. I'm Smoke. The man who can get in and out of any situation without being seen. But somehow I didn't even see that hole you were in until it was too late. That's not like me. You were put in my life for a reason, Molly, and I one hundred percent believe it wasn't just so I can witness you being hurt or killed by your ex. I've got this. Okay?"

She hesitated, and Smoke wanted to plead his case some more, but he kept quiet, letting her think. He was rewarded by her small nod.

"Why don't you close your eyes and rest," he suggested.

"You'll keep an eye out to make sure we aren't being followed?" she asked nervously.

"We aren't being followed," Gramps said from in front of them.

Molly sighed and relaxed.

Smoke held her, meeting Gramps's gaze in the rearview mirror after she'd started snoring lightly against him.

"He won't touch her," Gramps said in a low voice.

Smoke gave his friend a chin lift and held Molly tighter. Everyone would have to be on high alert until the Chicago detectives could find the evidence they needed to take Weldon down for the murder of Molly's grandparents. He wasn't so conceited as to believe the man couldn't get to Molly. He had once—it was possible he'd luck out a second time. Smoke would do everything in his power to make sure that didn't happen, but after experiencing what both Skylar and Taylor had gone through, he knew no security system was infallible. No plan was perfect.

He had to hope that Weldon was too much of a coward to come to Indianapolis to try anything. But if he wasn't, if he showed his face, he'd wish he hadn't.

If Preston Weldon dared come after Molly, he was a dead man. Period. Silverstone would kill him and make his body disappear. No one would find him, nor would they find his killer.

He loved Molly. It was unbelievable how fast it had happened, but there it was. He had no idea how she felt, but with the way she clung to him, he knew there was more than friendship and gratitude.

He had to be patient. If it was meant to be—and he honestly thought it was; he hadn't fallen into that hole by accident—it would happen when the time was right.

Chapter Thirteen

A week and a half had passed since they'd returned from Chicago, and things seemed to be very . . . normal. Molly had walked on eggshells at first, but each day had passed quietly, much like the one before it. Mark would either go to Silverstone Towing, and she'd go with him, or they'd stay at his house. They'd laughed, watched television, and cooked meals together.

Mark had planted the cutting from Nana's rosebush in his backyard, and it seemed to be thriving.

Molly had talked to the lawyer, Maggie Melton, and she'd overnighted paperwork for her to sign. Nana and Papa hadn't had a large estate, but what there was would all go to her. The insurance people had reassured her they were working on her case, but generally the process for an insurance payout took time, especially for something as expensive as a house.

It was all very . . . *normal.*

Though, she loved hanging out with Mark. She'd gotten to know him even more, and it was getting harder and harder to not let her feelings for him show. He wasn't perfect, as he'd warned her. There were things he did that annoyed her, but in the scope of life, they weren't that big of a deal. Some days she had the feeling he wanted her as more than simply a roommate or friend, and other days he seemed very distant. It was confusing . . . but then again, neither of them had ever lived with someone of the opposite sex.

Either way, despite Mark coming right out and saying he was interested in her when they'd first arrived in Indianapolis, lately he'd been treating her with kid gloves. Maybe it was because of Preston's attack . . . or, worse, he'd just changed his mind about wanting to be more than friends.

He held her hand, hugged her, gave her chaste kisses on the forehead, but nothing more intimate. Molly feared that he'd decided to just help her get back on her feet before sending her on her way, treating her in an almost sisterly manner in the meantime to gently let her know he'd changed his mind about wanting a romantic relationship.

The thought was too depressing to dwell on.

Molly had plans to hang out with Taylor tomorrow at Silverstone, and she was looking forward to seeing her, to getting out of her own head for a while. Between Taylor and Skylar, Molly rarely felt lonely. They texted nonstop, and having friends like them was something Molly hadn't ever experienced. She was looking forward to chilling with Taylor while the guys worked a tow shift.

There had been no sign of Preston, but Molly knew she wasn't lucky enough to have heard the last from him. He wouldn't give up so easily. He was regrouping, planning . . . she knew that as surely as she knew her name. And when he struck, it was going to be bad.

But she refused to live her life in fear. Mark had taught her that. He had every confidence she was safe. So she had to believe it.

Looking over at the clock, Molly saw it was almost eight thirty. She was being lazy but couldn't bring herself to care. She'd heard Mark get up three hours ago to work out, and she'd gladly gone back to sleep. Now the sun was peeking in through the windows, lifting her mood. It felt wonderful to stretch out. It still wasn't so long ago that she'd been stuck in a tiny hole with little room to move.

The door to her bedroom opened, scaring the shit out of Molly. She jumped and immediately threw herself off the side of her bed farthest from the door.

"Molly? Shit! I'm sorry. It's me!" Mark said, his tone remorseful.

Molly peeked over the edge of the mattress and took a huge breath. "Jeez, Mark, you scared me!"

"I'm so sorry. I had planned to open your door quietly, just to peek in to see if you were awake, but I caught my foot on the carpet and kinda fell against it."

Molly couldn't help it. She burst out laughing. When she had herself under control, she said, "The legendary Smoke, the man who prides himself on being the sneakiest member of his team, tripped over the *carpet*?"

He winced, but since he was smiling, Molly knew he hadn't taken offense. It was one of the dozens of things she'd learned since moving in that she loved about him. His surprising clumsiness . . . and his ability to laugh at himself.

"Yeah, well, now that you're up, wanna do something fun today?"

Molly knew the time was coming when she'd have to figure out what to do with her life. If she wasn't working at Apex as an environmental engineer, she needed to decide what she *did* want to do. The problem was, the one thing she wanted wasn't exactly an option at the moment.

Pushing that thought to the back of her mind, she stood and climbed onto the bed. She sat cross-legged and nodded at Mark. "Of course. What did you have in mind?"

"Is that my shirt?" Mark asked instead of answering her question.

Molly blushed. She'd started wearing his black T-shirt, the one she'd worn out of the jungle, to bed. She didn't know why, other than maybe she found it comforting in its familiarity. She'd gained back much of the weight she'd lost, thanks to Mark constantly feeding her nutritious meals and shakes—and sweets—but she still swam in the shirt.

She brought her knees up and pulled the shirt down over them. "Yes," she said, tilting her chin up in feigned confidence.

He stared at her for a long moment before saying, "I'm not going to take it back, Mol. I like it better on *you*."

Licking her lips, Molly saw his gaze fix on her mouth, and for a second she thought he was going to join her on the bed and finally kiss her the way she'd dreamed of. He actually took a step forward, but seemed to get control over himself at the last second.

"I'm not telling you where I'm taking you. It's a surprise."

"I'm not good at surprises," Molly admitted. "If it's not something I'm all that thrilled about, I have to pretend I'm superexcited, and things get awkward."

"I never want you to lie to me. If I take you to a restaurant you hate, I expect you to tell me before we walk through the doors. If I buy you a present you know you'll never use or you don't like, you can return it, and I won't feel bad. Life's too short to pretend you like something when you don't."

Molly's heartbeat increased at the thought of him buying her gifts in the future. It *sounded* like he wanted her around for a long time, but a present could be something as simple as a birthday gift or a chocolate bar he picked up somewhere. "I don't want to hurt your feelings," she told him.

"You'll hurt my feelings more if I find out you hate something I've done for you or given to you," was his simple reply.

He had a good point. "Okay, but you have to do the same. I know I've bought a lot of crap, and somehow it's managed to migrate past my room. If you don't like the throw blanket I left on your couch, or if you hate that picture of the swimming turtle you let me put in the dining room, you have to tell me."

"My house has felt more like a home since you moved in," Mark said, the sincerity easy to hear in his tone.

They stared at each other for a beat, then he said, "Wear jeans and a comfortable shirt. Any shoes you want."

"Okay," she said.

"Take your time getting ready. It's still early. I'll make some breakfast for us . . . western omelet for you?"

"Sounds great," she told him, and it did. Eggs had a lot of protein, so she ate them often, but Mark went out of his way to make each dish different so she wouldn't get sick of eating the foods her body needed.

"Thank you, Mark. Seriously. Without your generous offer to stay here, I would probably be cowering in a hotel room up in Oak Park, wondering when Preston was going to get to me. Not only do I feel perfectly safe here with you, you've helped me regain my strength, eased my transition back into the real world, and introduced me to Taylor and Skylar. I can never repay you."

"I don't want repayment," he told her. "I just want you to be happy, healthy, safe, and able to live the life you want." And with that, he turned and exited the guest room. He shut the door quietly behind him.

Molly listened as he walked back through the hall, then down the stairs. She took her knees out of the shirt and flopped backward. She lay spread-eagle on the bed and stared up at the ceiling.

Live the life she wanted. Mark would probably have been shocked if he knew what she *really* wanted.

And at thirty-five, time was ticking away.

She used to think she had lots of time, but as one year ran into the next, she realized that her dream was probably never going to happen.

Realizing she was sinking into the doldrums, Molly forced herself to roll off the bed and head into the bathroom. Mark hadn't been kidding the first day he'd brought her home when he'd said he'd spared no expense remodeling the bathrooms. The only room Molly liked more than the bathroom attached to her room was the master bath.

One day she'd taken a bath in the huge tub in his room. She could practically swim in the thing, but the seats alongside the edge made it easy to keep her head above water. She'd filled the tub, using extra bubble bath, and had stayed in the hot water for almost an hour, relaxing and reading a book Taylor had loaned her. The heated floors and towel racks, the marble countertops, and the fancy fixtures seemed so unlike Mark, but she definitely wasn't complaining.

Molly took her time showering and getting ready, and it was an hour before she headed down the stairs toward the kitchen. She stopped at the edge of the great room and watched Mark for a brief moment. He was unaware of her presence, and she could drool over him all she wanted without him knowing.

He had on a pair of black jeans that hugged his ass. His shirt was heather gray, and Molly could just see a bit of chest hair at the opening. His arm muscles bulged when he moved, and when he reached for the saltshaker on the counter, his forearm flexed, making Molly want to swoon. His brown hair was cut short, and he currently had a five-o'clock shadow. It wasn't enough to cover up that adorable dimple in his cheek, though.

She must've made some sort of noise, or Mark had felt her staring at him, because he looked up and caught her in the act. But he didn't call her on it.

"Hey," he said quietly.

"Hi," Molly returned, pushing off the wall and walking toward him. He held out an arm, and it felt completely natural to walk straight into his embrace. Resting her cheek against his chest, Molly once again realized they fit together perfectly. She'd always felt as if she was too short. Too small. Too thin. But around Mark, she didn't feel any of those things, despite his size.

"I didn't want to start your eggs until you were here so your omelet wouldn't get cold. I've got everything else ready, though. Grab a cup of coffee, and have a seat—I'll have your omelet done in five minutes or so."

He let go of her, and Molly padded over to the Keurig. They moved around the kitchen as if they'd been living together for years rather than thrown together by circumstance a few weeks ago.

She pulled herself up onto one of the barstools at the granite island and sipped her coffee as Mark cooked.

"A girl could get used to this," she quipped after a moment.

"So could a guy," Mark returned.

This morning felt . . . different. Mark seemed quiet, thoughtful. He'd also been more touchy-feely than usual. Molly loved it, but it made her nervous too. Was she reading too much into his behavior? Had she gotten so comfortable in his house that she was imagining things that weren't true? Things she wanted to believe?

"You're thinking too hard again," Mark said as he tilted the skillet, and a perfect omelet plopped onto a plate. He put the plate in front of her, along with a tub of sour cream and a jar of salsa. He'd quickly learned that she liked to slather her eggs with both.

Molly cut off a bite of her omelet after she'd put on the condiments and sighed with contentment as she chewed. He always seemed to put the perfect ratio of filling to egg.

"You sleep okay?" Mark asked as he sipped his coffee.

Molly knew he'd already eaten, as she'd seen his empty plate in the sink. She swallowed, then nodded. "Yeah."

"No nightmares?"

"No. I only had a couple when I first got here, but now, once I fall asleep, I seem to *stay* asleep."

"Good. I looked in on you last night around two, and you were out," Mark said nonchalantly.

Molly stilled with the bite of omelet halfway to her mouth. "You looked in on me?" she asked.

The pink that bloomed on Mark's cheeks was surprising. She hadn't meant to embarrass him.

"Yeah. If I wake up at night, I usually do a walk-around to make sure all the doors are locked, the alarm is on, and everything looks normal. Your door was cracked, and I peeked in. You were sleeping on your back with your arms and legs spread out, like normal," he said with a grin.

"Did you do this walk-around before I started staying here?" she asked.

Mark shrugged. "Yeah. I'm a bit paranoid. But it didn't happen every night. Now it does."

"I don't like that you do that because of me," Molly admitted.

"It's not *because* of you," Mark countered. "I did it before you got here too. But because we don't know what your ex is planning, I just feel better knowing he can't get to you without setting off my alarms."

"Me too," Molly admitted. "I get that no house or security system is foolproof, but after accidentally setting it off last week, I now know how fast you respond." She'd been embarrassed that she'd forgotten all about the alarm when she'd seen a small herd of deer along the fence at the back of his property. She'd opened the back door to go outside while Mark was in the shower, hoping to get closer for a picture—without turning off the alarm.

There hadn't been any sirens blaring or anything, but when she'd gone back inside after snapping her picture, Mark had rushed into the room with a skimpy towel around his waist, dripping wet, looking completely freaked out.

The entire situation had been mortifying, especially her having to admit she'd simply forgotten about the alarm. But despite a short lecture about the importance of staying safe, Smoke had been pretty understanding, all things considered.

"You know what Silverstone does, and I'm not talking about the towing business. We're very careful. *Very* careful not to let our job follow us home, but I'm a paranoid son of a bitch. That's why I installed the security system in the first place. But I have to admit, I'm also glad it makes you feel protected and safe. Now, finish your breakfast so we can get going," he ordered.

Molly had long since put down her forkful of food, but picked it back up at his insistence. She was getting too fond of being in Mark's house. It was going to suck when she had to move out.

After she finished her omelet, Mark put her plate and fork in the sink and returned the sour cream and salsa to the fridge. Not putting any water on the dishes to soak was one of the minor things that irked her about him, but she let it go, curious as to where he was taking her.

She put on a pair of sneakers, then met him at the door to the garage. He set the alarm and closed the door to the house. As he held the passenger-side door for her, Molly thought again about how gentlemanly he was. And not just in public, where it was expected or where someone could see him. *All* the time. Cooking, holding doors open, getting up after he'd already gotten settled on the couch to get her a snack . . . the little things that were so much more important than larger gestures like flowers.

He pulled out of the garage and waited until the door shut before heading down the long driveway. As he neared the electronic gate, it opened automatically when he ran over the sensor in the asphalt. It closed immediately after his bumper cleared the gate.

Molly pulled out her phone, as she hadn't bothered to check her messages that morning. She'd been too busy ogling Mark, which she didn't regret in the least.

Still smiling, she unlocked her phone—and stared down at the screen in confusion.

It wasn't unusual for her to get ten or twenty emails overnight. Most were junk mail that she just deleted without opening. Before she'd gone to Nigeria, there had been some days when she hadn't bothered to even check her email. But lately, she'd been sure to check every day in case the insurance company or the lawyer emailed needing a signature or document or something.

But next to her email app was the number 1,523.

She'd received over fifteen hundred emails *overnight?*

"What's wrong?" Mark asked, in tune with her as always.

"I'm not sure," Molly said.

She had a few text notifications, and she figured those were from Skylar and Taylor. At the moment, she was too curious as to why she'd gotten such an influx of emails.

Opening the app, she flinched when she saw some of the subject lines on the emails in her in-box.

Stupid bitch!

Go kill yourself!

Who the fuck you think you are?

Die!

They went on and on. Molly gasped in confusion and shock.

"Molly, what?" Mark asked, concerned now.

Ignoring him, Molly clicked on the first email.

You're a stupid bitch! I hope you aren't breeding because any kid of yours would certainly be just as stupid as you.

The words were hurtful—and Molly had no idea what could've made her the target of such vitriol. She clicked on another email.

OMG! People like you don't deserve to be walking around on this earth! Why don't you just go kill yourself already. We'd all be better off with you dead.

Tears sprang to her eyes. So much hate—and in just the first two emails—was almost unbearable to read.

She was a good person. She did her best to be nice to everyone she met. But after being on the receiving end of Preston's animosity for so long, this kind of meanness made her feel even more vulnerable than she already did. And the fact that there were *hundreds* of emails, all of them likely filled with the same kind of disgust and loathing . . .

It was enough to push her over the edge.

Her phone was jerked from her grasp, and Molly looked up in surprise. She hadn't even felt Mark pulling over to the side of the road. He looked down at her phone and scowled.

"What the fuck?" he muttered as he scrolled through her in-box.

"I don't know," Molly said. "I have no clue what's going on." She watched as a muscle in Mark's jaw ticced as he read some of the emails she'd received. He seemed to stop on one for a long moment—then he reached for his own phone.

"Mark?"

He held up a finger, asking her to hang on. She pressed her lips together and wiped her eyes.

"Eagle? This is Smoke. Are you at the garage? Good. I need your help. Someone posted a nasty, untrue story about Molly in an animal rights group on Facebook. And whoever it was, they also encouraged people to email and tell her how they felt about what she did. She's received over fifteen hundred messages so far this morning . . . no, but you can log into her account and read them yourself. At least one of them mentions the post. I don't think it's any big mystery who did this. I need you to find that shit and get it taken down. Then follow up with the Oak Park detectives and inform them of what happened.

"This is Weldon's work. I'd bet everything I have on it, but he won't be stupid enough to post under his own name. I won't be in today, I'm taking Molly out for some fun. Yes, she's still on for tomorrow and hanging with Taylor at the garage. We need to nail this asshole. Right. Thanks. I'll email you her password so you can get into her account. Later."

Mark disconnected the call with Eagle, then tapped on his keyboard before looking over at her. "What's your email username and password?"

Molly didn't even think about refusing to tell him. He was helping her. She told him, and he emailed the information to Eagle. Then he put both his phone *and* hers into the pocket in his door and gripped the steering wheel hard enough that his knuckles turned white.

"Mark?" she asked tentatively. She was having a hard time processing what Mark had just told Eagle.

"I *hate* that asshole," he said between clenched teeth.

"Me too," Molly agreed immediately. "Preston posted something about me on Facebook?"

"I'm assuming it was him, yes."

"What'd he say?"

"Doesn't matter."

"It does to me," Molly insisted. When Mark didn't say anything, she pleaded, "Please?"

Sighing, Mark eventually said, "One of the emails included a screenshot of the post. From what I could tell, he posted a picture of a bag of dead puppies . . . and said he'd caught you in the act of putting them in a grill to burn them, to hide the fact that you'd killed them. He posted your email address and encouraged people to tell you what they thought of your actions."

Molly inhaled sharply. Just thinking about the picture Mark had described was enough to make her want to cry. But knowing that thousands of people out there thought she would do something so abhorrent was overwhelming. It didn't matter that they didn't actually know her at all. That was still a lot of hate aimed her way. It hurt. So damn bad.

Molly would no more hurt a defenseless puppy than say something bad about someone on social media. Looking over at Mark, she saw that he was on the verge of losing it. His face was red, and his biceps were flexing over and over again, as if the steering wheel was Preston's neck.

And the longer she watched him, and the more she thought about it, the angrier Molly became as well.

Preston *was* a bully. A petty, pathetic excuse for a man. He couldn't handle her dumping him because he was an asshole and a controlling jerk. The people emailing her had a right to be mad about that story; she would've been, too, if she'd happened across it on social media. But they didn't know *her*. Didn't know that Preston was a fucking liar.

At the moment, her anger took a back seat. She needed to calm Mark.

She reached over and placed a hand on his forearm. "Mark."

"What?" he growled.

"Look at me," she begged.

He turned his head, and Molly had never seen such fury in someone's eyes before. "I'm okay," she told him.

But he shook his head. "Weldon's a piece of shit. A cowardly, spineless, pusillanimous motherfucker."

Molly couldn't help it—she laughed.

"What the fuck are you laughing about?" Mark asked.

"Pusillanimous?" she asked.

"Yes!"

"Right. But Eagle is on it. And I'm sure he'll call Gramps and Bull if he needs to. I'm here with you, and safe. Preston *is* a coward and a bully, and if he thinks making up stories about me and getting strangers to flood my email is going to make me want to go back to him, he's even stupider than we thought."

The fury in Mark's eyes lessened a bit. "You aren't reading any more of those emails," he told her.

"Okay," Molly agreed. She didn't want to read them anyway.

"We'll have to get you a new email address. You can inform your insurance company and Maggie what it is later."

"Okay," she said again.

Mark grabbed the hand that was on his forearm and brought it up to his lips. He kissed her palm, then sighed.

Goose bumps broke out on Molly's arms. Mark had kissed her a few times. On the top of the head. On the forehead. And she'd kissed him that once, right at the edge of his mouth. But feeling his lips on the tender skin of her palm sent electricity shooting right between her legs.

"I don't know what my surprise is for today, but you can't tell a girl that you're taking her out, then go back on your word," she teased.

She saw Mark's lips twitch. He shook his head. "Strong as fuck," he muttered. Then, louder, "Okay, Mol. I won't change our plans. But we don't know if that dickhead is anywhere around or not. I'm not going to take any chances with your life or well-being."

"I'm okay with that," she told him.

"You'll do what I tell you, as soon as I tell you," Mark said sternly. "If I say *drop*, you get down on your belly immediately. No matter if we're in a parking lot or inside a building. Understand?"

"Yes."

"If I tell you to run, you run. If I tell you to freeze, you freeze."

"Okay, Mark. I have no problem with any of that." She squeezed his fingers. He hadn't let go of her hand after he'd kissed it. "But I still want us to enjoy ourselves. If you can't relax enough to do that, then we might as well go home. I'd rather be locked behind the walls of your house, where we both feel safe, than have you stressed out and overly cautious. Preston Weldon is a jerk. And he tried to get inside my head. I admit that he succeeded for a second, but I'm stronger than that. He won't break me."

Mark stared at her for a long moment before he closed his eyes. They popped open almost immediately, though, and he said, "Folly Molly my ass. You've got nerves of steel."

"Not really. I just don't want my surprise ruined by that jerk. I'm sure I'll be freaked out later, and you'll have to remind me that I'm trying to be a more positive person. But for now, I want to be normal. I want to go out and be Molly Smith, not a victim."

"You *are* Molly Smith, and you are the least victim-like person I've ever met," Mark told her.

"Right, so can we go, then? We're sitting on the side of the road, and the last thing I want is to end up on *Live PD* when the cops stop to check out what we're doing."

Mark chuckled. "They film in Lawrence, Molly, that's northeast of Indianapolis, nowhere near us. Exactly opposite of us here in the southwest part of the city, in fact."

"You never know, there might be a roving band of Lawrence cops looking for some action for the show," Molly joked.

"Right. So I'd better get going. You aren't getting your phone back today, though."

"Okay. But can you ask Bull and Eagle to tell Skylar and Taylor what's going on? I don't want them to think I'm ignoring their texts."

"I'll tell them," Mark reassured her. He looked over his shoulder and pulled back onto the road, but didn't let go of her hand. Molly had no problem with that.

It looked like her respite from being harassed by Preston was at an end. He'd done the same thing before she'd left. Started out with petty stuff, given her time to let down her guard, then escalated again. She had no doubt he'd do the same thing now. She might have been in Indianapolis, but nowhere was going to be far enough away to make him stop, she realized. Molly just hoped Silverstone or the police could stop him before he went too far.

Chapter Fourteen

Smoke was doing his best to put his fury behind him, but it was extremely difficult. He'd seen the shock and horror in Molly's eyes as she'd read the filth people had sent her. He knew without a doubt that Weldon didn't give a rat's ass about any protection order. He'd probably seen it as a challenge. And with this move, he'd thrown down the gauntlet. Smoke had given him a chance to slink away with his tail between his legs, but it was now game on.

"Bowling?" Molly said in excitement as he pulled into the parking lot of their destination.

When he'd checked in on her in the middle of the night, he'd had the strongest urge to take her out. She'd been such a trooper, never complaining about not going anywhere but Silverstone Towing and his house. He wanted to get her out of the house, let her experience some of the fun things that Indianapolis had to offer. That *he* had to offer.

Smoke wanted Molly to stay. Every day, he braced himself to hear her say she was ready to move out on her own, to go back to her life. And every day, he said good night and watched her walk up the stairs, wishing she was headed for the master bedroom and *his* bed.

He was trying to go slow. Give her time to get used to him. Show her that he wasn't like Weldon or any of her other asshole ex-boyfriends.

He loved having her things intermingled with his in the house. Her blanket, the picture of the turtle, the cute mug Taylor had bought for her. His pantry had more junk food in it than it had ever seen, and he loved that too.

Molly Smith was the woman for him . . . he just had to make her never want to leave. And the next step in doing that was to take her out on a date. Bowling was something he'd done all the time when he'd been in the Army, but it had been almost five years since he'd stepped inside a bowling alley. Smoke had no idea if Molly had ever bowled, but there was a first time for everything.

He parked his Explorer and scoped out the parking lot. He didn't see any sign of anyone who made him nervous. Gramps had found out that Weldon drove an older-model Crown Victoria. He'd bought it at a police auction. It was a former patrol car, stripped down.

Eagle had been the one to find out that Molly's ex had applied to the police academy, and had been denied. The man definitely had an inferiority complex when it came to the cops. His job in security was probably an attempt to assuage his ego, and now his need for power had manifested itself in an inability to let go of Molly.

But all seemed quiet in the bowling alley parking lot. Smoke was on edge, but he was also determined to make this date a good one. He did his best to relax his shoulders and held out his hand. "Climb over the console, and come out this side," he told her. Just getting out and walking around the SUV to open her door could give someone a chance to get to it first and snatch her—or put a few bullets into her.

Molly raised an eyebrow but didn't protest, much to Smoke's relief. Because she was so slight, she could easily climb across the seat. He took hold of her hand, helping her maneuver past the steering wheel and out of the vehicle.

"I haven't been bowling in ages!" she chirped happily. "I have to warn you, I used to be pretty good," she said with a spark in her eye.

"Me too," Smoke agreed.

"Shall we make a bet?" she asked a little cockily.

"You're that good?" Smoke put an arm around Molly's shoulders and held her against his side as he hurried them to the door. If needed, he could pick her up and run, or drop and cover her with his body.

"I'm that good," Molly bragged.

They entered the bowling alley without incident, but Smoke knew he wouldn't be able to relax if he didn't make sure Weldon wasn't on the premises. He was taking a chance, leaving Molly at the desk to get their shoes, but he needed to do a run-through of the building.

"Stay here. Do. Not. Move. I need to clear the building. I don't want to leave you here, but I don't want to take you with me either. If you hear anything that makes you nervous, take my keys, get the hell out of here, and go to Silverstone Towing. Understand?"

She nodded with wide eyes as she took the keys he held out to her.

Smoke took a deep breath and turned to do what he needed to do.

He was back at her side within four and a half minutes. He hadn't seen Weldon or anything out of the ordinary. There was no way he could've known where they were going today, and Smoke would've felt better canceling their outing and going to either the garage or back to his house, but honestly, he'd been looking forward to anything resembling a date for quite a while, and he didn't want to ruin the day.

Molly had chosen the lane against the far wall, which pleased him.

"Everything okay?" she asked, a slight wrinkle in her brow the only indication she was worried.

"It's fine," he told her, leaning over and kissing the top of her head before sitting next to her and reaching for the shoes she'd gotten for him.

"If you think it's better that we leave, I'm okay with that," she told him softly.

"Well, I'm not," Smoke said, concentrating on tying his shoe.

"He's not going to stop," Molly said.

Smoke looked up at that. "He is," he insisted.

Molly pressed her lips together.

He put a hand on her shoulder and leaned into her. "The guys are on this. They'll get the information they need and pass it on to the cops. In the meantime, we'll continue to do our thing, and he'll either get bored or so pissed off that he'll make his move. And if it's the latter, we'll catch him, and he'll go to jail. What I'm *not* going to do, however, is put you in danger in the meantime. You will never be bait for him. Ever. That's not how Silverstone works. Understand?"

Molly nodded, and Smoke couldn't miss the look of relief that flashed across her face. He wished he'd reassured her on that point before now.

"I need to look for a new job. What if it's time for me to go back to work and he's still being his assholey self?" Molly asked.

Smoke wanted to smile at her choice of words, but he didn't. "You don't *need* to find a job right this second, Mol. And before you complain that you're a mooch, you aren't. We've been over this. I *like* having you in my house. You more than do your share of the housekeeping, and money is not an issue."

She didn't answer, simply stared at him. He could practically hear her brain working.

"For today, you don't have to think about it. All you have to do is *try* to beat me in bowling."

His words did what he'd hoped. She arched a brow. "Try?" she asked haughtily.

"Yup."

"I'm gonna make you eat those words," she threatened.

Smoke grinned as she stood and went over to the stand to choose her bowling ball. As he looked around once more, his smile dimmed. Thinking about what Weldon had done made his blood boil, but now wasn't the time or place to dwell on it. He'd wanted to take Molly out and hopefully let her forget about her douche of an ex for a little while, and that was just what he was going to do.

~

Molly sighed in happiness as she settled into the Explorer. She and Mark had played five games. What she'd enjoyed most was that Mark hadn't let her win. He was as cutthroat about winning as she was. He'd won four of the five games, but only by a few points each time. They were well matched, and the morning and afternoon had been really fun.

They'd taken a break after three games to eat greasy bowling alley food, and for the first time in a very long time, she didn't feel like she was a stuffed turkey after only eating a few bites. She hadn't thought about Preston in hours—she had instead relaxed and had a fun time with Mark.

They hadn't run out of things to talk about, and she loved being able to tease him and be teased back without worrying about hurting his feelings.

"We need to find a tournament," Mark said, smiling over at her as he drove. "Together, we'd be unbeatable for sure."

"I'd love that. Do you think they have them here?"

"If not at this alley, they have to have them somewhere."

Molly laid her head back on the headrest and turned so she was looking at him. "Thank you for a great day," she said.

"My pleasure," Mark returned. "It's been a long time since I've done something so . . . normal. Do you want to go out for dinner or eat in?"

"In," Molly said immediately. "Ever since you said you didn't like eating out and why, I can't get that out of my head. And after eating all that crap for lunch, I think I need something green."

Mark chuckled. "Yeah, I'm gonna pay for eating all those nachos and the three hot dogs, but it felt good to splurge."

"So . . . salad for dinner?" Molly asked.

"Sounds good."

As they drove back toward his place, he asked, "You still want to go in to Silverstone Towing tomorrow?"

"Yeah. Taylor said she was going to be there, and I'd love to hang with her for a while . . . if you still think it's okay."

"It's more than okay," Mark said quickly. "But I would understand if you wanted to hole up at the house too."

"I don't want him to scare me from my normal activities," Molly told him. "I mean, I know I can't take long walks in the woods or anything like that, but I feel safe both at your house and at the garage. If he's stupid enough to do anything while I'm at either of those places, he'll get caught, and this will be over."

"I'm proud of you."

Molly shrugged. "I'm doing what anyone else in my situation would," she protested.

"Maybe, maybe not, but your attitude about it is remarkable. You've come a long way from that negative person you claimed to be back in Nigeria. That Molly would be lamenting that everything Weldon did was her fault and that she deserved it."

Molly was stunned to realize Mark was right. Somehow over the last few weeks, she'd already changed significantly. And she had a feeling it was from hanging around Mark and his friends. They were all so . . . satisfied with their lives. Her parents and grandparents hadn't been that way. She'd loved them dearly, and they'd loved her, but they'd been prone to dwell on the bad things in life rather than the good. Despite what Mark and the others did on their missions—*killing* people who did horrible things to others—they were still generally positive.

"I think you're rubbing off on me," she said honestly.

She got a huge smile in response. And that dimple. Damn, Molly would've done anything to see it every day for the rest of her life.

Mark turned onto the gravel drive leading to his property. It was off a main road, and continued for about a half mile before the security gate.

He stopped his Explorer after only half that distance and stared at the road in front of him.

Molly squinted, trying to figure out what she was looking at.

When it registered, she gasped.

Someone had thrown nails on the driveway. Not just a few either. It looked like hundreds.

And there was only one person she knew who would do something like that. Something so petty and childish.

Preston.

Without a word, Mark turned his wheel sharply to the right and pulled off the road. The car bumped and jolted as he drove in the grass a few yards away from the gravel.

"Preston did this," Molly said quietly.

"Probably," Mark responded.

"Did your camera thing go off?" she asked, already knowing the answer. It hadn't. If it had, Mark would've done something about it. But he hadn't gotten any notification on his watch all day.

"No. He was smart enough to stay far away from the gate and the cameras there." He looked over at her. "He can't get near the fence or the house without me knowing," he said. "As long as it's set, my alarm is nearly foolproof. I guarantee he can't get past the gate without me being notified."

Molly nodded.

Just as Mark had suggested, the nails on the road were only put down for a short distance before the gravel was clear again.

"I'll ask Gramps or someone to come by and clear it so we don't pop a tire when we leave tomorrow," Mark said.

Molly nodded.

He pulled up to the gate and quickly put in the impossibly long code. The gate opened, and Molly didn't think she breathed normally until it was closed behind them. Mark's head was constantly on a swivel, looking for anything out of the ordinary as they drove toward the house before pulling into the garage. When the door was shut, he turned to her and took her hand in his.

"I've said it once, and I'll say it again—you're safe here, Mol."

"I know."

"I hope you do. If I didn't think we were safe here, I'd take you to Silverstone Towing and lock you in our safe room until Weldon was behind bars."

The confident way he spoke made Molly nod. "Okay."

"Okay. Come on, I don't know about you, but my body's screaming for some greens."

She smiled at him, appreciating that he was trying to make light of what Preston had done—and the fact that he could be out there watching them right now.

They walked inside, and Mark made her disarm the alarm, ensuring she remembered the code. Every time she turned the complicated system on or off, it increased her familiarity. Arming it from inside the house was easier than disarming it. All she had to do was push the Arm button. She did that and turned to see Mark nodding at her with approval.

"You want to shower before dinner?" he asked.

She didn't really feel like she'd worked up that much of a sweat bowling, but Molly realized that Mark needed to call his friends. And she was astute enough to understand that he probably didn't want her overhearing his conversation. She decided to give him that.

"Sure."

"Okay, go on up. I'll get stuff ready so we can start chopping when you're done."

Nodding, Molly turned to head up the stairs, but Mark caught her hand in his. He pulled her back to him and wrapped his arms around her.

Molly loved his hugs. There was nowhere she felt safer than in his arms. His heartbeat was strong and steady under her cheek . . . and she couldn't help but wonder how it would feel to be held like this with nothing between them.

"This is gonna end soon. I promise. Then you can take all the long walks in the woods that you want," he vowed.

Molly's throat felt tight, and she didn't want him to hear her voice wobble, so she simply nodded against him.

He held her for a beat longer, then kissed her on the forehead and stepped away. Without a word, Molly headed up the stairs to the room she'd been staying in. She closed the door and leaned against it, sliding down to sit on the thick, soft carpet under her.

Sometimes Nigeria felt like it was just yesterday. Like when she woke up in the middle of the night and forgot where she was for a split second. But most of the time it felt as though someone *else* had been kidnapped and thrown into a hole as if she was nothing but trash.

Mark and his friends had made it possible for her to move on with her life. To feel strong.

She wanted Preston to leave her alone. To forget about her. For a while, she'd thought maybe he had during her months away. But after seeing him in Oak Park, she understood that he would *never* give up. In his mind, she was his. It made no sense.

She just hoped and prayed that in the process of trying to get her back—by physical force, if necessary—he didn't hurt anyone she'd come to care about.

But he'd already killed Nana and Papa. Molly instinctively knew he wouldn't let anyone else stand in the way of what he wanted.

Taking a deep breath, she slowly stood and headed into the bathroom to shower. For tonight at least, she was safe. Locked behind the walls of Mark's house. She'd take one day at a time and hope Silverstone and the police could find what they needed to make Preston leave her alone for good.

~

Preston spied on the house through his binoculars from his hiding spot a quarter mile from the fence that surrounded the asshole's house. He was inside. With *his* girlfriend.

And Molly was definitely his. He'd found her first.

The cameras and security around the entire perimeter of the property were problems. He knew enough about both to know the setup was top of the line, which was a nasty surprise he hadn't expected, especially from a dumb mechanic. He wouldn't be able to breach it and steal Molly away before the cops or the asshole himself were on him. He'd just have to be patient and wait for his opportunity.

The blinking light of the camera closest to his hiding spot taunted him. Letting him know that if he went any closer, he'd be caught on video.

Molly was going to suffer for cheating on him. He just knew she was in there fucking that asshole. He'd used his resources to look up the license plate and had learned all he needed to know about the man she was shacking up with.

Mark Chamberlin. Thirty-eight years old, six-one, brown hair, brown eyes.

Almost *forty*. Over the fucking hill. He was in good shape, though, which pissed Preston off further.

He flexed his arm, pleased at how ripped he was. "I could take 'im," he said out loud. "Fucker thinks he's so damn awesome. He'd be no damn match for *me*." He reached for another beer in the bag at his feet and chugged it. He crushed the empty can in his fist, flexing his biceps again, then stuffed it back into the bag. He knew better than to leave his DNA lying around for someone to find.

Until he could snatch her, Preston would take pleasure in fucking with Molly and her new fuck buddy. He'd laughed the entire time he'd spread the nails on the driveway. He'd planned to spread them out more, but he'd tripped and dropped the entire bag in a clump. Then he'd tried to disperse them with his foot, but it had taken too long, and he'd gotten nervous that someone would see him.

He'd hoped the jerk Molly was with wouldn't be paying attention. When Preston had seen him maneuver around the nails on the driveway, it had ruined some of his fun.

But it didn't matter. He'd get her back. He wasn't done with her. No bitch *ever* said no to him. He was the one who decided when they were done. And he wasn't anywhere near done with Molly Smith.

She had no one now. She was all alone in the world. The guy she was fucking didn't count. He'd get sick of her soon enough. Preston had no doubt about that. Molly was an annoying bitch, but that didn't mean she got to call the shots. Women like Molly needed to be put in their place.

Preston hadn't actually meant to kill her damn grandparents, but they wouldn't tell him where she was, and he *knew* they'd had the information. Even after he'd slapped the old woman, trying to get her husband to break, they'd continued to resist. When the woman had started screaming, he'd had to do something to shut her up, so he'd punched her as hard as he could, knocking her out.

Then the old man had opened *his* mouth.

It was their own faults they were dead.

He'd wrapped his hands around the old man's throat, and the feeling of *power* that had filled him as he'd watched the man struggle to breathe . . . Preston had never felt anything like it. When the man was dead, he'd turned to the woman. She'd begun to come around, so he'd strangled her too. Then, knowing his DNA was probably all over the scene, he'd torched the house.

Preston had been *positive* when Molly heard about her precious grandparents being dead, she'd come home.

But she hadn't. Not for over a month. It had been frustrating and infuriating. But eventually she'd shown up, just like he'd known she would.

He'd been elated to see her again—except for the fact that she'd shown up with not one, but *two* men. He wouldn't have been surprised if she was fucking them both!

Preston grabbed another beer, draining that one just as quickly, chasing it with a shot from the bourbon stashed in his bag. Molly's punishment for daring to give herself to someone else would be severe.

Despite his fury that she'd gone and hooked up with another man—or men—he'd still been relieved to see her after failing to track her down for so long. She'd lost some weight, but it didn't matter what she looked like. He'd fuck her anyway.

He turned his attention back to the binoculars, to the house in the distance. The curtains or blinds were all shut, so he couldn't see anything going on inside. As he watched and drank, disgust and rage filled him. He *hated* that his bitch girlfriend was cheating on him—but he'd punish her for that.

Then convince her that he'd put it behind him. That they were good . . .

It was fun to fuck with her head. He knew she must have freaked out after seeing her emails that morning. He had no idea how many people might have contacted her, but if the responses to his post were any indication, it had to have been a lot. Just the thought of her panic and confusion made him smile.

While messing with her head was a good time, he had to be careful because of the damn protective order she'd placed on him. He couldn't be caught communicating with her, or on camera anywhere near her. But eventually, either she or that asshole she was living with would fuck up, and he'd be there.

Smiling, Preston whispered, "Soon."

He headed back to where he'd left his car, another quarter of a mile away, a little less steady on his feet. When he arrived, he took a large swig from the whiskey bottle he'd left under the passenger seat before starting the engine and pulling out onto the road. He had to get back to Chicago. But he'd return, ready to take his Molly back to where she belonged.

Chapter Fifteen

Molly had awoken early the next day and sighed in relief when she'd checked her phone and didn't have thousands of horrible emails or texts waiting for her. She'd created a new email address the night before and sent it out to only those few people who needed it.

The only text that morning was from Taylor, asking if they were still on for hanging out at Silverstone Towing.

Molly reassured her they were, and got up to shower. She went downstairs before Mark finished his workout in the garage and had his protein shake waiting for him when he came back in the house.

She had to admit that she loved the look of pleasure on his face when he saw her. He went up to shower, and Molly couldn't help but fantasize about how he'd look naked with water cascading down his body.

After he came back downstairs, they'd chatted about the day ahead. When they'd left, the driveway had already been cleared of nails, and Molly had seen Mark looking around carefully as he'd pulled out onto the road. When his muscles had stayed relaxed, she'd figured Preston wasn't following them.

They'd just arrived at Silverstone without incident, and Mark turned to her before they got out of his car. "Let me know when you're ready to leave."

"I don't want to rush you if you have work to do," she said. "I can hang out for as long as you need. The last thing I want is to interrupt whatever you're doing with your team. I know firsthand how important it is."

She couldn't read the look on Mark's face.

"What?" she asked.

"A lot of women wouldn't be as understanding or patient," he said.

"A lot of women weren't being held captive in a hole in the middle of a jungle, knowing no one was looking for her," Molly quipped.

"Good point," Mark said quietly.

"If you need to be here all night, discussing plans and studying maps, I can sleep in one of the rooms upstairs. I don't ever want to rush you, because your safety is at stake. I'm aware that what you do is dangerous. Take as much time as you need—I'll never complain about your meetings with the others taking too long."

Mark reached for her then. Put a hand on her nape and pulled her toward him. Molly braced herself on the console between them. He touched his forehead to hers and simply held her for a moment. Molly could feel his warm breath against her lips, and she wanted nothing more than to press her mouth to his, but fear held her back. She was afraid that, despite how often he touched her, she was misreading things, and he was merely being a supportive friend.

Being around Mark and pretending she didn't love him was killing her, but not being around him would hurt more.

"You're one of a kind," Mark said after a minute. Then he pulled back. "Come on, I'm sure Taylor's waiting for you."

It took Molly a second to get her equilibrium back, but she climbed out of her side of the truck and walked up to Mark, who was waiting for her at the front of his car. They continued side by side into Silverstone, grabbing their name tags off the metal board next to the door on their way.

As soon as they entered the great room, Shawn called out a greeting from the kitchen. The smell of cinnamon rolls was thick in the air, making Molly hungry all over again, even though she'd just eaten breakfast not too long ago.

Taylor came up to them, and Molly saw her eyes flick to their name tags. At first it had been a huge adjustment knowing that Taylor didn't know who she was every time she saw her, but it barely registered now. Taylor was who she was, and Molly adored hanging out with her.

"Hey," Taylor said, giving Molly a hug. Then Mark hugged Taylor, grinning when he pulled back. "I think you get more pregnant every time I see you," he remarked.

Taylor put a hand on her tiny belly. "Whatever. I think the little guy is growing extrafast."

Molly felt a pang of jealousy, but she pushed it back. This was Taylor, her friend, and she was thrilled for her. "Guy?" she asked, raising an eyebrow.

Taylor shrugged. "We've decided not to find out the baby's gender. Some days I'm convinced he's a boy, especially when he's kicking me, and other times I'm positive she's a girl. Today's a boy day."

"I don't think I'd be able to stand the anticipation. I'd need to know what I was having," Molly said.

"I've been pretty good about that . . . so far. Come on," Taylor said, grabbing Molly's hand. "Shawn made a batch of extra-cinnamony rolls for you."

"Is that a word?" Molly asked.

Taylor shrugged.

"I'm shocked that a renowned grammar nut like you would dare use a fake word," Molly teased.

"Hey, when Shawn says he used double the amount of cinnamon sugar in the pastries because he knows how much of a sweet tooth you have, I'm allowed to make up words to help describe the goodness," Taylor told her. "Besides, this week I'm craving sugar, so I benefit too."

Molly heard Mark chuckling behind her. He followed them to the edge of the kitchen, then caught her hand. "I'm going to head downstairs with the guys. If you need me, just text or knock on the door, okay?"

"Okay."

It looked like he was going to say something else, but Shawn interrupted him by bringing over a round tray of the most decadent-looking cinnamon rolls Molly had ever seen in her life.

"Holy crap," she breathed out in excitement.

"Lord, if you go into a sugar coma, try to make it to a bed before you collapse."

She giggled and glanced up at Mark.

He was looking down at her with an expression of amusement and—dare she think it—affection.

"Have a good visit with Taylor." Then he leaned down, kissed the top of her head, and headed for the hallway that led to the stairwell to the basement.

"Giiiirl," Taylor said after he'd left.

Molly spun around and found both Shawn and Taylor smiling at her.

"Looks like our visit is gonna be extra entertaining today," Taylor said.

Knowing she was going to be grilled about what was going on between her and Mark, Molly wrinkled her nose. If she knew what the hell was happening, she'd gladly spill the beans, but she was as confused as ever.

"Here, sugar always makes things better," Shawn told her, holding out a plate with an ooey-gooey mess of frosting and pastry.

"Thanks," Molly told him.

"And here's a huge cup of water; you're gonna need it," Taylor said with a grin, passing it over. Molly took the offered cup as Taylor grabbed her own plate and drink. Within a couple of minutes, they were sitting in the comfortable chairs in the basement, enjoying their sugary treats.

The two women started their conversation by talking about the emails Molly had received. Taylor had obviously heard about them from Eagle, and was suitably outraged. Then they discussed Taylor's pregnancy and how it was progressing.

"I'm scared," Taylor admitted.

"About what? The birth itself?" Molly asked.

"No."

"You can't be nervous about Eagle being a father. He dotes on you. He's gonna love that baby more than anything. He'll be so protective, the kid won't be able to do *anything* without him hovering."

"I know, isn't it awesome?" Taylor asked. "He's already said that he has no problem being the one to get up in the middle of the night. I mean, I'll have to feed the baby, but Eagle will just bring him or her *to* me rather than me always having to get up."

Molly put a hand to her chest and closed her eyes. "Swoon," she said.

Taylor laughed. "Right?"

"So, what are you nervous about?" Molly asked.

"You know about my condition. I'm scared my kid's gonna have the same thing. It runs in families. And even if he doesn't . . . I'm not going to recognize my own baby."

Molly leaned forward. "I have no doubt that you'll figure out a way to make it work. You're an amazing person, Taylor. You and Eagle already love that baby more than anything. I don't know everything there is to know about prosopagnosia, but I *do* know that the love you and Eagle share will make everything work out."

"Thanks," Taylor said softly.

"You're welcome."

"Enough about me. Let's talk about *you*," Taylor said with a smile.

"Do we have to?" Molly asked on a groan.

"Tell me about your job. You're an environmental engineer, right?"

"I was, yes."

"Was?" Taylor asked.

"I mean, I am," Molly backpedaled.

"I think your first answer was more honest. Were you fired?"

"Not exactly. But I just can't muster up any excitement for the job. I already called my boss and told him I wouldn't be coming back. The relief I felt after making the call was almost crippling."

"Have you thought about writing a book about what happened to you?" Taylor asked.

Molly looked at her friend with wide eyes. "What?"

"A book. An autobiography of sorts."

"I don't think anyone cares."

"That's not true," Taylor argued. "*I* care." She took a deep breath before continuing. "You haven't talked much about it, and I can respect that. I don't like thinking about that serial killer hunting me. But I really think people would be interested in what happened to you. Channels that show all those crime shows on TV are superpopular. People get sucked into that kind of thing. They want to know all the details. Remember Elizabeth Smart? People were desperate to know what happened to her when she was held by that psycho all those years. *She* wrote a book. And Jaycee Dugard has a book. The girls who were held by Ariel Castro wrote books.

"There are even a lot of books by former prisoners of war. Remember the woman soldier who was taken captive in Turkey? The one the press dubbed the American Princess? Sometimes people called her the Army Princess too. I proofread her book, and it was on the bestseller lists for *weeks.*"

"I don't want to be an object of morbid fascination," Molly said.

Taylor sat forward on her chair and put a hand on Molly's knee. "I don't really think that's what it is. I think we're fascinated about how some people survive the awful situations they find themselves in. I also suspect people are proud of the strength of the men and women who make it through horrible things like that. We can't imagine it happening to us, but we hope that we can be as strong as the people we read about if we're ever in a similar situation.

"What happened to you in Nigeria was horrible, and it was a freak thing. I talked to the author of that princess book, and she said it was cathartic to write it. And I know a lot of people in the industry. If you didn't want to actually write it yourself, we could find you a ghostwriter. But I think it's important to get your story out there."

Molly couldn't believe she was even contemplating writing about her experience. On the one hand, she wanted to forget it had ever happened, but on the other, helping others be strong appealed to her. Especially since she never thought she was all that brave or strong herself. But she'd made it out alive. "I'll think about it," she finally told Taylor.

"Good. And of course I'll proofread it for you."

Molly rolled her eyes and smiled. "Of course."

Taylor opened her mouth to say something else, but was interrupted by the door to the safe room opening. Bull, Eagle, Mark, and Gramps all piled out and ran for the stairwell.

"What's happening?" Molly asked, but the men were already gone.

"Help me up," Taylor asked, holding out a hand.

Molly pulled her out of the chair, and they followed the men up the stairs. They were all standing in the small dispatch room talking with Jose, who was on duty that morning.

"When did you last talk to him?" Bull asked.

"About an hour ago. He said he was going to grab something to eat, then he'd let me know when he was back on duty. I honestly forgot about it until we got a call, and I was going to assign it to him. He didn't answer the radio. I called his cell, and there's no answer on that either," Jose explained quickly.

"Did you trace his tow truck?" Eagle asked.

"Yeah, it's in a parking lot at Fifth and Main."

"Call the police. Let them know we need a welfare check," Gramps told Jose.

Jose nodded and reached for the phone.

The men of Silverstone all turned in tandem, stopping short when they saw Taylor and Molly in the hallway.

"What's wrong?" Taylor asked.

"We can't get ahold of Bart," Eagle told her. "We're gonna go check on him."

"All of you?" she asked.

"I'm staying," Mark said. "The others will go. Eagle can drive. If he's been hurt, Bull can drive the truck back here, and Gramps can go to the hospital with Eagle and Bart. I'll stay here and monitor the situation, and can call his family if it comes to that."

The men all nodded, approving Mark's plan, and filed by Molly and Taylor.

Following behind them, Molly saw Eagle kiss Taylor, then head for the door with the others. She turned to Mark. "If you need to go with them, go. I'll be fine here."

"I know you will, but honestly, I'd feel better staying here with you. We have no idea if this is Weldon's doing or something else entirely. I'd rather not take any chances."

Molly swallowed hard. This was her worst fear coming true. That Preston would strike out against others because of her.

Then something else occurred to her. No one had hesitated to act when they'd realized Bart was missing. They'd sprung into action without thought. The bottom line was that Bart was one of their own, and Silverstone obviously took care of their employees.

Unlike what had happened to her.

Maybe she wasn't being fair, but it hadn't seemed like Apex had done anything but run scared after she'd been taken. They hadn't left anyone behind to spearhead a search party, or to try to work with the Nigerian government. They'd simply left her behind.

"Can you give us a second?" Mark asked Taylor. She immediately nodded and went into the kitchen to talk with Shawn. "What are you thinking?" Mark asked, putting his finger under Molly's chin and meeting her gaze with his own.

She loved how sensitive he was when it came to her feelings. "I can't help but compare Silverstone's reaction to that of Apex . . . my former employer. Did they even try to find me? I don't think they did. Bart hasn't even been out of contact for an hour, and you guys are pulling out all the stops to find him."

"Listen to me. Are you listening?"

Molly nodded.

"I can't change the past. I wish I'd known you before you went overseas. But I was damn worried about you before I even knew you. You can ask the guys if you want. When we got the reports that an American had been taken along with the Nigerian schoolgirls, I was *not* happy. I pushed them to leave sooner than we were honestly ready, but I couldn't stand the thought of you being out there somewhere. Our job was Shekau . . . but my mind was on *you.*

"Apex is stupid not to realize that their greatest assets are the people who work for them. And that they're worth any amount of money to keep safe. Silverstone Towing is nothing without our employees. But Bart is more than just an employee. He's a friend. One we all like and respect. If he decided to take an extralong break and forgot to take his radio, fine. He'll be embarrassed, and he'll never do it again. But if he's been robbed, or he's hurt, or something else has happened, we'll do whatever it takes to help him."

"I know, and I respect you guys so much because of it."

"Rest assured, Molly, now that I *do* know you, nothing will stand in the way of me and the rest of Silverstone finding *you* if you go radio silent."

His words reassured her in a way she hadn't even known she needed to be reassured.

Once again, she found herself in his embrace. She'd hugged Mark more in the last few weeks than she'd ever hugged anyone before, save perhaps her grandparents. It should've surprised her, but it simply felt right.

It was a tense forty-five minutes as they waited to hear from the rest of the guys about Bart. When Mark's phone finally rang, Shawn, Taylor, and Molly unabashedly eavesdropped.

"You find him, Eagle?" Mark asked. "Good!"

Every muscle in Mark's body relaxed, and Molly sighed in relief.

"I'm going to put you on speaker, hang on," Mark said. "Okay, go ahead. What happened?"

"The cops were on scene when we got here. Looks like his blood sugar got too low. He decided to take a short power nap instead of eating—which, believe me, he won't do again. Gramps is on the way to the hospital with him to make sure he's good. Bull and I should be back soon. Taylor?"

"I'm here," she told her husband.

"You good?"

"Yeah, Eagle. I'm fine."

"So nothing looks out of place? Tampered with?" Mark asked his friend.

"No. His doors were locked, and I guess it took the cops quite a bit to rouse him enough to unlock them. This wasn't Weldon. I'd bet your entire fortune on it."

"Betting *my* fortune, huh?" He chuckled. "Okay, that makes me feel better. Thank you."

"I'll be back at the garage soon."

"Okay. Drive safe."

"Always."

Mark clicked off the phone and smiled at Molly. "Excitement for the day seems to be over. At least, let's hope it is."

Molly nodded. "Definitely."

"I'll start packing some lunch boxes for the drivers," Shawn said. "I should've thought about doing that already. They can still take a break and eat, but if Bart needs sugar immediately, he won't have to choose between getting fast food or a nap."

"Thanks, Archer. I'm sure everyone will appreciate that."

"And I'll make sure lunch is ready for Eagle and Bull when they get back. Gramps, too, when he returns from the hospital. I thought I'd make a grilled-lemon-chicken salad. Sound good?"

"Sounds perfect," Mark reassured him. "You want to stay?" he asked Molly.

She nodded. "If that's okay."

"Of course. Go on back downstairs with Taylor. I'll bring lunch down to you both."

"You sure?"

"Yup."

"Thanks."

"Anytime."

And Molly had a feeling Mark truly meant that. Taylor thanked him, too, and they headed back to the basement.

It wasn't until an hour and a half later—after the guys had gotten back, and after Molly and Taylor had eaten, and after Bull and Gramps had left for the day, and while Eagle was upstairs talking to Shawn—that the women resumed their previous conversation.

"I know I'd stepped away upstairs, but I couldn't help but overhear what you said about your old company," Taylor told Molly. "I was as surprised as you were when I found out how well the Silverstone employees have it. They have literally zero turnover. It's unheard of. But everyone who works here knows how good they have it. They work their asses off too. I wasn't surprised that the guys immediately headed out to check on Bart. It's just who they are."

Molly nodded. "I agree. They didn't have to take me with them after they found me. It would've been easier, and they would've been home sooner, if they hadn't."

"So . . . you don't want to work for Apex anymore. I may or may not have convinced you to write a book on your experiences. But then . . . what? What do you *really* want to do?"

Molly glanced at the door to the safe room uneasily.

"It's soundproof. Smoke can't hear you, if that's what you're worried about," Taylor said.

It *was* what she was nervous about. But trusting Taylor, she took a deep breath to admit her deepest desire.

~

After finding Bart, the team hadn't really been able to fully concentrate on researching for their next mission anymore. So they'd called it a day and agreed to try again soon. Smoke had stayed in the safe room, giving Taylor and Molly time to continue to get to know each other. He loved that they were getting along so well. He knew Molly had accepted an offer to visit Skylar's kindergarten classroom at some point in the near future as well. He was hoping both ladies would ultimately contribute to Molly's staying in the area. Surely having close friends here in Indianapolis would be a deterrent to leaving, right?

His phone buzzed with a text, and Smoke looked down.

Eagle: Check on Taylor for me, would ya? I want to make sure she really is all right after everything that happened. Stress isn't good for the baby.

Smoke: Will do. But you could come down the stairs and do it yourself.

Eagle: I could. But she's been telling me I've gotten too protective lately, so I'm trying to back off.

Smoke: So you want to get me in trouble?

Eagle: You can use the camera. Just check to make sure they're good. Please?

Smoke: Fine. But you owe me.

It wasn't really a hardship to check on the women; Smoke didn't mind making sure Molly was all right after everything that had happened. He headed over to the bank of computer screens and brought up the security camera in the basement. The two women looked comfortable, and Taylor definitely didn't look stressed.

He reached over to turn it off and report back to Eagle . . . when something Molly was saying to Taylor made him hesitate.

"Living with Mark has been both the best and worst thing to happen to me in my life."

Smoke frowned. He hadn't thought Molly was unhappy in the slightest.

Knowing he was crossing a line by listening to a conversation she thought was private, but not able to move from his spot in front of the camera, Smoke leaned in so he didn't miss a word.

"What do you mean?" Taylor asked. "I thought you were happy there."

"I am! I mean, it's great. I feel safe. Mark has enough security there to keep the president secure. I just . . . he's amazing. And funny. And so damn good looking. Every time he smiles at me with that dimple, my knees go weak."

"And that's a bad thing?" Taylor asked, her brow raised in clear skepticism.

"No. But . . . I'm pretty sure I'm in love with him, Taylor. And it kills me to suspect he's just being nice. That he'd keep anyone safe if they needed it."

Smoke's mouth fell open.

Molly was in love with him?

Fuck! He'd been trying to go slow because he didn't want to freak her out with how much *he* was falling for *her*. What a mess.

Taylor laughed and shook her head. "If you think Smoke would let just any woman move into his house, you're insane. That's *his* safe place too. We've all been over to his house more since you moved in than before they went to Nigeria. He might do whatever he could to help someone else he'd rescued from a horrible situation—find an apartment for them, set up a security system, etcetera—but he wouldn't just move them into his house."

"Really?" Molly asked.

"Really. Now stop beating around the bush, and answer my question. What is it you *really* want to do with your life? You're living with a man you think you love, you aren't sure how he feels about you, and you've quit your job. Are you going to go back to Chicago? Are you going to find another environmental engineering job after you write your book? Don't think about it. Just tell me what your heart wants to do."

Write a book? Smoke had no idea what Taylor was talking about, but he didn't have time to wonder before Molly was talking again.

"You're going to think I'm completely crazy."

"No, I'm not. Trust me."

Molly took a deep breath and looked over at the safe-room door. Smoke felt bad once again that he was listening in, but he couldn't shut off the camera *now*. Not before hearing what Molly truly wanted.

"I want to be a mother," she admitted softly. So quietly he almost didn't hear. "I thought I had lots of time. But I'm in my midthirties, and I swear I can hear my biological clock ticking. Maybe it's ridiculous and antifeminist, but I thought I'd be married by now. I never wanted to work for Apex for long. I thought I'd meet someone, marry, get pregnant, then I'd quit to stay home and raise our child." She paused for a long moment, then put a hand over her eyes. "It's stupid, I know!"

"It's *not* stupid," Taylor protested. "You're allowed to want what you want."

"So many women would've killed to get where I was at Apex. I feel like it's frowned upon for women to *not* want to work in today's society. To want to be a stay-at-home mom. But . . . ever since losing my own parents, I've wanted to give someone else the kind of love they gave me."

"And you don't think you can do that now?" Taylor asked.

"As I said, I'm not getting any younger. And now . . . I'm not sure I can imagine having kids with anyone other than Mark. Which is insane, since I'm sure he just sees me as a fragile damsel in distress, what with all his forehead kisses."

Smoke couldn't believe what he was hearing.

Molly not only loved him—she wanted *children* with him?

It was all he could do to not spring out of his chair, barge into the basement, throw Molly over his shoulder, and run to the nearest bed.

"He does *not* see you as a damsel in distress," Taylor argued. "If you ask me, the man more than wants you right back."

"You think he does? I'd thought maybe, but . . ." Molly shook her head. "No, you're just being nice."

"I'm not. Hell, with my condition, I don't even always understand facial expressions. But Smoke can't take his eyes off you, Molly. And didn't you tell me earlier that he took you bowling? Girl, that was a *date*. Not to mention how crazy he gets when he thinks about your ex harassing you. Men who only think of a woman as a friend, or as someone who just needs protection, don't act like that."

Smoke grinned. He'd thought he was being sneaky up to now by watching Molly when she wasn't aware, but apparently he hadn't been as smooth as he'd thought. Taylor had sure noticed.

"You want my advice?" Taylor asked.

Molly nodded.

"Tell him what you want."

"Tell him I love him and want to have his babies?" Molly asked, her eyes wide with disbelief. "Um . . . *no!*"

Taylor laughed. "Okay, maybe not quite like that. But if neither of you makes the first move, you're just going to continue to be miserable."

"I've looked up apartments that I could rent," Molly admitted quietly.

Every muscle in Smoke's body went taut. The *hell* she was going to move out of his house, not after he'd heard how she really felt about him.

"You have?" Taylor asked.

"Yeah. I've decided that I want to stay here in the Indianapolis area, but I can't live with Smoke forever. And I'm already dreading the day he asks me to move out. And God forbid he meets a woman he wants to date before then. I couldn't deal with that. So it's just smarter to make the first move."

"Do me a favor and talk to him before you do anything crazy like sign a lease," Taylor said.

"Of course," Molly said. "He probably knows which parts of the city are better than others for renters."

"Yeah, that too," Taylor said dryly.

Smoke was done. He clicked off the camera. If Molly thought she was moving out of his house, she was sorely mistaken. She wasn't nearly as safe elsewhere. And if she wanted babies, he'd happily do his best to give them to her. She was probably right about her biological clock, and if they were going to have kids, they needed to get on that as soon as possible.

He had no problem with that whatsoever.

Smoke turned off all the computers in the room and made sure any security-sensitive materials were locked away before he headed for the door. He didn't know if the women were done talking, but it was time he had a heart-to-heart with Molly. At home. Where they couldn't be interrupted.

Both women looked up at him in surprise when he entered the basement. Molly flushed . . . and he couldn't help but wonder if she turned pink all over when she blushed.

He couldn't wait to find out.

"You ready to go home?" he asked.

"Um . . . yeah. Is everything all right?" Molly asked as she stood.

"Yup."

"Oh, okay." She turned to Taylor and gave her a hug. Smoke saw Taylor whisper something in her ear, and Molly nodded. Then she turned to face him. "I'm ready."

Smoke held out his hand and relaxed when she took it. They all headed up the stairs and entered the great room just as Eagle was entering from outside.

"Eagle, good timing. I'm headed home with Molly," Smoke told his friend. He hadn't texted him back to let him know the women were good, but he figured Eagle could see that for himself.

"Okay. Hey, flower," Eagle said, heading for his wife.

Smoke didn't even slow down as he towed Molly toward the door. He was impatient to get her home. Now that he knew how she felt about him, nothing was going to stop him from making his move.

Chapter Sixteen

Molly was nervous for some reason. Maybe it was because she'd admitted her deepest desires out loud. Or maybe because Mark hadn't said much on the drive back to his house.

He parked inside the garage and waited for her to come around the car. He took her hand and practically dragged her inside. He stopped at the alarm pad long enough to disarm, then arm it again, then he pulled her through the great room, up the stairs, and into his bedroom.

Molly had no idea what was going on.

Mark pulled her over to the bed and sat her on the side. Then he knelt in front of her and put his hands on her knees. He looked extremely serious . . . and Molly licked her lips nervously.

"I'm going to just come out and say this to get it out of the way," Mark said. "Eagle texted and wanted me to check on Taylor. I turned on the security camera. You know we have them in every room at the garage, right? Every room but the bathrooms."

Molly nodded. She *did* know that. He'd told her the first time he'd given her a tour of Silverstone Towing.

"Right. I didn't mean to eavesdrop . . . but I *had* to know what it was about living with me you didn't like so I could fix it."

Molly gasped. "Oh shit!" she whispered.

Mark's hands tightened. "Do *not* panic," he ordered.

"Too late," Molly retorted, remembering everything she'd told Taylor.

"Why do you think I kept this house?" he asked.

She was confused about the abrupt change in topic, but relieved too. "Because it was your uncle's."

"No. I mean, I loved the old coot, but I could've sold the property and bought a house with a lot less upkeep. There's no way I needed a five-bedroom house. I remodeled it and added a couple of bathrooms . . . because kids are messy as hell, and when they're teenagers, they take forever to get ready."

Molly stared at Mark, barely breathing.

"I wanted kids, Molly. A large family. I wanted to fill this old house with laughter, and sisters shouting at brothers, and a ton of mayhem. But with each year that went by, I realized that I'd probably never have any of that."

They stared at each other for a long moment. Molly could hardly believe what she was hearing.

"I want to offer a proposition," Mark said lightly, breaking the silence.

Molly's mouth was dry, so she didn't say anything, merely waited to hear what he was going to offer.

"I'll give you all the children you want," he said bluntly. "But I want to be involved in their lives—and yours. I know things between us started off on an unusual footing, but having you here, in my house, makes me happy. Happier than I've been in a very long time.

"I don't want to freak you out, but . . . you're *it* for me, Mol. You're everything I've ever wanted in a woman, and I've thought about nothing but taking you in my arms and making love to you every damn time you head up to bed, every damn night. Let me love you. Give you children. You can stay here with me, have our child, and never have to work again."

Molly knew her mouth was hanging open, but she couldn't help it. "You can't be serious."

"I'm dead serious," he countered. He moved suddenly, pushing her back until she was lying on the bed, Mark hovering over her. She could feel his hard cock against her thigh, and she unconsciously spread her legs wider, wanting more of his weight.

"I love you, Molly. And I'm not just saying that because you said it first. It's because of who you are. You're everything I've ever wanted in a partner. Stay with me. Let me make love to you. Let me give you the children we both want."

She wanted to say yes. Wanted that so bad . . . but this seemed too fast.

Her heart was beating a million miles an hour, and she was panting, as if she'd just run a marathon. All her life she'd been cautious, especially after her parents had been killed. She didn't take chances. Going to Nigeria was the biggest risk she'd ever taken, and look how that had turned out.

"I've been hurt too much in my life to believe this is true," she whispered honestly.

"I admit that I probably wouldn't have said anything tonight if I hadn't overheard your conversation," Mark said. "But that doesn't change the fact that I get up in the middle of the night just to check on you. To watch you sleep in your bed and wish I could join you. It doesn't change the fact that I've gotten myself off in the shower every morning for the last two weeks.

"This is new for me, too, Molly. It scares me how much I already love you. The thought of Weldon putting his hands on you makes me *insane*. We both want the same thing, but if for some reason we realize in the future we don't love each other anymore, we can still coparent our children. I have enough money to make sure you and our kids won't want for anything. And I can give you as much time as you want to decide—nothing has to happen right this second."

Molly swallowed hard and licked her lips. She tightened her hold on his biceps. She could practically hear Taylor screaming "Say yes!" in her ear.

The fact that she was seriously considering this was nuts. But she couldn't deny he was offering everything she'd ever wanted.

Mark was offering her heart's desire on a silver platter—and his love as well.

"Okay," she whispered.

"Okay?" he asked. "You'll let me give you a baby?"

Molly nodded.

"You want to wait?"

"No."

His eyes dilated, and Molly actually felt his dick twitch against her leg.

"I'm clean. It's been a long time since I've been with anyone, and I got tested right after that relationship, just in case I met someone I wanted to be with," Mark said.

Molly wrinkled her nose. She hated this part. The sex talk was uncomfortable and awkward, but they were adults. It had to be done. "Me too. I mean, it's been a few years for me, and I had to have a million tests done before going overseas to make sure I was healthy."

"To be clear," Mark said in a low tone that made goose bumps break out on her arms. "I'm going to take you bare. Right now. I've never—and I mean *never*—made love to a woman without a condom. I might've wanted children, but I didn't want to have them with the wrong person."

"How do you know I'm the right person?" Molly blurted, still having a hard time wrapping her mind around what was happening.

"Because I feel it here," Mark said, putting a hand over his heart. Then he picked up one of her hands and put it on his chest. "Feel that? Feel how hard my heart's beating? That's for you, Mol. I can't wait to sink inside you like I've dreamed of doing for so many nights. You make me laugh, you scare the shit out of me, and you've made me happier than I can ever remember being."

He was killing her.

"Are you sure about this? I mean, we haven't even kissed. How can we love each other when we haven't even done more than hug?" she asked.

Mark leaned down and put his forehead against hers. "I love how when you sleep, you take up as much of the bed as you can. I love how you bite your lip when you're concentrating. I love how your eyes light up when you see the deer that like to hang out on my property. I love how deeply you cared for your nana and papa, and how you savor your first cup of coffee in the morning, and how we can have long discussions about everything from politics to whether penguins used to be able to fly, without getting upset at each other. I love that you enjoy bowling, and that you're willing to try new things simply because I recommend them. I love that you love my friends and how well you fit in with them. But most of all, I love the way I feel when I'm around you. As if I've finally found the reason I do what I do . . . to keep you safe from all the bad in the world."

"Mark," Molly whispered, overwhelmed.

"Love is more than sex," he went on. "But trust me, I have no doubt we're going to be great together. Again, I'm sorry I listened in on your conversation with Taylor, but I'm not sorry it's brought us to this point. It saved us from wasting a lot more time. I love you, Molly. I'm thirty-eight years old. I know what I feel. I'm only sorry it took so long for us to find each other."

Molly closed her eyes and sighed. "I'm scared," she admitted, then opened her eyes and met Mark's gaze. He'd pulled back and was looking down at her with concern. "But I do love you. I've never met someone like you. You take me as I am, faults and all. I'm terrified that you'll wake up one day and wonder what the hell you're doing with me. Everyone I've ever loved has left me. If you do, too, it'll break me."

"I'm not going to leave you," Mark said in as serious a tone as she'd ever heard from him. "I've waited a long time for you. I'd be an idiot to let you go now that I've found you."

Molly opened her mouth to say that he could change his mind down the road, but she didn't get the chance. He shifted upward so he was straddling her hips. His hands gathered the material of her shirt, and he ordered, "Arms up."

She was so surprised, she did as he asked without thought. Then she was lying under him, wearing just her bra.

But that didn't slow Mark down. "Arch your back."

She did, and he unhooked her bra and drew it down her arms.

Her nipples puckered, both from the chilly air and the lust-filled look in his eyes. But he didn't touch them. His hands went to her jeans. He deftly undid the button and unzipped them. He straightened to his knees and shoved the pants, with her panties, down her thighs. Molly toed off her shoes, and then wiggled out of the pants.

Then Mark stilled above her—and Molly panicked. She'd gained back much of the weight she'd lost, but she still wasn't very curvy. Her breasts were only a full A cup, and she'd overheard way too many comments in her life about how she needed to eat more to be comfortable naked in front of Mark.

"Fuck," he breathed.

His hands went to her breasts and covered them. His hands were so big, they almost spanned her entire chest. He pinched one nipple, and Molly almost came out of her skin. She arched into him and moaned. She gripped his wrists, holding on for dear life. He continued to play with her nipples, and when she looked up at him, she saw a huge smile on his face. His damn dimple seemed to be winking at her.

"They're sensitive," he said, sounding way too pleased about that.

"They're small," Molly countered.

"They're fucking perfect," Mark corrected, then he leaned down and replaced his fingers with his lips, and she nearly lost her mind once more. Molly wiggled and squirmed against him, not able to lie still. When her hands slipped up his arms and encountered material, she groaned in protest.

She tried to pull his shirt off, but didn't make much headway since he wouldn't let go of her nipple long enough for her to get it over his head.

"Mark," she whined.

"Yeah?" he asked distractedly.

"I want you naked too."

That seemed to shake him out of his trance. He went up on his knees and ripped his shirt over his head. As Molly was staring at his honest-to-God six-pack abs, they flexed as he stood up next to the bed.

He stripped off the rest of his clothes, then ordered, "Scoot up."

Molly moved to the center of his bed and pushed the covers down so she was lying on the bottom sheet. Then he came back to her, crawling on his hands and knees, as if he were stalking prey.

He climbed up her body and didn't stop until he was once again over her. But this time he came down so his flesh pressed against her own. Molly could feel how wet she was as he nestled between her legs.

She couldn't believe this man loved her. It made no sense . . . but she believed him. He'd never lied to her, had even come right out and admitted he'd spied on her and Taylor.

"I wanted to go slow, but the thought of being inside you bare has me so worked up, I think if you so much as touch me, I'm gonna explode," he admitted.

Molly opened her mouth to tell him he didn't need to go slow when his hand moved between their bodies and brushed against her clit.

Her hips immediately thrust upward. She wanted more of that.

Mark grinned. "Fuck, I love how sensitive you are."

She wanted to hold back, wanted to be coy, but couldn't. It was as if Mark had little electric probes connected to his fingers. Every time he touched her, she jerked and writhed and craved more. He dipped his finger lower, scooping up some of the juices dripping out of her, and lubricated her clit lazily.

"Mark," she protested. "More."

He eased his body to the side, propping himself up with an elbow and looking down her body as he began to play with her. His finger never really gave her what she wanted. He teased, running it along one side of her clit, then playing in her folds, then going back up to circle around to the other side.

Molly thought she might go out of her skin. When he lowered his head and once more took a nipple into his mouth, she practically screeched in frustration. "Please," she begged. "Please, I need you inside me!"

~

Smoke was holding on to his control by a thread. Molly was a wildcat beneath him. Her hips were thrusting up against his hand, and she was writhing and moaning, touching him wherever she could. It was all he could do to keep hold of her. It was exciting, and something he'd experienced with few women before. Too often they'd lain docile and submissive under him.

Not his Molly. He knew if she had the strength, she would've flipped him onto his back by now and had her way with him.

That thought definitely appealed too. He could picture her on top, taking his cock inside her body, then riding him hard and fast, her hair tumbling around her, small tits bouncing on her chest.

"Fuck," he muttered as his cock jerked, and precome oozed from the tip. He was losing the battle to stay in control. He needed to be inside Molly. Now.

He lifted his head from her chest and looked down her body. She was thin, yes, but he loved every fucking inch of her. She was perfectly made as far as he was concerned. He stopped teasing and began to work her clit furiously, hoping it wouldn't take too long for her to go over the edge. He paid attention to what she seemed to like, and it was mere minutes before her mouth fell open, and her body began to shake.

She was so beautiful as she orgasmed. Smoke knew he'd want to see her like this every fucking night.

He moved even as she tried to close her thighs. She groaned long and low as Smoke used his knees to keep her legs open. He notched the head of his weeping cock to her soaking-wet folds and pushed inside.

The first feel of her hot warmth against the bare skin of his dick almost had him spurting prematurely. He grabbed the base of his cock and squeezed hard, staving off his orgasm.

"Damn, Mol," he groaned.

Her hands found his ass, and she pulled him toward her, hard. Grunting at her unexpected strength, Smoke had to put both hands against the mattress to catch himself so he wouldn't crush her.

"More!" she begged, wrapping her legs around him, hooking her ankles together over his ass.

He could feel little tremors deep inside her body from the orgasm he'd just given her, and as he sank balls deep into her body, he groaned, closed his eyes, and threw his head back. She was burning him alive. He'd never felt such intense pleasure while making love to a woman. Ever.

He opened his eyes and looked down at Molly. She was smiling at him and had the most satisfied look on her face. Her hair was in disarray on his pillow . . . and he vowed right then and there that she'd never spend a night away from him again. She belonged right here. In his bed. Under him, over him, next to him.

"Mine," he growled, shoving himself deeper inside her.

Her eyes widened, and she inhaled sharply. "Yours!" she agreed. "And you're mine. No one else gets this."

Smoke couldn't help but smile.

"I'm serious," she said fiercely.

"I'm yours, and you're mine," he said, pulling back, then thrusting hard. Again, he wanted to go slow, but now that he was inside her, and it was the most amazing thing he'd ever felt in his life, he couldn't. Later, he'd worship her properly. He'd eat her out and feel her orgasm on his tongue. Then he'd take her from behind, and let her ride him, and fuck her in the shower.

But for now, all he could think about was filling her up with his come.

She wanted a baby? He'd fucking give them one.

"Hold on, this is gonna be hard and fast," he warned.

"Fuck me," Molly breathed.

The swear word coming from her lips and her declaration that he was hers pushed Smoke over the edge. He knelt up and grabbed her hips, holding her still for his thrusts. He easily glided in and out of her body since she was soaked from her earlier orgasm. Her tits jiggled with every thrust, and Smoke wished he had another set of hands to squeeze and pinch her nipples as he took her.

He had no idea how long he fucked his woman, but knew it wasn't nearly long enough. It would *never* be enough. One second he was enjoying how she felt around him, and the next he was done for.

Ropes of come flew out of his cock, coating her channel and making it even easier to slide in and out of her body. Amazingly, Smoke stayed semihard afterward. He supposed it was because he'd waited so damn long to fuck Molly, even his cock didn't want to stop.

"Holy shit, Mark," she panted as she gripped his arms.

Regretting she hadn't come a second time, he said, "Touch yourself. I want to feel you come around me."

Without hesitation, she moved one of her hands between them. He could feel the back of her hand against his pubic hair as she fingered her clit.

"Yeah, like that. God, that's so sexy," he muttered, looking down between them. He kept up his thrusts, though no longer as desperate as he'd been.

Molly wasn't docile in this either. Her fingers moved as fast as lightning over her bundle of nerves. Her hips pumped up and down in time with his glides, her whole body writhing sensually under him.

"I'm close!" she huffed.

Mark wanted to keep thrusting, but instead forced himself to push inside her as far as he could go and hold still. Molly moaned loudly, and she almost strangled his cock. Her inner muscles clenched so hard around him it felt as if he wouldn't be able to pull out of her . . . not that he would mind staying inside Molly forever.

She thrashed under him, and it took both hands on her hips to keep himself lodged inside her body as she squeezed the life out of him. When her orgasm subsided, he began fucking her hard and fast once more. It only took a dozen thrusts before he was coming a second time. Not as hard as before, but just as satisfying.

They were both sweating and out of breath . . . and Smoke could think of nothing other than how much he loved the woman beneath him.

Holding her to him so he wouldn't get dislodged, Smoke rolled until Molly was straddling him. She sat up just a bit to look at him. Smoke could feel their combined juices dripping down his balls, but didn't care that he'd be lying in a wet spot before too much longer.

"I love you," he told her, gazing up into her eyes.

He saw a sheen of tears fill them, but she didn't look away. "I love you too," she whispered.

Smoke pulled her down so her head was resting on his shoulder.

"I should get up and clean off."

"No," Smoke said quickly. "Stay. My little swimmers need to stay right where they are for the time being."

Molly chuckled against him. "You know the odds of me getting pregnant after one time are low, right?"

Smoke shrugged. "Then we'll have to do that again later."

Molly picked her head up. "Are you sure?" she asked.

"One hundred percent. I hate the circumstances that made you flee all the way to Nigeria, but I can't be sorry you were there," he said honestly. "You've changed my life for the better. And if you get pregnant, it'll be the happiest day of my life yet. You may have always wanted to be a mother, but I've always wanted to be a dad too."

Molly put her head back on his shoulder, and he could feel the wetness of her tears against his skin. He didn't say anything, as he felt as if *he* could cry right then himself.

Lying there with Molly, he finally felt complete. All his life he'd wanted a woman with similar dreams of a big family, and now, here she was. And she loved *him*. His cock was still deep inside her; his come was coating her channel, inside her body, looking for an egg to impregnate; and he was truly, blissfully happy.

"I'll give you space to spread out in a second," he whispered, but to his surprise, he heard Molly give a slight snore. He looked down at her without moving and saw that she was fast asleep. She'd passed out on top of him.

Figuring she'd move when she got uncomfortable, Smoke sighed. Molly felt absolutely perfect right where she was.

It was still early—the sun hadn't even set yet—but he didn't resist the urge to close his eyes. He needed to feed his woman in an hour or two, and he couldn't wait to see her padding around his house in nothing but one of his T-shirts. He'd worked her hard—and had plans to let her do the work next time—but for now, he was content to fall asleep with her breath on his neck and her slight weight pinning him to the mattress.

Chapter Seventeen

"That's it . . . harder, Mol!" Mark ordered.

Molly braced her hands on Mark's chest and rode him faster, the sun just beginning to brighten the room around them. The sound of their skin slapping together was loud in the otherwise quiet morning.

She looked down as she fucked the man she was head over heels in love with, and couldn't keep the smile from her face. He was staring where they were joined as she moved, and she could just imagine what he saw. She'd done the same thing when he'd made love to her last night. The sight of his cock covered in their juices sliding in and out of her body had been erotic and exciting as hell.

As she'd expected, Mark didn't let her stay in control for long. It wasn't in his nature. He flexed his stomach muscles and flipped her over onto her back, thrusting into her even harder and faster than she'd been able to take him. In less than a minute, he pushed inside her so far it almost hurt, and held himself there as he came.

She'd lost count of how many times he'd come inside her. Her hips were sore, her pussy was sore, even her nipples were sore from when he'd played with them earlier, but she couldn't have been happier.

She had no idea where she was in her cycle, if it was even possible for her to get pregnant right now, but if she wasn't already carrying his child, it wasn't for lack of trying.

Mark had blown her mind the night before when he'd offered to give her the children she wanted. Then he'd blown it further by admitting he loved her.

She had everything she wanted in her life right here in her arms. And she was terrified of losing it. Of doing something stupid to make Mark regret his offer. Of Preston ruining what she'd found.

"No negative thoughts when I'm inside you," Mark ordered.

Molly smiled. "Sorry."

"This is going to work. *We* work," he insisted, as if he could read her mind.

Molly was grateful that he didn't harp on her when she started thinking negatively. He merely helped her adjust her thoughts. "We do. It's almost scary how well we know each other after such a short period of time," she commented.

Mark shifted, not pulling out of her as they cuddled. "Tell me about this book Taylor wants you to write."

Molly realized they'd never gotten around to talking about that the night before. After a short nap, Mark had woken her up, and they'd made dinner together. Then he'd taken her back up to his room, where he'd eaten her to two orgasms, then made love to her again.

He'd woken her up in the middle of the night to take her from behind, then this morning, insisting she ride *him* this time.

"She thinks I should write a book about my kidnapping." Molly waited for him to frown and tell her it wasn't a good idea. But instead, he nodded.

"I think that's a great idea. People are fascinated by that sort of thing."

"I wouldn't talk about you guys . . . well, at least not by name," she told him.

"And we appreciate that. We can do what we do because people don't know who we are and don't expect us. We're only four men, but many times that works in our favor. We can move faster than larger teams, and because we don't have to worry about government red tape, we can act when we need to—we don't need to ask anyone's permission."

"I'm proud of you," Molly told him.

"Thanks. You have no idea how much that means to me. Most people would think we're murderers."

"That's just stupid," Molly said heatedly. "You're doing the world a favor, and if people can't see that, it's their problem, not yours."

Molly screeched in surprise when he rolled them, then sat up with her in his arms. He picked her up and walked toward his bathroom.

"I can walk," Molly protested, even as she snuggled into his chest.

"I know. But why walk when I can carry you?"

"You're going to spoil me," Molly told him.

"Good. You need more spoiling," Mark said easily.

He sat her down on the counter, and Molly winced at the cold marble under her ass. He put his hands on either side of her hips and leaned close. Molly placed her hands on his sides and held on to him.

"It's funny, every time I've seen you sleeping, you've taken up as much of the bed as possible. Spread eagle. Your limbs stretched toward each corner of the bed. I thought I was going to have to get used to sleeping on a small sliver of the mattress at the very edge. But every time you fall asleep in my arms, you don't move an inch. You clung to me last night as if I was a teddy bear. No spread limbs. No taking up all the space in the bed. I have to say . . . I fucking love that, Mol. Love that you cling to me as if you don't want me to move even one inch away from you."

Molly knew she was blushing, but she did her best to meet his eye. "I'm not sure what to say to that."

"You don't have to say anything. Just letting you know how much I love having you in my bed. I'm going to turn on the water to let it warm up. Brush your teeth, use the bathroom . . . but know that I'm going to take you again when we're in that shower. I can't seem to get enough of you. I might get blisters on my damn dick, but you feel so incredible it's hard to care. Coming inside of you brings out the caveman in me. I'm sorry."

"Don't apologize," Molly told him. "I like your caveman."

He smiled, and his damn dimple made her instantly wet once more. "Good. Me Tarzan, you Jane. Now get your ass in gear, and get in that shower."

Molly laughed and rolled her eyes. "If you'd scoot back, I could move."

But Mark didn't step away from her. His face lost the teasing look, and he leaned down and kissed her.

They'd shared their first kiss last night, after she'd said something when they were making dinner about how they'd made love but still hadn't kissed. Mark had made sure to remedy that thoroughly. He'd kissed her so passionately that her knees had gotten weak, and they'd almost burned their dinner.

Since then, he'd gone out of his way to kiss her as much as possible.

The kiss he gave her right then wasn't passionate— it was affectionate. "This is the first day of the rest of our lives," he said quietly. "I can't promise I won't irritate you, because I'm sure I will. We'll fight and bicker, and get sick of each other. We'll wonder what the hell we're doing and if we're fit to be parents. But no matter what happens, I'll never stop loving you. I'll move heaven and earth to keep you and our children safe. No one hurts you. No one hurts them. Understand?"

Molly nodded.

Then he kissed her on the forehead and stepped back. He cranked on the water in the huge shower and headed for the sink on the left side of the bathroom. They'd moved her stuff into the bathroom after dinner, and Molly hopped off the counter and went to "her" sink. She might've felt self-conscious walking around naked, but Mark had already made sure she knew beyond a shadow of a doubt that he loved her body.

After brushing her teeth, Molly stepped into the shower, where Mark was already waiting for her. He pulled her toward him, and she couldn't help but thank her lucky stars for bringing her this man.

～

"What are your plans for the rest of the week?" Molly asked him.

Smoke had skipped working out that morning, for obvious reasons, and he'd made Molly her favorite omelet. They'd just finished, and were still sitting side by side at his dining room table.

"It depends on you, really," he told her.

"I'm sure you have stuff you and your team need to discuss," she protested.

They did. Willis had sent over a huge packet of information about a situation in Jamaica that he said needed their attention. They hadn't had a chance to dig into it yet. "Are you going over to Skylar's school to help in her class?" he asked.

"Yeah, I think we want to do it in the next couple of days. She told me they're finishing up a unit on colors and they're going to do some huge art project. Apparently, it's going to be a mess, and Skylar said she could use all the help she can get."

Smoke chuckled. "I can imagine."

"Yeah, kindergartners and paint—I'm not sure about that combination."

"Are you really going to write that book?" he asked.

Molly shrugged. "I don't know. But I have to admit that writing down everything that happened, and how I felt during the experience, is appealing. I don't have nightmares about it anymore, but I can't help but think getting it all on paper could be cathartic."

"I agree. You know you can talk to me about anything if you need to. Or if you aren't comfortable with that, I can find a psychologist for you to meet with."

"I know, and thank you. The thing is, I think I'm more upset about Nana's and Papa's deaths than I am about what happened to me. It was bad, and I was beaten once, but I wasn't sexually assaulted. I was pretty much ignored most of the time. I don't know if the cops will ever find out exactly how my grandparents died . . . and I'm not sure I want to know if they do. I wouldn't be able to take hearing about their last minutes on earth. It might destroy me."

Smoke pushed back his chair and held out a hand. "Come here."

Molly immediately moved from her chair to his and settled on his lap. She laid her head on his shoulder and snuggled into him. He loved this. Loved being able to hold her close whenever he wanted. It was a huge change from having to hold himself back, as he'd been doing. It felt like such a blessing.

"I'm really sorry about Nana and Papa. I know I've said that before, but I am. I regret that I never got to meet them. Never got to tell them what an amazing job they did raising you. That they'll never get to see how well I treat you, or meet their great-grandchildren."

Smoke felt Molly inhale deeply against him. "Me too," she said softly. "They would've loved you. But, more importantly, they would've loved you for *me*."

Her words felt good. Really good.

"So . . . how about if, for now, we continue alternating spending time here at home and at Silverstone Towing? I can get work done while I'm there, and you can start putting your thoughts down on the computer. Taylor can help you organize and arrange the story, and I'm sure she can find someone to rewrite if necessary."

"If you're needed by the guys, you'll go in, though, right?" Molly asked.

"*We'll* go in. I don't want to leave you here by yourself," Smoke told her.

She looked at him. "I'm safe here," she said.

Smoke loved that she felt that way. But regardless, with Weldon still out there stalking her, he didn't feel good leaving her by herself. "I know, but"—he moved his hand to her inner thigh and caressed her through the cotton lounge pants she'd put on after their shower, much to his disappointment—"I like being with you."

Molly rolled her eyes. "I like being with you, too, but we can't just stay home and fuck all the time."

Smoke smiled.

"Figures you'd smile at that," she said.

"Actually, I'm smiling at you calling this *home*," Smoke admitted. "Although the fucking part was good too."

"Are we really doing this?" Molly asked softly. "Is this real?"

"Yes. And yes," Smoke told her. "And for the record, I want to marry you, Molly. But I didn't want to freak you out last night. I figured the baby thing was enough. I'm willing to wait as long as it takes for you to be comfortable with that, though . . . as long as you get comfortable with it before our first child is born."

Molly stared at him with wide eyes. "Was that a proposal?"

"No. It was a statement of my intent," Smoke told her.

"Oh, that's so much less stressful," she said with a roll of her eyes.

"Look at me," Smoke ordered, secretly thrilled when she immediately met his gaze. "I love you. That isn't going to change a day from now, or nine months from now. I know what I want, and that's you."

"What if I can't get pregnant? What if something's wrong?" she asked.

"That's not going to make me love you any less. And we'll deal with it if we need to. I'll get tested to make sure my sperm is viable, and you can get tested too. We both want to be parents, and we'll make that happen one way or another. Adoption, surrogacy, fertility treatments, whatever it takes. I've got the money to make our dreams come true, Molly. I'll bend over backward to make you happy, but I want you to be Mrs. Molly Chamberlin when we become parents for the first time."

"I don't think I'm ready for that yet," she told him.

Mark nodded. "I know. And that's why I'm telling you, so you can think about it and get used to the idea. I'm in this for the long haul. We might've started out our relationship in an intense way, but that doesn't make my love any less real."

"You scare me, Mark."

"You said that last night. You'll learn you have nothing to be afraid of when it comes to me. With you, I'm a pussycat."

"Oh yeah, *that* I don't believe. You're more like a grizzly bear. Taking what you want, when you want, and damn the consequences," she teased.

"Well, when what I want is you, damn straight," Smoke said.

"How about we go to Silverstone today, then we can stay home tomorrow," she suggested.

Smoke pouted. "I wanted to stay home today."

Molly laughed. "I know. But I'm sore. And at least if we take a few hours off from ravishing each other, I can be ready to go again tonight."

Smoke frowned. "Did I hurt you? You should've said something."

Molly put her hand on his cheek. "You didn't hurt me, Mark. Promise. I just need a little break."

"We can stay here. I can keep my hands off you. I think." The last bit was added softly.

She smiled. "I don't trust *myself*," she admitted, running her hands down his chest. "You're pretty sexy."

"Right, the garage it is," Smoke said, abruptly standing and putting Molly on her feet in front of him.

She giggled as they brought their dishes to the kitchen. "I'll call Skylar and figure out when she wants me to come to her classroom."

Smoke put his dishes in the sink and pulled Molly against him. "Thank you," he said.

"For what?" she asked.

"For trusting me. For being here. For just being you."

"I don't know how to be anything else. And honestly, I should be freaking out about Preston. Worrying about what he's planning next. But I trust you and your team to deal with him. It's a big deal for me to let that go. So thank *you*." Then she went up on her tiptoes and kissed him before hugging him tightly. "I'm going to go upstairs and change."

"Move all your shit to my closet," he called out as she walked toward the stairs.

She looked back. "Are you sure?"

Smoke wanted to shake his head in disbelief, but merely said, "Yes!"

"Okay. It might take me a bit. I seem to have accumulated a lot of stuff for someone who had nothing not too long ago."

"Do you want my help?" he asked.

"No, I got it. Thanks, though." Then Molly turned and headed up the stairs. She stopped halfway up and said, "Mark?"

"Yeah, Mol?"

"I don't mind that you spied on me and Taylor. Not in the least." Then she spun and took the stairs two at a time until she was out of sight.

Smoke sighed in relief. She could've been really upset with him over invading her privacy, even if he hadn't meant to at first. But instead, she was as thankful as he was that their relationship had moved forward. She was an amazing woman, and Smoke knew he was damn lucky to have her.

Now he just had to figure out this Weldon shit and make sure the man forgot about her. He needed to contact the Oak Park police and see if they'd been able to connect Weldon to her grandparents' deaths. See what they'd found out about the email harassment she'd been through. Weldon was obviously smart . . . but he wasn't smarter than Silverstone.

"You touch my woman, and you're a dead man," he vowed before turning to the task of loading the dishwasher.

Chapter Eighteen

Two days later, Molly was sitting on the floor with a group of kids surrounding her as she read a book about colors. They'd spent the morning with the paints, and it had been utter chaos, but Molly had loved it.

Mostly she'd had a good time because Skylar was such a wonderful teacher. She hadn't gotten upset when Becky had spilled an entire jar of paint. She hadn't lost it when Muhammad had decided he wanted to paint his neighbor instead of his paper. She hadn't even raised her voice when Abby and Sarah had started a paint war by flicking their paintbrushes at each other.

Anyone who thought kindergartners were a breeze was sadly mistaken. But Skylar handled everything with patience and kindness. Molly's respect for the other woman had skyrocketed.

The children's paintings were all hanging up to dry so they could be displayed later, then at the end of next week, the kids would take them home.

Molly had spent much of her time with a little Black girl named Leteisha and her best friend, Lena. Lena was from Vietnam, and Skylar had explained that when she'd first started the class, the little girl had hardly ever talked. But after meeting Leteisha, she'd opened up quickly, and the two chattered like little magpies now. The girls were as different as oil and water, but they'd connected on a level Molly hadn't seen before in kids so young. Leteisha was blind, and Lena had taken her under her wing, literally. The two girls didn't do anything separately, with Lena often holding Leteisha's hand and helping her friend navigate the seeing world. It was heartwarming, and seeing their sweet friendship gave Molly a little more hope for humanity.

A boy named Rob climbed into her lap as she read, and Molly's heart almost melted. He popped his thumb into his mouth and leaned against her. She couldn't help but think about her own child sitting like this someday.

And about how hard Mark was working trying to get her pregnant.

She knew what they were doing was crazy, but she'd never been as happy as she was right now.

Molly closed the book just as Rob sneezed—all over it and her hand. Chuckling, she reached for a tissue and helped him blow his nose. The poor thing had been coughing and sneezing all day.

Come to think of it, a lot of the children in the class had runny noses. Molly had been wiping noses and helping kids wash their hands all day.

"Recess time!" Skylar told the class.

The children leaped up from their positions around her, and Molly helped Rob stand before rising herself. Then she helped get the kids lined up, smiling at seeing Lena and Leteisha standing hand in hand. They headed outside, and Molly couldn't help but laugh when the kids immediately started running the second they hit the grass in the playground.

A security officer was walking around the perimeter of the playground, and the woman waved and said hello to some of the kids.

"She was hired after Sandra and I were taken," Skylar said softly from beside her. They were standing near the door, watching over the class like hawks. "The administration balked at having to pay a full-time security officer, and I don't blame them. But with all the violence in the world, it was something that needed to be done. Smoke stepped up and donated the money for the woman's salary."

"He did?" Molly asked in surprise.

"Yeah. And he insisted on the school board hiring someone young and highly motivated. He didn't want a retired police officer or someone who might just want some extra money in their pocket. They hired Officer Williams after an intensive search and interview process. She was an officer for the Memphis Police Department who wanted a change of pace for her and her son."

Molly looked over at the officer. Her black braids were pulled back, and she had a huge smile on her face as she knelt by the fence to talk to Lena and Leteisha. She was wearing black cargo pants, and a yellow polo shirt with the elementary school's logo. She had a full utility belt with everything a full-time police officer would carry. Even as she spoke with the girls, Molly could see her eyes roaming the grounds, looking for danger.

"All the kids love Destiny," Skylar went on. "As do us teachers. She makes us all feel safer. She doesn't leave until the last teacher does. I remember all the times when I was the last one out of here, and how it was a little scary walking to my car in the parking lot in the dark. Without Smoke's generosity, I know we'd all be a little more on edge."

Molly had known Mark was generous, but with every day that passed, she was learning exactly how much of a philanthropist he really was.

"I love your class," Molly told Skylar.

"Thanks. They're a handful. Much more energetic than last year's. Sandra, as well as the rest of that class, spoiled me for sure. But that's just how it works. Some years are easier than others, but I love seeing their zest for life."

Molly nodded. "There were a lot of kids out today, though, right? I mean, you don't usually only have ten in your class, do you?"

"No. I've got fifteen. Five have been out because of the flu. I try really hard to convince my parents to keep their children home if they have a fever, but many can't afford to take the time off work to stay home with them, so they end up in school anyway. We stay on top of things the best we can with the disinfectant wipes and the handwashing, but kids are little petri dishes. It's a miracle I'm not sick more than I am. But then again, I diligently make sure I get my flu shot every year, and I'm constantly washing my hands. You've gotten the shot, right?" Skylar asked.

Molly shrugged. "I was vaccinated against everything under the sun before I went to Nigeria. I'm sure that was probably one of them."

"Good. I think I've built up a kind of immunity since I'm around kids all the time."

"Taylor told me something, and I hope you don't think I'm being rude . . . but you don't want children of your own?" Molly asked.

"Don't get me wrong. I love my job, and I love children. But I also love my alone time. I can't imagine being around kids all day, then going home to more. Some people would call me selfish for not wanting to have babies, but I like my life. I've just never felt that maternal instinct. You want them?"

"Oh yes," Molly said with a sigh as she watched Rob chase Maria around the playground.

"With anyone in particular?" Skylar teased.

Molly knew she was blushing as she turned to smile at her friend. "Mark and I are . . . I guess you'd say . . . dating."

Skylar squealed in delight, and even bounced up and down on her toes, and she clapped lightly. "Yay!"

Molly couldn't help but laugh. Then she asked, "You don't think it's too fast? Or weird?"

"No!" Skylar said immediately. "Look, every relationship moves at its own pace. When you click with someone, you click. I know Carson and I moved really fast too. Don't get bogged down in what you think your relationship is *supposed* to be like. It is what it is."

"He says that he wants kids. It's one of the reasons he kept his uncle's big house," Molly admitted.

"I love that for you," Skylar said, the sincerity easy to hear in her tone. "Seriously, you guys are perfect for each other. And since you're already living with him, that makes things easier," she teased.

"Yeah, he's, uh . . . one hundred percent committed to the baby thing," Molly admitted.

Skylar's eyes got round, then she grinned. "You're gonna be knocked up before the month is up," she predicted. "Our Silverstone men are so damn masculine, I swear I worry sometimes that my ovaries will spontaneously impregnate themselves just by looking at Carson."

Molly snorted. "Right?"

"Carson's been asking me daily to marry him," Skylar admitted. "But I've been putting it off."

"Why?"

"That's just it . . . I'm not sure. I love the man more than life itself, but I keep thinking that . . . I don't know . . . maybe he's going to change his mind? It sounds dramatic, but I think I would literally die if he decided he didn't want to be with me anymore. I guess I'm holding back because I'm scared it'll change our relationship."

"From what I can see, there's no way Bull is going to change his mind about you. I'm new to the Silverstone circle, but he doesn't have eyes for anyone but you. Being married isn't going to change that, I don't think. Society puts a lot of pressure on couples to be married. But in the end, I don't think it has to change anything about relationships. They work, or they don't. A ring and a piece of paper have nothing to do with it," Molly said.

Skylar nodded. "Deep down, I know that. But it helps to hear it from someone else. Thanks."

"Of course." It felt good to be able to help her friend. Molly felt like she'd been doing all the taking recently, so it was nice to be the one being leaned on for once.

"What about you and Smoke? You gonna get married?"

"Mark said he wanted to marry me, but that he would wait until I was comfortable with the idea. But he also warned me that if I get pregnant, he wants his ring on my finger before our baby is due."

Skylar burst out laughing. "So you'll be married before the year is out. Good to know. You better start thinking about what kind of ceremony you want. Something quick and easy? Or the full-blown shindig with fifteen bridesmaids and groomsmen?"

"Oh Lord, no. I don't even know that many people," Molly said with a shudder. "I think maybe something between the two extremes. I don't really have any friends other than you guys and the people who work at Silverstone. So maybe something low key but where I'd still get to wear a fancy dress. Oh, and I want the party. Maybe we could even have it at Silverstone."

"I think that sounds like a great idea," Skylar said with a smile.

"And . . . maybe, if you wanted . . . we could have a double ceremony," Molly said shyly. "I mean, Mark hasn't even officially asked me, but I know I'd be super nervous with all that attention on me. I'd love to share a wedding day with someone."

Skylar's eyes got big. "Seriously?"

"Well, yeah, unless you want your own ceremony. I know lots of people *do* like all the attention on them for the big day."

"Not me," Skylar said with a shake of her head. "That's so sweet. Thank you!"

"Look at us, planning our weddings when neither of us has said yes." Molly laughed nervously. "Isn't that bad luck or something?"

"None of that," Skylar said. "I know you're trying to be more positive, so you can't even think that. Besides, apparently it's only a matter of time before Smoke puts his ring on your finger and his baby in your belly."

Molly loved the thought of both those things.

A loud bell interrupted their talk, and Skylar immediately stepped forward and raised her hand. The children were running toward them from all corners of the playground. Skylar turned to look at Molly. "I'd love to share a wedding day with you. It means the world that you'd even ask. I'm glad Smoke found you; I think we'll keep you." She grinned.

Molly opened her mouth to respond, but they were inundated by kids laughing and talking about how much fun they'd had at recess.

At the end of the day, she was exhausted. She felt as if she'd run a marathon.

Mark had arrived to pick her up, and after she climbed into his SUV, he leaned over and kissed her. "How was it?"

"Exhausting, chaotic, and really fun," Molly said.

"Change your mind about your future career?" he asked with a grin.

"Oh heck no," Molly said. "I'd rather stay home with a baby, or two, or three, than deal with a classroom full of them five days of the week."

"Babies can be harder than grade-schoolers," Mark said as he pulled out of the lot.

"And you know this how?"

"Research," he told her.

Molly wanted to know more, but she felt somewhat shy around him all of a sudden. Talking about babies made her nervous. She was still pinching herself that her life seemed to be going so well. "How was work today?"

Mark sighed. "Tough."

Molly put her hand on his arm. "I'm sorry." She knew better than to ask for details. What he and Silverstone did was dangerous, and she knew he wouldn't put *her* in danger by telling her where they might be going next, or upset her with details about what some monster was doing to others.

"Thanks," Mark said. "We've been in touch with our FBI contact, who's let us know that there's been a development in one of the cases we've been researching, and he'll be sending us more intel."

"Does that mean you'll be going on a mission soon?" Molly asked.

"It's possible. But we all agree that we don't want to leave until this thing with Weldon is done," Mark said.

She was shocked. "But Preston might decide to lay low for weeks."

Mark shrugged, seemingly unconcerned.

"You can't just stop what you're doing for weeks," she argued.

"Why not?" he asked.

"Because! There might be someone else out there who needs help. What if you'd waited weeks to go to Nigeria? I might not have made it out of there. And more of those schoolgirls might've been sold off. You aren't allowed to wait," Molly informed him. "If something comes up, you guys have to go. I'll be fine. I've dealt with Preston in the past, and I'll deal with him if he decides to do something while you're gone."

Mark's lips were pressed together, and he didn't say anything as they traversed his driveway. He punched in the code for the gate, and when he pulled into the garage, he turned off the car and got out.

Molly was nervous since he hadn't responded to anything she'd said, but it was obvious he had thoughts on it as he grabbed her hand and pulled her into the house. He dealt with the alarm, then practically dragged her up the stairs. He did that a lot, but she didn't mind.

He put his hands around her waist and picked her up, practically throwing her onto the bed. Then he quickly climbed on top of her.

"Listen to me, Molly. Are you listening?"

She was kinda concerned because he'd never manhandled her quite like that before. He hadn't hurt her in the least, but he was obviously feeling something very intense at the moment. She nodded.

"Good. Because I need you to hear this. Weldon's an asshole, and I'm not going to give him an opening to get to you by leaving. All of the team is in agreement on this. We know he's out there. Watching and waiting to do something. The man *killed* your grandparents when they wouldn't tell him where you were.

"I hate that someone might be in need of our help, but I'm not leaving you on your own. I know my security is excellent, but all Weldon needs is a tiny slipup, and he'll take advantage. I love you, Molly. And now that I've found you, I'm not going to lose you. We've got decades ahead of us. You could be pregnant right now." His hand went down to rest on her flat belly, and Molly's heart melted.

"We've had a discussion about this. We all agree—even Gramps— our families come first. Skylar, Taylor, you, any children we have—they *all* come before Silverstone. If it comes to that, we'll retire from going on missions. Eventually we'll get too old anyway. It's important to us to do our part to make the world a safer place, but the people we love are even *more* important. Understand?"

Molly nodded and closed her eyes, overcome with emotion.

Mark lowered his head and nuzzled her neck, giving her a chance to regain her composure.

Then she opened her eyes and blurted, "I told Skylar that she and Bull could share our wedding day."

He lifted his head and smiled down at her. "Okay."

"You aren't upset? I didn't even ask you."

"Bull is one of my best friends. And if you're thinking about our wedding day and what kind of ceremony you want, that means you're going to say yes when I ask you to marry me. So, no, I'm not upset."

"I might ask *you*," she said, just to be contrary.

"If you did, I'd say yes," he returned, still grinning, his dimple making her absolutely crazy with longing.

Reaching up, Molly grabbed the back of his neck and pulled him down to her. She kissed him with every bit of love she had in her soul. When they separated, she said breathlessly, "Look at us. In a bed. Whatever shall we do?"

He burst out laughing. His head went back, and Molly could only stare up at him in a lust-filled haze. She felt his dick against her thigh, and suddenly wanted him inside her more than she wanted her next breath.

"Whoever gets naked first gets to choose the position," she declared.

And that was all it took. Clothes went flying, and within seconds, they were both naked. "Who won?" she asked when he fell on top of her once more, his hot, hard body sending shivers through her own.

"We both did," Mark said, then scooted down her body, his intent clear.

Molly opened her legs, giving him room, and she moaned at the first touch of his tongue.

It was over an hour later when they were both sated and he finally climbed out of bed to go grab some snacks to replenish their energy. Molly was exhausted, but completely satisfied.

Meeting Mark had been the best thing that had ever happened to her.

Closing her eyes, she fell into a deep sleep before he returned.

~

Preston glared at the house in the distance. As night fell, the damn blinking red light from the security camera over the gate continued to mock him, just like it had the last time he'd been here. He'd walked the entire perimeter of the property, noting the same damn lights blinking all around the fence.

He'd be hard pressed to get through the gate, get Molly, then escape before the police arrived. He was well aware of how security systems worked, and that he'd have to wait for the perfect time and place to take back what was his.

The time would come. He had to be patient, even though he hated waiting. He'd waited for months! He *hated* the stupid bitch for putting him through this ridiculous shit, but she did not get to decide when their relationship ended. *He* was in charge.

He tipped up the bottle of whiskey he'd brought with him and almost fell over as he drank deeply. He wasn't feeling any pain after all the alcohol he'd consumed that afternoon. He needed it. Needed to be drunk to get through the pain of knowing *his* woman was fucking someone else.

He saw the way they'd held hands. How they'd kissed that afternoon when he'd picked her up from the elementary school. They were probably going at it right now—which infuriated Preston.

She was going to pay for that too. She had to pay for so many things, he couldn't even remember them all right that moment.

Weaving and swaying, he walked back toward his car. His precious Crown Vic. He'd been so excited to win it at the police auction. He may not have been accepted into the police academy, but he was still a cop. People bowed down to his authority. He had the gun, the uniform, and the car.

Molly would respect him before he was done with her. He'd make sure of it.

He walked the half mile to the gas station where he'd parked his car, stumbling occasionally, and practically fell into the driver's seat. He'd parked in the back, where there were no security cameras . . . he'd checked. It took several attempts to get the key into the ignition. Once the car started, he finished off the whiskey and threw the bottle onto the floor of the passenger side.

He picked up his gun, which was sitting on the seat next to him, and petted it lovingly, as if it were a living, breathing thing.

"If she doesn't reshpect me, she'll reshpect *you*," Preston slurred as he fondled the weapon. He threw it on the seat once again and put the car in gear, slowly pulling out of the gas station to go to the shitty motel where he'd been staying.

His money was slowly running out. He'd have to make his move soon. His job was gone—he'd missed several shifts, and his boss had finally had enough. But the man had always hated him because he knew

Preston was so much better than him. He was jealous of Preston's looks, authority, and obvious skill at being an officer.

His thoughts floating around in his head, Preston felt surprisingly calm, considering the situation with Molly. He'd returned to Indianapolis after a couple of Oak Park homicide detectives had knocked on his door up in Chicago. They'd wanted him to come down to the police station to talk, but he knew his rights. Unless they were arresting him, he didn't have to do jack shit. Assholes thought he didn't know anything about the law, but he knew. He'd studied it. He would've made better damn officers than those two combined.

The detectives had asked him some questions, obviously trying to get him to admit to what he'd done, but he'd given them a bogus alibi and sent them on their way, knowing by the time they'd checked out his story—and found out he'd lied—he'd be long gone. He wasn't going to be thrown in jail, no way. Not because of one dumb bitch.

Inmates notoriously didn't like cops. And Preston was practically a police officer. The only reason he didn't have the official badge was because the psychologist hadn't liked him, had blackballed him.

Preston had thought for sure he'd gotten away with offing the bitch's useless grandparents, but obviously she'd ratted him out. He'd get his revenge for that, just as he would for all her other misdeeds.

His plan was to take care of the loose ends in his life—namely, one Molly Smith—then go out in a blaze of glory.

The cops were on his tail, and after a lot of thinking, Preston decided to give up the long game of wasting time messing with Molly's head. She was a stupid bitch—saying no to him, disappearing, shacking up with a fucking loser.

But *he* wasn't stupid, even if he *was* having a hard time thinking straight with all the alcohol in his veins. He had no woman, no job, no home. Couldn't go back to Chicago. And even if he could, he knew how cops worked. They wouldn't give up. They'd keep hounding him no matter where he went.

His new plan was to take out Molly fucking Smith once and for all, then force the police's hand. See if the pansy asses could even shoot their damn weapons. And do his damnedest to take out a few of the mother-fuckers before they killed him. Payback for denying Preston his badge.

Yes, it was a good plan.

If Preston couldn't have Molly, no one could have her.

She'd pay for rejecting him. As would the cops.

No one rejected Preston Weldon.

He pulled into the parking lot of the motel, running over two curbs in the process, and managed to get his car almost between the white lines of the parking spot. He'd stopped at the end of the row, knowing better than to put his car right outside his room. Only idiots who didn't know how police investigations worked did that. And Preston wasn't an idiot. He was a badass police officer who should be feared.

He stumbled out of his car and to his room. Once inside, he fell face-first onto the bed, the smell of the not-so-clean comforter barely registering in his inebriated state. The last thing he thought before pass-ing out was that shacking up with some asshole was the worst thing Molly Smith had ever done. Preston would make sure of it.

Chapter Nineteen

Molly was dying. That was all there was to it.

"How do you feel, Mol?" Mark asked.

She could only moan.

"I was hoping you'd be better today," he said quietly. He was sitting next to her on the couch and rubbing her shoulder lightly.

Molly was on her side, curled into a little ball. She felt like death warmed over. She hated being sick. Loathed it. And yet here she was, freezing to death even though she had a fever of 102, surrounded by tissues, coughing, and sneezing, and she even had a damn puke bowl sitting on the floor by the couch. It was pathetic, and all she wanted to do was die.

Without opening her eyes, she said, "I'm not."

"So I see."

Molly had camped out on the couch earlier that morning after getting up to grab a Sprite from the kitchen. She didn't have the energy to go all the way upstairs to bed, or to one of the guest rooms. She also didn't want to get Mark sick, although it was probably too late anyway. They'd shared much more than the same air in the day or two since she'd helped in Skylar's kindergarten class, before she'd fallen sick. It was obvious the flu vaccine hadn't been one of the shots she'd gotten before she'd headed overseas, after all.

Mark had wanted to take her to the doctor, but she'd refused; she'd had the flu enough to know that the virus just needed to work its way through her system. Mark had agreed to give her one more day, but if she wasn't better, he was taking her to the doctor no matter *what* she wanted.

Molly was equally determined to stay right there on the couch for the rest of her miserable life.

"Do you need anything?" Mark asked gently.

"No," she told him.

"I hate seeing you like this," he said.

"I hate *being* like this," she agreed.

"I'll be in my office if you need me," he said. Then he leaned down, kissed her temple, and stood.

Molly didn't even watch him go. She closed her eyes and tried to get comfortable. Every muscle in her body ached, and she didn't think she was ever going to get warm again. She didn't think she'd slept, *really* slept, more than an hour or two at a time in two days. The flu sucked. Big time.

∼

Smoke sat down in his office after what seemed like the hundredth time he'd checked on Molly. She'd been in the same position as the last time he'd checked on her. On her side, curled into a ball. Only this time, she'd been moaning in her sleep. He hated to see her sick, wished he could take her place.

Skylar had felt terrible when she'd heard how sick Molly was. Obviously she'd caught the flu from the kids in Skylar's class. Hindsight being what it was, Smoke wished he'd thought about having her get the flu shot before she'd gone to visit. All he could do now was try to keep her hydrated and hope her fever broke soon.

He heard Molly dry heaving and stood to go to her, but his phone rang. He glanced at it, hoping to ignore whoever it was, but saw it was Gramps calling.

"What's up?" he said in lieu of greeting.

"We got the latest intel from Willis. We need to meet."

"Now?" Smoke asked.

"Yeah. I know Molly's sick, but this is important. It's bad, Smoke, otherwise I wouldn't ask you to come in. We'd come to you . . . but this is Silverstone business."

Smoke sighed. The team had made a decision long ago to not talk about their Silverstone jobs anywhere, *ever*, but within the security of their safe room. Even though Molly knew about what he and his friends did, as did Skylar and Taylor, they were still reluctant to have them be privy to the exact details of their missions.

He was also well aware, without Gramps having to say anything, that whatever Willis had sent was something major, if his friend even considered asking him to come in when Molly was sick. They'd been following the case of a notorious drug dealer down in Jamaica for several weeks now. Drug dealers weren't new. Unfortunately, they were a dime a dozen. But this guy was serious bad news. Like, a nine or ten on their scale of bad news, and it was obvious whatever information Willis had sent over was concerning.

"Okay. Let me get Molly up. We'll be there as soon as we can."

"I'm sorry," Gramps said again. "Is she feeling any better today?"

"No. I'm hoping today's the worst of it, though. If we can get over this hump and get her fever down, I think she'll get better soon."

"Okay. Eagle's leaving Taylor at home—not that she's happy about it. He doesn't want her around Molly because of the baby. He doesn't want to risk her getting sick and it harming the kid."

"Understood. I'd do the same thing," Smoke said, not offended in the least.

"But I think Skylar's coming with Bull. Today's an administrative day at her school, and she's already been to the mandatory meetings, so she got off earlier this afternoon. I'm sure she wouldn't mind looking after Mol until we're done."

"Appreciate it. I'll let you know when we're on our way."

"Drive safe."

"Will do. Later." Smoke clicked off his phone and ran a hand through his hair. Convincing Molly that she needed to get up and go with him to Silverstone Towing wasn't going to be easy.

He walked into the living room—and his heart broke all over again when he looked at her. Her cheeks were flushed, and her brow was furrowed, as if she were in pain.

He crouched next to the sofa and put his hand on her shoulder. "Mol?"

"Hmmm?"

"I need to go to Silverstone. Something's come up that the team needs to discuss."

"Have fun," she mumbled.

"I want you to come with me so I can keep my eye on you."

"*No.*"

Smoke's brow rose in surprise. Her tone was almost fierce. "It won't be so bad. We can get you set up in one of the sleeping rooms."

Her eyes opened into slits, and she glared at him. "I'm not moving from this couch, Mark. Maybe not ever."

Smoke grinned, but wiped the humor from his face when he saw Molly wasn't amused. "I know you feel like crap, but I really do need to go in and take care of this."

"Then go," she said.

"I don't want to leave you here alone."

Molly moved, coming up on an elbow. Smoke saw the way her muscles quaked as she did her best to be strong while arguing with him.

"Mark, I feel awful. Like, I can't go more than thirty minutes without dry heaving. I'm freezing, and my head hurts. When I stand up to pee, the room spins. I'm not going to go anywhere if you leave. I'm going to stay right here on the couch and try not to die. I've been single a long time, and I can manage to be sick all by myself. I love you, but hovering over me isn't helping me feel any better. It actually makes me feel worse because I know you feel helpless."

Smoke took a deep breath and watched as she lowered herself back down to the couch and shivered. He reached out and tucked the blankets back around her shoulders. He couldn't stand to see the misery in her eyes and wished there was something he could do to make her feel better.

"I'm safe here," she said quietly. "I'm not going to do anything but sleep. Promise. Go without me. Please. Don't make me get up and go with you. I also don't want to infect anyone at Silverstone either. It's better if I just stay here."

"How would you feel about Skylar stopping by?" Smoke asked.

Molly sighed. "It's not necessary, Mark."

"I know, but she feels guilty that you got so sick. I'm sure she'd like to check in on you."

"Would it make you feel better?" Molly asked.

"Yes."

"If I agree, does that mean I can stay here?"

"Yes," Smoke repeated.

"Then fine. But honestly, I'm going to be crap company. The last thing I want is someone else watching me throw up. But if it means I don't have to move from here, then fine."

"Okay, Mol. Your phone is fully charged. It's right here on the table next to you. I can reset the alarm when I leave, but you're going to have to get up when Skylar gets here to disable it so she can get in. I'll give her the code to the gate, but you'll have to answer the door."

"'Kay."

"You think you can get up to do that?"

"Yeah," Molly said with a small nod. "I'll probably need to pee in a bit anyway."

"All right. I'll send her over as soon as I get to the garage. I love you, and I'm so sorry you feel horrible."

"Through sickness and health, right?" she said.

Those words went straight to Smoke's heart. "Absolutely," he agreed. Then he kissed her again. "Love you, Mol."

"Love you," she echoed.

Smoke stood and looked down at his pathetic woman. She looked even smaller under the covers than usual. Most of the time he forgot just how petite she was. But seeing her sick just made him want to gather her in his arms and rock her like a baby.

He went upstairs and changed his clothes, and when he returned to the living room, Molly seemed to be asleep. He tucked her phone in her hand, since she'd need to hear it ring when Skylar arrived so she could get up to turn off the alarm and let her friend in.

Smoke had second and third thoughts about leaving, but knew she wasn't going to do anything other than what she'd said . . . lie there and try to get better.

"I'll bring home some more vanilla ice cream," he whispered against her temple.

"Thanks. Drive safe. Love you," she woke enough to mumble.

"I love you."

Then Smoke forced himself to stand and head for the garage. It was already late afternoon. The sooner he left, the sooner he could get back to her. He made sure the alarm was set before he pulled out of the garage, but the worry in the pit of his stomach didn't subside. He had no idea if it was because he felt bad he was leaving Molly when she was so sick, or if it was something more.

Telling himself that he'd be back as soon as possible, and that his security system would alert him if anything went awry, Smoke did his best to concentrate on the road.

∽

Molly felt her phone vibrating against her fingers and heard the ringing through what felt like cotton-stuffed ears.

"'Lo?" she mumbled into the receiver.

"It's me, Skylar. I'm here outside your door."

"'Kay, I'll be there in a second," Molly told her friend. She clicked off the phone and put it back on the table next to the couch. She'd thought Mark had literally just left. She'd obviously dozed since then, though. Pushing herself upright, Molly waited until the room stopped spinning before she slowly stood. Using the back of the couch, then a chair at the table, then the island counter in the kitchen to keep her balance, she made her way to the alarm keypad. She punched in the numbers, only messing up once, but thankfully not setting off the alarm, then slowly shuffled to the front door.

After letting Skylar in, she went back to the alarm panel and rearmed the system. Skylar put her arm around Molly's waist and helped her back to the couch.

"Lord, Mol, I had no idea you felt *this* awful."

She tried to smile at her friend. She really wanted to lie back down, but forced herself to stay sitting up for the moment. "I told Mark in no uncertain terms that I was not leaving this house."

Skylar nodded. "I don't blame you. Taylor really wanted to come, but Eagle said no because of the baby."

"I would've kicked her ass if she came over here," Molly said. "I'm sure I'll be better soon. It's just the flu."

"Still, ugh," Skylar commiserated.

"Must've been all that sneezing on me that the kids did."

"Yeah, there were five more kids out this week," Skylar said with a nod. "Can I get you anything?"

Molly looked over at the small table. "Maybe some more Pedialyte?"

"Of course," Skylar said, grabbing the plastic cup Molly had been drinking out of. "Do you want me to make you some soup or anything?"

At the thought of food, Molly's stomach tightened. She pressed her lips together and shook her head.

"Right. Okay, I'll be right back."

The second Skylar went into the kitchen, Molly's stomach rebelled. She leaned over and grabbed the plastic bowl Mark had left for her. Her mouth watered, and she spit into the bowl, praying she wouldn't start dry heaving again. Her stomach hurt as it was, and the last thing she wanted was to make those horrible retching noises in front of her friend.

Luckily, by the time Skylar returned with a cupful of the electrolyte water, the nausea had passed for the moment. The room was spinning again, though, so Molly reclined. "Is it cold in here, or is it me?" she asked.

"It's you," Skylar said immediately, placing the cup on the table.

Molly closed her eyes and prayed the room would stop spinning.

"Lord, what am I doing here?" Skylar asked. "You're not up to talking, I can tell. Is there anything else I can do for you?"

Molly shook her head but didn't open her eyes.

"I'm sorry you feel so bad," Skylar said. "I know Smoke wanted me to come over and keep watch over you because he can't . . . but you feel like shit. And my being here isn't going to help. I know when I'm sick, I don't want to talk to anyone."

"You can stay," Molly said, but there wasn't much oomph behind her words. "And I'll be fine."

Skylar chuckled a bit. "I know you will. You're going to sleep. I'll go back to the garage and tell Smoke that you're good. Sleeping. Make sure you drink as much liquid as you can. If you get too dehydrated, you'll have to go to the hospital, and I know you don't want that."

Molly forced her eyes open. "Thanks for coming by to check on me. I really do appreciate it."

"I know you do. Do you have to let me out?"

"Shit, yes. Give me a second," Molly said. She wished she could close her eyes and sleep, or at least try to, but she had to get up and let Skylar out, then turn the alarm back on. She pushed herself upright once more. The nausea returned, but she willed it aside.

"I'll help," Skylar said, holding out her hand.

"Be sure to use some antibacterial gel when you get back to your car," Molly said as she took her friend's hand. "And don't touch your face for a while."

"Okay," Skylar reassured her.

"Are the guys going to be mad that you didn't stay long?" Molly asked.

"No. And if they are, tough. Guys might like people waiting on them hand and foot when they have a little man cold, but when you're really sick, like you are, sleep and being alone in your misery is the best thing."

"Amen, sister," Molly quipped. She detoured to the alarm panel by the garage and turned the system off, then headed to the front door, where Skylar was waiting for her. She tried to smile at her. "Thanks again for coming over. Seriously." Her mouth started watering again, and Molly hoped her discomfort didn't show on her face.

"Of course. Call me when you feel more human."

"I will."

"Bye, Mol."

"Bye."

The second the door shut behind Skylar, Molly knew she was going to throw up again. She took three quick steps toward the bathroom, but didn't make it before her stomach clenched. She bent over in the hallway, shivering and doing her best not to fall on her face as her stomach heaved. What small amount of water she'd managed to keep down since the last time she'd puked came back up.

Her eyes watering, and feeling as if she were standing in the middle of Antarctica without a coat on, Molly shuffled to the kitchen. She grabbed some paper towels and did the best she could to clean up the mess she'd made in the hallway.

Thankful she hadn't eaten anything for her to throw up, Molly swayed on her feet. She was two seconds away from falling flat on her face. The couch looked like it was ten miles away. Moving slowly, praying the nausea wouldn't return, Molly headed for it. It seemed to take a year, but she finally reached her nest of blankets and pillows. Lying down and pulling the covers up to her chin, Molly shivered for several minutes before feeling as if maybe she wouldn't freeze to death.

Turning back onto her side, she brought her knees up to her chest.

Closing her eyes, she forgot about everything except how miserable she felt. If she didn't feel any better when Mark got home, she was going to tell him she was ready to go to the doctor. She didn't want to get up. Didn't want to leave. But she was kinda scaring herself with how horrible she felt. And the last thing she wanted was for Mark to get sick too.

Thoughts of both of them being miserable and sick ran through her head as Molly fell into a state of semiconsciousness on the couch.

~

Preston was drunk again. He'd been drunk for what seemed like days. But he didn't care. Didn't give a shit about anything. Well . . . other than getting his hands on the bitch who'd snubbed him.

He was watching from his spot in the trees, near the gate that led to the asshole's house, the one who'd stolen his girlfriend, when a car pulled up and went down the driveway. He recognized the woman. His Molly hung out with her sometimes.

He was still chugging his whiskey, thinking of all the ways he was going to punish Molly for her sins against him, when he saw the woman coming back up the driveway not too long after she'd arrived.

He was stewing in his own hate when he happened to look up at the camera on the gate after she'd pulled back onto the road.

Preston couldn't believe what he was seeing.

He rubbed his eyes, hoping he wasn't hallucinating.

No, he wasn't.

The camera wasn't blinking.

It wasn't on.

He looked from the camera to the house, then back at the camera. Preston had no idea how much time he had, but he knew he needed to act fast. He couldn't remember a time since he'd been stalking Molly that the alarm system hadn't been armed. He'd seen the asshole leave earlier, before the other woman had arrived. He wasn't sure if anyone else was in the house—he didn't think so—but ultimately it didn't matter. He'd shoot anyone who got between him and Molly.

Time for her to pay for what she'd put him through. For disappearing on him. For rejecting him. For *all* of it.

Preston stumbled as fast as he could back to his car. He drove down the driveway and nervously looked up at the camera from a safe distance. It was still off.

Smiling evilly, he took one more swig of whiskey, then a deep breath.

He floored the gas.

Grunting in pain as his head hit the steering wheel when he struck the gate, Preston looked up. He'd bent the metal barrier but hadn't quite broken through. Damn the man and his fucking security!

It took a few more tries, with Preston backing up and ramming the gate, but he let out a shout of triumph as his Crown Vic finally slammed through and went bumping down the gravel driveway.

The alarm being off might've given him some time, but he still needed to work quickly. Get in, kill whoever he had to, grab Molly, and leave. That was the plan.

After that, he'd get the hell out of Indianapolis and find a good place to hole up . . . and show Molly *exactly* how wrong she'd been to reject him.

Skidding to a halt outside the front of the house, he leaped out, almost falling on his face, and went around to the trunk. He grabbed a crowbar and headed for the door. Molly was coming with him, one way or another. This would be fun.

Chapter Twenty

Smoke couldn't believe what he was seeing. Gramps, usually so calm, was actually pacing the safe room at Silverstone Towing in clear agitation. "I *know* her," Gramps said in a low voice. "Cassidy Hewitt. She grew up in El Paso, and we went to the same high school for a year. She was a freshman when I was a senior. She was in the band, played flute, and was funny as shit. My parents and her parents knew each other, hung out in the same circles."

"What the hell was she thinking going to Jamaica?" Bull asked. "And working for Michael Coke, the most notorious drug dealer the country's ever had?"

"I don't know!" Gramps barked. "The last I'd heard from her was years ago. She'd married this dude and then divorced. They had a son, I think. He'd be around ten or eleven now. This is so fucked."

It *was* fucked. Smoke looked down at the copy of the letter in his hand. It was handwritten, the letters feminine and ornate. The ugliness the words depicted was at odds with the beautiful script.

> To Whom It May Concern,
> My name is Cassidy Hewitt. I'm from El Paso, Texas.
> I work at Michael Coke's estate in Kingston, Jamaica.
> I had no idea who he was when I accepted the job
> as a live-in teacher. I want to leave, but I know he'll

kill me and my son if we try to escape. I'm willing to do whatever it takes to get my son out of here alive. I know how Coke's operation works, where the drug houses are, who's working for him. All of it. I'll tell you everything if you just help us escape. If he finds out I mailed this letter, he'll torture my boy and make me watch. He'll kill me either way, eventually. I know it. Please help me.

Sincerely,

Cassidy, a desperate American citizen

Silverstone had been studying Coke and his drug network for weeks. Coke's father had started the Shower Posse, a violent drug gang, and had passed it down to his children. He'd been killed many years earlier, as had Michael's brother and sister. Michael was even more ruthless, and paranoid, than his siblings had been. It served him well, as his enemies and the authorities hadn't been able to get close to him.

He had hundreds of loyal followers who would do anything for him, including murdering anyone dumb enough to ask too many questions and kidnapping children from their homes and forcing them to work for his operation. Rumor had it he had dozens of kids living on his vast property in West Kingston. That he was brainwashing the children, telling them their parents had sold them, that *he* was now their father.

"As I said, I knew her a long time ago," Gramps said. "I liked her. A lot. We even exchanged letters back and forth for a while when I was in the Army. She's the kind of girl you would love to bring home to your parents. To settle down and marry. A *good* girl. I knew she was so far out of my league it wasn't even funny. Then she got married, and that was that. Any chance I might've had with her was gone," Gramps said.

Smoke narrowed his eyes. He'd never heard of this Cassidy chick, ever. And the fact that Gramps was obviously distressed was surprising as hell. He was always the unflappable one. The steady one.

"But knowing that she's living with that scum, that she's scared . . . it cuts. Deep," Gramps said.

"This isn't like most of our missions," Eagle said quietly. "Coke is almost impossible to get to. Because of the unemployment rate and poverty in Jamaica, the people he employs are extremely loyal . . . mostly because they don't want to lose their income stream, but still. Many people have tried to take Coke down over the years and haven't succeeded."

Gramps growled and leaned over and snatched the letter off the table. He leaned toward Eagle and waved the paper at him. "So Cassidy and her son are expendable?"

"I didn't say that," Eagle told Gramps.

"Fuck!" Gramps shouted, throwing the paper onto the table and resuming his pacing.

"Look, I think we all agree Coke needs to go," Bull said calmly.

Everyone nodded.

"And that if we decide to take this on, it'll be unlike any mission we've done before."

They nodded again.

"This is personal for Gramps. I can't remember a time when we've gone into a mission knowing someone personally who was affected. We might see pictures of the victims, or know our mark is holding hostages. Or we might stumble across someone like Molly who needs our help, but this is different. I'm up for the challenge. What do you guys think?"

The other three men all agreed immediately.

"It's gonna take a lot of research and planning," Eagle warned.

"What are *you* thinking?" Smoke asked Gramps.

"Undercover," Gramps blurted. "Willis can help with connections. I know they've got some UCs there already. It's how we've gotten some of the information he's already sent us."

Eagle frowned. "That's dangerous as fuck," he said.

"I know. But because this *is* personal, I'm going in by myself," Gramps said.

"The fuck you are!"

"No fucking way!"

"Not happening!"

Bull, Eagle, and Smoke all spoke at the same time.

"Look, you guys have families now. There's no way any of you can do this."

"Right, but you aren't doing this by yourself," Eagle growled. "We're a fucking team. We *work* as a team. I happen to agree that there are aspects to this op that might be better executed by a single person, but that doesn't mean you're going to hop on down to Jamaica by yourself while we sit on our asses here in Indiana."

The four men all stared at each other. Smoke was in complete agreement with Eagle, but he also knew Gramps had a point. It *would* be easier for one man to infiltrate Coke's operation. He held his breath as he waited for Gramps's reaction.

Finally, he nodded. "I just . . . you don't know Cassidy. I mean, I guess *I* don't really know her anymore either. But thinking of her scared out of her mind, and risking everything to mail a fucking letter to the FBI . . . Jesus . . . it makes me crazy."

Smoke stood and put a hand on Gramps's arm. "We'll do everything we can to get her *and* her son out."

Gramps sighed heavily. "'Preciate it."

"Let's all sit down and go over everything we've gotten from Willis so far," Bull suggested. "Now that we know we aren't just thinking about this, that we're actually doing it, we can ask specific questions. Ask for more detailed information. We need to know about all of Coke's associates, who's working for him, what the layout of his mansion is, what the routine is. *All* of it. Knowledge is power, and if we're going to be sending Gramps into the lion's den, we need to know what we're up against and where best to strike. Agreed?"

Everyone nodded, and Gramps seemed a little less amped up now that he knew Silverstone was on the same page in regard to rescuing the woman he was once close to.

When they'd all gathered around the table, Bull lifted his chin at Smoke. "Skylar's back," he said, holding up his phone. "She says Molly's good, but she just wanted to sleep. She left her safe and sound resting on your couch."

"Thanks," Smoke told his friend. He was relieved to know Molly was okay, but the nagging pull to go home and see for himself that she was safe wouldn't go away.

"Let's start at the beginning," Eagle said. "With Coke's father and how he started his empire."

Knowing they were probably going to be there longer than he wanted, Smoke forced himself to turn his thoughts from Molly. She probably wouldn't have any idea how long he was gone anyway—she'd sleep through the afternoon and hopefully be feeling better by the time he got home.

∼

Preston looked through one of the windows at the front of the house and saw a formal dining room table. There were no other obstructions if he broke the window and climbed inside.

Taking a deep breath, he checked his watch. He didn't know how much time he'd have. Even without the alarm being on, there still might be a separate camera system. He needed to get in, get Molly, and get the fuck out.

He drew back his arm and slammed the crowbar against the window.

Surprisingly, the window didn't break. It shattered but held together. Tempered glass. *Fuck!*

He smashed the glass several more times, not even worried that someone might hear him, until he could push the entire frame inside the house. Preston shoved his way in, breathing heavily already, falling onto his hands and knees. "Goddamn tempered glass is good for *one* thing," he muttered. Thankful he hadn't cut himself to ribbons when he'd fallen, he quickly stood and stumbled into the next room.

Molly was on the couch, sitting up and looking around in confusion.

He pulled the Glock pistol out of its side holster and pointed it at her. "Get up," he barked.

"Preston?"

"Yeah, honey. It's me! Now get up."

"How did you get in?"

Pissed that she wasn't immediately obeying, Preston strode over to the couch and hit her with his pistol. She screeched and fell sideways onto the couch.

A sweet, heady feeling of control rushing over him, he stalked around the couch and grabbed her arm. "I said, *get up!*" He wrenched her upward until she was standing. Then he put the gun right between her eyes and leaned in. "You're going to do what I say, when I say it, if you want to live, understand?"

He saw Molly swallow hard, then nod.

"Good." Kicking a plastic bowl out of his way, Preston spun Molly until her back was to him and put an arm around her chest diagonally. He pressed the gun against her temple. "Now, walk."

Without a word, she did as he said.

Not knowing why he hadn't done this before, savoring the huge adrenaline rush from how powerful he felt in that moment, Preston smiled as they made their way toward the door.

"Unlock it. And don't do anything funny," he threatened.

Molly reached out and undid the dead bolt. Then the chain. She opened the door.

He pushed her through with his body, laughing when her legs almost gave out on the steps. Only his hold on her kept her from face planting. He rushed her to his car and opened the back door, shoving her inside.

Then Preston did a happy drunken jig right there in the driveway. He'd done it! He had her! She couldn't get out of the back seat. Not until he let her out. The old cruiser he'd bought had some of the police features removed after it had been taken out of service, but he'd paid good money to restore them. Plastic molded seat in the back, wire separating the back from the front. Doors that wouldn't open from the inside.

As he looked around, his fuzzy brain finally remembering that he needed to get the hell out of there, Preston opened his door and got in. He looked back at Molly and grinned. She had blood oozing from a cut on her temple where he'd hit her—and she looked absolutely terrified.

He fucking *loved* that.

"Not so fuckin' sure of yourself now, are you?" he asked before reaching for his whiskey bottle. He chugged down a few swallows, shuddering at the heated rush of the alcohol running through his bloodstream, then turned his car around and gunned it back down the driveway.

He'd stolen his woman fair and square. He couldn't wait to teach her a few lessons . . . and to make her regret humiliating him.

∼

An hour and a half later, Smoke was done. They still had a lot more work to do, but his uneasy feeling had only grown. He needed to get home to Molly.

"I'm out," he told his friends. "I told Molly I'd stop on the way home and get her more ice cream." He looked at Gramps. "I'm sorry about Cassidy. From everything you've told us, she sounds like she's got a good head on her shoulders. She's gonna be fine until we can get to her."

"I hope so," Gramps said.

Checking his watch for the thousandth time, Smoke saw that he hadn't received any notifications from his alarm system. Relieved, he decided to check the cameras on the app on his phone. He'd not done so since arriving at Silverstone. He'd been too engrossed in their research into the Shower Posse gang and Coke's world in Jamaica.

He clicked on the app and waited for it to boot up. The first camera he checked was at the gate.

What he saw made his blood run cold.

The gate was demolished, lying crumpled and barely hanging on by one hinge.

"Smoke? What?" Eagle asked, clearly noticing the panic on his face.

"*Fuck!*" Smoke swore. He quickly brought up more cameras—and couldn't believe what he was seeing. Someone had broken the window at the front of his house in his dining room . . . and the front door was standing wide open.

He immediately dialed Molly's number, swearing again when it rang and eventually went to voice mail.

"Weldon's got Molly," Smoke said, standing so fast, the chair he'd been sitting in went flying.

He turned and headed for the door without another word, but Bull caught his arm. "You can't go off half-cocked. We need info," he said.

"Fuck that! He's *got* her," Smoke shouted. "I don't know why the alarm didn't go off."

He jerked his arm out of Bull's grasp and opened the safe-room door. He ran through the basement and took the stairs two at a time, his friends right on his heels.

Skylar was sitting upstairs watching TV, and she stood when the four men rushed into the room.

"Did Molly turn the alarm back on when you left?" he asked without preamble. As soon as the question came out, he knew Skylar wouldn't know. He was panicking, which wasn't like him.

"Um . . . I don't know. I think so? I mean, she turned it on when I came in, and turned it off right before I left."

Smoke didn't need to hear any more. It didn't matter what had happened. What mattered was that Molly was in trouble.

"Go with him," Gramps ordered Eagle and Bull. "I'll call the cops, give them a description of Weldon's car. They can put out a 'Be on the lookout' for it."

"Call the drivers too," Bull said. "They can keep their eyes out while they're on the roads."

Gramps nodded.

"I'm driving," Eagle told Smoke. "Give me your keys."

Smoke handed them over. He didn't give a shit who drove, although he knew deep down it would be better if it wasn't him. He'd probably kill someone in his rush to get home or to find Weldon's Crown Vic.

Within seconds, they were in his Explorer and headed for his house. The trip took half as long as it usually did because Eagle was driving like a bat out of hell.

The destruction of his security gate was even worse than he'd thought from looking at it on the cameras. Someone had obviously rammed right through it. Someone determined . . . because Smoke *knew* it hadn't been easy.

"That would've left a mark," Eagle said. "The front of his car's got to be fucked."

Smoke agreed, but his teeth were clenched together so hard he couldn't get any words out.

The Explorer flew over the gravel, and Eagle skidded to a halt in front of the house. Smoke was out and running toward the door before anyone could stop him.

"Smoke! Stop! Let *me* go in!" Bull yelled, but Smoke ignored him. He knew his friend was simply trying to protect him. To keep him from seeing Molly if she was deceased, but he didn't care. Couldn't stop himself from going in.

"Molly!" he bellowed the second he was inside, but somehow he already knew that she wasn't there. The house just felt empty. She'd filled it with her presence since she'd moved in, and now it already seemed cold and barren.

He ran by the kitchen and looked down at the couch where he'd last seen Molly. The blankets she'd been snuggled under were half on and half off the cushions. The bowl she'd been using to throw up in was knocked over, and her phone was still sitting on the table. Any chance of tracing her through the phone was moot.

Then something else caught his eye. Leaning down to get a closer look, Smoke froze.

Blood.

He didn't touch it, knowing crime scene investigators would need to take photos, but it made his own blood boil.

He stood abruptly and headed for the front door once more.

"Smoke?" Bull asked. "We need to search the house."

"No need. She's not here. Weldon took her, and I'd bet everything I own he's bringing her back to Chicago."

"Yeah, that's where he's comfortable," Eagle agreed. "It's his home turf."

"I'll call Chicago PD," Bull said as they all headed for the Explorer once more.

"Let Gramps know. He'll want to come too," Eagle said.

Smoke heard his friends planning, but he wasn't really listening. All he could think about was Molly and how scared she had to be. He'd promised her she'd be safe in his house, and she hadn't been.

He never should've left her. He'd known it as soon as he'd stepped out the door. He'd never again doubt his own judgment. Smoke would bring her home if it was the last thing he did.

He climbed into the passenger seat and clenched his hands together in his lap, staring down at them as Eagle turned the car around and headed for the interstate. He thought about how those big hands looked on Molly's petite body. How her fingers looked intertwined with his. How he'd placed his hand on her belly before she'd gotten sick, wondering if she was pregnant yet . . .

Weldon was a dead man. He'd hurt Smoke's woman. No matter how long it took, or how many laws he had to break, Smoke would make sure the man suffered for daring to put a hand on Molly.

There wasn't anywhere Preston could hide from him. His days were numbered.

Chapter Twenty-One

Molly shivered in the back seat of Preston's car. The seat was uncomfortable. She'd already tried to open the door when they'd been at a stoplight, but it hadn't budged. They were now on the interstate heading north toward Chicago.

Every muscle in Molly's body hurt. The nausea had returned with a vengeance now that she was in a moving vehicle, and her fever was still as high as ever. As if it wasn't bad enough to be kidnapped by her crazy ex-boyfriend, she was deathly ill on top of it.

Folly Molly.

The old nickname flashed through her brain, but she did her best to push it back. She couldn't get sucked into her old way of thinking right now. She needed to be as clearheaded and positive as possible to try to get out of this. Molly also had no doubt Mark would be looking for her. She remembered how he and his friends had dropped everything to find Bart. They'd do the same for her. She knew it just as well as she knew her name.

Recalling the conversation she'd had with Mark about fighting a captor or trying to talk her way out of a situation, Molly took a deep breath. She couldn't fight, not when she was trapped in Preston's back seat, but she could talk.

"Preston, what's going on?"

"What's going on?" he echoed. "You disrespected me. *No one* does that, Molly!"

"I'm sorry," she said as contritely as possible.

"You will be," Preston agreed darkly.

Molly shivered. She wasn't sure if it was a byproduct of the fever or because Preston sounded so damn scary. She watched as he took another swig out of the bottle next to him. He swerved across the center line, then overcorrected, going onto the shoulder before he steered back into his lane. Shit, he was going to get them both killed in a car accident.

"Thank you for coming to get me," she said quietly, testing the waters to see if she could con him into believing her.

He looked back at her, and Molly cringed as he swerved all over the highway again. He focused on the road and chuckled. The sound was chilling, and goose bumps rose on her arms. "It's too late for that, bitch," he told her. "You can't trick me by being all nice and sweet now. First, you broke up with me. Second, you left without telling me where you were going. For *months*! And for the record, at first I asked your grandparents nicely where you were. If they'd told me, they'd still be alive today. But instead they *disrespected* me! Told me to get out of their house. That they'd never stop protecting you, even if it was the last thing they did. And you know what? It was!"

Preston laughed hard then. He threw his head back and slammed his hand on the steering wheel, as if what he'd said was the funniest thing he'd ever heard in his life.

Molly couldn't help it; nausea overwhelmed her. Both from thinking about what her poor nana and papa had been through at the hands of her ex, how scared they must've been, and from the weaving back and forth Preston was doing as he drove. She leaned sideways and dry heaved. As usual, nothing came up but some of the Pedialyte she'd been trying to drink.

"That's the good thing about a plastic seat . . . it doesn't matter what you do back there . . . it's easily cleaned up!" Preston crowed. "You can shit yourself, piss everywhere, and throw up all you want . . . but all I have to do is take a hose to the back, and it's gone. Poof! No DNA evidence you were here at all. So do your worst. It won't change what's gonna happen to you."

Molly wiped her mouth with the back of her hand and tried not to pass out. She was dizzy, feeling like she was going to keel over and die any second. Being sick sucked on a regular day. When your ex kidnapped you and threatened to do all sorts of horrible things, it was even worse.

"What are you going to do with me?" she asked, deciding she had nothing to lose.

"Since you asked so nicely, I'll tell you," Preston replied. "At first I thought about bringing you back to Chicago. To my home. I was gonna show you how good we could be together. I was gonna treat you like my queen, prove we were meant for each other. That you were wrong, wanting to break up with me. But now that you've let someone else defile your body—*cheated* on me, talked to the cops and made them suspicious of me—I've changed my mind."

Molly shivered again. She'd had no inkling that Preston was so insane. If she had, she would've steered clear of him and wouldn't have gone on even one date. She had so many regrets in regard to him, but nothing would change what was happening right this second.

"Now I'm going to find some desolate exit, drive around until I find the perfect spot, then kill you just like I did your precious nana and papa. What do you think about that?" he asked.

Molly was still scared . . . but at that moment, she also got pissed. How *dare* he think he could kill her, as if she were nothing but a piece of trash? "I don't like it," she answered bluntly.

For a second, she thought she'd made him even angrier. But then he laughed once more. He took another swig of the alcohol and held it up. "I don't give a shit if you like it or not. And I'd let you have some of my whiskey, but I can't get it through the bars. Sorry!" he told her. "It's a shame, really. We could'a been so good together. But I wouldn't want you now, even if you hadn't disrespected me by not givin' us a chance, by thinkin' you could break up with me. You fucked another man when you were *mine*. That, I can't fuckin' forgive!"

Molly opened her mouth to respond, but he went on.

"Where did you go, bitch? I demand you tell me! I looked for you *everywhere*! I stole your grandparents' mail looking for any fucking letters. I stalked Apex, and you weren't going to work. Do you know how embarrassing it was for me to face my coworkers? I'd told them all about my beautiful, sweet girlfriend, how much she loved me, and then you disappeared! They wanted to meet you. I bragged about you, then I couldn't produce you. They thought I'd made you up! Everyone started talkin' behind my back. I'd catch them when I walked into a room, then they'd all shut up. You ruined me—and it's not *fair*! I would've been accepted into the police academy if it wasn't for you messing everything up!"

Molly tuned Preston out, telling him nothing. Everything he was saying was a lie. And he was delusional. He'd applied for the police academy long before he'd met her. She'd had nothing to do with his not being accepted. Thank God whoever was doing the recruiting had realized there was something wrong with him. The thought of Preston in a position of power over others was horrifying. His job as a security guard had obviously done enough to make him think he was untouchable.

When Preston swerved once more, almost taking out another car, Molly reached for her seat belt. Realizing in dismay that there wasn't one, she closed her eyes and prayed they wouldn't wreck. Although, that would probably be the best thing that could happen to her right now. The police would be called, and maybe she could make a run for it if the glass in the windows was broken out.

"Are you listening to me?" Preston screamed.

"Yes," she said automatically.

"Damn straight you are," he growled with satisfaction. He continued with his rant against her, Oak Park, her grandparents, the cops, and even the color of the sky at the moment. He was truly insane—and Molly had a feeling this wasn't going to end well for her.

She had no idea how long they drove. Time passed without meaning. She was semidelirious from her fever, but Molly noted it was fully dark now. The sun had just been beginning to set when Preston had snatched her from Mark's house. She assumed they had to be closer to Chicago than Indianapolis, that they'd probably been driving for a couple of hours.

Molly looked up when she realized they'd slowed down. How Preston hadn't wrecked yet was a complete mystery. For a while, the car had seemed to be going faster and faster, and the weaving and swerving hadn't helped with her nausea. Preston also hadn't shut up once, continuing to drink and rant, and the only way to keep him semiappeased was to acknowledge what he was saying with the occasional "uh-huh" and "I'm sorry."

Molly tensed when she realized that Preston had pulled off the interstate and was speeding down a very dark, very deserted road. "Preston, we can start over. Make things between us work," she said out of desperation.

"Ish too late," he slurred. "You've defiled your lady garden by allowin' a poishonous snake in."

She wanted to laugh at his ridiculous analogy, but this was definitely no laughing matter. Molly put a hand over her belly and closed her eyes. She had no idea if she was pregnant, but if she was, her death, possibly along with that of their child, was going to destroy Mark.

Preston drove the back roads of rural Indiana for what seemed like forever. He seemed to be lost, and being hammered wasn't helping him navigate. Molly prayed he'd get his car stuck and would have to go for help, but she wasn't that lucky.

He finally stopped and turned off the engine. "Thish is it," he slurred thickly. Then he got out of the car, leaving his headlights shining toward a large overgrown field. There was a small copse of trees beyond the field . . . and no other lights anywhere.

Preston's head slipped out of view, and Molly guessed he'd fallen on his ass. She prayed that he was too drunk to stand, but she almost cried when he popped back up.

Folly Molly.

She mentally told her brain to shut up—and when Preston opened the back door, she moved.

Throwing herself toward Preston, she hoped to startle him enough that she could run into the darkness and hide.

But even drunk, Preston was surprisingly agile . . . and she was not. With the virus coursing through her body, she was weak and unsteady on her feet. She managed to hit Preston, but instead of falling backward away from her, his arms went around Molly, and he took her to the ground with him. He rolled until she was under him.

His leaned down so his lips were practically touching hers. Molly turned her face but could still smell the whiskey on his breath, making her stomach clench.

"You won't get away from me again," he told her.

Molly couldn't help it—she gagged. From fear, from the motion of her attempted escape, from the smell of the alcohol . . . it all combined to work against her.

Preston moved quickly, getting off and shoving her over so she couldn't puke on him. Of course, there was nothing left in her belly to throw up, but he apparently didn't know that.

"Gross," he muttered as she dry heaved into the dirt under her. When she was done, he hauled her upright and began to force march her across the pitch-black field.

Molly had no idea where they were, but she knew this was it. He was going to kill her and leave her body here to rot. She could only hope that someone would find her quickly. The thought of Mark agonizing over what had happened to her was more painful than anything she could think of.

The death of her grandparents was extremely hard, but she couldn't even fathom Mark being there one day, then gone the next. The agony of wondering what had happened would be more than she could bear, and she hated that Mark might feel a tenth of that same agony over her.

She stumbled on the uneven ground, feeling completely frozen. She was wearing the black T-shirt Mark had given her when he'd first met her down in that hole. It comforted her when she was sick, and now it would comfort her in death. She didn't have shoes on, only a pair of fuzzy socks. It felt as if it was below freezing outside, but she knew that was because of the fever.

"Preston," she blurted, having no idea what she was going to say, but needing to try one more time to get through to him.

"Shut up, bitch," he barked. "Here's good," he declared, pulling her to a stop. "Stand right there," he slurred in a menacing tone.

Molly's muscles were frozen. She couldn't move an inch. Her back was to Preston, and she thought about making a run for it, but she was literally too sick to do anything other than stand there and quake.

She closed her eyes and thought about Mark. How he'd looked the last time he'd made love to her. His pupils dilated, cheeks flushed, every muscle in his body rock hard and tense as he'd orgasmed. He was the best thing that had ever happened to her, and it wasn't fair that she was being taken from him so soon. That she wouldn't get to experience motherhood. But for the first time in her life, she'd had a place where she felt she could be herself and not be judged. She'd found new friends and had experienced what a truly loving relationship should be like.

Molly wasn't sure what Preston was waiting for. She could hear him breathing heavily behind her, but she didn't dare turn around.

"You shouldn't've tried to break up with me," Preston finally said in a surprisingly calm, lucid tone. "I would've gotten sick of you pretty quickly and tossed you aside. You aren't good enough for me, never were. But you had to go and disrespect me. Tell me you wanted to be *friends*. Men and women can't be friends. Goodbye, Molly."

The thought of what was about to happen was enough to make her nausea rear its ugly head once again. Bile filled her throat, and Molly couldn't hold it in.

She opened her mouth and leaned over to barf—just as the gun went off.

Pain exploded in her head, and she pitched forward, falling on her face.

Another shot rang out, but Molly didn't hear or feel anything more.

~

Eagle was driving almost a hundred miles an hour. Bull had turned on the state police scanner app on his phone, and they were listening as half a dozen troopers were on the heels of a drunk driver someone had called in. Normally, Smoke wouldn't have given a shit about such a chase—but because the car in question was an older-model Crown Victoria with Weldon's license plate, he couldn't breathe.

The car was apparently weaving in and out of traffic, trying to elude the police. All Smoke could think of was Molly being in the car with him.

The troopers were already aware that the person driving might possibly have a hostage, and they were doing everything they could to stay on his tail but not agitate him enough to make him lose control. They obviously weren't succeeding. They were driving at speeds of 110 or more, and Smoke couldn't even swallow, his mouth was so dry.

No one said a word, everyone in the vehicle tense as they listened to the chase progress. Surprisingly, they weren't that far behind Weldon. Smoke had no idea what he'd been doing, why he wasn't already in

Chicago. He didn't want to think about what he might've done to Molly.

The troopers were trying to arrange to get Stop Sticks placed across the interstate. They would pierce Weldon's tires, and the air would slowly leak out, making it all but impossible for him to continue to drive at high rates of speed.

It seemed that everything was going as planned—but then all hell broke loose.

"He's swerving. Ah shit, he's crossed the median! Suspect driving northbound in the southbound lanes . . . fall back! Fall back! Ten-fifty, ten-fifty! Start EMS!"

Smoke couldn't breathe. He knew a ten-fifty meant an accident. Weldon had been driving on the wrong side of the road, and he'd wrecked.

He closed his eyes and prayed harder than he'd ever prayed before.

The chatter on the scanner was hard to understand as the troopers barked information to their fellow officers and dispatch. Within minutes, Smoke could see red and blue lights flashing in the darkness ahead. Traffic was at a standstill, but Eagle barely slowed down. He pulled over onto the left shoulder and flew by the stopped vehicles.

Of course Eagle would know how desperate Smoke was to get to the scene and find Molly. Just the thought of his woman, his love, broken and bleeding or trapped in Weldon's car . . . the fear was almost overwhelming.

"She's gonna be fine," he whispered.

Bull reached forward and placed a hand on his arm from the back seat. "Of course she is. No matter what happens, we'll take care of her."

Smoke nodded. He was grateful he and Molly had such supportive friends.

Eagle slammed on the brakes, and Smoke flew out of the car, running toward the chaotic scene ahead of them. Police cars were everywhere, and traffic was stopped on both sides of the interstate. He spotted Weldon's demolished vehicle in the median. It had obviously rolled several times.

He glanced around, headlights from the stopped traffic revealing a damaged guardrail on the far side of the opposing lanes. Smoke guessed Weldon had hit the rail, bounced back across, and rolled over and over in the median, coming to a stop in the grass in the middle of the four lanes of traffic. Miraculously, it seemed no other vehicles were damaged. Somehow, Weldon had missed hitting anyone else.

But to Smoke's horror, the Crown Vic was on fire.

The troopers were doing their best to get the mangled driver's side door open, but even as Smoke watched, they quickly backed off when the flames shot higher.

"No!" Smoke cried, running for the car, which was already fully engulfed.

He was tackled from behind and went flying forward, his chin hitting the grass in the median hard enough for him to bite his tongue. Smoke immediately fought to get up.

"Stop!" Gramps yelled.

Smoke knew his teammate had been following them in his own car, but he didn't feel any relief that he was there. "Get off me!" Smoke shouted. "I have to get to Molly!"

"It's too late!" Gramps yelled back. "You can't help her!"

Smoke struggled harder, then realized Eagle and Bull had joined Gramps in restraining him.

Pinned on his belly, his friends sitting on him, he watched in agony as the flames reached the gas tank—exploding in a spectacular fireball.

Tears fell from his eyes as he stared disbelievingly at the carnage. "Molly," he rasped, letting his head drop. His forehead landed in the fresh-smelling grass, and he felt his heart break into a thousand pieces.

He'd failed her. How many times had he told Molly she was safe? That he'd protect her?

Too many. And now she was dead.

Smoke felt his friends ease off him, but he didn't move. He couldn't. He felt as if he was paralyzed. A sob moved up his throat, and he felt his entire body convulse as it left him. Tears poured from his eyes as he lay on the ground and mourned the loss of the woman he loved more than life itself.

~

Smoke couldn't make himself leave the scene. Eagle, Bull, and Gramps had stayed by his side through every unbearable hour, giving him the unconditional support he needed. The fire department had shown up, and it had taken a while for them to put out the fire. When they were done, there was almost nothing left of the vehicle.

Night had fallen hours ago, and Smoke watched numbly from a distance as the troopers and detectives from the nearest town examined every inch of Weldon's Crown Vic, bagging what evidence they could. To Smoke, it seemed the work was excruciatingly slow.

He and his friends had been allowed to stay after their FBI contact, Willis, had made a few phone calls and greased some wheels. Smoke knew Gramps had arranged it, and he was grateful. Because he couldn't leave. Couldn't look away. He needed to be there when they found Molly's body.

Someone pulled out a sheet and draped it over Weldon's remains in the front seat. He'd been burned to a crisp in the explosion. Earlier, when Smoke had seen an officer bag a whiskey bottle, his fingernails had dug into his palms hard enough to draw blood. It wasn't bad enough that Weldon had kidnapped Molly, but he'd been fucking drunk too? It was a miracle that he hadn't killed anyone else.

But that thought didn't comfort Smoke at the moment.

After what seemed like ages, he finally saw the firefighters pry open the trunk . . .

And Smoke frowned in confusion when they walked away from the car seconds later.

He looked over at Eagle. "What's going on?"

"I don't know."

He kept his eyes on the vehicle. They didn't grab another sheet . . . didn't cover the remains of another body.

For the first time in hours, a spark of hope swept through Smoke. Did that mean Molly *hadn't* been inside?

"I'm on it," Bull said, already rushing toward the officers.

Smoke wanted to move. Wanted to go over and listen to what the officer was telling Bull, but he was frozen in place. Every muscle tense. Waiting to hear what was found inside Weldon's trunk.

After what seemed like an eternity, Bull ran back over to them.

"There was only one occupant in the car," he said without preamble. "No one in the trunk. No one in the back seat."

"She wasn't in there?" Smoke breathed.

"Doesn't look like it," Bull agreed.

For just a moment, Smoke sagged in relief—but then panic hit. "Then where is she, and what did he do with her?" he asked.

"I don't know, but we're gonna find her," Gramps said.

~

When Molly regained consciousness, it was still dark outside. It took a moment for her to remember what had happened.

Groaning, she reached back and felt her head. Her hair was sticky, and she knew without a doubt Preston had shot her. She had a horrible headache but didn't feel much else. Her lips parted on a deep breath—and Molly winced when pain shot through her face at even that slight movement. Gingerly touching her face, she felt more blood near her jaw. It seemed as if she'd been shot in the head twice, but she wasn't dead. It seemed impossible.

Somehow, probably because she'd been moving to throw up, the bullet had missed going into her brain.

She attempted to roll over, but even more excruciating pain in her leg made her freeze.

As she lay still, panting and trying to get her bearings, she listened to determine if Preston was still lurking somewhere nearby. She heard nothing but the sound of cicadas.

Knowing she couldn't stay there—Preston could return to make sure he'd actually killed her—Molly forced herself to turn over and sit up. It took almost five minutes for her to get to her hands and knees. Her calf was burning, as if someone was stabbing her with a hot poker, but she did her best to ignore it. She had to move. She would die if she stayed in that field.

She slowly began to crawl. Shuffling one hand forward, then a knee. Then the other hand and opposite knee. She moved inch by inch through the grass and dirt, barely feeling the pebbles as they dug into the skin of her palms and knees. Between the fever from the virus racking her body and the freaking gunshots, she was almost numb. Almost.

She crawled for five minutes, then lay down on her stomach to take a break. She forced herself back up and crawled for another six minutes before resting again. She counted each second of each minute, occupying her mind by keeping track of how long she crawled before allowing herself to stop. Every now and then she'd look up to see if she could spot anything, or anyone.

You're doing great, Molly. I'm proud of you.

The first time she heard Mark's voice, she honestly thought he was there.

She turned, excited to see him, but found nothing but darkness.

"I'm losing it," she mumbled. But hearing his voice, even if it was just in her head, gave her the strength to continue.

Her energy soon began to wane. She wanted to stand, to walk—it would be so much faster—but the first time she tried, the pain in her leg was just too much.

She fell in a heap to the ground, sobbing.

Don't give up. I know you can do this.

"I can't," she whispered.

You can. Do it for our babies.

Thinking that was kind of a low blow, Molly took a deep breath anyway and got back on her hands and knees. She swore the darkness didn't seem as all-encompassing, but she figured that was wishful thinking. She couldn't see where she was going, and once she thought she was crawling in circles when she entered a copse of trees, but eventually she realized that all the trees simply looked the same.

When she first saw what she thought was a light, Molly assumed she was hallucinating. She squeezed her eyes shut, then opened them again.

The light was still there.

It gave her renewed hope. It might not've been anything—and who in the hell would open a door to her in the middle of the night—but she had to try.

You're almost there. I love you, you've got this.

Mark's voice was the only thing keeping her going at this point. She had no energy, was shaking from the fever ravaging her system, and knew she'd lost a good amount of blood. She was so cold.

By the time she realized what she was seeing was a farmhouse, she'd almost convinced herself it was just another figment of her imagination. There was literally nothing else around. A dirt driveway that probably led to a road, but Molly had no more strength to get to it. If no one was home, or if they refused to help her, she knew she would die.

You aren't going to die.

"Mark . . . I need you!"

He didn't respond.

Molly couldn't think straight anymore. Didn't know what was real and what wasn't. Several times she'd lain down and decided to sleep until morning arrived, but then she'd heard Mark ordering her to get up again. To keep going. She hadn't wanted to. It was too hard. Too painful. But each and every time, she'd done what Mark had demanded. She'd do anything for him. Even keep going when every cell in her body was telling her to stop.

Almost there, Mol. You can do it!

Looking at the steps that led to the front door of the farmhouse, Molly almost gave up again. After everything she'd been through, those stairs seemed insurmountable.

When you get to the top, I can find you, Mark's voice whispered.

And that was what gave her the strength to climb— one painful step at a time.

Finally, she reached the door. Molly lifted a hand and slapped it weakly against the surface.

It barely made a sound. She was going to have to do better.

After curling her hand into a fist, Molly realized how much her palm hurt. She looked at it and saw nothing but blood. It was as if she was looking at someone else's hand. As if it wasn't *her* lying on the porch of a stranger's house.

Knock again, Molly. Do it. Do it now!

Hating Mark at that moment, she made another fist and rapped her knuckles on the door.

Louder!

"Bossy," Molly muttered, but she knocked again, harder, using the last of her strength. She lay down in front of the door and closed her eyes. "I'm done," she whispered.

You did good, Mol. So fucking good . . .

It could've been minutes or seconds, but a light came on above her, and Molly winced. Even through her closed eyelids, the light felt as if it were burning her retinas.

"What the hell?" a male voice exclaimed after Molly heard the door open. "Carol! Call the police!"

"What's wrong?" a female voice asked from somewhere inside the house.

"It's a girl! She's hurt. Covered in blood. Holy shit, can you hear me?" the man asked.

Tell him to call Silverstone.

Molly wanted to tell Mark to shut up. That she was tired and needed to sleep, but instead she opened her eyes into little slits. The light was still bright enough to hurt, but strangely she didn't really feel any pain from her body anymore. "Silverstone Towing . . . ," she whispered.

"What?" the man asked, bending over her.

"Call Silverstone Towing," Molly repeated.

"What'd she say?" the woman asked, her voice closer now.

"Dunno. Silver something or other," the man said.

"Here's a blanket—wrap it around her," the woman ordered.

The blanket was draped over her, and Molly almost moaned in pleasure. She was so cold. So fucking cold, and that blanket felt amazing.

"Here, you call the cops," the woman said, and Molly felt a hand on her shoulder. "Can you hear me?"

Molly nodded. At least she thought she did.

"The police are coming. What's your name?"

"Call Silverstone Towing," she managed to get out once more.

Good girl.

Molly closed her eyes, ignoring the commotion around her. Mark was proud of her—that was all she needed to know to let herself rest. She was tired of hurting. Tired of being sick. She wanted to sleep. She didn't hurt in her sleep.

～

Smoke wasn't sure where to tell Eagle to go. Molly was out there somewhere, but without any clues, they had nothing to go on. But he couldn't go back to Indianapolis. Couldn't check into a hotel to get some sleep. Not when Molly needed him. And he knew without a doubt that she did.

He could practically feel her desperation.

Whatever Weldon had done, he hadn't managed to kill her. He knew that without a doubt. No matter what the odds told him, his *gut* said Molly was alive.

Closing his eyes, he did his best to send her positive thoughts.

You're doing great, Molly. I'm proud of you.

Don't give up. I know you can do this.

Do it for our babies.

I love you, you've got this.

You aren't going to die.

"I think he left her somewhere," Eagle said. "We need to call the cops and see where they picked up the chase. Since Molly wasn't in the car, he had to have dumped her somewhere before the cops saw him swerving all over the road. That would at least give us a starting point to look for her."

It was a good suggestion, but Smoke knew it would still be a long shot. There was no telling how long Weldon'd had her. Where he might've left her.

The sun would be rising soon. It was hard to believe so much time had passed. It seemed like an eternity since he'd discovered Molly was missing. And he definitely didn't want to think about what Weldon might've done to Molly before leaving her somewhere. They were searching for a needle in a haystack, and Smoke needed a miracle.

His phone rang, scaring the shit out of him. Looking down, he saw it was Archer from Silverstone Towing. The last thing they needed was some sort of emergency back home.

"Smoke here."

"Smoke, thank God I got you!" Archer shouted, his words fast and breathless. "We got a call. From a woman near someplace called Deer Park, Indiana. She said her and her husband found a bloody girl on their doorstep. She didn't say what her name was, only told them to call Silverstone Towing."

"It's Molly!" Smoke nearly stopped breathing. "Where is she *exactly*?"

"The woman said the ambulance was there now, and they were Life Flighting her to Mount Sinai in Chicago."

"Did you get her name? The woman who called?" Smoke asked.

"Name and number."

Smoke mentally sighed in relief. The couple was going to get a hell of a thank-you gift, but for now, he needed to get to that hospital. "Thanks, Archer."

"You really think it's Molly?" he asked.

"Without a doubt," Smoke said. "I'll call when I know more," he told his employee, then hung up.

"They found her?" Eagle asked.

"Yes. In Deer Park. She's being flown to Mount Sinai in Chicago. How fast can you get me there?"

With no verbal response from Eagle, Smoke felt the Explorer surge forward with a burst of speed.

"Deer Park isn't far from here," Bull said. "Weldon wrecked not too long after he dumped her."

Smoke winced at the phrase but didn't say anything.

"I'll tell Gramps what's up," Bull added, lifting his phone to his ear.

Smoke only half listened to what Bull was telling their teammate. He hated to know that Molly had been bleeding when she'd shown up on that couple's doorstep, but she was alive. That was all that mattered.

I'm coming, Molly. Hang on.

Chapter Twenty-Two

Molly frowned at the incessant beeping. It was annoying, and she reached out to grab her phone to turn off the alarm—but realized almost immediately that moving wasn't a good idea. Every muscle in her body hurt. She had no idea why.

Moaning a bit, she tried to open her eyes, but even that seemed to hurt.

"Mol? Thank God! That's it, open your eyes . . . you can do it."

Mark's voice was scratchy, and he sounded tired. Frowning, Molly wanted to ask him why he was so tired. Tell him that he'd been working too hard and needed to rest. "Mark?"

His name was nothing more than a croak. God, why was it so hard to talk, and why did she feel so weak?

"I'm here, Molly. I'm here," he said. "Can you please open your beautiful brown eyes so I can see them?"

Squinting, Molly did her best to do as Mark had asked. She opened them in slits—and got her first look at him.

He looked like shit. It seemed like he hadn't shaved in days. Maybe a week or more. He had dark circles under his bloodshot eyes.

"You look like crap," she blurted.

But instead of being upset with her, he smiled. And the dimple she loved so much was still barely visible through his facial hair.

"And you are so fucking beautiful, I can't stand it," he told her. "How do you feel? Are you hurting?"

Swallowing, Molly nodded. "Yeah. Where am I?"

"At a hospital in Chicago. What do you remember about what happened?"

Panic filled her. *Chicago?* She didn't want to be in Chicago! That was where Preston was!

"It's okay. Concentrate on me, Molly. What do you remember?" Mark asked.

"Um . . . I-I have the flu," she said. "Did it get worse?"

"Yeah, it got worse, but Weldon kidnapped you. Do you remember that?" Mark asked.

The second his words sank in, she remembered.

Her eyes popped open, and she ignored the pain from the light in the room. "He shot me!" she exclaimed.

"Yeah, twice," Mark said solemnly. "But he's a shit shot. One bullet entered the back of your head, but the angle was extreme, and it came out just in front of your ear, missing just about everything vital. It basically skimmed just along your skull. But it bled like a son of a bitch. The other shot went into your calf."

"He was drunk. And I keeled over to throw up," Molly admitted. "That's when he shot me the first time. I passed out and don't remember the second."

Mark closed his eyes and took a deep breath. Then he looked back down at her. "Thank God he was too drunk to shoot straight."

"Where is he? I want to testify," Molly said firmly.

"You don't have to. The cops found him when he got back on the interstate, and he ran. He flipped his car, and it burst into flames."

Molly could only stare up at Mark in disbelief. "Was anyone else hurt?"

"How did I know you'd be worried about everyone else but yourself? No, by some miracle he didn't run into anyone else. But for a few hours, I thought you'd died inside that vehicle with him. When the fire started, Gramps had to tackle me to keep me from throwing myself at the burning car."

"Oh, Mark," Molly whispered, hurting for him.

"You were so sick when you got here, the doctors were extremely worried. Your fever was over a hundred and four. You'd been shot twice, but they were more concerned about the fucking flu taking you down," Mark said, shaking his head.

He picked up her hand and kissed the back of it, and Molly noticed for the first time that it was bandaged.

"The cops aren't sure how far you crawled, as they haven't found where Weldon shot you, but you did a number on your hands and knees. They'll heal, though. You're free of him, Molly. He can't hurt you or anyone else again."

Molly smiled weakly. A weight she'd unconsciously been carrying around ever since she'd fled the country lifted from her shoulders. "I'm not sorry he's dead," she said.

"Good. I'm not either. In fact, if he'd lived, I would've found a way to kill him myself," Mark told her.

His anger didn't scare her. Instead, it made her feel loved.

Her eyes closed, and it took a minute for her to open them again.

"You're tired," Mark said. "Sleep."

"I heard you, you know," Molly said.

"What?"

"When I was crawling, looking for someone to help me. I heard you in my head. Telling me not to give up. To keep going. You were the only reason I didn't lie down and go to sleep."

Mark's eyes teared up, which made Molly's do the same.

"I didn't know where you were, but I wasn't going to stop looking until I found you," Mark replied. "The only thing I could do after learning you weren't in his car was mentally send you as many positive vibes as I could."

"I heard them," Molly reassured him.

Mark leaned forward and put his hand on her belly. "You aren't pregnant, so thank God we didn't have to worry about that asshole murdering our child. But I want to remedy that as soon as possible. After you're healed, of course."

Molly gave him a sleepy smile. "Of course."

"I love you, Molly. You'll never know how much."

"I *do* know, because I love you just as much," she returned.

"Sleep. You have a lot of people waiting to see you," Mark told her. "Bull, Skylar, Eagle, Taylor, and Gramps have been taking turns camping out in the waiting room."

"How long have I been here?" Molly asked.

"Six nights. This is the seventh day."

"Really?"

"Yeah. Really."

"You need to go shower. And sleep. And eat," she scolded.

"I will, now that I know you're going to be okay," he agreed.

"When can we go home?"

Mark chuckled. "You just woke up! I'm sure the doctors are going to want to keep you here for a few more days to make sure you're good."

"'Kay," she mumbled, feeling extremely exhausted all of a sudden. It was too much of an effort to talk.

Molly felt Mark's lips on her forehead.

"Love you, Molly."

"Love you," she mumbled, then everything went dark as she fell into a healing sleep.

∼

Smoke felt as if he could take a full breath for the first time in a week. Molly was going to be all right. She had some scars that might bother

her later, but they could deal with those. The detectives were also going to want to talk to her, hear her version of what happened.

Smoke had already gifted the couple who'd helped her with a generous reward. He'd talked to them over the phone, and they'd insisted they'd simply done what anyone with a heart would do, but he didn't care. They'd helped his Molly when she'd needed it most—and, more importantly, they hadn't dismissed her ramblings about Silverstone Towing and had actually done a Google search and called. Their call had allowed him to be at Molly's side almost immediately. He could never fully repay that.

Eagle, Bull, and Gramps had been by his side through everything, and Skylar and Taylor had also driven up to be with them. Molly had scared everyone, but now that she was awake, and he knew she'd be okay, he could finally breathe again.

He walked into the waiting room, which Silverstone had practically taken over, and said, "She woke up. She remembers everything, and she's gonna be just fine."

Skylar and Taylor cried. Bull, Eagle, and Gramps smiled in relief.

"Does that mean you'll finally let us take you to the hotel for a fucking shower?" Gramps bitched. "You stink, bro."

Everyone laughed, including Smoke. "Yeah, I'm starved too. Maybe we can find a good deep-dish-pizza place on the way?"

Bull came over and hugged Smoke hard. Then he pulled back, leaving his hands on his shoulders. "Happy for you, Smoke."

"Thanks."

Eagle joined them, putting one arm around Smoke and the other around Bull. "Your woman is strong as fuck."

"She is," Smoke agreed.

Gramps completed the circle, joining his friends. "I swear our job seems pretty damn tame right about now."

Everyone chuckled.

Smoke agreed with Gramps. Lately, it seemed as if most of the drama in their lives was in their own backyard, so to speak, not a result of the missions they went on to eliminate evil men or women.

Evil was all around them, and it had touched most of them in the most intimate ways possible.

The four men stood like that for a long moment, soaking in the camaraderie that had begun years ago in the Army when they'd been Delta Force soldiers. It felt as if they'd just survived another battle, and come out intact on the other side.

Skylar ducked under Bull's arm and hugged him, and Taylor did the same with Eagle.

"When can we see her?" Taylor asked.

"She's sleeping right now, and I know the doctor will want to check her over while we're gone. We'll go grab something decent to eat, I'll shower, then we'll come back and see if she's awake and up to visitors," Smoke told her.

"Good. I've missed her," Skylar said.

"Me too," Smoke agreed. "Me too."

⁓

"You need to stop treating me like I'm an invalid," Molly complained when Mark lifted her out of his Explorer and carried her into their house.

"I know you're not," Mark said. "I just like carrying you around."

Molly wanted to roll her eyes, but she had to admit that *she* liked him carrying her around just as much. He leaned over, and she disarmed the alarm, then immediately armed it again. He carried her into the kitchen and sat her on the counter.

It had been five months since Preston had kidnapped her from the house and tried to kill her. Things had mostly been wonderful . . . but every now and then, Molly fell into her old negative thinking. Sure that everything that had happened was her fault.

She should've said no when Preston had asked her out the first time. She shouldn't have gone to Nigeria.

If she hadn't, maybe Nana and Papa wouldn't have been murdered.

She'd forgotten to turn on the alarm after Skylar had left that day after her visit, giving Preston the chance he'd been waiting for.

But each time she'd gotten depressed, Mark had been there to reassure her. To tell her that he loved her. Remind her that she wasn't responsible for Preston's actions. And rally their amazing friends around her.

But today was a good day. They'd just gotten back from the hospital. Taylor had given birth to a beautiful baby boy. Molly would never forget the tender moment she'd accidentally witnessed. Just thinking about it made her want to cry.

She and Mark had gone up to Taylor's room to visit the new family, when he'd been stopped by someone he knew on the staff. Leaving him to chat, Molly continued down the hall and quietly pushed open the door, and she heard them behind the privacy curtain stretched across the room.

"Do you think it's going to fade?" Taylor asked her husband.

"I honestly don't know," Eagle said. "Does it bother you?"

"Bother me?" Taylor said incredulously. "That birthmark on his cheek is a miracle, Eagle! I can look at our son and *recognize* him. He'll probably hate it when he gets older, but knowing I can just glance at our son's face and *know* who he is . . ."

Then her voice had trailed off. When Molly peeked around the curtain, she saw both Taylor and Eagle silently crying. Their heads were pressed together, and they were gazing down at their newborn son with such absolute looks of love on their faces, it felt like barging in to say hello was completely intrusive.

Molly had backed out of the room silently and informed Mark that they'd visit their friends later. He'd been concerned, but quickly understood when she told him what she'd overheard.

"I picked up a present for you today," Mark told her as he reached for a paper bag sitting on the counter. Molly hadn't noticed it before now, and she wondered when he'd gone shopping. He might've sent out one of his employees at Silverstone Towing while they'd been hanging out in the basement. She'd spent a lot of time there recently; she could relax completely at Silverstone.

She'd also started working on her book, about what had happened to her—both in Nigeria *and* with Preston. She'd taken the job in Nigeria to get away from him, after all. And in the end, she'd had to face the very thing that had made her run in the first place. Nigeria actually seemed like another lifetime, and the events from all those months ago paled in comparison to being shot twice by her ex.

"What is it?" Molly asked, her eyes lighting up. She loved getting presents from Mark . . . well, the ones that weren't too expensive. She was still working on trying to get him to chill out when it came to buying her things. Something completely goofy—like a key chain or a funny-shaped tomato from the grocery store—was one thing, but the brand-new Volvo XC90 had been a bit too much.

Although she couldn't deny she loved her new SUV. So much so, she hadn't complained when Mark had loaded it with every upgrade possible, including every safety feature he could get.

"Open it and see," Mark said with a tender smile.

He'd spread her legs and was standing as close to her as possible as she sat on the counter, giving her a thrill. Molly had run out of patience with him several weeks after her release from the hospital. He'd refused to touch her sexually, even after the doctor had cleared her. She'd had to resort to sneaking into his shower, going to her knees to suck his cock, before he'd lost his iron control.

He'd taken her to bed and hadn't let her leave for the next twelve hours. Not that Molly had complained. He'd made love to her tenderly, then almost desperately. She'd been sore as hell when they'd finally left the bedroom, but she'd never mentioned it to Mark. Every ache had been worth it.

Molly pulled out a small cardboard box from the bag. "A pregnancy test?" she asked.

Mark nodded. "Yeah. You haven't felt good in the mornings lately, and your taste buds have changed. You've eaten eggs almost every morning since you moved in . . . until recently. Your tits are also swollen, and you've been more emotional than usual."

"And you think it's because I'm pregnant?" Molly asked. She tried to tamp down her excitement, but wasn't sure she succeeded. She'd also begun to wonder if she was pregnant, because she simply felt . . . off, but leave it to her ultraobservant boyfriend to pick up on all the other slight changes.

"Yes," he said. He gripped her waist and lifted her off the counter. "Come on, let's do it." He took hold of her hand and pulled her toward the stairs.

Molly laughed. She didn't think she'd ever get tired of Mark hauling her around. They went into their bedroom, and she held up a hand. "I can pee on the stick without your help."

She knew he wanted to complain, but he wisely refrained. "Okay. Let me know when you're done, and we can wait for it to change together."

Molly nodded and went into the bathroom. Her hands shook as she opened the packaging. Mark hadn't brought up getting married again, but she knew he wanted to. She'd caught him and Bull talking about what they wanted for their joint ceremony. She hadn't thought guys cared much about their wedding details, but obviously that wasn't the case with Bull and Mark.

Knowing Mark was probably on the verge of bursting into the small room if she didn't hurry up, Molly read the directions, which were straightforward enough, and did her thing.

Putting a washcloth on the counter next to the sink, she placed the stick on it, washed her hands, then turned toward Mark as he entered the bathroom. He was clearly unable to wait another second and immediately put his arms around her.

"Mark, can I ask you something?" Molly asked.

"Of course. You can ask me anything. You know that," Mark told her.

Molly smiled. "Will you marry me?"

Mark stared down at her with his mouth half-open. She was thrilled that she could shock him.

"I mean, I want to marry you no matter if I'm pregnant or not. I love you, and even if we never have children, I'll still want to spend the rest of my life with you."

"God, Mol," Mark whispered, lifting her up against him.

Molly wrapped her legs around his waist and clung to him as their foreheads touched, and she could see emotions swirling in Mark's eyes. Finally, he lifted his head and looked deep into her eyes. "Yes, I'll marry you. I love you so much, you just don't know. And we're going to have the family we've always wanted, no matter what we have to do to get it."

He walked out of the bathroom, still carrying her. He sat on the side of the bed, Molly straddling his lap, and reached for the drawer in his nightstand.

He pulled out a black ring box and held it up between them. "If it's not what you want, we can get something else, but I thought this was perfect."

Molly opened the box with shaking hands—and stared silently at the ring inside.

She swallowed hard, but that didn't stop the tears from falling. She grasped the antique ring delicately and held it up. "What . . . ? How . . . ?"

"It's your nana's ring," Mark told her unnecessarily. Molly would've recognized the ring anywhere. She'd played with it more times than she could count, spinning it around her grandmother's finger as she'd sat next to her, holding her hand. She'd memorized the story about how Papa had asked Nana to marry him, gifting her with this very ring.

"When the case of your grandparents' deaths was closed, after the investigation was completed and the case wrapped up, the items sitting in evidence were sent here. I looked through the box, and there wasn't anything worth keeping . . . except for the rings. I hated keeping them from you, but I was waiting for the right moment to propose. I have your papa's ring, too, and if it's okay with you, I'd love to wear it once we're married."

"Oh my God, Mark! Yes! A thousand times yes!" Molly cried.

He took the ring from her and slid it down her left-hand ring finger. It fit perfectly, which she'd known it would. Nana had let her try it on a few times, and it had always fit.

Then Mark was hugging her once more.

She couldn't believe this was her life. That she'd somehow found a man who put her first. Who went out of his way to do whatever he could to make her happy. She didn't need material possessions, although having her grandparents' rings was a miracle she'd never expected.

Mark moved then, and Molly expected him to roll her onto her back in their bed and make passionate love to her—but instead he carried her back toward the bathroom.

"Um . . . what are we doing?" she asked.

He didn't answer, just loosened his arms and let her slide down his body until she was standing once more.

"You ready to look?" he asked.

It took Molly a moment before she remembered the pregnancy test. Upon seeing her nana's ring, she'd completely forgotten about it. Her belly doing flip-flops, she nodded. They both leaned over the counter to see the results.

Two lines.

For a second, Molly had no idea what that meant. Then she saw the explanation printed right there on the plastic device. One line for not pregnant. Two for pregnant.

She looked up at Mark and saw the beautiful dimple in his cheek. He was smiling from ear to ear. His hand covered her belly, and he said reverently, "I knew it. I knocked you up!"

It was such a guy thing to say, Molly could only laugh. "Yes, you did."

Then he picked her up once more and went back into the bedroom. That time he *did* drop her on the bed before hovering over her. "I love you, soon-to-be Molly Chamberlin."

"And I love you, Mark Chamberlin."

They grinned at each other for a beat, then Molly said, "The first to get naked gets to choose the position."

Clothes went flying, and Molly laughed joyfully. Life with Mark would never be dull, and he'd be the best husband and father a woman could ask for.

Folly Molly indeed.

She was the luckiest woman in the world.

∼

To Whom It May Concern:

It's Cassidy again. Are you getting these letters? Please, I'm begging you. Not for me, but for my son. They're going to get him killed. They're forcing him to deliver drugs now, and I'm scared to death. I'll do anything you ask, if you only save him from this hell. If you don't help me, I'm going to have to try to get out of here on my own. I know I'll probably be caught, as everyone on this compound loves Michael and is loyal to him . . . but I'm desperate. I'll be on the lookout for anyone you might send in to help me, and I'll do everything I can to assist. But please, come help us!

~Cassidy Hewitt

Gramps reread the latest letter for the hundredth time. Cassidy's desperation ate at him. She didn't deserve this. She'd reached out to her government for help and, as far as she knew, was being ignored. He hated that.

But it was time. Silverstone had worked closely with Willis and had put a plan in place. It had taken months of preparation, and it was *finally* time to move. Gramps would go in undercover. He was going to pose as a drug dealer from Dallas, someone who wanted to meet Michael Coke and get into his distribution network.

It was risky as hell, and something Silverstone hadn't done before, but Gramps was ready. Cassidy and her son were waiting for someone to rescue them, and Silverstone could take out another despicable human being in the process. Bull, Eagle, and Smoke would be in Jamaica as well, but they were taking secondary roles. They were backup. He'd be alone when he went into the lion's den, so to speak.

Closing his eyes, Gramps recalled the last time he'd seen Cassidy. He'd gone back to El Paso to visit. His parents had started arguing, as usual, and he'd needed a break from their squabbling. He'd gone to one of the bars near their home, and Cassidy had been there with a friend. It had been great to catch up with her. Laugh. Talk.

They hadn't done anything else, but the pull between them had still been there.

They'd always danced around their attraction. He'd left her alone in high school because he'd thought he was too old for her. But he'd seen her now and then over the years, and each time he'd toyed with the idea of asking her to warm his bed. To spend a night together. To find out if they could purge the crazy connection they seemed to have. But every time, he'd chickened out, not wanting to ruin their easy friendship.

He remembered a particular letter he'd received from her when he'd been deployed. Gramps supposed she must've gotten his address from his parents at some point. The letter wasn't the first she'd sent, but in it, she'd told him how miserable she was in her marriage. She'd said the only good thing to come from it was her son.

Mario.

He was eleven now. It was a delicate age, when kids were easily influenced. If he was brainwashed by Coke and his gang, he would eventually end up in jail.

His jaw hardening, Gramps inhaled deeply. They were headed to Jamaica soon. He'd get Cassidy to safety or die trying. He just hoped she wouldn't blow his cover the first time she saw him.

Cassidy Hewitt was a wild card in this op. She could be the key to everyone getting out in one piece, or she could be his downfall. But she was worth the risk. Gramps wasn't leaving Jamaica without her and her son.

About the Author

Susan Stoker is a *New York Times, USA Today*, and *Wall Street Journal* bestselling author whose series include Badge of Honor: Texas Heroes, SEAL of Protection, and Delta Force Heroes. Married to a retired army noncommissioned officer, Stoker has lived all over the country—from Missouri and California to Colorado and Texas—and currently resides under the big skies of Tennessee. A true believer in happily ever after, Stoker enjoys writing novels in which romance turns to love. To learn more about the author and her work, visit her website, www.stokeraces.com, or find her on Facebook at www.facebook.com/authorsusanstoker.

Connect with Susan Online

Susan's Facebook Profile and Page

www.facebook.com/authorsstoker

www.facebook.com/authorsusanstoker

Follow Susan on Twitter

www.twitter.com/Susan_Stoker

Find Susan's Books on Goodreads

www.goodreads.com/SusanStoker

Email

Susan@StokerAces.com

Website

www.StokerAces.com